TARGETS OF OPPORTUNITY

TARGETS OF OPPORTUNITY

by JOE WEBER

G. P. PUTNAM'S SONS
New York

G. P. Putnam's Sons
Publishers Since 1838
200 Madison Avenue
New York, NY 10016

Library of Congress Cataloging-in-Publication Data

Weber, Joe, date
   Targets of opportunity / Joe Weber.
       p.   cm.
     ISBN 0-399-13804-8 (alk. paper)
     I. title.
   PS3573.E219T37   1993
   813'.54—dc20   92-26962 CIP

Printed in the United States of America

1   2   3   4   5   6   7   8   9   10

This book is printed on acid-free paper.

ACKNOWLEDGMENTS

In appreciation for their kindness in offering technical advice to embellish this novel, the author wishes to thank Colonel Hugh Longmire, USAF (Ret.); Lieutenant Colonel Bill Johnson, USMC (Ret.); Colonel Jerry W. Marvel, USMC (Ret.); Larry Hodgden; and Commander Fred Hudleston.

Other contributors who provided invaluable information wish to remain anonymous.

A special thanks to my wife, Jeannie, who patiently assists me with every phase of my labors.

Of all the animals, man is the only one that is cruel. He is the only one that inflicts pain for the pleasure of doing it. It is a trait that is not known to the higher animals.

The higher animals engage in individual fights, but never in organized masses. Man is the only animal that deals in that atrocity of atrocities, War.

SAMUEL LANGHORNE CLEMENS
("Mark Twain")

This book is dedicated to those unsung military heroes who have volunteered for hazardous missions under extraordinary conditions. Especially to those men and women who made the ultimate sacrifice while performing their duties under a cloak of secrecy.

TARGETS OF OPPORTUNITY

CHAPTER ONE

Da Nang Air Base, South Vietnam

Brad Austin shoved the throttles forward to military power, then simultaneously released the Phantom's brakes and spoke to the control tower. "Rhino One and Two are on the roll."

"Roger, Rhino. Maintain runway heading and contact departure control when safely airborne."

"Rhino One."

Rhino was the tactical call sign for the Alert Five Hot Pad marine fighter crews. Responding to any threat, the flight crews were responsible for scrambling into the air within five minutes of an alert.

Pressed back into his ejection seat, Captain Brad Austin scanned his engine gauges and selected afterburner. His feet momentarily lifted from the rudder pedals during the sudden surge of acceleration.

Twin white-hot flames belched from the fighter's jet exhaust as the F-4B Phantom blasted down the runway. The blazing afterburners kicked up spray from the rain-drenched concrete.

Holding the control stick in the full-aft position, Austin watched the runway markers flash by. The nose gear began to extend as the F-4 accelerated past 120 knots. Four seconds later the main tires lifted off the wet runway.

Snapping the gear handle up, Brad tweaked the nose down and raised the flaps as the powerful fighter thundered over the end of the runway.

Passing 300 knots, Austin pulled the throttles out of afterburner and established a normal climb attitude. "Hang on, guys," he said to himself. "The first team is on the way."

"Rhino Two closing," Austin's wingman, First Lieutenant Stew Robinett, radioed as he slid into parade formation.

Robinett, who was supposed to begin his takeoff ten seconds after his flight leader, had commenced his roll after waiting only three seconds. The lieutenant had a reputation for expediting his running rendezvous.

"Button Four," Brad ordered, checking his instruments and master caution light. Button Four was a preselected radio frequency for Da Nang Departure Control.

Stew Robinett, following normal procedures, switched frequencies without acknowledging the call.

"Departure," Brad said as the fighters crossed the beach, "Rhino Lead is with you."

"Roger, Rhino One," the controller answered in a staccato manner. "Radar contact. You've got two fast movers at ten o'clock, three miles. They're descending out of one-one-thousand . . . and have you in sight."

Austin quickly searched the sky to his left, then sighted the black exhaust trails behind the inbound Phantoms. "Tally—no factor."

"Rhino One, maintain your present heading and contact Casper Two Seven on Black." Casper Two Seven was a two-seat TA-4F Skyhawk tactical air coordinator.

"Copy, button Black," Austin replied, gazing at the descending F-4s. "Rhinos, switch."

Glancing at Monkey Mountain, Brad keyed his intercom and spoke to his radar-intercept officer. "Randy, keep me honest . . . if we have to scud-run." Scud-running was flying under the low monsoon rain clouds.

First Lieutenant Randy Wyatt, checking Robinett's Phantom for leaking fuel or hydraulic fluid, swiveled his head to the front. "You can bet on it."

After inspecting Austin's F-4, Stew Robinett drifted into a loose combat cruise formation while the fighters clawed for altitude. "Rhino One looks good."

"You, too," Wyatt answered.

"Casper Two Seven, Rhino One is up with two Fox-4s carrying snake and nape." Both aircraft, loaded with Snakeye bombs and napalm, were configured for close air support.

"Copy, Rhino. We'll keep you feet-wet until we have permission to drop."

"Okay," Brad replied evenly in an effort to conceal his contempt for the restrictive rules of engagement.

"Come left to three one zero," the tactical coordinator said with a sense of urgency in his voice. "Anchor on the Quang Tri one zero five for fifteen at base plus three." The F-4s would remain over water east of the navigation aid at Quang Tri.

Surveying the swollen rain clouds, Brad eased the Phantom's nose down. "Roger. What have you got?"

"Stand by. I'm on the other horn."

Brad clicked his mike twice, then looked down as Hai Van Peninsula passed under his left wing. "Well, the Cong is really taking advantage of the monsoon season."

"You got that right," Randy Wyatt replied, shaking his head in resignation. "The bastards are keeping us humping . . . day and night."

"Rhino, Casper Two Seven." The voice sounded metallic.

"Rhino," Brad answered, checking his armament panel and engine gauges.

"We've got a recon team trapped in a valley. Their Huey was shot up when they landed, and a second gunship is trying to extract them. The helo pilot is in contact with the recon lieutenant."

"Copy," Austin replied, leveling the flight. "What's the ceiling in the valley?"

"Thumper One Nine," the Skyhawk observer radioed to the marine helicopter crew, "say ceiling."

Brad heard a garbled reply from the low-flying Huey. He also detected the rattling sounds of machine guns. "It sounds like they're in deep shit."

"Yeah," Wyatt cautiously responded. "I hope we're not flying into a setup."

"Rhino, they estimate between five and six hundred feet. It's ragged, with light rain."

Brad studied the coastline, judging the tops of the overcast to be 2,500 feet. He peered down at the flat, greasy-looking sea. "Can we get in?"

"I think so," the coordinator responded in a confident voice. "I've already eyeballed the entrance to the valley, so we'll lead you in for the first run."

"Okay." Brad inched the throttles forward. "We'll be with you in six minutes."

"Roger," the tactical coordinator replied, then explained the urgency of the situation.

The Huey had been hit while the marine reconnaissance team was exiting the helicopter. The pilot had attempted to lift off, but lost control and crash-landed when the tail rotor had been blown off. The recon lieutenant, two of his men, and the helicopter flight crew were injured. Both aviators were in critical condition and needed immediate medical attention.

The gunship pilot was trying to extract the trapped men, but two machine guns were making it impossible for him to approach the landing zone.

The recon lieutenant had reported that the enemy troops were slowly surrounding their position. Every time the gunship stopped firing, the soldiers advanced a few meters closer to the stranded men.

Worse yet, the helicopter was running low on fuel. The tactical coordinator had been in contact with an army helicopter, but the pilot would have to refuel before he could relieve the Huey gunship. The situation was rapidly becoming desperate. Brad and his wingman were the last hope for their fellow marines.

"Casper, Rhino One has you in sight at eleven o'clock. Come starboard and we'll join on the inside."

"Ah . . . roger, we've got you," the backseat observer replied as the Skyhawk banked into a shallow turn. "You're cleared in hot. Out of the turn, we'll lead you up the valley. Call the helo in sight."

"Copy," Brad replied, flipping his master arm to ON. "Dash Two, switches hot, drop in pairs." Each pilot would drop two bombs on the first pass.

"Switches hot," Robinett acknowledged. "What kind of pattern are you going to use?"

Brad glanced at the entrance to the valley. The dark clouds extended across the opening, obscuring everything but the tops of the mountains. *Christ, who knows?*

"We'll just fly in," Austin radioed as he banked steeply to rendezvous with the Skyhawk. "I'll work on a plan as we go. Drop back in trail—half mile—and keep me in sight."

A long pause followed.

"Brad," Stew Robinett replied as he surveyed the thick cloud cover, "are you sure about this? We're going up rising terrain . . . with a low overcast and poor visibility."

Austin thumbed his mike switch. "We've got stranded marines up there. Keep me in sight."

Robinett slowly exhaled. "We're hanging on."

"Thumper One Nine," the Skyhawk pilot said as he crossed the coastline, "Casper is rolling in with two Fox-4s."

"Bring 'em in!" The gunship's vibrating rotor blades made the pilot sound as if he was beating his chest while he talked. "We're taking heavy fire."

The three airplanes dove, screeching low over the hamlets on the east side of Route One.

"Thumper," the Skyhawk pilot radioed as they passed over the highway, "we're entering the valley. Mark the target with Willie Peter."

"Roger," the Huey pilot responded, turning to fire a white phosphorus rocket at the front line of the advancing enemy soldiers.

The streaking projectile impacted twenty meters in front of the nearest machine gun. Smoke rose through the trees while the Vietnamese retreated several meters.

"Drop your ordnance," the gunship pilot said over the beating rotor blades, "at twelve o'clock for thirty meters. We're clear to your right."

"Roger," Brad acknowledged, "twelve at thirty." *This is going to be close.*

Seconds later, Austin detected a wisp of rising smoke to his right. "I've got a visual . . . at one o'clock. Dash Two, we'll pull off vertical."

"Two," Robinett responded, gulping oxygen.

"Nail 'em," the Skyhawk pilot radioed, pulling straight up into the dark overcast.

Brad let his Phantom drift up to the base of the thick clouds. They would not be able to use their normal bombing approach. He had maintained 450 knots, but there was no way to establish a thirty-degree dive from 600 feet above the ground. Brad and his wingman would have to rely on their pilot's instincts.

"Thumper," Brad said, breathing rapidly, "tell them to get their heads down."

Austin heard the *whump-whump* from the gunship when the pilot replied. Brad hesitated a moment, calculating his release point. He savagely popped the Phantom's nose down, released the Snakeyes, then snapped the stick back.

"Ohhh . . . shit," Randy Wyatt groaned under the g load as their F-4 plunged into the low rain clouds. "This is totally insane . . . I'm telling you."

The Phantom shot out of the clouds at 2,800 feet. Brad pulled the fighter through the top of a loop, let the nose drop below the horizon, then rolled the F-4 right side up and leveled off. "Dash Two, I'm on top. You'll be out at two point eight."

"We're clear," Robinett responded, observing the tops of the surrounding mountains protruding through the overcast, "and I've got you at twelve."

"Roger," Brad replied, looking for the Skyhawk. "Thumper, call the hits."

"You're both a little long—'bout twenty meters, but you got their attention."

Brad swore to himself before keying his radio. "Okay, we're coming in with napalm . . . one minute apart. Suggest you try to extract them after the first pass."

"Roger that."

"Dash Two copies," Robinett said, selecting his napalm stations. "I'll roll in at sixty seconds."

"Rhino, Casper," the reassuring voice sounded in Brad's earphones. "I'm orbiting over the mouth of the valley."

"Tally," Brad replied, catching sight of the Skyhawk while he switched his armament panel. "I'm in hot."

Brad reefed the F-4 around and thundered up the valley. The rain was intensifying, which obscured his forward visibility.

"Dash Two," Brad warned, pulling the throttles back, "the vis is dropping. I'll call my final speed."

"Copy."

Brad squinted through the rainswept windshield at the gray, foggy haze. "Randy, call my speeds while I try to see where the hell we're going."

"Three-ninety . . ." Wyatt tightened his shoulder restraints. "Three-eighty . . ."

"Thumper," Austin said, concentrating on maintaining visual contact with the ground, "can you mark again?"

"Affirmative."

A pause followed before the gunship pilot again replied. "Your target is eleven o'clock for twenty-five to thirty meters. I'm going in as soon as you drop."

"Roger," Brad responded at the same moment he saw the white smoke. "I've got a visual."

"Three-sixty," Wyatt prompted. "I hope we don't take out our own troops."

"Dash Two," Brad radioed, shoving the throttles forward, "three-eighty is a good speed."

"Two is rolling in," Vic Lowenstein, Robinett's RIO, answered for his busy pilot. "Copy three-eighty."

Brad eased the nose down, boring in on the rising smoke. He could see the Huey moving toward the trapped marines. "Get on with it," he muttered to himself.

"Holy Mother of Jesus," Wyatt shouted through clenched teeth. "You're going to take off their heads."

Waiting till the last second, Brad dropped the napalm bombs and snatched the stick into his stomach. "One's off!" He selected afterburner and rocketed through the clouds, rolling upright over the gloomy mass.

Searching for the Skyhawk, Brad listened to the helo pilot, then keyed his cockpit intercom. "That son of a bitch deserves the Medal of Honor."

Wyatt remained quiet while he mentally reviewed the ejection-seat procedures.

"Thumper is taking hits," the gunship pilot shouted over the rattle of machine-gun fire. "They're advancing toward us. Dash Two, lay it down forty meters in front of us, and walk it into the trees!"

"Two has you in sight," Robinett excitedly replied. "Here it comes . . . hang in there."

"Roger," the Huey pilot yelled above the confusion. "We've got the last man coming aboard."

The napalm containers tumbled from the howling Phantom, decimating the center of the enemy patrol. Men ran screaming through the trees, hopelessly attempting to extinguish the flames that had engulfed them.

"Two's off," Robinett reported as his fighter entered the murky clouds.

Brad saw the TAC Skyhawk at the same time he heard the frantic helicopter pilot. The tense voice sent a chill down his spine.

"We're overloaded—can't get off the ground! We need cover while we jettison our weapons and ammo!"

Brad detected the desperation in the pilot's voice. He sounded resigned to facing death.

Austin yanked the throttles to idle, popped the speed brakes open, snapped the fighter to an almost inverted position, and pulled the nose down. "Thumper, Dash One is in."

Randy Wyatt gripped the sides of the canopy. "We can't dive through the clouds!"

The shrieking Phantom plummeted into the dark clouds while Brad tugged on the stick to pull out of the steep dive. "We don't have time to go out and enter underneath."

"These sonuvabitches," the gunship pilot yelled, "are fanatical. They're almost on us!"

Dropping out of the leaden undercast, Austin and Wyatt cringed when their fighter's right wingtip skimmed along the sharply rising hills.

"That was close," Wyatt exclaimed while Brad simultaneously slapped the stick to the left, retracted the speed brakes, and shoved the throttles forward.

"Just a few seconds, Thumper," Austin radioed, yanking the Phantom back on course. "I'm going to ripple the whole load."

Brad reset his armament panel, checked his speed at 390 knots, then caught sight of the Huey. The gunship pilot was struggling to head down the valley. The landing skids bounced across the ground while the crew frantically hurled guns and ammunition out of the helicopter.

Brad made a slight heading change, then lowered the nose. He had the gunship boresighted. *God, be with me.*

"Holy shit . . ." Wyatt moaned over the intercom, "we're gonna hit the ground."

Raising the F-4's nose, Brad pickled his entire load of ordnance. The Snakeyes and napalm hurtled over the top of the helicopter, enveloping the right flank of the enemy soldiers in a pulsing black, orange, and red fireball.

Brad pulled hard on the stick, then felt the Phantom shudder from the impact of gunfire. He instinctively shot a glance at the master caution light. It remained dark. "Stay calm," he told himself.

Concentrating on his primary flight instruments, Austin let out a sigh of relief as they emerged from the clouds. "I think we took some hits."

Wyatt nervously keyed his intercom. "Everything is okay back here . . . so far."

Brad scanned the gray sky. "Dash Two, say posit."

The radio was eerily quiet.

"Casper, Rhino One. Do you copy?"

Brad's earphones remained silent. "Randy, give Casper and Stew a call."

"Casper Two Seven and Rhino Two," Wyatt radioed, swiveling his head from side to side, "Rhino Dash One. Do you read?"

The absence of sound confirmed that they had lost radio contact.

The rounds that had impacted the Phantom had destroyed their communications link.

"Shit," Brad said, looking for the Skyhawk. "We're nordo." Nordo was shorthand for no radio.

"I've got the TAC at two o'clock . . . level," Wyatt replied, tuning his radio to the 243.0 guard frequency. "Casper Two Seven, Rhino Lead on guard. Do you read?"

Still no reply.

Brad slowed the fighter and rendezvoused with the Skyhawk. The tactical coordinator had surmised that Rhino One's radio had malfunctioned.

Coasting into formation with the Skyhawk, Brad glanced at the observer in the rear cockpit. He was gesturing for Austin and Wyatt to look down.

Directing his attention below the right wing, Brad was relieved to see the Huey gunship racing from under the low clouds. "Randy, they made it."

"Yeah, they'll be feet-wet in a couple of minutes." Wyatt flexed his fingers to relieve the tension. "That guy won't have to buy any drinks for a long time."

A moment later, Stew Robinett glided into position off Brad's wing. Vic Lowenstein looked Rhino One over, then gave Wyatt a thumbs-up signal.

Pulling his power back, Austin tapped his helmet and pointed to Robinett. Dash Two, who was now the leader, had the responsibility of guiding the flight home.

The Skyhawk pilot waved, then banked and climbed away as the F-4s departed for Da Nang.

The two Phantoms skimmed through the tops of the clouds while Brad prepared for the instrument letdown. He selected the approach plate for the runway that they had departed from. Robinett would fly the approach for both pilots, but Brad had always monitored the instrument procedures when he flew as a wingman.

"All set back there?" Brad asked Wyatt as the lead Phantom started the descent.

"Yeah," Randy replied with a nervous chuckle. "I'm ready for a cold beer."

"That makes two of us." Brad laughed as the fighters entered the gloomy overcast. He raised his helmet visor in order to see better.

When the Phantoms began bouncing around in the rain and turbulence, Brad increased the separation to twenty-five feet. After leveling off for a short period, Stew Robinett turned south and again descended.

"I think," Brad said as he concentrated on keeping his leader in sight, "that our TACAN is out, too. It's frozen." The tactical air navigation system provided distance and azimuth between the aircraft and the airfield.

Wyatt keyed his intercom. "Do you have any idea where the hell we are?"

Brad paused a moment, trying to reestablish his situational awareness. His soiled flight gloves were damp with salty perspiration. "No . . . we may be too low to get a lock on the TACAN. Just relax."

"I'll relax when you get this sonuvabitch on the ground."

Robinett banked to a new heading, then commenced a slow descent. The rain increased and the clouds grew darker as the Phantoms continued their approach. Both aircraft yawed as the turbulence increased.

"Jesus Christ!" Wyatt swore as he darted looks out of both sides of the cockpit.

"What?" Brad asked, feeling a constriction in his chest.

"We're almost in the trees!" Wyatt snapped his head to the other side of the canopy, then glanced at the altimeter. "We're letting down over a mountain. We gotta climb!"

"Oh!" Brad cried out, yanking the stick back at the instant a bright flash blinded him. His heart pounded as he slammed the throttles into afterburner and waited for the impact.

Wyatt's voice reflected panic. "What happened? Where's—"

"They went in—hit something!" Brad was fighting his own overpowering fear. "Keep broadcasting on guard. We're nordo and declaring an emergency."

"What are you going to do?"

The Phantom shot out of the clouds while Brad rapidly considered their choices. He pulled the throttles back to conserve fuel, then headed for the coastline. "If we can find Casper, he can lead us down."

Feeling a surge of adrenaline, Wyatt searched for any aircraft. "What if we can't? We're almost out of fuel . . . and we can't fly back north."

"Then we'll drop down and follow the coast—see if we can locate the runway."

"I can't believe it," Wyatt said anxiously. "Are you sure they hit something?"

"Positive. They exploded right in front of us." Brad's pulse was racing. "They midaired, or hit the ground."

Wyatt remained quiet a moment, then spoke in a hesitant voice. "Maybe we should think about jumping out."

Brad scanned the empty sky. "Goddamnit, we aren't getting out while we still have gas."

They remained silent while Brad descended to 200 feet above the water. Slowing the F-4 to 180 knots, he hugged the shoreline under the thick clouds and stared at the coastline. If they did locate the runway, Brad planned to land in the opposite direction from their takeoff. He could not risk a dual flameout while he maneuvered to the other end of the airfield.

Brad checked his fuel quantity and thought about a controlled ejection. Minutes seemed to turn into hours as the Phantom gulped fuel and the rain increased.

"Randy," Brad ordered in a calm voice, "keep talking on guard. Someone may hear— There it is!"

"You see the runway?"

"No," Brad shot back, "but there's Hai Van . . . and that little island off the tip."

"Hon Son Tra?"

"Yes," Brad answered while he pointed at the islet. "Right below us. See it?"

"I've got it!"

Banking steeply over the small island, Brad lowered the landing gear and flaps. "That's it. We just need to turn south—be lined up for a straight in."

"I hope," Wyatt replied, straining to see the base, "that they're painting us on radar."

"We're probably too low."

Slowing to approach speed as they crossed the bay, Austin went through his landing checklist and looked at the gear indicators. Satisfied, he glanced out at the runway. Brad was startled to see two F-4s accelerating toward them. The dull-gray fighters were almost obscure against the rain clouds.

Snapping into a tight turn, Brad shoved the throttles forward as the two Phantoms roared past. He could feel his heart pound.

"Get this thing on the ground," Wyatt uttered in shock.

Brad continued in a complete circle, yanking the power back as he rolled on final. Stabilizing at 130 knots, he touched down in a spray of water, popped his drag chute, then rolled to the end of the runway.

After entering the dearming area, Austin noticed a vehicle racing toward their Phantom. The unannounced landing would certainly cause a major flap.

Brad also noticed that his hands were shaking.

CHAPTER TWO

SOUTHERN CALIFORNIA

Hollis Spencer, CIA agent, tugged his utility cap over his forehead as the navy helicopter flared over the darkened hangar. He checked his watch when the wheels touched the moonlit ramp, then grasped his briefcase and jumped to the pavement. The Southern Air Transport C-130 Hercules, operating under government contract, was expected to land in twelve minutes.

Spencer, a former naval aviator, lowered his head and held a firm hand on his cap. He quickly walked away from the beating rotor blades as the pilot added power to begin his return trip to Miramar Naval Air Station.

Hollis Spencer, known as "Cap" to his colleagues in the Agency, had been selected as the project officer for Operation Achilles. The months of delicate negotiations and in-depth logistical planning were over. The United States Navy was about to add a unique asset to its airplane inventory.

The project officer, a lanky man in his early forties, approached the sentry at the entrance to the blacked-out hangar. After Spencer presented his identification badge, the guard switched off his flashlight and stepped aside. The young sentry knew the affable CIA officer well, as did the rest of the security specialists, but the identification routine was not taken for granted.

Entering the light trap, Spencer strode into the huge building and walked toward his office. The red-tinted floodlights cast soft shadows on the faces of the technicians and engineers who were waiting for the prized airplane to arrive. Each had been handpicked for the operation.

"Morning, Cap," the senior military adviser said, stirring his steaming coffee.

"Good morning," Spencer replied, thinking about how many days had commenced at two o'clock in the morning. "This is going to be a special day."

"You bet," the portly naval officer replied. "I haven't been able to sleep for three nights. My wife thinks I'm seeing another woman."

Spencer chuckled as he reached for the doorknob, then paused. "Hank, give me a holler when the Herc is on final."

"I'll do that." Captain Henry Murray raised his mug. "They should be on time."

Spencer flipped the light switch, opened his leather briefcase, then tossed four file folders onto his cluttered desk. He sat down and opened the top personnel record. Three navy pilots, along with one marine aviator, had been selected to participate in the first step of Operation Achilles.

Each of the four fighter pilots had distinguished himself in aerial combat. Two of the navy pilots, with one MiG kill each, had already been approached. Each had enthusiastically accepted the offer without knowing any of the specifics.

Now Spencer had to interview the last two aviators and offer them the chance to volunteer.

He studied the material in the folder, noting that marine Captain Bradley Carlyle Austin was an alumnus of the Naval Academy. He had been a member of the swimming team, and competed as a diver. Graduating with honors, Austin had selected a commission in the Marine Corps. After a tour of duty at Quantico, Virginia, he had reported for flight training at Pensacola, Florida.

He looked carefully at the black-and-white photograph and read the brief description in the file. At five feet ten and 165 pounds, Austin appeared to be trim and athletic. Spencer noted the tanned face, the direct look in the hazel eyes, the modest, faint smile. Like the other three pilots, Brad Austin was a bachelor.

Spencer remembered his own first visit to the Marine Corps base at Quantico. That eventful trip had changed the course of his life.

It was after his F9F Cougar had been struck by flak during the Korean War that Lieutenant (junior grade) Hollis Spencer had crash-landed the jet near Seoul.

The accident had cost him his right eye and left a long, jagged scar across the top of his head. From that time forward, Spencer had worn a patch over his blind eye and a hat to cover the wide gap of wrinkled skin.

The navy had medically retired him at the age of twenty-six. Afterward, Spencer had traveled to Washington, D.C., hoping to join the Federal Bureau of Investigation. Turned down because of the lost eye, he had driven to Quantico to visit his brother, a second lieutenant who was going through Basic School.

His brother had consoled him, suggesting that he apply to the Central Intelligence Agency. He was especially qualified since he had a degree in psychology, and had been a highly decorated navy combat pilot.

The rest—Spencer smiled to himself—was history: a rewarding career that had budded at Quantico, Virginia.

Spencer glanced back to Brad Austin's folder. The young aviator had performed extremely well in the advanced jet strike syllabus, graduating first in his class. Skimming the fitness reports, Spencer was impressed by the comments from Austin's senior officers. His previous commanding officer had written that Austin was a mature, professional young officer with a straightforward personality and excellent flying skills. Another CO called him a gregarious officer who fulfilled his responsibilities while maintaining a sense of humor. Spencer also read a brief note explaining that Austin's father, Vice Admiral Carlyle Whitney Austin, had recently retired.

"Cap," Henry Murray bellowed, "the aluminum overcast is on final."

"Thanks," Spencer replied, slipping Brad Austin's file to the bottom of the stack. "Be right there."

He turned off the lights and walked to the entrance of the hangar. Trying to contain his excitement, Hollis grinned when he passed the sentry.

"Mister Spencer," the guard said enthusiastically, "is that the bird bringing in the secret plane?"

"It sure is," Spencer answered, smiling to himself. He searched the sky as he walked across the ramp to join Hank Murray and the other men.

"I hear it," Spencer said to Murray, "but my eye hasn't adjusted to the darkness."

The navy captain pointed toward the end of the dry lake. "He's just coming over the runway . . . made a wide, flat approach."

Spencer spotted the four-engined turboprop in the bright moonlight.

The C-130, flying with the external lights extinguished, had started to flare. The pilot snapped on the landing lights a few seconds before the cargo plane smoothly touched down. The lights went out as the pilot placed the propellers in reverse pitch.

Hollis Spencer watched the lumbering plane roll to the end of the wide runway, then awkwardly turn and follow the flight-line jeep.

Spencer and Murray stepped away from the group of men.

"Hank," the CIA officer said as the Hercules approached the hangar, "how soon do you think you can have the aircraft ready to fly, without cutting any corners?"

The noisy C-130 taxied past, turning ninety degrees to point the tail at the closed hangar doors.

"We should have it," Murray paused, bracing himself against the gale-force propwash, "ready for the first hop in ten days . . . fifteen at the outside."

"That'll fit just right," Spencer responded, turning away from the pungent odor of burned jet fuel.

They looked at the back of the plane when the cargo ramp was lowered. The engines wound down, then mercifully spun to a stop as the hangar doors opened. Shielded red floodlights illuminated the aircraft parking area as the men hurried to unload the airplane components.

"I'm going to take a walk," Spencer said, rubbing his hands for warmth, "and see if I can work off some of my anxiety."

"I know what you mean," Murray responded, glancing at the gray forklift approaching the airplane. "We'll all breathe a sigh of relief when the parts are in the hangar."

Out of habit, Spencer looked at his watch. "Let's hope the other Herc is on time."

"It will be," Murray assured him, then walked toward the cargo plane. "You know CIA Air better than anyone."

"You're probably right," Hollis laughed, then turned and set off toward the runway.

He had worked with the CIA airlines before, including Civil Air Transport, Air Asia, Intermountain, Southern Air Transport, and Air America. His most recent assignment had been in the Agency's Directorate for Plans. The department engaged in covert operations throughout the world.

The activities of the Directorate for Plans were handled with the utmost secrecy. The department was exempt from the CIA's internal review procedures, a step many senior CIA officials continued to question. The answer was standard. A review might compromise national security, or place key agents in life-threatening situations.

Spencer had worked for an extended period of time with Air America, the agency's largest airline. Incorporated in Delaware, the CIA airline operated as a civilian organization. The company was able to bypass the bureaucracy and endless red tape of the military, fly international routes with a minimum of interference, and break rules and restrictions if a mission called for it.

Spencer stopped, concerned that a nervous sentry might mistake him for an infiltrator. He scanned the star-studded sky, then looked back toward the hangar. The huge cargo plane was barely discernible in the gentle red glow.

Turning, Spencer retraced his steps. He smiled to himself, remembering the days and nights of frustration spent tracking the operations of the Air America fleet. The organization, functioning behind a smoke screen of secrecy, constantly shuffled planes around to other companies in the network. Engine serial numbers were routinely changed, along with the aircraft registration numbers on the tails.

Spencer remembered seeing a classified photograph showing three Curtiss C-46 Commandos with the same tail number. During certain clandestine operations, one C-46 was left in plain sight at a major airport, for the purpose of having witnesses view it, while the other two aircraft were involved in their assigned activities.

Damaged aircraft were cannibalized to keep other planes flying. Many Air America pilots laughed about flying airplanes that were composed of major parts from a half-dozen other aircraft.

Spencer angled across the aircraft parking ramp, reviewing the various elements in the top-secret project. Time had somehow telescoped, and it seemed that it was only yesterday when he had learned about the operation. From the beginning, Spencer had hungered to see the covert plan come to fruition. It was the type of venture that quickened his pulse, and, knowing that it would have a significant impact on the war effort, gave him satisfaction. Cap Spencer would never admit it, but high-risk operations were an indispensable source of vitality in his life.

He had been working with Air America in Vientiane, Laos, when the Agency had rushed him to Langley. Though he did not realize it at the time, his experience with the clandestinely operated airline would prove invaluable to Operation Achilles.

Stopping seventy yards from the transport plane, Spencer watched while the crew started the engines and raised the aft ramp. When the C-130 taxied away, Spencer continued toward the darkened hangar. The large doors were sliding closed when Hank Murray stepped through to the ramp.

Spencer noticed the smile on his face. "Well, what do you think about our prize?"

"It's in mint condition," Murray answered, giving Spencer the okay sign, "at least what I've seen so far."

Both men turned when the second cargo plane's landing lights caught their attention. Like the first C-130, the lights came on a moment before touchdown, then flickered off when the pilot selected reverse thrust. The secret weapon, plus a large quantity of spare parts, was now safely in the hands of the CIA project officer.

"What's your next step?" Murray asked, watching the first Hercules taxi for takeoff.

"I'm flying to Alameda this morning to meet another navy pilot, our third candidate. Then I'm off to Bangkok to interview the marine pilot."

Murray nodded, then beamed. "Let's take a look at our baby while they unload the rest of the parts."

CHAPTER THREE

DA NANG AIR BASE

Brad Austin and Randy Wyatt played acey-deucey at a battered card table in the Hot Pad trailer. Their wingman and his RIO were reading at the opposite end of the narrow room. The sound of shrieking engines filled the trailer as a continuous stream of jets thundered into the air, punctuated by the *whop-whop* of helicopter rotor blades.

A dented air conditioner, set for maximum cooling on its high blower, occasionally rattled and spit drops of water on the floor. Brad had set a bucket under the dilapidated machine in order to catch the water.

Outside on the Hot Pad at the north end of Da Nang, two armed and fueled F-4 Phantoms sat in the searing heat. The fighter-bombers, each carrying twelve 250-pound fragmentation bombs and sixteen five-inch zuni rockets, had been configured for close air support. If army or marine ground units needed emergency air cover, the Hot Pad crews could be airborne in five minutes.

Both aircraft were connected to ground power units to expedite starting the General Electric J-79 engines. Support crews, sweltering in the shimmering heat and damp humidity, lounged near the fierce-looking Phantoms.

The waiting went on around the clock, wearing nerves thin and sapping everyone's strength. The oppressive heat combined with the underlying tension made Hot Pad duty an exercise in personal discipline.

Randy Wyatt tossed the dice through the homemade chute, watching them tumble across the stained game board. "Bird balls," he said listlessly as the two cubes presented him with a pair of aces.

Wyatt's close-cropped red hair was thinning at the temples. His aqua-blue eyes stood out in a sea of freckles on his angular face. An inch over six feet, the country-western aficionado had been a star pitcher on the Oklahoma State University baseball team.

"Let's take a short break," Brad suggested, unzipping his torso harness and flight suit. "It's so goddamn hot in here, I can't think."

He walked to the chattering air conditioner and stuck his face next to the grille. "I can't believe that the same company that made this piece of shit manufactured the engines in our Fox-4."

Wyatt feigned a look through the window. "Yeah, they've got a bucket under the plane, too."

Brad closed his eyes and inhaled the semi-cool air. "What I wouldn't give for a swimming pool . . . even a kiddie pool."

"Why don't you draft a missive to the commandant," Wyatt said with a straight face, "and tell him this stinking hole he sent us to is lacking in certain amenities?"

Austin ignored the remark and returned to the table. "You know, Randy, I can't get over Stew and Vic hitting the mountain . . . nine feet from the top."

Wyatt looked down, sharing the same frustration about the tragic accident. "Stew was a damn good pilot, no doubt about that." He paused, observing his friend. "Brad, you need to put it behind you and think about the present. We'll never know what they were thinking."

"I know," Brad frowned, "but there has to be a plausible reason for Stew's actions. I would have flown his wing anywhere. He was a bright guy, and a good stick."

Wyatt noticed that their wingman's RIO was listening to the conversation.

"Brad," Randy said quietly, "at least they didn't know what hit them."

Austin sighed. "True, but that's little consolation for their families."

They flinched at the dull buzz from the Hot Pad phone. Everyone leaped to their feet while Wyatt yanked the receiver from its cradle.

As Brad and the other crew headed for the door, Randy Wyatt waved for them to stop. "No scramble," he mouthed, covering the mouthpiece, then thanked the controller. "Twenty-three is on the way back with extensive damage."

Brad looked at the tattered flight schedule. "Chitwood and Davey Perkins."

The four men hurried outside to watch the arrival of Rhino 23. Brad asked his plane captain to man the Hot Pad phone until the aircrews returned to the trailer.

Walking parallel to the runway, Austin and Wyatt passed a crushed water buffalo. The portable water cistern, with the wheels angled out forty-five degrees, was mangled beyond repair. Twenty-five minutes after Brad and Randy had reported to the Hot Pad trailer, a CH-46 helicopter had inadvertently dropped the water container from a height of 200 feet.

"I'm sure as hell glad," Wyatt laughed, "that that mother didn't land on our shack."

"Yeah." Brad grimaced. "We'd have been about three feet shorter."

They both saw the black smoke from Rhino 23 as the Phantom turned on a two-mile final approach.

Brad shielded his eyes as Captain Alec Chitwood lowered the F-4's landing gear. "It looks like they've got . . . there's something burning."

"Look at the left wing." Randy pointed. "The ejector rack and pylon are gone."

Brad waited until the howling Phantom was closer. "You're right. The left wing has taken a hit."

Paralyzed, they watched the stricken fighter-bomber cross the runway threshold and touch down in a puff of tire smoke. A fraction of a second later, the left main landing gear sheared off, causing the drop tank to separate from the wing.

"Oh, shit," Austin exclaimed as the air base crash equipment started chasing the Phantom.

The fuel tank burst into yellow-orange flames before it slid off the runway, tumbling end over end.

The heavily damaged F-4 continued to slide as the left wing ground along the pavement. Slowly, the aircraft slewed around and stopped sideways next to the edge of the runway. A small fire erupted under the fuselage, then flashed into billowing black-and-orange flames.

Motionless, Brad stared at the conflagration, then yelled in futility. "Get some foam on 'em, for Christ's sake."

Austin and Wyatt were stunned when the ejection seats fired.

Brad watched Perkins and Chitwood arc through the air, separate from their seats, then drift to a landing next to a fire truck.

"I think," Brad paused to take a deep breath, "they'll be debriefing over a couple of stiff drinks."

The recent rain had left the air heavy with humidity. Dark clouds surrounded the base, carrying the threat of another torrential downpour. The rumbling sound of thunder rolled across the flight line.

Fuel and ordnance handlers, along with maintenance and support personnel, continued their duties in defiance of the miserable weather.

Four of the squadron's F-4s, assigned to barrier combat air patrol for the ships at Yankee Station, continued to cycle back and forth in around-the-clock operations. The rest of the Phantoms, with the exception of the Hot Pad aircraft, were tasked with interdiction and close air support missions.

Brad sat alone in the mess hall, tuning out the ever-present sound of jet engines and helicopter rotors. He reached for his wallet and carefully removed a picture of Leigh Ann Ladasau. Brad studied the black-and-white photograph, thinking about the first time he had seen her. Vacationing in Hawaii, he had been mesmerized by the petite brunette with the sparkling blue eyes and radiant smile.

Closing his eyes, Brad remembered her pleasant laughter and beautifully sculptured face. They had shared one night of passion in San Francisco, and Brad would never forget it. He reread Leigh Ann's latest letter, savoring every word, especially the part where she wrote that she dearly missed him and could not wait to see him again.

"Hey, guy," Randy Wyatt said as he placed his tray down across from Brad. "We've been rescheduled for the nineteen-hundred launch."

"Good," Brad replied, folding the letter. "I'll have time to drop my girl a note."

Wyatt reached for the black-and-white photograph. "No doubt about it . . . for sure."

Brad gave Randy a wry grin. "What?"

Handing the picture back, Wyatt shook his head. "She is definitely a knockout."

Randy tasted a bite of the ham and beans, chewed slowly and thoughtfully, then plopped his fork on the tray. A look of contempt crossed his ruddy face. "I wouldn't feed this shit to the Cong."

"Yeah, I agree." Brad chuckled. "The navy spoiled me while I was aboard the carrier."

Wyatt's response was cut off when he noticed their commanding officer entering the mess hall.

Lieutenant Colonel Bud Parnell was an enigma to most everyone. Short and barrel-chested, Parnell, nicknamed "The Bulldog," was a tenacious and cocky fighter pilot from the old school. But Parnell was also kind and considerate. Shifting from one phase of his personality to the other, he never allowed anyone to know the whole of the real man behind the facade.

Parnell walked straight to Brad's side, taking the seat next to him.

"Austin," the CO said as he unfolded a message form, "do you know anything about this directive?"

Brad accepted the piece of paper, scanned the contents, then reread the message slowly. The instructions, from the commanding general of the air wing, ordered Brad to report to Marine Colonel Charles Thornton, U.S. Military Liaison Office, Bangkok, Thailand. He was to report no later than 1600 hours, two days hence.

Confused, Brad handed Parnell the message. "Sir, this is a total surprise to me. I don't have any idea," he paused while Wyatt hastily excused himself and left the table, "what this is about. . . ."

"Well," Parnell scratched his earlobe, "I don't either. I made a couple of inquiries, and no one seems to know diddly-shit . . . including the general's aide."

Brad started to reply, then decided to remain quiet when he saw the crimson streak creep up Parnell's neck.

"What's strange," the CO said with a hint of anger, "is that this isn't temporary duty. You are checking out of the squadron, lock, stock, and personnel record."

Parnell jammed the message in the breast pocket of his damp utilities. "We're short of pilots and RIOs, so some staff puke decides to take an experienced aviator and turn him into a paper pusher."

Brad's mind raced, trying to think of a reason for the unexpected orders. He had only recently suppressed his fears that his breach of the rules of engagement over Phuc Yen would not return to haunt him.

"You can stand down from any further duties," Parnell said as he rose. "You better get to humpin', if you plan to get out of here today."

"Yes, sir," Brad replied, rising out of respect. "I'm sorry, Skipper."

"Hell," Parnell spat, "it isn't your fault. Stop by and see me," the CO somberly continued, "last thing before you leave."

A warning bell sounded in Brad's mind. "Yes, sir."

* * *

Lieutenant Colonel Bud Parnell's dusty hootch was indistinguishable from the quarters of his pilots and radar-intercept officers. One side of the CO's temporary shelter had been severely damaged during a midnight mortar and rocket attack.

Brad dropped his two custom-made canvas bags by the entrance and smartly rapped on the screen door. In the Marine Corps, Austin had learned as a newly minted second lieutenant, one did not tap lightly on a door. Marines were expected boldly to announce their arrival.

"Come in, Brad," Parnell greeted while the squadron safety officer excused himself and left the hootch.

"Sit down," Parnell gestured toward a worn folding chair. "I know you've got to hurry to catch the trash hauler, so I'll just take a minute."

Don't bullshit me, Skipper. You'll take as long as you want.

Parnell propped his boots on his wooden footlocker and clasped his hands behind his head. "Brad, do you think your sudden departure has anything to do with the rumors I've heard about Phuc Yen . . . and the purported cover-up?"

I knew this was coming.

The CO was referring to an incident that Austin had initiated while he had been an exchange pilot on an aircraft carrier. Variations of the story had traveled throughout the naval aviation community, expanding with each telling. The yarn had the earmark of a classic aviation anecdote.

"Sir," Brad cautiously answered, "as I said before, I honestly don't know."

Parnell leaned back and stared at the ceiling for a moment, then gave Austin a thin smile. "Out of curiosity, what really happened at Phuc Yen?"

You're going to nail me to the wall, aren't you . . . ?

"Skipper," Brad squirmed, "I've been ordered not to say anything about Phuc Yen."

Phuc Yen, at the time of Austin's breach of the rules of engagement, had been an off-limits MiG airfield twelve miles north of Hanoi. The base had become a sanctuary for Communist fighter pilots who happened to be getting the worst end of an aerial engagement. At the first sign of trouble, the MiG pilots would race for the protection of Phuc Yen.

"Well, let me tell you what I've heard," Parnell shifted his feet, "and if my info is in the ballpark, you can nod your head as you go out the door."

Come on, Skipper, give me a break.

"With one MiG to your credit," Parnell reached for his cigar, "you went after North Vietnam's second-leading ace."

Out of the corner of his eye, Parnell caught the quick frown that creased Brad's forehead.

The CO maintained his poker face. "Major Nguyen Thanh Dao shot down your flight leader, you chased Dao to Phuc Yen, made up your own rules, then blew his ass out of the air and blasted another MiG on the taxiway."

Parnell hesitated a moment. "Is that about on target?"

"Bull's-eye," Brad answered, and rose from the chair. "Skipper, I've got to get underway."

Bud Parnell smiled, then stood and shook hands with Austin.

"Brad, if they're trying to pigeonhole you, or give you any grief, let me know. I've got a couple of friends who are wearing stars."

Brad pumped Parnell's hand. "Thank you, sir."

"That's a great story." The CO laughed, and slapped Brad on the back. "Someday, you'll have to tell me how you got away with it . . . without shitting in your mess kit."

CHAPTER FOUR

Brad had checked into the New Thai Hotel, showered, changed into a fresh uniform, then called the Military Liaison Office. He had been surprised when the duty officer had asked for his telephone number and explained that a Hollis Spencer would contact him.

Twenty minutes later, Spencer had called and instructed Brad to meet him at 5 P.M. on the deck of the restaurant facing his hotel. Brad was tempted to ask for the secret password, but decided that would be too frivolous. If the Marine Corps had found it necessary to send him all the way to Bangkok under unexplained circumstances, the matter must be serious.

Brad sat at the ornate table, wanting a beer but ordering a glass of iced tea instead. He looked out over the sprawling city that was the capital of Thailand. He had been astonished at his first sight of Bangkok's elaborate temples. They looked to him as if they had been formed from gold and marzipan. The major hindrance both to travel and sightseeing, he had learned in his fifty-five-minute taxi ride from the airport, was the impenetrable congestion in the streets.

Brad checked his watch: one minute to five. He looked up to see a man in a crisp tan suit approaching him. Mister Hollis Spencer, he presumed. Slightly taller than Brad, the man was trim and wore a patch over his right eye. He walked directly toward Austin's table.

Rising, Brad came to attention before he realized that he didn't have to salute. "Good afternoon, sir."

"Afternoon," Spencer pleasantly responded. "You are Captain Austin?"

"Yes, sir," Brad answered with a trace of caution in his response.

The project officer extended his hand. "Hollis Spencer."

Brad shook hands with the agent and avoided glancing at the dark eye patch.

Spencer noted the guarded manner as he placed his briefcase on the table. "It's cocktail hour." He smiled as he reached for the chair across from Brad. "How about a beer."

"That sounds good," Brad replied, motioning for a waiter. He suddenly felt surprisingly relaxed with this stranger, but curious as to why a civilian was meeting him.

After ordering for both of them, Spencer glanced at the vessels on the river before turning his head to Brad. "Well, Captain, I know you have many questions, and I won't keep you in suspense."

Brad nodded, but remained quiet.

"I am a liaison between the military and certain civilian agencies in charge of special operations." Anticipating a reaction from the marine, Spencer was pleased to see that Austin was quietly digesting the information. "You have been sent to meet me through all the proper channels.

"The fact that I have your service records here," Spencer tapped his briefcase, "and your future orders, if we come to an agreement, should reassure you as to the legitimacy of my offer."

Although his curiosity was thoroughly aroused, Brad showed no emotion.

"However," Spencer continued in a low voice, "if you need more proof, more credentials—"

Brad waved his hand to indicate that it was all right. He trusted Spencer, so far. The man had a military bearing, though dressed as a civilian. Could he be an aviator? With an eye patch? In any case, Spencer was right; Brad had been sent through all the proper channels.

"I've got an interesting assignment for you." Spencer paused while the beers were delivered. "But you are at liberty to refuse it . . . without any questions asked."

Oh, shit, Brad thought to himself, *here it comes. Chief file clerk in the bowels of some civilian agency. Is the Marine Corps behind this? Are they putting me on ice and out of sight because of the incident at Phuc Yen?*

After the waiter left, Spencer turned casually, but slowly and carefully scanned the occupants of the other outdoor tables. He looked Brad in the eye. "How would you like to become a test pilot?"

Caught off guard, Brad forgot about his beer. "A test pilot? That's it?"

Spencer sipped his beer slowly. "That's right. To start with." He could see the relief on Austin's face as a grin appeared at one corner of the captain's mouth. "The project is top secret, strictly voluntary."

Brad's eyes questioned the agent. *Is this on the level?*

"I cannot say much about the project at this point," Spencer smiled reassuringly, "but we believe that you're the Marine Corps representative we need. You'll learn more at the right time. For now you'll just have to trust me."

Trying to start at the beginning, Brad carefully formed his reply. "Mister Spencer, I haven't been through Pax River." He was referring to the Test Pilot School at the Patuxent Naval Air Test Center in Maryland.

"That doesn't matter, son." Spencer smiled. "You know how to fly an airplane . . . mighty well, according to your records. Besides, we will have a Pax River grad who will be flying the aircraft before you take your shot."

"Well," Brad said slowly, still feeling that something strange was going on and wishing he could ask for the real story, "I really appreciate the compliment, but you're not giving me very much information on which to make a reasonable decision."

Spencer raised his glass. "I know, and I wish I could say more, but you will just have to trust me." He really liked this young man; his intelligence, his caution. "Brad, it is sometimes a little hard to categorize things in special projects, but let's say for now that the job will be as a test pilot. At least in the beginning."

And in the end? Brad thought to himself. But he knew better than to ask. The end of any operation in war is unpredictable. Like in life.

"If you come aboard, you'll be reporting to me in San Diego, California." Spencer paused a long moment. "You'll have a thorough briefing as soon as you check in."

Brad still wondered why Spencer had traveled all the way to Bangkok to recruit him to be a test pilot. The Marine Corps certainly had hundreds of highly qualified pilots, some with extensive backgrounds as test pilots. He decided to try one more approach.

"Sir, can you tell me what I'll be flying?"

"I'm afraid not." Spencer chuckled. "If you volunteer, I can tell you when you arrive in California."

"What's the alternative," Brad tentatively asked, "if I don't volunteer?"

Placing his forearms on the table, Spencer cast a look around. "You'll be reassigned to a different squadron at Da Nang . . . and we will never have had this conversation."

Austin smiled and shook his head. It sounded intriguing. And if it meant going stateside for a while and not getting shot at every day, he would be stupid not to volunteer.

Brad slowly reached for his beer and gave Spencer a long look. "Count me in."

"Good." Spencer smiled. "I don't think you'll find it boring, to say the least."

The afternoon heat had slowly dissipated after the sun had dropped below the horizon.

Brad watched the delicate Thai dancers perform their traditional rituals on the lawn adjacent to his hotel. The blazing torches around the perimeter of the courtyard cast a cheerful glow on the evening river traffic.

"Would you care for another drink?" the slender young man asked Brad.

"Oh, I don't think so," Brad answered, swirling his tall scotch and soda. "I'll go ahead and order."

When the waiter had gone, Brad tried again to unravel the puzzling situation posed by Hollis Spencer. The Marine Corps did not function in riddles like this. He felt as if he were a character in a spy novel, or an agent of the Central Intelligence Agency.

Brad reached for the vinyl packet Spencer had given him. It contained all manner of instructions and an indication that at some point Brad would be assuming another identity. He was to send his uniforms and identification papers to Hollis Spencer at the Miramar Naval Air Station's Personal Property Shipping Office.

There were four hundred dollars in cash and a travel voucher to fly on an airliner leased to the Department of Defense. He was to wear civilian clothes, return to Da Nang Air Base in three days, and board a World Airways jetliner bound for Travis Air Force Base, California.

Brad's meal arrived, and he absently dabbled with a few bites of the

Panang red curry with chicken and prawns. Losing interest in the meal, he looked at the packet as if it were a snake. *What am I getting into?*

The essence of the most significant memorandum in the packet— something Hollis Spencer had only hinted at in their last moments of conversation—was that though Brad was still in the Marine Corps, he would not be so recognized until the project was terminated. His service record, which Spencer had taken with him, would be in a secure place. Brad would be paid in cash, and, if he was killed, he would be listed as missing in action en route to Bangkok.

Hollis Spencer had explained that Brad's name had been deleted from the passenger manifest of the cargo plane that had flown him to Bangkok. He would return to Da Nang using a fictitious identity. The whereabouts of marine Captain Brad Austin, from the time he had checked out of his fighter squadron at Da Nang, would remain unknown.

Brad had been instructed to rent an automobile after his arrival at Travis, drive to San Diego, check into a prearranged room at the Miramar Bachelor Officers' Quarters, and wait to be contacted.

Spencer had also made it clear that Brad would not be restricted to the base. However, he was not to communicate with his family, or let friends or acquaintances know that he had returned to the United States.

Lifting his glass, Brad tossed back the last of his drink. He realized that it had been assumed that he had no close attachments, but he was determined to find a way to see Leigh Ann.

CHAPTER FIVE

A high-pitched shriek and accompanying sonic boom announced the arrival of Lieutenant Commander Grady Stanfield. Hollis Spencer flinched from the explosive sound, then casually raised his arm from a wingtip and walked out to the aircraft ramp.

Spencer shielded his eye from the dazzling glare of the early-morning sunshine. He smiled inwardly as the sleek F-8 Crusader snapped upright from knife-edge flight. The large speed brake protruding from the belly rapidly slowed the aircraft while Stanfield lowered the landing gear and raised the wing-incidence handle.

Every time Spencer watched a jet blast over the runway and snap into a ninety-degree break, he longed to be at the controls of a fighter plane again.

Spencer caught a glance of Hank Murray as he walked out of the hangar. The chubby navy captain had a scowl on his face.

"Quite an arrival." Spencer smiled.

"I ought to ream that sonuvabitch's ass out," Murray growled. An engineer by profession, he had never appreciated the mind-set of fighter pilots. "I almost dropped the goddamned altimeter on the cockpit floor."

"Well," Spencer calmly said, "you know the old cliché."

"I sure as hell do." Murray shook his head in disgust. "You can always tell a fighter pilot, but you can't tell him much."

"I'll talk to him," Spencer replied in an attempt to placate Murray, then turned and walked back to the hangar. Although Hank Murray outranked the Crusader pilot, Hollis Spencer had jurisdiction over everyone at the secret base.

Spencer paused in the shade near the hangar entrance and watched Stanfield land and taxi to the ramp. After the engine spooled down, Spencer walked out to greet the senior aviator assigned to the operation.

Grady Stanfield was a small man with a perpetual smile and a gleam in his brown eyes. Young for his rank, Stanfield had finished college in three years. Highly motivated, he had learned to fly in high school and had obtained his commercial pilot's license in college.

Five weeks after graduating from Notre Dame, Stanfield had reported to Pensacola Naval Air Station for flight training. Graduating with honors, he spent a tour of duty as a fleet fighter pilot, attended graduate school, then reported to the Naval Test Pilot School.

After completing the rigorous course at Patuxent River, Stanfield had been sent to a squadron preparing to deploy for a cruise to Southeast Asia. Four and a half months later, flying an F-8E Crusader, Grady Stanfield had shot down his first and only MiG.

"Welcome aboard," Spencer greeted while Stanfield climbed down from the cockpit.

"Thank you, sir," the pilot replied, beaming, and then reached for Spencer's outstretched hand. "It's a privilege to be here."

Unlike the other three pilots who had been selected for the highly classified project, Stanfield had known from their first meeting that Hollis Spencer was a senior CIA agent. Grady Stanfield, the ranking officer among the four pilots, would be the officer-in-charge of the aviators.

"Come on in," Spencer motioned as he grasped the pilot's helmet bag, "and I'll show you where the flight-gear locker is located."

"Great," Stanfield said, spotting the almost assembled airplane. "Sir, may I take a look . . . ? I can't believe it's actually here."

"Sure." Spencer chuckled. "I can't believe it either."

They slowly walked around the aircraft, stopping occasionally to inspect the wings and fuselage. Stanfield looked at the leading edge of the wing, pausing at the point where it attached to the fuselage. He ran his hand along the top and bottom of the metal wing, frowning at the wrinkles in the skin. "It looks like this was manufactured in a machine shop."

"That's probably right," Spencer replied dryly, "but I don't have any complaints."

"Amazing," Stanfield said as he approached the nose of the airplane. He examined the split air intake and gun camera opening before dropping to one knee to study the gun pods and blast-protection panel. He noticed that two rivets were missing from under the engine air intake. "When will the Mark-12s be installed?"

Spencer knelt down and looked at the gun pods. "I expect it will take three or four days to install the cannons."

Spencer's right knee popped when he rose. "We want to complete the aerial gunnery testing as soon as possible."

Stanfield nodded and removed his sunglasses. "Is it okay if I look in the cockpit?"

"Be my guest," Spencer answered as the test pilot mounted the narrow steps on the makeshift platform next to the smooth fuselage.

Hank Murray stood on an elevated bench on the opposite side of the canopy. Attired in work khakis, Murray grudgingly shook hands when Grady Stanfield introduced himself.

A technician sat in the pilot's seat, adjusting the flight instruments and checking the controls. He leaned back to allow the test pilot to have a better view.

Stanfield thoroughly inspected the cramped cockpit and glanced at Spencer. "It looks like they stuffed things wherever they could find a spot."

"Yeah," Cap Spencer chuckled, "but it sure goes like a bat out of hell."

Grady smiled and looked at the navy captain. "Do you have any manuals or technical info I could borrow?"

Unsmiling, Murray gave Hollis Spencer a hasty look before addressing Stanfield. "Briefing folders are being prepared, to include the aircraft performance and systems operations manual. The information should be available Monday morning."

Noticing Murray's quiet restraint, Stanfield decided not to ask any more questions, at least until his relationship with the crusty captain warmed. "Thank you, sir," Stanfield said as he backed down the wooden steps.

"You're welcome," the engineer acknowledged, returning to his conversation with the instrumentation specialist.

"Let's stow your gear," Spencer suggested with a smile, "and we'll go over the program we've outlined."

"Yes, sir," the fresh-faced pilot replied, shaking his head. "This is

really incredible. The cockpit looks like it was designed by a committee where no one talked with each other."

The wind whipped across the top of Brad's hair as he wheeled the
Mustang convertible through the turn leading to the Miramar Naval
Air Station. Brad had spent the night in Santa Ana, but he had followed
his orders and had not contacted any of his friends at the El Toro
Marine Corps Air Station. He had started to call Leigh Ann, then
decided to wait until he was situated in his new quarters.

After a hearty breakfast, Brad had checked on his stored Corvette
before departing for San Diego. He longed to drive the 427-cubic-inch
Stingray, but he had been explicitly instructed to use a rental car
without a base sticker.

Approaching the gate to the air station, Brad slowed and brought the
car to a smooth stop. The guard scrutinized Brad's government identification card, scanned the wrinkled sheet on his clipboard, then gave
Brad permission to enter the base.

The bar in the officers' club was unusually quiet for a weekend afternoon. Brad selected a stool near the end of the counter, ordered a beer,
and let his mind drift to more pleasant things. He pictured sailing with
Leigh Ann across San Diego Bay.

"Brad Austin!" a voice exclaimed from across the room.

Startled, Brad turned to see Nick Palmer walking toward him.

"You son of a bitch," Palmer said, thrusting his hand toward his
friend, "it's good to see you."

"It's good to see you, too," Brad replied as the two pilots shook
hands enthusiastically. "What the hell are you doing in this part of the
world?"

"I'm in the navy, remember?" Palmer laughed aloud. "And this is a
naval air station."

Cautiously, Brad glanced around the room. "Let's grab a table, and
I'll buy you a cold one."

"Fair enough." Palmer grinned and grasped Brad on the shoulder.
"We've missed you."

The two men had become close friends when Brad was serving as an
exchange pilot with a carrier-based navy fighter squadron. They had
flown together on a number of combat missions, alternating between
flight leader and wingman.

Considered the two best aviators in the F-4 Phantom squadron, each had an "official" MiG kill to his credit. Austin had destroyed two additional MiGs at Phuc Yen, but they had not been disclosed in the ensuing bureaucratic cover-up.

An inch short of six feet, Nick Palmer had an athletic physique and movie-idol looks. His light-brown hair and easy smile never failed to attract women. A graduate of Princeton University, "Nick the Stick" Palmer was the oldest son of a wealthy manufacturing mogul.

The bar was almost empty, and Brad relaxed. He ordered two beers and followed Nick to a table.

"Seriously," Palmer asked as they sat down, "what is a jarhead doing at Miramar?"

Feeling a pang of trepidation, Brad hesitated a moment. He did not want to lie to his friend. "Actually, Nick, it's a crazy story. One that I'm not at liberty to discuss . . . even with close friends."

The look of surprise was clearly evident on Palmer's face. He took a quick swig of his beer. "You've been recruited—actually you volunteered—to become a test pilot, right?"

Austin blanched, then leaned closer to Palmer. "Nick, what the hell are you talking about?"

Palmer inhaled deeply while he cast a quick look at the bar. No one was paying any attention to them.

"Brad, I have been invited to become a test pilot. Only thing is, the job is not at Pax River."

"Jesus H. Christ," Brad whispered through his unmoving lips. "I'm in the same shit."

Palmer tilted his glass up, swallowing the remaining contents in three gulps. "What were you told?"

"I was offered the assignment by a civilian—some kind of adviser to the military."

"What'd he say?"

"Basically," Brad softly chuckled, "he said his project—or whatever the hell it is—is so secret that the Marine Corps would have to forget about me while I'm assigned to the operation."

Palmer signaled for the cocktail waitress. "That's the same spiel that I heard. I was also informed that the fastest way to a court-martial is to even mention the project."

"The craziest thing," Brad shook his head, "is the fact that the Marine Corps sent me all the way to Bangkok to meet this guy with an eye patch—"

"Goddamn," Palmer interrupted in shock. "It sounds to me like the same fellow. . . ."

Brad sat back and looked at Nick intently. "Do you feel like we're in the Twilight Zone?"

Palmer nodded and looked up at the waitress. "I'll have a double scotch and soda."

The sun had just dipped below the horizon when Austin and Palmer drove into the parking lot of the Snug Harbor Lounge. They had chosen the nondescript lounge after deciding to leave the officers' club. Both men had agreed that, sooner or later, someone they knew would walk in and discover them.

They locked the convertible and took in the sights and sounds of San Diego Bay. The natural harbor was the home of a vast armada of navy warships and their support vessels.

Brad became absorbed in watching a sloop preparing to dock at a marina below them. "If we're going to be here for any length of time, let's get an apartment close to the water."

"If they'll let us," Nick responded, giving his attention to a destroyer entering the mouth of the harbor. "What do you think this test-pilot deal is about?"

"I don't know," Brad answered, turning toward the door of the cocktail lounge. "Since we've both shot down MiGs, they may have some new top-secret tactics that they want us to try. That, or some 'gee whiz' type of experimental gun pod . . . to augment our missiles."

Palmer stopped short, prompting Austin to hesitate and face him. "Brad, why would anyone—the military in particular—go to such trouble to sign us up for some off-the-wall scheme . . . like being test pilots when we aren't test pilots?"

Brad's eyes followed a shapely blonde as she got out of a white Mercedes roadster and entered the club. "Nick, I'm not sure what the guy sporting the eye patch was about, but he definitely has the horse-power to make things happen."

A worried look crossed Palmer's face while both pilots thought about the situation.

"We are no longer in the military," Brad remarked at last. "The guy had the authority to give us travel vouchers, orders, money, and when we got here, we had BOQ rooms . . . but he isn't in the military."

Palmer stated the obvious conclusion for them both. "He's with the spooks—the cloak-and-dagger crew."

Unsmiling, Brad darted a look at two couples approaching the entrance to the lounge. "Like in the trench coats and wide-brimmed hats?"

"That's right."

"Nick," Austin laughed aloud, "why in the world would the CIA be screwing around with a couple of guys like us?"

"Level with me, Brad." Palmer eyed him with suspicion. "Don't bullshit me. If you know what's going on, and you're giving me a runaround, I'm going to—"

"How would I know what this is about?" Austin interrupted, feeling a sudden sense of foreboding. "Nick, I don't have the foggiest idea why we're here."

A hint of a smile creased Palmer's face. "Doesn't it seem coincidental to you that we are together again—from the same squadron on the same carrier—on some kind of harebrained 'I led three lives' type of operation?"

Brad raised his hands, palms up, and shrugged. "Look, we both have MiG kills to our credit. That's all I know, except that we can't take for granted that we're the only ones involved in this test-pilot crock of shit." He shook his head. "Besides, we'll probably find out what's going on tomorrow."

"I hope you're right," Palmer said curtly.

Brad turned and walked through the door of the smoke-filled lounge. He spied two empty bar stools, and they sat down and ordered drinks.

"Have you let anyone," Nick quietly asked, "know that you're in the States?"

Brad caught the eye of the attractive blonde who had walked in while they were in the parking lot. Embarrassed, he looked at Nick. "No, I haven't. I started to call Leigh Ann, but the more I think about it, the more paranoid I become."

Palmer nodded, eyeing the stylishly dressed blonde. The woman glanced at Nick and extracted a cigarette from a holder that matched her handbag. She definitely looked out of place in the small lounge.

Raising his glass, Brad stared at it a moment, then set it down. "Screw it . . . I'm going to call her."

"Why not," Palmer said as he formulated a plan to meet the stunning woman at the end of the bar.

After getting change for a five-dollar bill, Brad walked to the pay telephone next to the rest rooms. The continuous noise distracted him while he waited for Leigh Ann's phone to ring.

"Hello."

"Leigh Ann, this is Brad."

"Brad!" she said ecstatically. "Where are you? Your voice sounds so clear."

He hesitated, cupping the phone receiver in his hand. "Ah, I'm in California . . . on a special assignment."

"You're kidding." Leigh Ann's voice reflected her excitement. "Can you come to Memphis? I miss you so much!"

Brad watched Nick walk toward the comely blonde.

"I don't think so, at least not very soon. Any chance you could fly here?"

The line remained quiet for a moment. "I have finals coming up in a couple of weeks, but I could join you for a weekend."

"Great," Brad exclaimed as he saw Nick introduce himself to the woman. "Why don't you check on airline reservations, and I'll call you tomorrow evening to get your flight number and arrival time."

"Brad, where am I supposed to meet you?"

"Sorry," he said, distracted by Nick and the woman. "I'm in San Diego."

Leigh Ann paused, sensing a degree of tenseness in his response. "Brad, are you okay?"

"Yes, I'm fine . . . really."

"You don't sound like your normal self." There was concern in her voice. "Why are you in San Diego?"

Brad watched the woman smile at one of Palmer's comments. "Leigh Ann, I can't discuss why I'm here. Just do me a favor, please."

"Sure, but can you tell me what is going on?"

"No, not at the moment." Brad laughed. "Trust me, and don't tell anyone—not even your parents—that I called. It's very important that no one knows that I'm in the States."

He inhaled, then slowly let the air out. "Leigh Ann, I hold a secret clearance, so there are certain things that I cannot discuss . . . even with you. I hope you understand."

"Okay, whatever you say. I can't wait to see you."

He assured her once again that he was fine, and returned to his bar stool. He directed his attention to the neon beer logos over the mirror behind the counter. Out of the corner of his eye, he noticed Nick walking toward him.

"Brad, my man," Palmer beamed, "I hit pay dirt. Come on over and meet Allison."

"Give me a break." Brad quietly laughed. "I don't need to get involved with your pickup."

Nick chortled. "She's new in town, and she'd like to meet my long-lost friend."

"You're a real dandy," Brad said. "What did you tell her we do for a living?"

Palmer turned his head so the blonde could not see his face. "I told her that we work for the government."

Brad shook his head. "Games, games."

Feeling uncomfortable, Brad reluctantly followed Palmer to the end of the bar.

"Allison," Palmer smiled, "this is my friend, Brad Austin. Brad, Allison van Ingen."

"Hello," the woman said in a deep voice, extending her slender hand. She had an air of nonchalance and self-assurance. Definitely old money.

"It's a pleasure, Allison," Brad replied, shaking the delicate hand. "Ah, Nick told me that you are new to the San Diego area."

"Yes," she smiled, "I've been a resident of Philadelphia most of my life."

Brad noticed that she was not wearing a wedding band or engagement ring. Instead, Allison's left ring finger was adorned with a diamond-and-emerald cocktail ring.

"What made you decide," Brad cautiously asked, "to move to San Diego?"

She looked at them with amusement. "My father bought a company here, and a yacht that had been used for customers was included in the package."

Nick and Brad exchanged puzzled looks.

"So," she sipped her martini, "father asked me to supervise the redecorating. *Bellwether* is going to be refurbished for his personal use."

Allison van Ingen was obviously rich, but she didn't seem to hold herself above other people. "I just arrived this morning, so I've been busy looking for a nice home to lease."

"Did you find anything?" Nick asked, lighting her cigarette with her jeweled lighter.

"Yes." She smiled. "I was on my way to look at it again," she paused, "when I decided it was past the cocktail hour . . . and I saw this place." She gazed around the austere environment. "It's rather quaint, in its own special way."

"Yes," Nick chuckled, "it certainly is different."

Allison gave Palmer a radiant smile. "I don't know about the two of you, but I'm famished."

Palmer tried to hide his glee.

"Would you, both of you," Allison asked before Nick could say anything, "care to join me for dinner? Perhaps you could tell me all about San Diego?"

Brad started to reply, then hesitated.

Showing his surprise, Nick shoved his glass across the bar. "Sure. I know a nice place overlooking the bay."

Brad and Allison's eyes met for a moment.

"Thanks," Brad said, "but I'll let Nick give you the tour. He has spent more time here than I have."

"Won't you join us? Safety in numbers." She laughed, then added, "Besides, my father is paying for the evening."

Brad was captivated by her soft brown eyes. "Okay, I'll go—if you'll let us pay for everything," he said, without noticing the *hit the road* signal Palmer was giving him.

"Well, how nice of you to offer," she replied with a coy glance at Brad.

CHAPTER SIX

Brad gently raised his head from the pillow and swung his legs over the side of the bed. His head throbbed and his mouth tasted like sawdust. The night on the town with Allison van Ingen had been a nonstop drinking marathon. The former debutante from a Philadelphia Main Line family could more than hold her own with the two fighter pilots.

Reaching for his watch, Austin remembered the message that had been taped to his BOQ door. Palmer had received the same instructions. They were to report to Hollis Spencer at 0800 in the VF-121 training squadron hangar.

After quickly shaving and showering, Brad dressed in tan slacks and a polo shirt, then walked to Nick Palmer's room.

"Are you alive?" Brad asked after loudly knocking on Palmer's door.

Nick opened the door, then slumped on his bed. "Barely," he groaned. "If I last until noon, I may pull through."

Brad looked at Palmer's bloodshot eyes before turning to gaze at his own in the mirror over the washbasin. "What the shit were we drinking—at the time of our last conscious thoughts?"

"Cocktails from hell," Palmer slowly whispered, "and they tasted like pelican piss."

Brad noticed that his friend's hair had not been combed. "We better get a move on, 'cause we're due at the hangar in fifteen minutes."

Palmer heaved himself off the rumpled bed and walked unsteadily toward the bathroom. "Don't ever let me do that again . . . even with Allison."

"I thought you Ivy Leaguers," Brad chuckled, "would have the common sense not to drink something that had been set on fire."

"It was your idea," Nick snorted, "to introduce her to Flaming Hookers."

Dehydrated, Brad walked to the sink and filled a glass with water. "Get it together. We can't afford to be late."

"Don't talk so loud. It echoes in here."

The drive to the hangar had been quiet. An early-morning rain had left the air cool and damp. The low gray clouds provided Austin and Palmer with a welcome shield from the blazing California sun. After parking the rental car, Brad and Nick entered the large building and approached a senior officer in the passageway.

"Excuse me, sir," Brad said, catching the curious look from the commander. "Do you happen to know where we can find Mister Hollis Spencer?"

The executive officer of VF-121 gave them clear directions, then continued down the hallway. He glanced back once, curious about the strange people in his hangar. He and the commanding officer had been ordered to provide a secure space for a group of government employees, but he had been taken aback by Hollis Spencer's air of authority. No one knew his real function . . . but he certainly had the power to command whatever he wanted.

Brad looked at Nick and laughed. "Did you notice the look that he gave us?"

"I sure did . . . like we're some kind of slimy reptiles."

"Well," Brad paused while a group of sailors walked by, "we do look a little strange . . . stumbling around in civilian clothes."

"And," Nick chimed in, "without a clue as to what in the hell is in store for us."

"Well, let's go for it."

They walked to the training room that had been assigned to Hollis Spencer.

The space was well-lighted and uncluttered. Sitting in the middle of the front row of chairs sat a tall man in a red and white shirt, jeans, and cowboy boots. Like Austin and Palmer, the stranger had the short, neat haircut of a fighter pilot.

"Howdy," the cowboy said as he stood to shake hands. "Lex Blackwell."

Austin and Palmer introduced themselves, then surveyed the room and podium.

Brad grinned. "Are you in the test-pilot business, too?"

"Well," Blackwell nodded, "that's what I've been told."

From Waxahachie, Texas, Layton "Lex" Blackwell looked like a lean bull rider. All he needed to complete the picture was a cowboy hat.

"Lex," Nick asked, "have you been through Pax River?"

"Nope, can't say as I have."

"That," Brad commented, "makes three of us who are unqualified to be test pilots."

"Yeah," Blackwell replied as he sat down, "two weeks ago I was on the *Oriskany*, driving Crusaders. Next thing I know, my ass was yanked to Alameda."

"Let me guess," Palmer said as he and Brad took their seats. "You have at least one MiG to your credit, and you were recruited by a civilian adjunct to the military."

"That's right," Lex responded. "Special mission; do-or-die–type thing."

Brad leaned back. "Did he have a patch over his right eye?"

Blackwell gave Austin a suspicious look. "What's going on here?"

"We don't know any more than you know," Palmer interjected, "but we—Brad's a marine—were independently approached by this fellow in civilian clothes who was wearing an eye patch."

Blackwell rotated the class ring on his left hand and glanced at Brad. "You're a marine?"

Austin smiled. "That I am, but I bathe every day."

"Brad," Palmer explained, "graduated from Canoe U., but he had a mental lapse and accepted a commission in the Corps."

Blackwell's reply was interrupted when Hollis Spencer and Grady Stanfield entered the room and closed the door. Spencer was wearing his usual utilities, complete with starched cap and black eye patch, while Stanfield was dressed in a sage-green flight suit. The test pilot carried a bundle of manuals under his left arm.

The junior pilots were surprised, and it showed. Brad and Nick exchanged a brief look before Hollis Spencer stepped behind the lectern.

"Good morning, gentlemen," Spencer began, then added boldly, "and welcome to the Central Intelligence Agency." The blunt statement had the exact effect Spencer had wanted to achieve. "Now that I have your attention, I want to explain the seriousness of the operation you are about to join.

"Since we have met before, I'll get right to the point." Spencer smiled warmly. "To refresh you, my name is Hollis Spencer . . . and I am the CIA project officer for Operation Achilles."

The three pilots sat transfixed, waiting to hear the rest.

"Lieutenant Commander Stanfield," Spencer continued, nodding toward the senior pilot, "will be your officer-in-charge while we are in the field. This is a top-secret operation, and I must impress upon you the gravity of any breaches of confidence."

Spencer paused, studying the reactions of the men. A look almost of relief, now that their questions were being answered, registered on each pilot's face.

"You are not to discuss anything that is said in this room, or at our field site, with anyone . . . and I mean anyone." He briefly stared at each pilot. "Have I made myself clear?"

"Yes, sir," Austin and Palmer replied, while Blackwell dipped his head.

Brad found his voice. "Mister Spencer, I don't know about Nick and Lex, but I'm a little confused."

Spencer stepped to the right side of the podium and rested his forearm on top. "Brad, I like to work on a first-name basis, and most everyone calls me Cap."

Grady Stanfield displayed his infectious smile. "Cap is a member of the brotherhood. He's a tailhooker who flew Cougars in Korea."

The tension immediately eased, replaced by a growing feeling of trust—Spencer was, or had been, a naval aviator.

"I'll clear the confusion," Spencer continued, "and then turn the brief over to Grady, our resident test jockey."

Brad could feel the rapport between the two men.

"Sorry about all the secrecy, but that is the nature of this business. You will understand the need for anonymity when I explain what you will be doing."

Spencer watched for a reaction from the recruits. No one moved or made a sound.

"We are not going to hold you hostage during the course of this project. As a general routine, you can expect to work from early Monday morning—three A.M.—to early Friday afternoon. If you care to live off base, and I'm going to leave that to Grady's discretion, you will rent an apartment. But you are not to tell anyone the nature of your work."

Spencer saw the relief on the pilots' faces.

"The Agency has been directed to keep all information strictly confidential," the CIA agent hesitated, "for reasons that will be disclosed if we receive permission to carry the project to its conclusion."

Spencer gave each man a brief look. "You will maintain very low profiles, and not frequent places where you might encounter people you know . . . like the officers' club, or other aviator haunts. Any questions?"

"Yes, sir," Brad answered, wondering about Leigh Ann's visit. "How long can we expect to be here?"

"Three to four weeks, depending on the decisions being made in Washington."

Spencer gave Stanfield a casual look before turning his attention back to the men. "Now, the four of you, including Grady, are going to have an opportunity that few fighter pilots ever get. An opportunity to share invaluable information with your fellow aviators." Spencer paused for effect. "You are going to fly one of the enemy's airplanes . . . a MiG-17."

The collective looks from the three pilots reflected their shock and disbelief.

Austin and Palmer sat on the balcony of their apartment, studying the intricacies of the aircraft they had flown against in combat. The stubby Mikoyan-Gurevich MiG-17F, known to NATO as "Fresco-C," was over 20 feet shorter than an F-4 Phantom and weighed approximately 40,000 pounds less than the twin-engine warplane. Known as an aerial hot rod, the smaller fighter had superior wing loading, which made it extremely agile. The compact size of the aircraft, combined with its maneuverability, made the Soviet-built fighter a formidable opponent for any adversary.

While Nick and Brad absorbed the English version of the aircraft performance and systems operations manual, the MiG technicians were busy converting the airspeed readings from kilometers to nautical miles per hour. They had also changed the instructions and placards in the cockpit to English.

The MiG-17, manufactured by State Industries in the Soviet Union, had been obtained from Czechoslovakia in a complex exchange of military technology. The information that the United States had provided was outdated and essentially useless, but served the purpose.

While Operation Achilles was getting underway, diplomatic efforts to acquire the highly touted MiG-21 were continuing.

With their lawn chairs tilted back and their feet propped on the railing, Brad and Nick had a commanding view of Mission Bay and the Pacific Ocean.

Grady Stanfield, who had opted to remain in his BOQ, had granted his three charges permission to live off base. Lex Blackwell had elected to rent an apartment in the same complex. The three men had studied the MiG information together during the previous three days, then confined themselves to their apartment grounds during the evenings.

"Can you believe," Palmer asked with a grin, "that we're actually going to blast off in a Russian-manufactured flying machine?"

"After I've got it up and down in one piece," Brad looked over the top of his sunglasses, "I'll believe it."

Brad dropped his feet to the deck and closed his systems manual. "This is a jerry-built Spam can . . . something like Spanky and Alfalfa would have designed."

"That's true," Nick replied, marking his place in the MiG folder, "but it's a very effective fighter if it's flown by a competent pilot."

Acknowledging the remark, Brad opened his manual and leaned toward Nick. "Look at this Mickey Mouse pump. It activates the flaps and landing gear?"

Palmer suppressed a laugh. "Hell, I've seen washing machines that were more sophisticated than this bag of trash."

"According to my calculations," Austin grumbled, "it's going to take about a minute to lower the landing gear. You have to lift a toggle switch, flip the pump on, wait until the pressure comes up, then lower the gear. If you're fortunate enough to have the rollers lock in place, you turn the pump off and cover the toggle switch." Brad looked at the blue sea and watched the swells roll toward shore. "Nothing but the best."

"That," Nick chuckled to himself, "is what you get when you pull Ivan off the tractor assembly line and tell him to go build a jet airplane."

Brad shook his head. "It's amazing that something built so crudely, at least by our standards, performs so well."

"Here's an item," Palmer exclaimed, "from the bad news–good news department. They've got an air cylinder mounted on the front of the engine. If you have a flameout, which I'd guess is likely to happen above forty thousand feet, you pull this switch, and presto—the Klimov gets a gulp of pressurized air . . . and you're off and motoring again." Nick leaned back and closed his eyes. "Why didn't our aero engineers think of that?"

"Too simple."

The telephone rang in the middle of the MiG discussion. Brad was pleasantly surprised when he lifted the receiver and heard Allison van Ingen's distinct voice. It had been four days since their adventure on the town.

After a short conversation, Brad opened two beers and walked out to the balcony.

"Who was it?" Nick asked as he clutched one of the cold bottles.

"None other than your debutante friend."

Nick looked up with a broad smile. "You're kidding. I gave her our telephone number after we got our apartment, but I figured she had written us off since we haven't heard from her."

"Well, that is obviously not the case," Brad replied, leaning against the railing. "She invited us to a cocktail buffet on her daddy's yacht. She gave me the directions."

"No shit?"

"This evening." Brad grinned. "She apologized for the short notice, but remembered that we would be gone for a week, starting tomorrow."

Nick tossed his folder into his flight bag. "I'll give her a call and see if Lex can join us."

"I already asked. He's invited too."

"I wonder," Palmer tilted his head, "how old she is."

"Since when did age make a difference? I've seen you stalk them from sixteen to sixty."

Nick formed a crooked smile. "She's gotta be late twenties, early thirties, wouldn't you say?"

"At least," Brad responded, then grew serious. "I think I'll pass on the invitation. Leigh Ann is going to be here a week from Saturday, and I want to avoid any further familiarity with Allison. She strikes me as the type who could get an innocent guy in a hell of a lot of trouble."

Nick gave Brad an inquisitive look. "Have you cleared Leigh Ann's visit with Spencer?" There was a hint of apprehension in his voice.

"Grady didn't say we couldn't have dates." Brad smiled, then added, "And who will tell? Leigh Ann is an old friend from Memphis. Coincidence."

"Well," Palmer awkwardly replied, "I'm not going to say anything, but you better keep her sequestered somewhere so she won't find out about the project."

"You're right." Brad rolled his eyes. "If Leigh Ann knows you're in town, she'll want to see you." She had met Nick when he and Brad had been stationed together on an aircraft carrier. "And she'll want to know what we're doing together."

"How long is she going to be here?"

Brad gazed thoughtfully across the bay. "Just for the weekend. I think she has finals a week later."

Palmer laughed quietly. "I'm sure she'll get a lot of studying done."

Brad gave him a sly smile, then finished his beer and stared at two sleek sailboats crossing the bay.

"Come on," Nick enthusiastically urged. "Let's get Lex," he jerked a thumb toward Blackwell's apartment, "and go see Allison's yacht."

Brad gave him a questioning look.

"It will do you good . . . take your mind off things."

Stretching his arms over his head, Brad laughed good-naturedly. "Yeah, I doubt if anyone on a yacht would recognize us."

With Palmer in the lead, Brad and Lex walked down the pier toward the 114-foot Feadship. The graceful vessel was gaily decorated and brightly lighted. Two crew members were taking in the colorful nautical flags as the horizon split the orange glow of the sun. Although *Bellwether* was impressive, she did appear to be in need of cosmetic repairs.

Nick was attired in a navy-blue sports coat adorned with a Larchmont Yacht Club crest. His white slacks and deck shoes completed the nautical theme.

Brad had selected a conservative gray suit, while Lex had dressed in dark slacks, polished cowboy boots, and a western shirt with pearl snaps.

Lex Blackwell was intrigued by all of the yachts, and the accompanying trappings of wealth. "Hey, Nick. Do you really belong to a yacht club?"

"Sure. Doesn't everyone?" he kidded. "It's de rigueur where my parents live. They have been members for years."

"Yeah," Lex drawled, "it was a tough decision."

"What was tough?" Brad asked while he looked at two other yachts that were nestled against the pier.

"Deciding which Waxahachie yacht club to join."

Blackwell heard laughter from a party on a gleaming Hatteras that was docked across from *Bellwether*. "How'd you guys stumble into this deal?" His nasal twang belied his intelligence.

"I'll tell you later," Brad answered as they caught sight of a group of people chatting on *Bellwether*'s open fantail.

Boarding the opulent yacht, Nick and Brad spotted Allison conversing with another woman in the saloon. Allison politely excused herself and walked toward them.

"Welcome aboard," she greeted with a warm smile, then introduced herself to Blackwell.

Wearing a red silk and satin cocktail dress that accentuated her curvaceous figure, Allison van Ingen commanded the attention of everyone in attendance. She summoned a steward who took their drink orders, then suggested the three men mingle among the other guests and introduce themselves.

After twenty minutes of small talk, the pilots became bored and gathered near the bow.

"So," Lex said with a mischievous grin, "which one of you is sleepin' with the little darlin'?"

Brad stifled a laugh when he saw Allison step from the companionway ladder to the deck. "Nick has her in his gun sight, but I think she's more than he can handle."

"Right," Palmer sarcastically replied, turning to Blackwell, "and this is the guy who is so p-w'ed by his girlfriend that he didn't want to come here this evening."

"Well, what have you two been doing," Allison asked Brad and Nick as she joined the men, "since our exciting tour of the hot spots of San Diego?"

"You mean," Brad smiled innocently, "after we got out of the intensive care unit?"

Allison gave Blackwell a coy look. "These two really know how to show a woman a good time."

"I'll bet they do," Lex replied, attempting to keep his eyes above the plunging neckline of Allison's dress. "This is a mighty fine boat you've got here."

"Thank you," she replied, and gave Brad a sly look. "I have your phone number, but you didn't tell me where you live."

A pregnant pause followed. "Actually," Brad finally said, "we live in an apartment complex."

"The three of you live in the same apartment?"

"No." Nick hesitated. "We have two apartments . . . with a nice view of the ocean."

Allison waved at a guest. "Does your complex have a swimming pool?"

"Yes," Palmer and Blackwell replied.

"My pool was a complete mess," Allison grinned, "so the pool people are in the process of draining the water and cleaning the bottom."

Nick was exuberant. "Would you like to join us for a swim and cookout when we get back next Friday?"

"Sure." She laughed with a rush of enthusiasm, then winked at Palmer. "You wouldn't turn down two more women, would you?"

"Heck no," Blackwell exclaimed. "We'll slap on some barbecue— Texas style. I think you'll like it."

"I'm sure I will," Allison purred, then turned to Brad.

"Let me show you what the interior decorators have done in the master stateroom."

CHAPTER SEVEN

Brad felt the aircraft yaw as the twin-engine C-1A Trader climbed through the turbulent clouds. He yawned and looked at his watch. It read 3:10 A.M.

The navy carrier on-board delivery plane, known as COD, had been loaned to the Central Intelligence Agency for an indefinite period of time. During the first phase of Operation Achilles, the aircraft would be used to ferry personnel, cargo, and mail between Miramar and the secret air base.

Brad listened to the radial engines change pitch as the command pilot reduced power after reaching their cruising altitude. The cockpit crew, dressed in navy-issue flight suits and helmets, were Agency pilots who had been handpicked by Hollis Spencer.

Leaning closer to Palmer, Austin had to speak loudly to be heard over the roar of the engines. "I can't wait to fly the MiG and find out what it will do."

"I agree," Nick responded as the Trader lurched and yawed. "It'll be interesting to see if the seventeen flies like we've been led to believe."

Brad remembered a previous conversation with Nick. "Are you talking about the wing warp that you told us about on the boat?" He was referring to a discussion they had had on the carrier prior to their first flight together.

"That's what I've been thinking about," Palmer continued as Lex Blackwell and Grady Stanfield moved within earshot in the dimly lighted cabin. "Apparently, the seventeen is flight-control limited. The information, we were told, came from a defector who had a lot of hours in the plane. The reason we didn't get his plane is because some jerk panicked and blew his machine out from under him."

"Welcome to your new country," Brad deadpanned.

Blackwell tilted his ear toward Nick. "Explain flight-control limited."

"The aircraft," Palmer said loudly, "as you have seen in the manual, is pretty elementary by our standards. We were informed that the seventeen goes left wing down if you push it to around 430 knots. Anything over 430 to 440, the pilot reverts to passenger status."

Stanfield whistled. "From what I deduce, you'll have to go to idle and throw out the anchor to recover the machine."

"If," Brad emphatically stated, "you have enough altitude to recover from whatever attitude you're in."

"That's right," Stanfield agreed. "You know you're in trouble when you run out of airspeed, altitude, and ideas at the same time."

"The MiG-17 drivers," Palmer said, "like to fight slow and tight, because of the lack of high-speed control authority. That, or slashing attacks and run like hell."

Brad cocked his head. "It seems like the thing to do is to get the gomer into a turning engagement, then keep adding power until the seventeen goes wing-rolling out of control."

"It works," Lex replied with a laugh. "That's exactly what I saw one of those little varmints do. Heck, I thought it was a trick maneuver . . . till the bastard hit the ground."

That brought a chorus of laughter.

"The way I figure it," Brad arched his eyebrows, "you keep your kinetic energy up around 500 to 550 knots. If the gomers go for a turning fight, pretty soon you're driving up their asses."

Palmer nodded in amusement. "If they don't lose control first. Did you notice the stick extender?"

Brad bounced against the side of the fuselage. "Yes. You have to engage a button to get the extender to slide out of the top of the stick." He laughed. "I wonder how many they've broken off . . . after they've gone out of control."

Palmer gave Austin a knowing look. "The defector, who apparently sang like a magpie, said they actually place their feet on the instrument panel and pull with both hands."

The Trader slewed from side to side, then suddenly flew out of the clouds and into smooth air.

"Thank God," Brad said as he loosened his seat belt. "Grady, what can you tell us about the project, if anything?"

Stanfield shrugged. "Not much, actually. Hollis doesn't discuss the big picture with me. I'm here because I have a test-pilot background and I've knocked down a MiG . . . same as you three."

"We're not test-pilot qualified, however," Blackwell stated matter-of-factly.

"I'm aware of that," Stanfield replied. "The three of you are here because you have demonstrated the intelligence and primal instincts to be 'fangs out' killers . . . if called upon to use your extraordinary skills."

"What's the plan of action?" Austin asked.

Pausing to collect his thoughts, Stanfield decided to be very candid. "Since Lex and I have F-8 backgrounds—I flew a Crusader to our test site—he will fly chase for me while I evaluate the MiG.

"Brad," Grady continued in a nonchalant manner, "when you and Nick fly the MiG, I will fly chase, or Lex will escort you around the patch."

Stanfield stopped for a moment, considering whether or not he should divulge another item of interest. "That's about it, except there is a lot more to this project than any of us can imagine."

Blackwell squinted his eyes. "You mean you're not gonna tell us why we have to be such experts in flying the MiG?"

Stanfield ignored the direct question. "There is apparently a tug-of-war going on between the CIA and the navy." Stanfield darted a look at the Agency pilots. "Spencer is eager to get on with this program, before VX-4 at Point Mugu gets his MiG." VX-4 was a special projects squadron.

"As I understand it," Stanfield continued, "the air force and navy will eventually receive seventeens and MiG-21s." Grady eyed the three. "Also, an item gleaned from a couple of conversations with Hollis. The navy is chapped off about the CIA grabbing three of their pilots—I don't know what the marines think."

"They're probably glad to get rid of Austin." Palmer chuckled, thinking about Brad's attack at Phuc Yen.

Austin gave Nick a cold, *do not say anything else* look.

"At any rate," Stanfield said, "this project, which is apparently centered around getting the MiG information out to fleet pilots ASAP, originated in the White House."

"What about our fictitious identities?" Brad asked. "When, where, and why are we going to need them? I know we are dealing with the CIA, but are we going to be taken prisoner by our own military?"

Stanfield glanced down at his flight boots, then back to Austin, and sighed. "Hollis assured me that we would understand . . . at the appropriate time."

That ended the conversation and left them as perplexed and uncertain about the future as before.

Brad had made reservations for Leigh Ann at the Hotel del Coronado on the peninsula across the bay from San Diego. He wondered about the wisdom of having her here under these circumstances, and with Allison in the picture.

When the C-1A began its descent, Palmer gave Austin a curious look. "Brad, why do you suppose Allison has been so friendly to us?"

"Probably because you charmed the hell out of her," Brad answered without cracking a smile.

"No, really."

Austin contemplated the question. "It was her first day in town, and we turned out to be nice guys. She doesn't seem concerned that we aren't in her social or economic stratum."

Palmer remained quiet until the landing gear was lowered. "You know, I think Allison has the hots for you."

"That's not going to be on the program," Brad replied, giving Palmer the safe sign like a baseball umpire. "Allison is your type, not mine."

The Trader touched down with a bark from the tires and turned off the runway at midfield. The pilots taxied to the hangar, then shut down one engine while the passengers exited the aircraft. After Spencer greeted the foursome and led them to the hangar's light trap, the CIA pilots started the engine and rolled toward the runway. They would return to Miramar before sunrise.

When the group of men entered the brightly illuminated hangar, they stopped and stared at the dazzling silver plane. Stanfield, who had seen the MiG before it had been completely assembled, took the lead.

"Go on, look it over," he encouraged, "because I'm going to be flying it in less than two hours."

The first rays of daylight were beginning to dim the stars when Grady Stanfield climbed into the cockpit of the MiG-17. Since the barren airfield was not equipped with landing lights, Grady would slowly taxi up and down the strip until the sun crept above the mountains.

Having previously spent several hours sitting in the MiG, Stanfield was familiar with every switch, control knob, and gauge in the fighter. He settled into the cramped ejection seat, connected his restraints, then double-checked the fasteners.

The armament crew was having difficulty fitting the American cannons into the MiG, so they had temporarily replaced the original guns with lead ballast. Stanfield had the men check the security of the lead retainers while he donned his helmet. Spencer and Hank Murray climbed the short ladders on each side of the cockpit to offer last-minute advice to the pilot.

Clutching a cup of steaming-hot tea, Brad stood next to Nick and a small group of technicians who had assembled the airplane. Lex Blackwell walked out of the flight-gear equipment room and leisurely strolled out to the F-8 Crusader parked next to the MiG-17.

"It seems incongruous," Brad mentioned to Palmer, "to see the two fighters on the same ramp."

"You're right," Nick replied while he compared the two airplanes. "I was trying to envision a Fox-4 sitting on the tarmac at Kep, or Phuc Yen."

While Blackwell preflighted the chase plane, Spencer and Murray climbed down from the edge of the MiG's cockpit. They stepped away from the fighter while Stanfield started the afterburning Klimov turbojet. After the engine had stabilized at idle, the makeshift power cart was unplugged and towed to the edge of the ramp.

Brad and Nick followed Spencer and Murray to an aircraft radio that was mounted in the hangar. The landing strip did not have a control tower. A speaker on the wall allowed everyone to hear the conversations between Stanfield, Blackwell, and the project officer.

Grady added power and the stubby-looking fighter moved straight ahead, then shifted from one course of direction to another. A moment later the MiG came to an abrupt halt as Stanfield's laughter reverberated from the speaker.

"This is like stuffing a marshmallow into a piggy bank."

The American fighter planes had hydraulically operated control systems, while the MiG-17 had pneumatically actuated controls for taxiing. The Communist pilots had to continuously thumb a switch to activate the compressed air to maneuver on the ground.

Spencer raised his microphone. "You look like you need a sobriety test."

"I think," Grady responded while he nudged the power up, "the hardest part of flying this sled . . . will be keeping it going straight until we reach the speed to rotate."

Brad and Nick laughed quietly to themselves, prompting a remark from Hank Murray.

"I wouldn't laugh too hard." He curled his lip. "We'll be watching you soon."

Palmer caught Brad's eye as Murray walked out to the ramp. "I wonder if the captain is always that pleasant, or if this is just one of his happier days."

"Don't worry about him," Brad responded, watching the paunchy engineer. "We've got our jobs to do, and that doesn't include placating him."

Stanfield made a number of high-speed taxi runs while the sun peeked above the distant mountains. The day promised to be clear and warm.

Blackwell followed a jeep to the runway, then taxied to the end and swung into position for takeoff. Returning from the opposite end of the strip, Grady brought the MiG to a stop on the right side of the Crusader. He and Lex talked with Spencer while the jeep driver and his observer drove the length of the runway. They stopped twice to allow the spotter to pick up debris that might be sucked into the inlets of the jet engines.

When the jeep cleared the runway, Grady keyed his mike. "You ready, Lex?"

"On the roll," Blackwell replied at the same moment he released the brakes and shoved the throttle forward.

The F-8 leaped ahead, then rapidly accelerated when Blackwell selected afterburner. The Crusader's Pratt & Whitney turbojet left a trail of white-hot flames as the sleek fighter blasted down the field. Lifting off the runway, Lex snapped the landing gear up and pulled the aircraft into a steep, climbing turn.

Stanfield taxied into position, said a silent prayer, then eased forward on the MiG's throttle and selected afterburner. He frantically thumbed the steering valve until he was going fast enough to use the rudder pedals. Once enough air flowed past the vertical stabilizer, Grady could control the MiG without the awkward switch.

Holding his breath, Stanfield eased back on the control stick. The nose rose slightly, but the aircraft was not ready to fly. Feeling a moment of indecision, Grady thought about aborting the takeoff. He darted a look at the engine instruments and pulled the stick into his lap.

The MiG vibrated before it lifted from the runway. He waited until the airspeed exceeded 140 knots before deselecting the afterburner. As per agreement with Spencer, Grady left the landing gear down for the duration of the test flight.

Brad watched the chase plane smoothly rendezvous with the MiG as Stanfield banked to circle the field. The first flight was designed to check all the controls and switches, except the landing gear. Stanfield wanted to remain over the field at an altitude high enough to make the runway if he had a flameout.

"Everything is still cooking," Grady radioed, "and the engine parameters are within limits."

"Copy," Spencer replied with visible relief.

Brad shielded his eyes and observed the F-8 slide under the MiG, stabilize for a few seconds, then move out to the other side of the fighter.

"You look clean," Blackwell said, checking for leaks.

"Roger."

Stanfield flew around the field for twenty-five minutes before he entered the landing pattern. After two touch-and-goes, he made a full-stop landing and taxied to the hangar. Blackwell buzzed the field, landed, and followed Stanfield to the hangar.

The jubilant crowd congratulated Grady while the MiG was thoroughly inspected and refueled. Forty-five minutes later, he and Blackwell were again airborne to explore the high-speed handling qualities of the compact fighter.

Climbing to 15,000 feet, the test pilot performed a series of aerobatic maneuvers, including aileron rolls, barrel rolls, and steep turns. Blackwell followed the MiG at a distance of 200 feet.

Lowering the MiG's nose, Grady let the airspeed build to 380 knots and pulled up into a loop. Coming down the backside, he let the airspeed build. Accelerating through 420 knots, Stanfield felt the controls begin to stiffen. 425 ... 430 ... 435 ... the MiG trembled.

The aircraft suddenly rolled to the left as Stanfield attempted to force the stick to the right.

"Trouble!" Blackwell radioed as he watched the MiG continue to the inverted position. The nose tucked down, pointing at the earth as the MiG rotated to the left.

"Get off the power!" Lex said while everyone raced out to the ramp area. "Do you copy?"

Transfixed, Hollis Spencer held the mike at his side. The wall-mounted speaker remained silent.

Brad searched the morning sky, spotting the corkscrewing MiG as it hurtled toward the ground. The sunlight glinted off the revolving wings, adding a dimension of surrealism to the situation.

"Oh, Jesus," Brad said to himself while Blackwell popped his speed brake and performed a split-S to follow the MiG. "Come on, Grady . . . get it together."

The spiraling fighter slowly stopped turning and started a high-speed recovery. Austin watched the MiG's nose rise in a punishing, high-g pullout. Almost level, the fighter disappeared behind a line of hills.

Unaware that he was holding his breath, Brad sharply exhaled when the MiG rocketed above the hilltops.

"Okay," Stanfield radioed in a tight voice, "I've got it collected. I'm turning final for a full stop."

"Sonuvabitch," Palmer exclaimed, and removed his sunglasses.

"Lesson number one," Brad remarked, trying to slow his breathing. "You have to believe the man who has flown the machine . . . when he says it locks up at 440 knots."

Nick let his head sag, then slowly shook it. "That was a close one, my friend."

Brad glanced at the MiG. "Say hallelujah. . . ."

CHAPTER EIGHT

The men on the parking ramp and in the hangar were subdued and quiet when Stanfield brought the MiG to a halt. He raised the highly polished canopy, shut down the engine, secured the systems and controls, then sat quietly in the cockpit, slowly recovering from his brush with death. Grady had had close calls before, but none that had been decided by a matter of thirty feet. He still felt the effects of the adrenaline racing through his body.

Two technicians placed the pilot's boarding ladder against the fuselage while Lex Blackwell brought the Crusader to a halt behind the MiG. Spencer walked to the ladder when Grady unstrapped and removed his helmet. Stanfield's hair was damp and his face was ashen.

Pilots often had a more extreme reaction after a traumatic incident was over. During the crisis, their minds went into a basic survival mode and often blanked out all other sensory inputs.

Spencer waited patiently for Grady to climb out of the cockpit. Brad and Nick joined the project officer as Stanfield stepped over the edge of the canopy railing and deftly backed down the ladder.

The usual twinkle in Grady's brown eyes was gone, along with the perpetual smile. The small pilot looked wilted, but steady on his feet.

Lex Blackwell hurried over to the group while Stanfield wiped his face with the sleeve of his flight suit.

"You okay, partner?" Lex asked with genuine concern. No one else said a word while Stanfield composed himself.

Grady inhaled. "Yeah . . . and I've got a recommendation."

The remark, delivered with a hint of a smile, broke the tension in the air.

"We had better not," Stanfield emphasized, pointing his thumb over his shoulder in the direction of the MiG, "fly that goddamn anvil over four hundred knots."

"Count on it," Spencer said, making the limitation an order. "What happened . . . exactly?"

"The beast—as a matter of fact—does go out of control above four hundred twenty to four hundred thirty knots." Grady pulled off one of his sweat-soaked flight gloves. "It just tucked under and started a left-wing roll. I couldn't talk to you," he glanced at Blackwell, "because I had both hands on the stick, trying to counter the roll and get that gomer-engineered stick extender to work.

"What a bucket of shit." Stanfield snorted in disgust. "If any of you get in that position, power to idle—as Lex was calling for—full right rudder and stick, wait until the speed bleeds off, stop the rotation, then pull out."

Grady hesitated a moment while he removed his other glove. "It's imperative that you stop the rotation before you stress the aircraft with a high-g load. I think if you make a rolling pullout, you could yank the wings off this bulldozer."

Spencer glanced at the radio speaker in the hangar. "How do the new radios work?"

"Number one is fine," Stanfield answered, stuffing his gloves into his helmet. "The squelch on number two isn't working, but I could hear okay."

Spencer nodded and gave the MiG a cursory look. "Grady, shall we call it a day?"

Stanfield finally smiled. "With all due respect, sir, I believe we should continue to march. It's better if I get back in that Spam can, rather than sit around and think about what almost happened."

The three junior pilots looked at Stanfield, then at Hollis Spencer. Would the project officer overrule the senior pilot?

"You're the test pilot," Spencer said, "so I'll go with your recommendation."

Brad watched as the MiG was towed into the hangar. The heat of the day was beginning to dissipate as Spencer and the four pilots gathered in a small room at the corner of the hangar. The rest of the men, regardless of rank or position, convened at the compact, unpretentious galley. The technicians had nicknamed it "the scarf and barf."

"Help yourself," Spencer encouraged as he opened the door of a well-worn refrigerator. The interior was filled to capacity with cold beer, soft drinks, and snacks. "The initial stock is on me, but it's your responsibility," he gestured to the pilots, "to keep it refilled."

"Will do." Stanfield replied, feeling the tension ebb as he plopped into a chair.

Brad opened a can of Budweiser and rested his elbows on the metal table. He, too, felt drained, even though he had not yet flown the MiG.

The debrief was short, but thorough. Stanfield had accomplished a great deal in one day. "We know one thing for sure," Grady said with a straight face. "Do not fly over four hundred knots in the MiG-17 . . . to give yourself a cushion."

Stanfield accepted a beer from Palmer before continuing. "The aircraft, other than the wing-warp tendency, is fairly straightforward in nature. The systems are simple and reliable, with no real surprises. As long as you remain inside the aircraft's operating envelope, the plane is stable and predictable."

Sipping his beer, Stanfield glanced through the door at the MiG. "We still have a nosewheel shimmy prior to lift-off, but I'm confident that we can move to the next stage. Tomorrow, the three of you will fly the MiG, with Lex and myself alternating in the chase position."

After a second beer, the tired group ate in the small galley and went to their bunk room. The four pilots would share the three sinks and two showers with the rest of the men assigned to Operation Achilles.

Palmer surveyed the cramped, simple surroundings. "They certainly didn't spare any expense on our living quarters."

"It beats foxholes." Brad laughed, remembering his experiences in the Basic School at Quantico. "I could sleep for three days."

His neck ached and he felt drowsy, but Brad swung one leg over the side of the bed, then the other. He had not slept well, even though he had been exhausted when he collapsed on the bunk.

Like his fellow pilots, Austin showered and shaved, slipped into his flight suit, and went to breakfast.

"You ready to go?" Nick asked as he sat down next to Brad.

"As soon as I get something in my stomach," Brad answered without looking up from his cereal bowl. "I didn't sleep worth a damn."

Stanfield waited until Lex Blackwell had filled his tray and joined them. The cowboy from Texas looked tired, too.

"Nick, you're going to fly first," Grady explained, blowing gently on his steaming coffee, "and Lex will fly chase for you."

"Sounds good," Palmer acknowledged in an attempt to keep any emotion from showing. Inside, the butterflies were beginning to take flight.

"We're going to use a higher rotation speed," Stanfield said, "because it's sluggish at the recommended takeoff speed cited in the manual."

Blackwell, who was forking his breakfast down like a man possessed, listened intently.

"Christ, Lex," Palmer uttered with mock disdain, "they're going to feed us again before Friday."

Blackwell gave him a scowl.

"What's on the agenda?" Palmer asked as he slid his bowl and orange juice away.

"Basic air work," Grady replied, looking at the list of items to be accomplished on each flight. "After you wring it out, you'll come back to the field for three or four touch-and-goes, depending on your fuel state."

Stanfield looked at Blackwell. "Don't let me slow you down," he teased, "but you'll fly second—same routine—and I'll man the chase plane for you and Brad."

Grady glanced around the table. "Any questions?"

"Yeah," Blackwell mumbled as the last remnant of his breakfast disappeared. "Do I have time for seconds?"

Along with Hollis Spencer, Brad and Grady watched Lex, followed by Nick, take off and climb to altitude. Stanfield stood next to the radio, giving instructions and providing suggestions to Palmer and Blackwell. After a couple of minutes, Nick's voice returned to its normal level.

Returning to the briefing room, Brad opened his battered MiG folder to refresh his memory. He reread all the pertinent information, then closed the manual and mentally checked off the "need to know" items. Fighter pilots filed all data into one of three categories: need to know, want to know, or who gives a shit.

He stared vacantly across the empty hangar, thinking about his future. What was Operation Achilles? Where was the one spot of vulnerability—the Achilles' heel—that could destroy them all?

Brad's head drooped. He looked at his watch, deciding to lie down and rest until Blackwell landed. He definitely wanted to hear the debrief.

The engine instruments looked stabilized as Brad hurtled down the runway. He felt a great sense of relief when the MiG responded to his inputs on the rudder pedals.

He had absorbed every detail of the previous flights, which gave him a degree of comfort on his first flight in the foreign fighter. Palmer and Blackwell had been elated by their flights, and had eagerly shared every detail with him.

Grady Stanfield, flying with the Crusader's gear and flaps down, joined on Brad's right wing as the MiG lifted from the long runway.

Continuing straight ahead, Austin pulled the throttle out of afterburner and went through the process of raising the landing gear. Flying next to him, Grady cleaned up the F-8 and reported that the MiG appeared to be free of leaks.

"Let's climb to twenty thousand," Stanfield suggested, "and you can put it through its paces."

"Roger, twenty thou," Brad radioed, feeling more comfortable with each foot of altitude he gained. He noticed the clouds and a rainbow over the mountains. Brad blocked out the war and the senseless killing that went with it as the exhilaration of flying returned.

Reaching 20,000 feet, Austin left the power at one hundred percent and accelerated to 380 knots. He rolled ninety degrees to the left and pulled 4 g's while completing a 360-degree turn. Stanfield remained close behind the MiG, vigilant for any signs of trouble.

Out of the turn, Brad raised the nose and executed an aileron roll. He noticed the attitude gyro tumble as the MiG passed through the inverted position.

"I wouldn't want to fly this thing in instrument conditions," Brad said to Stanfield as he pulled back on the throttle.

"That makes two of us," Grady replied, deploying the Crusader's speed brake to maintain his separation from the MiG.

Austin allowed the fighter to decelerate, exploring its slow-speed handling characteristics. Holding back-pressure on the stick, Brad leveled the wings and waited to feel the buffet prior to a full stall.

When the MiG began to tremble, Brad advanced the throttle to full power and tweaked the nose down. When the fighter reached 270 knots, he wrapped the aircraft into a tight turn to see how it responded to an accelerated stall.

Pulling 5 g's, the MiG completed a 180-degree course reversal before Brad felt the aircraft buck. Rolling wings level, he pulled the throttle to idle.

"Oh, shit!" Austin blurted, feeling his heart beat like a trip-hammer. The turbojet was developing full power while the throttle remained at idle. "Chase, I've got a runaway engine!"

"Stay with it!" Stanfield encouraged, adding power to stay close to the MiG. "We'll work it out."

Brad quickly analyzed his options while the MiG accelerated. He could not allow the fighter to exceed 420 knots, or his only option would be to make a high-speed ejection.

"If you can't save it," Hollis Spencer's voice came over the radio, "don't hesitate to get out."

"I'm okay for the moment," Brad replied as he scanned the instrument panel. The engine gauges were pegged at full power.

"Grady, I'm going to have to get enough g's on to slow it to flap and gear speed."

"Brad," Stanfield radioed with forced calmness, "keep your three-sixties tight, but work your way over the field."

"I'm trying," Austin replied, bending the MiG around in a gut-wrenching turn. Pointed toward the airstrip, he let the aircraft accelerate to 400 knots before he yanked it into another tight circle. "I'm going to cut off the fuel . . ." he grunted under the g forces, "and make a flameout approach."

"Don't chop the engine before you get the gear and flaps down . . ." Grady paused, "or you're going to be out of options."

"I won't," Brad labored, then released the back-pressure when the airfield came into view. After accelerating again, he banked into another hard turn and waited until the airspeed decayed to flap-deployment speed.

Austin's arm muscles ached from the constant pull on the control stick. He lowered the flaps and switched arms, grabbing the stick with his left hand. "What's the engine-out glide speed?"

A moment of silence followed.

"There's no mention of glide speed in the manual," Stanfield replied, "but keep it fast—at least one-fifty—until you've got the runway made."

"Okay," Brad acknowledged, and switched hands again. He reefed the nose skyward in a modified chandelle, watched the airspeed drop, then went through the laborious process of lowering the landing gear.

"You're doing great," Stanfield encouraged, then spoke to Spencer. "We'll need the crash truck at midfield."

"It's already in place," Spencer shot back, then talked to Austin. "Brad, if you get out of shape, I want you to jump out. Do you copy?"

"Roger," Austin managed while he completed the gear-lowering procedure. "I'm coming around one more time . . . before I shut down the engine."

Stanfield and Spencer answered at the same time, blocking out the radio transmission.

Brad checked his ejection-seat fittings before reaching for the fuel-cutoff valve. A half turn later he was at the high-key position over the runway.

Firmly grasping the fuel system actuator, he attempted to turn it to the off position, but the valve would not budge. "Sonuvabitch!" he grunted, grabbing the recalcitrant valve with both hands.

The MiG's nose dropped precariously low as Brad twisted with all his might. The valve snapped closed, and he frantically grabbed the stick. A moment later, the cockpit became deathly quiet as the Klimov turbojet spooled down.

"You okay?" Stanfield asked, breathing rapidly as he watched the MiG plummet toward the runway.

"Think so," Brad managed while he banked steeply toward the runway. He aimed for the first third of the airstrip. The lone crash truck came into view as he passed the ninety-degree position from the end of the runway.

A seat-of-the-pants aviator, Austin kept the airspeed above 150 knots, but realized he was not going to stretch the glide to the runway by completing the sweeping turn.

Brad sharply banked the MiG, angling toward the airstrip. The aircraft was sinking at a frightening rate when Brad approached the extended centerline of the runway.

Racking the MiG into a steep bank, Brad centered the aircraft in line with the pavement. Rolling wings level a moment before touchdown, Brad fought the stick as the MiG quit flying and thudded onto the runway.

CHAPTER NINE

Brad Austin sank into a chair in the briefing room and rested the back of his head against the wall. He could see the technicians and Hank Murray swarming over the MiG. Some of the men were removing access panels from the fuselage of the fighter, while others congregated around the cockpit.

The shrill whine of the Crusader's turbojet grew louder as Stanfield approached the hangar ramp. A minute later the engine spun to a stop, allowing Brad to hear the voices in the hangar.

Spencer entered the quiet room and laughed nervously. "How are you feeling?"

Brad gave him a blank look and shook his head.

"That good," Spencer said as he sat down across from the spent pilot. The project officer had made a decision, at least in his mind, that Brad Austin should be the primary pilot if Operation Achilles was allowed to run its course. The young aviator was a natural. "You certainly bring another dimension to the world of naval aviation."

"Not by design, sir," Brad replied just before Palmer and Blackwell entered the small room.

"What do you plan," Nick laughed sarcastically, "for your next show?"

Brad closed his eyes. "If I had the energy, I'd get up and kick your navy ass."

"We drove out in the jeep," Lex said. "You've gotta be the luckiest son of a bitch on this planet, bar none. Your tires touched down forty-four feet from the end of the runway."

"In all seriousness," Spencer said with unusual gravity, "we're going to have to concentrate on safety. We'll wait until Grady gets here, but I'm convinced that it is time to slow down . . . before someone gets killed."

Hank Murray and Grady Stanfield entered the room. The navy captain had a frown on his face.

"Find anything?" Spencer asked.

"We sure did," Murray replied, holding up a broken piece of throttle linkage. "It snapped just behind the throttle quadrant."

"I think," Brad mustered his energy, "that we should forget about flying the MiG, and let the navy use that shitbox for an anchor."

Brad relaxed slightly after the COD rose from the runway and the landing gear retracted. He did not enjoy riding in the back of planes being flown by other pilots. Especially people he did not know.

Hollis Spencer had decided to ground the MiG until a suitable throttle linkage could be machined. He had ordered Hank Murray to thoroughly examine the MiG for any other possible discrepancies. Flight testing would resume after Murray was confident that all of the MiG's components and systems were airworthy. Grady Stanfield had remained at the hangar to flight-check the fighter after the repairs had been made.

"Is it true," Palmer asked Blackwell, "that you guys from one-sixty-two used Sidewinders to knock out locomotives?" He was referring to the VF-162 squadron on board the carrier *Oriskany*. The Sidewinder was designed to be a heat-seeking air-to-air missile.

"That's right." Lex chuckled. "Those steam engines draw the little mothers like buzzards to a carcass. At the time I was shanghaied by the spooks, we had four engines to our credit."

Nick looked at Brad. "Tell him what you did with a Sidewinder."

"I'd just as soon forget it."

"Brad," Palmer proudly beamed, "who was an exchange pilot in our squadron, saved two of our guys who were in the drink. He used a 'Winder to take out a North Vietnamese patrol boat that was almost on top of the crew."

"No shit?" Blackwell exclaimed, glancing at Austin.

Brad nodded his head, feeling a tinge of embarrassment. He wished Palmer would drop the subject.

"I'm not kidding," Palmer continued. "He did a split-S, circled the boat, and attacked from the rear."

"What were you," Nick looked at Austin, "fifty to seventy-five feet above the water?"

Brad leaned his head back and closed his eyes. "Give it a rest, please."

"Anyway," Nick laughed, "he was down in the soup, steaming along at about four hundred fifty knots, when they opened fire with two machine guns. The jarhead just pressed on and cranked off a 'Winder."

Lex laughed, obviously enjoying the tale.

"That beauty tracked directly to their engine and blew the bastards straight out of the water." Palmer grinned with delight. "Trust me, it was a piece of work."

Palmer and Blackwell continued to swap sea stories and flying tales. Brad thought about what he would say to Leigh Ann on Saturday. He napped serenely until the Trader landed at Miramar.

Friday morning, Brad prepared breakfast while Palmer showered and dressed. After they had eaten their omelets, Brad got ready while Nick washed the dishes and read the paper.

"Spencer just called," Palmer said when Brad stepped out of the bathroom. "Grady flew the MiG this morning, and we're going to resume operations early Monday."

"When do we have to go back?"

Nick folded the paper and tossed it onto the kitchen counter. "He said the COD will be wheels in the wells at three A.M. Monday morning."

"That's great." Brad wrinkled his brow in displeasure. "We might as well stay up all night."

"I gather, from what he said, that we're going to be making up time." Palmer looked out the window, searching the ocean for ships. "He sounded pressured, sort of anxious."

Opening the refrigerator and small pantry, Brad made a brief note of the items they needed for the party that evening. "You sure you don't want to go with me?"

"No, thanks," Palmer replied, spying an aircraft carrier in the distance. "Lex and I will get the grill and charcoal. He wants to buy the meat at some place in Chula Vista."

Brad laughed. "If I know Lex, he probably found a barbecue joint, so all he has to do is warm the meat on the grill."

The phone rang as Austin reached for his keys and wallet. He snatched the receiver and was surprised to hear Allison van Ingen's soft, resonant voice.

"Hello, there."

He darted a look at Palmer. "Good morning, Allison."

"I didn't know if you would be back yet," she said, "but I wanted to confirm the cookout this evening . . . before I invited my friends. Actually," Allison continued before Brad could reply, "they're the two women who are redecorating *Bellwether*."

"Sure." Brad hesitated for a moment. "We're looking forward to seeing you this evening." He saw Nick hold up four fingers. "Would around four o'clock be all right?"

"That will be fine," Allison replied soothingly. "Is there anything we can help with, or bring?"

"Thanks, but we've got it under control," he chuckled lightly, "as soon as I go to the grocery store, and the other guys locate a grill."

"Under control, huh?" She laughed suspiciously. "I had better go to the supermarket with you."

Brad wondered what Leigh Ann would think about that. "That's okay . . . ," he said awkwardly. "I was just on my way out the door, but I appreciate the offer."

"Brad, I don't have a thing to do," Allison replied in her most convincing manner, "so I'll pick you up in thirty minutes, if you'll give me directions."

Brad's instincts told him this was not a good idea, but what could he say? He acquiesced and gave her the directions to the apartment complex. "I'll be out in front."

"I'll be looking for you," she said with a touch of excitement in her voice. "See you in half an hour."

He said good-bye and thought about asking Nick to go shopping with Allison. Rejecting the impulse as cowardly, he decided to handle the situation as best he could.

"She's got you nailed." Palmer laughed devilishly. "You had better check your six."

"I'll tell you something." Brad was serious, and it showed. "This whole deal—Achilles, keeping secrets, Allison and Leigh Ann coming—is getting out of hand."

"Not if we're careful," Palmer said cautiously.

"Allison, as she said she was going to do, is inviting two other friends over." Brad swore to himself and sat down. "She's bringing the women who are working on her father's yacht, so we've got to tell more lies."

They remained silent, realizing how careful they had to be not to reveal anything about their background or their jobs.

Palmer gave Brad a wry, fleeting smile. "Do you think we should cancel the shindig?"

"Logic tells me that we should," Brad replied, staring at Nick. "We're suppose to be low-key and out of sight . . . remember?"

"Well, maybe we should call it off," Nick said with more than a hint of frustration, "before something happens that puts us in a bind."

Brad thought for a minute. None of them knew what the future held. The stress of flying the MiG was taking a toll on their nerves. They deserved some fun and relaxation.

"To hell with it," Brad declared, thinking the party would be a good diversion. "Let's just go through with it, but not make any more commitments. And listen, Nick, don't let anybody get close to the truth. The consequences might be greater than we can imagine."

Palmer nodded thoughtfully.

"So," Brad said firmly, "on with it."

"Why not," Palmer was all too ready to agree. "I'm tired of this horseshit. It's time to enjoy life—live a little—with no serious commitments."

CHAPTER TEN

The white roadster curved down the entrance ramp to the freeway while Brad gazed at the distant shoreline. With the wind tousling her blond hair, Allison threaded her way through the late-morning traffic like a native Californian.

Overhead, the sky was clear and blue. The sun warmed Brad as the wind whipped around the convertible. He tried not to look at Allison's smooth, suntanned legs. She was wearing yellow short-shorts with a matching halter top that revealed a lot of cleavage. Brad was certain the halter could pass for a bikini top.

Allison glanced at Austin. "You haven't told me what you and your friends do for a living."

He had been waiting for the question. "We work on various government programs."

She smiled warmly. "I know you're with the government, but what is it that you actually do?" The accent on "actually" was pronounced.

Brad was clearly uncomfortable. "We test things," he answered, then immediately changed the subject. "When will your father's yacht be completed?"

"I'm not sure at this point." She slowed for the off ramp leading to the supermarket. "Brad, there's something about you that intrigues me."

"What's that?" he asked, trying to sound nonchalant. Was she prying, or just making conversation?

"You look like a military person." She laughed. "Like a pilot, with your short hair and aviator-style sunglasses."

"I've always worn aviator sunglasses," Brad replied truthfully. He was beginning to feel like an insect under a microscope, and he did not like the sensation.

"This is really a beautiful car," he declared in another attempt to divert the conversation.

"Why, thank you." She smiled. "My father knows how attached I am to it, so he had it driven out here for me."

Brad had noticed the Pennsylvania license plate. "That must be nice . . . to have your car delivered to you."

"It certainly is," she agreed without a trace of arrogance.

Allison parked the gleaming Mercedes and they got out. Brad had taken only a few steps when he almost panicked. The wife of a close friend from Annapolis was walking out of a store adjacent to the supermarket. Brad turned his head and stared across the parking lot, praying that she would not recognize him and call out his name. His heart was racing when the woman and her toddler passed by.

Safely inside the supermarket, Brad grabbed a shopping cart and opened his grocery list. Allison was very helpful during their stroll through the store, but she was definitely a showstopper. Brad felt an occasional twinge of embarrassment when people stared at the voluptuous blonde. After the leisurely shopping spree, Brad finally agreed to allow Allison to pay for half of the groceries.

On their return trip to the apartment, Allison mercifully did not ask Brad any further personal questions. They just exchanged small talk.

After arriving at the apartment, Allison helped Brad carry the sacks into the kitchen, then stepped out to the balcony.

"This is a beautiful view," she commented, scanning the blue ocean. After a moment, Allison gazed at the pool area. "What a gorgeous pool."

"It is, isn't it," Brad said while he stocked a cabinet. "We really enjoy it, when we have the time."

"When will Nick, and your other friend—I've forgotten his name—be here?"

Brad glanced at her. "Lex is our cowboy friend, and they should be back any time. Lex wanted to get some special meat and ribs."

"That sounds wonderful," Allison stated emphatically. She noticed the single lounge chair next to the railing. "Who's the sun worshiper?"

Brad laughed and looked at the lounge. "Nick likes to maintain his tennis tan at an even level."

"Would you mind if I work on my tan?" Allison asked with a sensuous smile. "I'll be happy to help you prepare everything when you're ready."

"Sure," he replied with a degree of trepidation. "Make yourself comfortable."

"Thanks." She slipped off her sandals and sat on the lounge. "I just can't get over this view. It's really incredible."

Brad agreed, and finished storing the groceries. He opened a cold beer and walked to the balcony door to see if Allison would like something to drink. Brad was unprepared for what he saw. Allison was lying on her stomach with her halter top resting on one of the lawn chairs. He noticed the conspicuous absence of white lines on her tanned back.

"Would you care for something to drink?" He couldn't take his eyes off Allison. *She is beautiful.*

"Oh, no thanks." Allison turned her head to see Brad. "Would you mind if I used one of your towels to lie on?"

Brad envisioned her lying nude on a bearskin rug in front of a crackling fireplace. "No, not at all . . . I'll get a fresh one out of the closet."

"You're a darling."

Smiling to himself, Brad walked to the linen cabinet. "Holy shit, what a body," he said to himself as he grabbed a large beach towel. He went out to the balcony and handed the thick towel to Allison.

"Thank you," she said, unfolding the navy-blue towel in front of her. She paused to look at the unique design. Brad cringed when he noticed the gold naval aviator wings adorning the center of Palmer's towel. His mind raced while he waited for the inevitable question.

Allison smoothly slid the beach towel under her breasts. She turned her head, searching his eyes. "Brad, you *are* a pilot, aren't you? A navy pilot."

Austin hesitated, tired of the ruse. "Well, I've been told to pile it here and pile it there," he answered lamely. "I've always been interested in aviation, so I collect flying paraphernalia."

She eyed Brad suspiciously and gave him a seductive smile. "Brad, I don't think you're telling me the truth. All three of you guys have an air about you."

Brad laughed and shook his head. "Hey, we're just normal people . . . who work for a paycheck."

She stared at him with a skeptical look.

"Allison," Brad said uncomfortably, "I work for the government, and that's it."

"I'm sure that you do," she smiled politely, "but what you do is hush-hush, isn't it?"

A grin spread across his face. "I think you've been watching too many movies."

"Right." She winked knowingly. "Would you mind putting some oil on my back?"

"I'd be happy to," he replied, relieved that she was apparently dropping the subject.

"I put it on the cabinet," Allison said, placing her hands under her chin, "next to the oven."

Taking a swig of his beer, Brad went to the kitchen and opened the Coppertone oil that Allison had purchased at the supermarket. He second-guessed the decision to go through with the cookout when he walked out on the balcony. After today, Brad reasoned, they would have to sever their ties to Allison van Ingen.

"Let me warm this," Brad offered, dropping to his knees, "before I spread it on your back."

"How thoughtful," she responded in a subdued voice.

Brad rubbed the Coppertone between his palms until it was body temperature, then applied the oil in long, smooth strokes. It would be easy to fall for Allison.

"Would you like some oil on your legs?"

"If you don't mind," she purred, totally relaxed by Brad's soothing hands. "That feels wonderful."

"Good."

When he had finished coating her legs, Brad started to rise.

"Have you got a couple of minutes," she softly asked, "to talk with me?"

Brad swallowed hard. "Sure. What's on your mind?"

Allison startled Brad when she abruptly turned over to face him. She held the beach towel over her breasts with one hand while she grasped Brad's arm with the other. "I was wondering if we could pack a picnic basket and—"

The doorbell rang, interrupting her in midsentence.

"It's open!" Brad shouted, thinking that it might be Lex at the door. Brad remembered that he had left the main door open, but he was unsure if he had locked the screen door.

"What were you going to say?" Brad asked, mesmerized by the beautiful, half-naked body.

"We'll discuss it later," Allison murmured as she turned on her stomach, "when we're alone."

Hearing the sound of footsteps behind him, Brad turned to see Leigh Ann staring at him with burning anger. Her luggage was next to the refrigerator.

"L-Leigh Ann," Brad stammered as he rose from his knees, "I thought— This is really a surprise. You're here a day early."

Leigh Ann's elegant, perfectly sculptured face reflected shock and humiliation.

Allison calmly looked over her shoulder. Leigh Ann's sudden appearance was the last thing Allison had expected, but she maintained her composure and reached for her halter top.

"Yes," the petite brunette said in a scathing tone. "Apparently, it's a surprise for everyone."

Brad's eyes captured Leigh Ann's silky brown hair and clear blue eyes, but her normally radiant smile had been replaced by a glare.

"Leigh Ann," Brad tried again, "this is not what you think . . . honestly."

"That's what they all say," Allison said lightly, "but this time you can believe him. I date his roommate, who should be returning any minute. My name is Allison van Ingen." She was cool and composed.

Brad was completely awed. Allison had saved him, rather than let him become shark bait.

Leigh Ann looked at Brad before she introduced herself to Allison. She was not sure the truth was being told. Her intuition told her not to trust Allison, and her confidence in Brad was shaken.

Leigh Ann turned to Brad. "Can I have a word with you . . ." she darted a cold glance at Allison, "alone?" She turned and walked into the kitchen before he could answer.

Brad followed, shaking his head in amazement. *How could this have happened to me?*

"I was so happy," Leigh Ann seethed, keeping her voice low, "about coming here a day early . . . to be with you." She paused to calm herself. "Then I walk in to find you rubbing suntan lotion on a woman who is wearing nothing but shorts that are a size too small."

"Leigh Ann, calm down and let—"

"I want to know what is going on," she demanded, "and I wouldn't believe that topless blonde for a minute."

"Leigh Ann," Brad gently coaxed while he wiped his hands on a kitchen towel, "let's take a drive. I need to explain a few things to you."

"You bet you do," she replied in an icy voice.

"Listen," Brad said, taking Leigh Ann by the shoulders. "There is nothing between Allison and me, or even between Allison and Nick. We're involv—"

"Nick Palmer?"

"Yes," he answered with a smile. "We're working on a special project, and I can't tell even you about it. Not until it's over."

She didn't look convinced.

"Right now," Brad continued uneasily, "we're just taking some time off to relax."

Leigh Ann nodded. "Yes, I can see that you're relaxing."

"Nick and I share this apartment," he explained, "and Allison simply asked if I would spread some oil on her back."

"Maybe so," Leigh Ann conceded, realizing that Brad was telling the truth, "but you can surely understand how it looked to me . . . when I walked in."

Brad gave her a convincing look. "I know, and I apologize, but there was nothing to it."

"I believe you." Leigh Ann smiled and placed her arms around his neck. "Why don't you take me to my hotel. It's been a long day."

"Excellent idea." Brad grinned suggestively.

CHAPTER ELEVEN

Leigh Ann was overwhelmed when she saw the Hotel del Coronado. The monarch of Pacific Coast resort hotels was a magnificent example of elegant Victorian architecture.

After checking in and depositing their belongings in the oceanfront room, Brad and Leigh Ann went for a tour of the grand hotel. They explored the lush grounds before returning to browse through the quaint shops.

Passing the Ocean Terrace, they decided to stop for a cocktail and unwind. Brad selected a table overlooking the ocean, and they ordered drinks.

When the waitress had left, Brad raised his glass, prompting Leigh Ann to do likewise. He clinked his glass against hers, then looked into her eyes. "To our weekend together."

"To us," she smiled gleefully, and tasted her cocktail.

Leigh Ann settled comfortably in her chair. "Can you tell me something about why you're in San Diego?"

Brad leaned closer to Leigh Ann. He hesitated a moment before answering.

"Nick and I have been asked, along with two other pilots, to evaluate a classified airplane."

A look of concern formed on Leigh Ann's face. "Is this secret airplane you're flying considered dangerous?"

"Honey," Brad teased, resorting to the black humor of all fighter pilots, "anytime you strap into something with an ejection seat, there is a certain amount of risk involved. That's the nature of my business."

They fell silent for a moment. Brad noticed that Leigh Ann nervously fingered her cocktail napkin.

"Leigh Ann, if I could tell you anything else, I would."

"I know." She knew Brad well enough to know that he thrived on excitement. How strange, she thought, that the same self-assurance and zest for life that made her fall in love with Brad, also made him pursue one of the most dangerous professions in the world.

They talked and laughed until the sun was barely suspended above the tranquil ocean.

Brad glanced at his watch. "I've got to give Nick a call. Excuse me," he apologized as he rose. "I'll be right back."

"Okay," Leigh Ann smiled with happiness, "but hurry."

Fortified by a second scotch and soda, Leigh Ann sat quietly and watched the golden sphere shimmer as it settled over the horizon. Her mind drifted back to the blonde at Brad's apartment. Although Leigh Ann had been initially outraged, she could now smile about the incident.

She turned to Brad when he returned and sat down. "Brad," she said sweetly, "tell me about Allison what's-her-name."

Unprepared for such a direct question, Brad stifled a nervous laugh and sat down.

"Actually," he began slowly, "Nick and I met her when we first got here. She had just arrived in San Diego to oversee the refurbishing of a yacht her father bought."

"Was that her Mercedes?" Leigh Ann asked dryly.

"Yes," Brad answered, wishing she would drop the subject.

"Where was Nick when I was at the apartment?"

Brad squirmed in his chair. "Nick and Lex Blackwell—one of the other pilots—had gone to find a barbecue grill and get some meat for a cookout this evening."

"So," Leigh Ann sipped her drink, "Miss Short-shorts slipped over to have tea with you, while the other guys were gone?"

Brad burst out laughing. "Jealousy doesn't become you."

She frowned. "I don't think it's funny. . . ."

"Leigh Ann, she drove me to the supermarket. That's all there is to it. End of story."

"She went into the supermarket wearing *that* outfit?"

"Yes," Brad replied, suppressing a laugh. "In *that* outfit."

"Unbelievable," she muttered, then looked Brad straight in the eyes. "Let me understand this. Allison—what did you say her last name is?"

"Van Ingen, with a small *v*. She's from a Main Line family in Philadelphia."

Leigh Ann considered all the information carefully. "This woman—who appears to be about thirty, has a new Mercedes convertible, is overseeing her father's yacht, and looks like a *Playboy* centerfold—is hanging out with three military pilots in an apartment." She paused, staring at Brad. "Does that seem a little strange to you?"

"Probably," Brad shrugged uncomfortably, "but the friendship has been platonic."

"So far," she replied with a taunting look.

Tilting her head, Leigh Ann gave Brad a smile. "Have you seen her father's yacht?"

"Come on, lighten up."

Leigh Ann was determined. "What's the name of the yacht?"

He gave her a sidelong glance. *"Bellwether."*

She remained silent, fixing him with a cold stare while she made a mental note of the name of the yacht.

"Yes," he laughed, "I've been on the yacht. She invited the three of us to a cocktail buffet. She had a lot of other people there, of all age groups."

"So," Leigh Ann gave him a knowing look, "you reciprocated and invited Allison over for a party the night before I was scheduled to arrive."

"Correction," Brad declared. "Nick invited her."

Leigh Ann leaned back and studied Brad. "We're missing it—the party, or cookout, as you refer to it."

Brad inhaled, then slowly let the air out while he signaled the cocktail waitress for another scotch. "We aren't going to attend . . . for reasons other than you probably suspect."

It was Leigh Ann's turn to laugh. "I can't *wait*," she crossed her arms, "to hear this."

"I'll tell you as soon as the waitress leaves." Brad smiled broadly, wondering how he could explain the delicate situation to her. *This should be interesting.*

Leigh Ann never took her eyes off him.

Brad accepted his drink with a smile, then turned serious. "Allison knows that the three of us work for the government, but she doesn't know what we do."

"She's getting curious," Leigh Ann finished the disclosure, "and you think that I might inadvertently say something."

"Leigh Ann," Brad began patiently, "my situation is complicated, and I'm not supposed to say anything to anyone . . . including you."

She gave him a suspicious look. "Why can't you tell her the truth? You're military pilots who are evaluating an airplane. You don't have to tell her the plane is secret."

Brad took a deep breath. "I'm not serving in the military at the present time," he confided, giving Leigh Ann time to digest that information. "I report to another organization in the government."

Leigh Ann sat for a moment, adding up the facts so far. "What part of our government," she asked with a skeptical look, "would get you out of Vietnam to fly some secret airplane?"

"I am not at liberty to discuss—"

"The CIA?" Leigh Ann asked with an ominous stare. "You're involved with the CIA, aren't you?"

His silence was her answer.

"Brad," Leigh Ann declared with a look of dismay, "this whole thing—the CIA, flying a secret plane, the mysterious blonde—is very weird. . . . It adds up to something dangerous for you, and it frightens me."

He placed his hand over hers. "Don't worry, okay? At least I'm not being shot at over North Vietnam."

Leigh Ann trembled. "Brad, I do worry about you . . . constantly." She gave him a brief smile. "And Allison sure seems strange."

"Do I detect another trace of jealousy?"

"Well," Leigh Ann hesitated, hiding her trepidation about Allison, "perhaps so, but you, Captain Austin, are naive where women are concerned."

Nick Palmer walked down to the patio next to the courtyard and swimming pool. He gave Allison's red bikini an admiring glance as she dove off the diving board. She had left the apartment late in the afternoon, returning an hour later with her bathing suit and a change of clothes.

Selecting a chair with a view of the spacious pool, Palmer watched Allison swim toward her two friends who were lounging in the shallow water. He darted a look at Lex Blackwell, then back to the women by the pool steps. "They're okay, but not in the same league with Allison."

"You're not going to hear any complaints out of me." Lex grinned, finishing another beer. "Where's the gyrene?"

"He just called a few minutes ago." Nick chuckled. "Seems as if Leigh Ann arrived a day early," he turned his head so Allison and her friends would not see him laugh, "and took a taxi to the apartment."

Lex opened another beer. "What's so funny?"

"Brad told me he was applying suntan oil to Allison's back—she was lying on her stomach, topless—when Leigh Ann rang the doorbell." Palmer punched Lex on the shoulder. "He thought it was you, and yelled that the screen door was open."

Blackwell doubled over and almost spit a mouthful of beer on the grass. "Jesus Christ," he guffawed, "is he in the hospital?"

"No," Nick replied, trying to contain himself, "but he said he took some battle damage."

"Yeah," Blackwell laughed and admired the three women. "I remember a little filly I dated back in Texas. She caught me at a motel, at one o'clock in the morning, with my high-school sweetheart."

Nick watched Allison and her friends climb out of the pool. "What did she do?"

"Set fire to my pickup truck," he drawled, then smiled at Allison while she dried herself.

"You gotta be kidding me!" Palmer was incredulous. "What kind of women do you date?"

"I like feisty ones," Lex replied as the three women approached the patio table.

Nick was concerned that Blackwell was beginning to slur his words. He had been drinking one beer after another since midafternoon.

"Reckon I better put on the chow," Lex said, then reached for another beer and stood to greet Allison. "Little dahlin'," he asked unsteadily, "you wanta help me with the vittles?"

Allison smiled widely as she reached for a towel to wrap around her waist. "I would be happy to help you," she teased, "in any way I can."

"My kind of gal." Lex grinned at Nick as he wrapped an arm around Allison's shoulder. "Hold the fort, Nick, while we rustle up the grub."

Palmer nodded, concealing his worry. He engaged Allison's friends in conversation while he watched Blackwell stagger toward the barbecue grill.

"I understand that the three of you," Allison said when she and Lex reached the grill, "do some kind of testing for the government?" The statement became a question.

Lex arched his brow. "Who told you that?"

"Brad mentioned that you test things, whatever they are, for a government agency."

Blackwell gave her a sly grin and started forking the meat on the cooker. "You wouldn't believe me if I told you."

"I might," Allison replied with mock innocence, "if you told me the truth. I asked Brad if he was in the military—the three of you look like pilots, you know, with the sunglasses and all—and he evaded my question."

Lex poured a thick sauce on the sizzling ribs and sliced beef. "We *are* in the military."

"Well," Allison huffed convincingly, "what's so secretive about what you do? Is it something that embarrasses you and your friends?"

Blackwell laughed and took a swig of beer. "This ain't for publication," Lex bragged, "but you're right, we are pilots . . . fighter pilots."

"I just knew it," Allison exclaimed. "I have an eye for guys like you. All of you have such a bold, reckless quality—sort of a carefree, cavalier air about you."

Flattered by her praise, Lex drained his beer. "If you promise me that you won't say anything to anyone, I'll tell ya what we're doin' here."

"Who would believe me?" Allison shrugged.

Blackwell glanced at Nick and the two women, then locked Allison in his stare. "We're testing an enemy fighter plane—a MiG that the CIA got aholt of."

"You're kidding?" she said, wide-eyed. "I won't tell a soul. Even I don't believe you."

"Nope," he burped drunkenly, "I'm not kiddin'."

CHAPTER TWELVE

Brad inhaled deeply and stared at the ceiling in the darkened bedroom. Leigh Ann's head rested on his shoulder and her leg sprawled across his groin. They began to breathe more slowly as their damp bodies cooled. Leigh Ann blew softly on Brad's chest, then tilted her head back to kiss him on the neck.

"I can't believe," she murmured, running a finger lightly over his muscled stomach, "that you have to leave in the middle of the night."

He reached for his wristwatch and squinted at the face. "Unfortunately, I don't have any choice."

Leigh Ann held him tighter, savoring their last few minutes together. "I could hold you all night."

"Don't tempt me." Brad laughed quietly while he gently caressed her back. "The last thing I want to do is report for duty when I know that you're lying here."

They remained silent, enjoying the quiet pleasure of the moment.

As much as she hated to see Brad leave, Leigh Ann was grateful that he was not going back into combat. The CIA program might be dangerous, she thought, but Brad would not be exposed to aerial combat.

Leigh Ann raised her head and looked into Brad's eyes. "When am I going to see you again?"

He brushed her forehead with his lips. "I don't know."

Leigh Ann nuzzled his chest. "I love you, Brad, and I'm worried about you. It would be different if I knew where you were and what you were doing."

"Not to worry." Brad sighed and caressed Leigh Ann's thigh. "What I'm doing at the present time is a hell of a lot safer than being shot at every day."

They remained quiet, each lost in their own thoughts. Leigh Ann was frightened by Brad's profession, but bravely kept most of her worries to herself.

A long silence followed before Brad roused himself. He slipped his arm from under Leigh Ann's neck. "I've got to shower and get out to Miramar."

Leigh Ann forced Brad down and eased on top of him. "There's room for two in the shower."

Leading Nick and Lex, Brad clambered into the C-1A Trader and thought about Leigh Ann while the pilots taxied to the runway. She said that she loved him, but he still felt that Allison's presence was harming their relationship. He felt guilty without really knowing why; maybe just having to deceive Leigh Ann was enough cause.

The two and a half nights with Leigh Ann had left him physically and mentally spent, but he had to take his mind off his personal problems and concentrate on the immediate future. He dozed off and slept fitfully during the flight to the isolated base.

Arriving before daylight, Brad was jostled awake when the COD touched down at the desert landing strip.

Still groggy, Brad slung his overnight bag over his shoulder and trundled into the hangar. The MiG was parked on the far side of the F-8 Crusader, nose pointed at the hangar doors.

Grady Stanfield and Hollis Spencer were huddled in the briefing room when the three pilots entered. A freshly brewed pot of coffee sat on the table next to a plate stacked high with pastries.

Brad noticed that Spencer's normal, amiable mood had changed. He seemed oddly stiff and awkward as he stared into his coffee cup.

When the pilots had taken their seats, Spencer finally spoke. "Gentlemen, before we continue flying, I want to share some information with you."

Total silence surrounded the table.

"Conducting secret operations," Spencer said with a grim set to his jaw, "in an open democracy presents some very special problems."

Spencer's hand tightened around his cup. "When the CIA is asked to subvert foreign governments, support fledgling democracies, undermine dictators, or conduct covert operations, people like me salute and smartly get underway. We realize the consequences of our actions, and we take our daily responsibilities seriously." His single eye probed each of the three junior pilots. "In other words, we keep our secret missions secret."

A sense of foreboding swept over the wary pilots.

"We have had a breach in security," Spencer bluntly announced, then focused on Blackwell and Austin. "Lieutenant Blackwell, you are one phone call away from being the laundry officer in Adak, Alaska."

Stunned by the denunciation, Blackwell slumped in his chair. "Sir, I'm afraid I'm not following you."

Brad cautiously looked at Lex, wondering if Hollis Spencer knew about Leigh Ann's visit. Something told him that Spencer knew everything.

With his jaw firmly clenched, Spencer gave Blackwell a look that would freeze water. "You told a civilian about this operation," he seethed. "A top-secret, White House–approved, covert operation! Do you know what you compromised?"

Mouth agape, Lex sat back in shock. His mind raced before he realized that Allison van Ingen was the only person he had spoken to about the MiG operation.

Before Lex could answer, Spencer turned to Brad. "And you violated my orders by inviting a lady friend to visit you in San Diego." Spencer hesitated a moment. "You were instructed not to contact anyone, were you not?"

Paralyzed, Brad glanced at Blackwell, wondering what Lex had revealed, and if he had said anything about Leigh Ann. Nothing made sense. "Yes, sir."

Ignoring their coffee, Nick Palmer and Grady Stanfield sat quietly, staring at the top of the table.

"However," Brad replied, suddenly growing angry, "I would like to make a statement. My 'lady friend' is not a threat to national security, and I have not compromised this operation by divulging what I am doing here."

Spencer's good eye narrowed. "The point is," he glared impatiently, "when you are told not to contact anyone, that's exactly what I mean." The words hissed from his mouth. "Do you read me?"

"Yes, I read you," Brad replied tightly.

Spencer swung around to face Blackwell. "Lex, you're in the bull-pen for now . . . until I decide if you'll remain a part of this operation or go back to a squadron."

Chagrined, Lex remained quiet, mentally kicking himself for getting plastered and shooting off his mouth. He wondered who in hell Allison had told about the MiG, and how it had reached Hollis Spencer so quickly.

"I want to explain something," Spencer declared as he reached to refill his mug. "We—the CIA—have an ongoing turf battle with the military intelligence empires. The navy, as I've previously mentioned, wants to take custody of our MiG."

"Sir," Brad interjected, "what difference does it make who controls the MiG, as long as we get the evaluation info to the pilots who are flying against it?"

Hollis Spencer stiffened as an awkward silence hung in the air. Finally, the project officer calmly folded his hands together. "Captain Austin, you do not understand the magnitude of Operation Achilles."

Everyone looked intently at Spencer, waiting to find out what the CIA agent had up his sleeve.

"I have received permission," Spencer continued patiently, "straight from Langley, to carry out the final phase of Operation Achilles."

The sounds of the hangar doors being opened momentarily interrupted him.

"Lex," Spencer said dryly, and paused. "Because of the time constraints of the mission, I'm going to keep you on the team . . . for now." He watched the sudden relief sweep across Blackwell's face. "One little peep—one more cranial-rectal inversion, and you'll wish that you'd joined the Foreign Legion."

Spencer's single eye probed Lex for a long moment. "Any questions, Mister Blackwell?"

"No, sir."

Hollis shifted to view the entire group. "We are going to take the MiG to a well-concealed base in Laos," he paused, studying their eyes, "to fly clandestine fighter sweeps over North Vietnam."

Each pilot reacted in the same way. A look of shock was followed by almost wide-eyed excitement.

"You are going to fly the MiG in the back door," Spencer announced in a low, controlled voice, "and go after North Vietnam's best pilots."

Nick Palmer found his voice. "Jesus Christ, that will be like shooting fish in a barrel."

"Not quite," Spencer replied, glancing at the MiG as it was being towed out of the hangar. "Your air force and navy friends in the Phantoms and Crusaders won't know that an American pilot is flying our MiG. Except for the few of us involved in this operation, no one will have any idea who you are."

The significance of this disclosure stunned Brad. "We won't have any identification, in case we're shot down."

"You'll have identification," Spencer explained, "but it won't be your own. That's the reason for the heightened security. You were never here; the MiG does not exist, and the White House does not want any culpability if you vanish."

Enjoying a light breakfast, Leigh Ann gazed serenely at the swooping seagulls and thought about Allison van Ingen. The woman piqued her curiosity. There was something not quite right about her, and Leigh Ann wanted to get to know her better. Perhaps they could have lunch before Leigh Ann had to go to the airport.

After Leigh Ann returned to her room, she sat by the window and stared at the ocean. She had second thoughts about calling Allison, then made a decision. She would contact Allison and attempt to befriend her.

"Yes, it's the right thing to do," Leigh Ann said to herself as she reached for the telephone. Remembering that Allison had only recently arrived, Leigh Ann called information and jotted the number on the small desk pad.

She dialed Allison's number, but no one answered. *Probably at her father's yacht,* Leigh Ann thought as she replaced the receiver.

With little else to do before her afternoon flight, Leigh Ann decided to explore San Diego and the yacht basins. If she happened to see *Bellwether,* fine. If not, there were plenty of other interesting things to see.

Leigh Ann packed her belongings and carried her bags to the front desk. She rented a car and got a map, then marked the routes to the largest marinas and other boat basins.

Minutes later, she was breathing in the invigorating air as she approached San Diego. The trip was relaxing, prompting her to drive to the most distant yacht basin.

After a lengthy and fruitless search for Allison's yacht, Leigh Ann drove to a second group of docks. San Diego, as she had discovered, was an endless stretch of sand, palm trees, and sailboat masts.

The morning had become hot when Leigh Ann stopped at the lush grounds of the yacht club. The foliage surrounding the clubhouse was dotted with hibiscus, bougainvillea, poinsettias, and geraniums. She parked the car and studied the interesting array of boats along the docks.

She strolled down the main pier, which provided access to the graceful vessels. Leigh Ann came to an abrupt halt when she spotted *Bellwether.* An elderly man wearing dungarees was working on the fantail.

Leigh Ann looked at the other yachts while she watched the wizened man from the corner of her eye. Apparently a crew member or caretaker, she thought as he polished *Bellwether*'s brass ornaments.

Mustering her courage, Leigh Ann walked to the afterdeck. "Good morning."

The old man turned to meet her gaze. "Morning," he replied while he continued to polish. His voice sounded gravelly. "What can I do for you?"

"I was wondering if Allison van Ingen is on board."

He gave her a curious look, then stopped polishing. "There ain't nobody on here, 'cept me and my cat."

"Do you know Miss van Ingen?"

"Never heard of her," he stated as he continued with his weekly chore.

Leigh Ann's curiosity was aroused. "Is this boat for sale, or did someone recently buy it?"

The man gave her a long, questioning look. "It's a yacht, ma'am, and it ain't for sale . . . as far as I know."

Leigh Ann could see that she was testing his patience. "Do you know who owns this yacht?"

"I wouldn't be workin' on it," he growled, "if I didn't know who owned it. This here yacht is leased to the government." He wiped the perspiration from his brow. "That's who pays me to keep her shipshape."

"I see," Leigh Ann absently replied. Warning bells were sounding in her mind. *Brad, what have you gotten yourself into?*

"Thanks," she said, turning to retrace her steps. Leigh Ann was fully convinced that *Bellwether* was leased to the Central Intelligence Agency. She walked to the shiny convertible, wondering what role Allison played in the operation.

Leigh Ann knew for a certainty that Brad had told her the truth—as much as he could. She had to inform Brad about *Bellwether* as soon as possible.

"Damn," Leigh Ann swore, suddenly remembering what Brad had told her about the remote test site. The only means of communication were secure lines, which the pilots were not allowed to use. She would have to wait until Friday afternoon to call Brad at his apartment.

CHAPTER THIRTEEN

"Who in the hell did you talk to?" Brad asked Lex while they waited for Palmer to take off in the MiG. He kept his voice low, even though the sound of the jet engine drowned their conversation.

Blackwell glanced at Hollis Spencer. The project officer was seventy feet away, standing inside the hangar next to the aircraft radio.

"I got drunk Friday night," Lex confessed self-consciously, "and told Allison we're testing a MiG for the CIA."

Brad was astonished. "For God's sake, Lex. Have you lost your mind?" He tossed a look at Spencer, who was speaking to Hank Murray. "You actually told her that we're testing a MiG for the Central Intelligence Agency?"

Blackwell exhaled softly. "Are you hard of hearing?"

"Jesus H. Christ," Brad answered, shaking his head. He thought about the beautiful blonde, especially remembering all the questions she had asked him. Allison van Ingen, besides Lex and Nick, was the only person who knew Leigh Ann was visiting him.

"I'll tell you something about our friend, Allison," Brad muttered, "that we should have figured out up front."

"I think I know what you're gonna say."

Brad caught Blackwell's eye. "She reports to Hollis Spencer, and we've been had."

"I wouldn't bet against you," Blackwell declared as he watched the howling MiG hurtle down the runway. "Think about it, Brad," Lex snorted, mad at himself. "She really bored in, innocently asking a lot of personal questions after I was completely shit-faced."

Grady Stanfield thundered across the landing strip, rendezvousing with Palmer as the MiG climbed straight ahead.

"You're right," Brad agreed at last. He felt a burning sensation in the pit of his stomach. "Her entire act was a test to see if we would disclose what we're doing."

"And I sure as hell did," Lex flared in disgust. "Like a drunken sailor in a Tijuana whorehouse."

"Well, that's water under the stern."

Blackwell gave Brad a quick glance. "Yeah, that's another classic to add to my reputation."

Brad listened to the pilots' voices blare from the loudspeaker and watched the two jets while he spoke to Blackwell. "You might want to consider talking to Spencer, and let him know she was the only one you said a word to."

"Yeah," Lex replied disgustedly. "After he cools down."

They remained quiet, watching the fighters claw for altitude. Spencer had moved the schedule forward, insisting that the air combat maneuvering evaluation be completed by Friday. They would fly back-to-back flights until they knew the MiG like their own fighters.

Stanfield and Palmer were preparing for the first round of fighter engagements. The object of the simulated aerial battles was to explore the MiG's weaknesses and strengths.

After the series of dogfights, Grady and Nick would land, have the planes fueled, debrief in minute detail, switch planes, then repeat the process.

Moving closer to the speaker, Austin and Blackwell paid close attention to the two straining pilots. They were about to reengage for the second battle. Nick Palmer, as talented as Stanfield in equal fighter aircraft, was getting the worse end of the aerial duel.

"Fight's on!" Grady called as the two jets passed nose to nose seventy feet apart.

Brad shielded his eyes and watched both aircraft pull into the vertical. Palmer was trying to use the MiG's slow-speed, tight-turning capability to outmaneuver the F-8 Crusader.

The struggle lasted almost a minute before Stanfield again gained the advantage. Palmer had been forced to lower the MiG's nose when the airspeed decayed. With an altitude and speed advantage, Grady rolled in on Nick's tail.

"Check six," Stanfield radioed in triumph. "Let's go for separation and try again."

"Roger," Palmer replied, breathing heavily. "Have you had enough humiliation yet?"

"Bring it on." Grady laughed.

"Why don't you jump me," Nick suggested stiffly, "and we'll go from there."

"You've got it," Stanfield agreed while he reefed the agile Crusader around. "Heads up. I'm high, coming in from your eight o'clock."

Brad and Lex watched the two aircraft converge. Nick pulled up into an Immelmann as Grady committed the Crusader's nose up. Coming over the top of a displacement roll, Stanfield appeared to have the advantage.

"I think," Brad laughed softly, "that Grady is about to receive a major surprise."

Blackwell gave him a curious glance, but remained quiet while he watched Palmer snap into a tight turn.

Stanfield was pulling inside of the MiG when Nick chopped his power and violently cross-controlled the nimble fighter. Grady tried to react to the ploy by snapping his throttle back and deploying his speed brake.

A second later, Stanfield recognized his mistake. In desperation, Grady simultaneously slammed the throttle into afterburner and retracted the speed brake. He hauled the sleek F-8 around in a last-ditch effort to extract himself from the stressful fight.

Brad watched Nick slide inside the diving Crusader, then heard his voice over the speaker.

"Gotcha!"

"You got lucky."

"The more creative one is," Palmer laughed enthusiastically, "the better one's luck gets."

"I won't fall for that again."

"That's what they all say."

The fighter engagements continued until Nick called low fuel. The score was Grady four wins and Nick two. When Palmer entered the break and turned downwind, Stanfield blasted across the center of the runway and yanked the screeching Crusader up into a victory roll.

Suddenly, as the F-8 reached the inverted position, a puff of black smoke erupted from the tail pipe.

Horrified, Brad watched the Crusader's nose drop as the roll rate decreased. He also saw a flock of birds scattering behind the jet. "Bird strike!"

"Eject! Eject!" Spencer shouted over the radio.

Two seconds later, as the Crusader's wings were perpendicular to the runway, Stanfield ejected.

"Oh, Jesus," Brad exclaimed as Grady rocketed sideways through the air. Stanfield's parachute opened a split second before he slammed into the ground and bounced to a stop.

The flash and explosion from the crashing jet shocked Brad into action. "Call a medevac!" he ordered the man standing next to the direct line to Miramar. "Get 'em out here on the double!"

Trailed by Blackwell and Spencer, Austin raced for the nearby jeep.

He clambered into the driver's seat while Hollis and Lex leaped into their seats. He started the engine and floorboarded the throttle. "Hang on!"

Careening down the taxiway, Brad skidded onto the runway behind the crash truck. Overhead, Nick Palmer climbed to reenter the landing pattern. Austin turned off the runway and lurched across the ground.

Brad's heart raced as the fire truck slowed to let a crewman jump off. The man tumbled, then leaped to his feet and ran toward Stanfield, arriving at the same time as the jeep.

Sliding to an abrupt halt, Brad leaped out and rushed to the inert form. "Son of a bitch," he said to himself as he knelt next to Grady. The pilot was battered and barely conscious.

The crash crewman, along with Spencer and Blackwell, joined Brad. Their faces reflected the anguish they felt. They could see the remnants of at least one bird on the side of Stanfield's scratched crash helmet.

"Don't move him," Austin said emphatically, "or touch him until the medevac gets here."

The burly man from the crash crew looked puzzled. He had been trained to pull pilots out of crashes.

"His neck may be broken," Brad explained as he glanced at Stanfield's contorted legs, "so we don't want to risk doing more damage. We'll leave his helmet on."

Lying on his side, Grady had one arm and one leg twisted under him. His helmet visor was shattered and his mouth was slightly open.

Hollis Spencer all too vividly recalled his own crash in Korea as he leaped up and ran to the jeep. Grabbing the radio microphone, he called the hangar to check on the status of the medevac helicopter.

Lex rose in stunned silence. He walked to the jeep, placed his hands on the hood, and let his head sag. "He took a bird through the canopy . . . and probably some down the intake."

Brad looked up at Blackwell. "You're right. Did you see that black puff of smoke fly out of the tail pipe?"

"Yes."

"That's what shelled the engine." Brad glanced at Stanfield. "Who knows how many birds went through the compressor."

Detecting a faint sound, Brad leaned next to Stanfield's face. "Grady, can you hear me?" The ear-splitting whine of the MiG taxiing to the hangar made hearing difficult. "Can you hear me?"

Stanfield's eyelids fluttered twice and his lips moved, allowing a trickle of blood to escape. "Brad, I . . . can't breathe. . . ."

"Grady," Brad comforted, "you've probably got some cracked ribs." Brad knew Stanfield's injuries were much more severe than broken ribs. "We've got a medevac on the way, so keep the faith."

Austin gently unhooked the parachute release fittings from Stanfield's torso harness. "Grady, we're going to use your chute to protect you from the sun."

Stanfield moved his lips, but no sound emerged.

Brad handed the fittings to the crash crewman, who gathered the parachute. He and Blackwell worked together to shelter Stanfield from the blazing sun.

"Brad . . . " Grady burbled in excruciating pain, "what . . . did I . . . what hit . . ."

"Don't try to talk," Brad said soothingly, and squeezed Stanfield's hand. "Just breathe easy and try to relax." *Easy words for me to say.*

Austin felt a slight pressure from Grady's fingers. "I'm going to stick with you," he consoled, then said a silent prayer.

CHAPTER FOURTEEN

Brad paced the long hallway adjacent to the emergency room. Grady Stanfield had been undergoing surgery for over three hours. Brad finally sat in a chair and let the back of his head sag against the wall. He felt exhausted from the shock and stress of the past few hours.

He thought about Leigh Ann and their future relationship. Would she trust him after the Allison incident? He had called the hotel when Grady went into surgery, but Leigh Ann had already checked out.

The memory of Allison van Ingen's tanned body crept into his mind. He wanted to confront Hollis Spencer and find out how he had known about Leigh Ann. *It had to be Allison,* he reasoned. *She must be some type of security specialist.*

Austin rubbed his temples to erase Allison's image. She had managed to entice Lex Blackwell into telling her the entire story about the MiG. Lex had been in the wrong, but she had definitely set the trap to snare him.

Grady had been admitted to the hospital without anyone's having to reveal the exact circumstances surrounding the accident. In order not to jeopardize the secret operation, Stanfield's unavoidable mishap would be investigated as part of a routine training-flight exercise.

Spencer had arranged to borrow a Phantom from VF-121. He had instructed Brad to fly the F-4 back to the test site after someone arrived to be with Grady.

Brad's thoughts were interrupted when two navy surgeons walked out of the operating room.

He rose to greet them.

"Is he going to be all right?" he asked, swallowing the lump in his throat.

"We have done everything we can," the taller of the two doctors assured him, "but the next twenty-four to forty-eight hours will be decisive."

"Lieutenant Commander Stanfield," the other doctor reluctantly offered, "is currently in critical and unstable condition. If he survives, he will be facing a long and arduous healing process."

Brad's heart sank. "Thank you. I know you did the best you could."

The taller surgeon patted Brad on the shoulder. "Get some rest. He's getting the best possible care we can provide."

"Yes, sir," Brad replied solemnly. *After I fly an F-4 back to the base.*

As soon as the doctors left, Brad went to the cafeteria and ate a sandwich. He ignored the stares at his flight suit as he methodically chewed his meal. Like a newsreel being played over and over, Grady's crash kept flashing through his mind. It had happened so quickly that the time sequence seemed to have been compressed.

After eating, Brad walked back to the waiting area. Bending over a water fountain, he was startled when an elderly couple burst through the double hospital doors. They went to the counter and announced themselves as the Stanfields.

Grateful that someone had arrived to be with Grady, Brad quietly slipped out of the hallway. He felt uneasy about not talking with Stanfield's parents, but he did not want to lie to them about the covert operation, or what had really happened to their son. The doctors would provide all the information the Stanfields needed.

The searing heat from the afternoon sun baked Brad Austin while he taxied the borrowed Phantom to the runway. VF-121, the Pacific Fleet replacement training squadron for navy F-4 crews, had hurriedly prepared the Phantom for departure. When Hollis Spencer made a request, he got results.

Although he could not erase Grady Stanfield from his thoughts, Brad was relaxed. It felt good to be in the cockpit of a Phantom again. The crash helmet the squadron executive officer had loaned him felt a little loose, but it would suffice for the short trip.

Closing the forward canopy, Brad switched from ground control to the Miramar control tower.

"Miramar, navy one-one-four is ready."

"Navy one-one-four," the terse voice responded, "cleared on course. Contact departure out of three thousand."

"On the roll," Brad replied, swinging the F-4 onto the runway. He shoved the throttles forward and felt the first chill from the air-conditioning system.

A moment later, Brad selected afterburner and watched the airspeed indicator. He gave his instruments and gauges a last peek before the Phantom clawed its way into the hot afternoon sky. He snapped the landing-gear lever up and glanced at the annunciator panel. Everything was functioning properly.

Passing 3,000 feet, Brad pulled the throttles out of afterburner and switched to departure control. A minute later he was switched to the Los Angeles air route traffic-control center.

Looking toward the Vallecito Mountains, Brad made a firm decision. He would talk with Hollis Spencer about the operation and get some straight answers. As much as Brad respected Spencer, he was disturbed about being deceived. Prior to Stanfield's disastrous crash, Brad had been debating whether to discuss Allison van Ingen with the project officer. Now he was positive that he would discuss her.

Spencer was certainly a driven man. While he had waited for the medevac helicopter to arrive at the crash site, Spencer had requested the F-4 from VF-121 at Miramar. The confirmation that a Phantom would be provided to Spencer had been received before the helicopter was on the scene.

Brad had been adamant about escorting Grady to the hospital, prompting Spencer to ask him to deliver the F-4.

Approaching 15,000 feet, Brad flicked the microphone switch and eased back further on the throttles.

"Los Angeles Center, navy one-one-four."

"Navy one-one-four, Los Angeles."

Brad glanced out at the area surrounding their secret base. "Navy one-fourteen will cancel and go VFR." He was changing his instrument flight plan, with the associated radar coverage, to a visual flight plan.

"Roger," the clipped voice acknowledged. "Squawk one two zero zero, and have a good day."

"Thanks," Brad radioed, switching the IFF to 1200. "One-fourteen is squawking twelve hundred."

Lowering the Phantom's nose, Brad adjusted the throttles and settled into a slow descent. Watching for air traffic, Brad analyzed his situation. If they did fly the MiG over North Vietnam, what were the chances that he might get shot down by an American fighter? Probably fifty-fifty, if he flew enough missions over an extended period of time.

Brad altered course a few degrees to pass behind a corporate jet. What if the North Vietnamese discovered what he was doing? That would double his chances of getting blown out of the sky.

The surface-to-air missiles were another factor to consider. The North Vietnamese regularly fired their SAM missiles right through any melee, often downing their own pilots.

There were a lot of ifs, but the most frightening aspect of the operation was the idea of being shot down and forgotten. The part about the White House disavowing his existence, if tragedy struck, particularly bothered Brad. At least, he thought cynically, the Marine Corps would make every effort to save him if he was downed while flying for them.

It was time for a frank discussion with Hollis Spencer. Surely, Brad thought with a gnawing anger, there must be some type of contingency plans for rescuing the pilots. The CIA damn sure could not expect them to become kamikaze pilots. Brad did not subscribe to the Divine Wind philosophy.

Reducing the power to idle, Brad descended to 500 feet above the ground. He deactivated the IFF, then turned to enter the narrow passage into the restricted airspace above their landing strip.

Slowing to 220 knots indicated airspeed, Brad slapped the landing-gear handle down and turned downwind. He had decided not to land out of a normal military break.

When the airspeed reached 170 knots, he lowered the flaps and turned base leg.

Banking to align himself with the runway, Brad noticed that the C-1A Trader was taxiing for takeoff. He found that unusual. The COD normally flew under cover of darkness.

Brad slowed to 135 knots and made a typical carrier landing. Without flaring, the Phantom slammed onto the pavement with a puff of white smoke.

He rolled to the end of the runway, turned around, then back-taxied to the midfield turnoff while the Trader held in position at the far end of the runway.

Taxiing along the right edge of the ramp area, Brad slowed to a crawl and swung the Phantom ninety degrees to the left. He opened the canopy, unsnapped his oxygen mask, and breathed in the warm, humid air from the rainstorm that had drenched the field prior to his arrival.

He peered at the ominous black clouds that had passed over the landing strip. Lightning continued to flash from the bottom of the angry-looking cells.

Brad watched the COD climb away as the F-4's engines spun to a halt. After removing the borrowed helmet, he saw Nick Palmer and Lex Blackwell approaching the Phantom.

"Thanks," Brad said, handing his helmet to the plane captain. He unstrapped his restraining harnesses and wearily climbed over the side of the canopy railing.

"How is Grady?" Nick asked when Brad reached the pavement. Lex handed Brad an ice-cold Budweiser.

"He is holding his own," Brad assured them, then gulped the chilled beer. Breathing through an oxygen mask always made his throat dry. "When I left, Grady was out of surgery, but in critical and unstable condition."

Lex shook his head in disbelief. "It's a goddamn shame."

Palmer gestured toward the blackened and twisted wreckage of the F-8 Crusader. "Murray found bird remains in the engine."

"I figured he would," Brad replied, staring at the charred ruins of the fighter.

"The explosion was so violent," Lex confided, "that it blew parts and blades plumb through the side of the fuselage."

"It's a miracle," Brad let out a low whistle, "that he got out of it in time."

"You're right," Palmer conceded. "Now we have to pray that God will grant him another miracle."

Brad took a long pull on his beer. "What's been happening around here since the crash?"

Blackwell and Palmer laughed nervously. "Brace yourself," Nick said, and smiled. "Our friend, Allison van Ingen, just flew in on the COD."

"Well, Lex, you were right," Brad responded with an edge of discomfort. "I may be a bit embarrassed, but it's time for some god-damned straight answers."

"Partner," Blackwell drawled, "you think you're embarrassed? Try lower than squid shit at the bottom of the Mariana Trench."

"We're going to have a brief," Nick grinned, "as soon as you're ready to join the happy group."

Brad asked his plane captain to put the borrowed helmet on the next

COD flight, then looked at the MiG in the open hangar. "Did you fly any more today?"

"Cap was beside himself," Nick informed Brad, "after the medevac left. So Lex and I waited until he settled down before suggesting that we resume flying."

"He agreed," Blackwell chimed in, "so we took turns till that toad strangler hit the field."

The atmosphere in the hangar was charged with tension when Brad entered the building. Hollis Spencer was in his office, speaking on one of the secure lines.

Austin started for the flight-gear equipment room when he spied Allison sitting alone in the briefing room. He changed course and walked to the door. Allison was as beautiful as ever in tailored utility trousers and khaki blouse.

"You did a real nice job," Brad declared, nodding his head. "They should give you a raise."

"Brad, that's hardly fair," Allison protested in earnest. "I had hoped we could put things in their proper perspective, and work together as professionals who have a job to do. You have yours . . . and I have mine."

Brad gazed at Allison without any visible emotion or hostility. "You have missed your calling," he deadpanned, fixing his hazel eyes on her. "You should have been an actress. They make a hell of a lot more money than a CIA employee."

Allison returned his gaze, unsure if he was being sarcastic or if he had complimented her in a backhanded way. Inside, she felt a stinging pain. Allison knew he had a reason to be angry.

She studied Brad, realizing how much she had come to respect him. "Would you mind if we take a walk later—after the briefing—and see if we can clear the air?"

Brad hesitated for a moment while he considered Allison's offer. He knew that she had only been doing her job.

"You mean," Brad answered with a faint grin, "mend some fences, as Lex would say?"

"Yes." Allison risked a thin smile. "I would like to mend fences, and start with a fresh slate."

"That sounds reasonable to me." Brad eyed her skeptically. "No more cloak-and-dagger stuff?"

She beamed her radiant smile. "Promise."

"Okay," he declared, and started to walk away, then stopped and turned to Allison. "One question that keeps going around in my mind."

She laughed quietly. "I'm sure you have more than one question."

Brad nodded and looked into her eyes. "When did you start following us," he smiled slowly, "the night you tracked us to the lounge . . . and we went on the tour of the city?"

"From the time you and Nick left the O club," she answered without a trace of embarrassment, and smiled like a Cheshire cat. "You two fighter pilots weren't checking your six."

Brad chuckled and gave her a long look. "You don't take any prisoners, do you?"

"Occasionally."

Instinctively, Austin knew not to respond to the remark. "When is Cap going to talk to us?"

"You have time for a shower," she informed him with a twinkle in her eye.

Turning to leave, Brad again paused to look back. "Would you mind using your influence to see if Cap will use the secure line to find out how Grady is doing?"

"That's already been taken care of," Allison assured him. Her expression grew serious. "His condition has improved to critical but stable."

"Thank God," Brad exclaimed, feeling the tension drain from his neck muscles.

"Our people are checking on Grady every hour," Allison explained as the ground crew maneuvered the lumbering F-4 into the hangar.

Brad searched deep into her eyes, curious about the nature of the real Allison van Ingen. "Thank you."

She smiled warmly, then returned to her neatly written notes.

CHAPTER FIFTEEN

Toweling himself dry, Brad reviewed the questions he intended to ask Hollis Spencer. A kaleidoscope of thoughts ran through his mind, with Stanfield's tragic crash and Allison's involvement in the secret operation dominating the others.

Dressed in a clean flight suit, Brad walked across the hangar to the small meeting room. Hollis Spencer and Hank Murray were huddled under the tail of the MiG, discussing a modification to the empennage of the fighter.

When Spencer noticed Brad, he rose and walked toward the briefing room. Nick Palmer and Lex Blackwell, absorbed in an animated conversation next to the Phantom, followed Spencer into the crowded space.

After an awkward silence, the project officer closed the door and sat down. "Before we get into specifics, I want to let you know that Grady's condition is improving."

The pilots silently acknowledged the update and glanced at Allison. Her face remained expressionless.

Spencer hesitated a moment, then addressed the three men. "As you are aware, Miss van Ingen is part of the nucleus of this operation. We have worked together for the past three and a half years."

Spencer stared at each pilot a brief second. "Don't let her looks fool you. I can assure you that she knows her job, and knows it well."

"I can attest to that," Lex agreed, and lowered his head.

The CIA agent paused. "It will serve you well," Spencer warned them, "to remember that."

Brad darted a look at Allison. She appeared composed and confident, as if she had heard it all before.

There was a hint of impatience in Spencer's voice. "Besides being an excellent security specialist," Spencer continued steadily, "Allison serves as my adjutant. She handles all logistical and administrative tasks associated with the operation."

Brad and Lex momentarily shifted their gaze to Allison. It was impossible not to be attracted to the vivacious blonde. Brad noticed that Nick could not take his eyes off her.

"She is intimately familiar with our destination," Spencer informed them, "having worked with me on an Air America project in Vientiane, Laos."

Spencer observed the looks of respect forming on the faces of the pilots. They were coming to grips with the fact that Allison was more than an attractive showpiece. She was an extremely intelligent and efficient woman.

"Everyone in this room," Spencer glanced at Blackwell, "along with a half-dozen maintenance people, will eventually be going to Laos."

Although elated about still being a part of the operation, Lex showed no emotion after the announcement.

"Excuse me, sir," Brad interrupted, "but it seems to me that we're going to be taking a hell of a risk to basically place a bandage on a hemorrhaging whale."

"Captain Austin," Spencer said in a pleasant tone, "let me explain something to you."

Brad's expression reflected the doubt he felt.

"The Vietnam situation—our undeclared war—is not going well . . . particularly the air war."

"How well I know," Brad agreed, refraining, for once, from expressing his contempt for the rules of engagement the administration in the White House had forced on the aircrews.

"Politically," Spencer declared, "this war has created a wide distrust of our government and its leadership. Our failure to win the war, combined with the ever-growing casualty list, have consumed an inordinate amount of public trust."

"Cap," Brad ventured, "with the growing resentment that is eroding the confidence in the military and the government, why aren't we using our full capability to end the conflict? We certainly have the means to win, and win quickly and decisively."

Blackwell nervously cleared his throat.

"Sir," Brad asked respectfully, "why are we pitting one American-flown MiG, with all the associated risks, against the entire North Vietnamese Air Force? I understand the unique concept, but I could probably be doing more damage flying a Phantom against the enemy."

Brad felt Nick tap his toe in a silent warning.

"Because," Spencer calmly replied, "we have been instructed to carry out the project. Operation Achilles, as I mentioned before, originated in the White House. They make the decisions, and we implement them . . . whether we agree with the concept or not."

Allison turned to Brad. "From what we have been told, off the record, there is a growing concern about the overall kill ratio in the air campaign. We are losing one of our aircraft for almost every four MiGs downed."

Her gaze briefly met Spencer's eyes. "The Pentagon believes we can increase the kill ratio from the current three point seven to one," she glanced at her notes, "to possibly four or five to one, using the MiGs that we acquire."

Spencer balled his right fist and squeezed it with his other hand. "Are you aware that the navy is preparing to start a postgraduate course in fighter weapons tactics?"

"We've heard scuttlebutt," Austin admitted.

"The school," Spencer said with an air of knowledge, "is going to be a part of VF-121 at Miramar. They've already nicknamed it Top Gun."

Allison looked at Brad. "The entire focus of Top Gun is to dramatically increase the kill ratios. The navy brass behind the new school believe we can, in the near future, be destroying nine or ten MiGs for every American aircraft lost." She paused to glance at Lex and Nick. "The three of you, at least in my estimation, would be prime candidates for Top Gun instructors . . . after you complete this operation."

Spencer reached into his breast pocket and withdrew his well-chewed pipe. "Gentlemen," he confided, "I'm going to tell you something that had better never go beyond this room . . . never in your lifetime."

The gravity of his words was not lost on the pilots.

"The bottom line of what we have been asked to do is this." He reached for his tobacco pouch. "Until the effects of Top Gun can begin making a difference in the fleet kill ratios, certain individuals want us to use other means to gradually increase the number of MiGs downed."

Brad tapped the table. "If we go after North Vietnam's best pilots using our deceptive MiG, then there will be less competition in the future . . . and more MiGs downed now?"

"That's how they see it in Washington," Spencer admitted. "We'll be turning out more and more finely tuned front-line fighter pilots, while the North Vietnamese will be losing their best pilots."

"Well," Brad replied, assessing the impact of the mission, "that does make sense, and I suppose the axiom about not having a rule book for war is true." His face was expressionless as he focused on Spencer. "In this business, as you well know, you win any way you can. If you finish second in this arena, you seldom get a rematch."

The room became as quiet as a tomb.

"That's absolutely true," Spencer agreed. "The days of chivalry in aerial warfare are long gone."

Brad thought about the risky assignment. "Before we charge the hill, I would like to make one statement." He met Allison's gaze, then stared at Spencer. "The North Vietnamese don't have any restrictions placed on their pilots. If our administration would lift the rules of engagement imposed on our aircrews, I guarantee you we would be kicking their asses all over the sky . . . even without Top Gun."

Brad again felt Palmer tap his boot.

"I understand what you're saying." Spencer nodded, concealing the same frustration that haunted Austin. "However, we are going to abide by our instructions, and deal with the situation that prevails at the moment. We're going to take advantage of the deception provided by the MiG."

Brad indicated that he had a question.

"Yes."

"I have a couple of questions," Brad paused, "that have been bothering me. First, how are we going to know when their best pilots are flying . . . and where to look for them?"

"A good question." Spencer thought for a moment. "I'm not going to expose all the details, but I can tell you how our intelligence sources will affect you."

Brad silently wondered why they could not be trusted with the intricacies of how the Agency gathered information.

"We have people," Spencer continued, "who pose as journalists, media representatives, foreign correspondents, et cetera, who closely observe the MiG bases."

The men were tensely attentive.

"They use binoculars, and other devices, to observe the pilots and their aircraft."

Brad was intrigued. "Cap, how do they get the information out? How will we know soon enough to do anything?"

"I'll get to that in a minute," Spencer assured him. "I want you to know what our people see, so you will have more confidence in our abilities."

Spencer furrowed his brow. "Our observers see the same pilots—the guys with the red stars painted on their fuselages—climb into the same aircraft time after time."

The project officer was unable to conceal the satisfaction he felt. "We know that a few Soviet pilots are flying with the North Vietnamese," Spencer shared a look with Allison, "and we'll get to that topic in a few minutes."

That announcement brought a surprised look from the pilots.

"When our observers see a particular pilot—one of the top jocks—climb into his aircraft," Spencer studied the intent faces, "they relay the side number and description of the MiG to an EC-121 flying over Laos.

"After the Warning Star receives the scrambled message, they will relay the data to our radio post, which they will believe is a new military intelligence operation."

Spencer anticipated Brad's next question.

"We can't have the surveillance aircraft talk directly to you," Spencer continued, "because that would jeopardize our cover. Remember, we don't exist, and never did exist."

Brad acknowledged with a nod. "Since our MiG doesn't have the capability to receive scrambled messages, I assume we will use some type of code."

"That's correct," Spencer sighed with weariness, "but we'll cover that in detail later."

The room remained quiet while Spencer packed and lighted his pipe. "The White House has instructed the Agency to keep this operation off the record. It never happened," he emphasized, blowing a ring of smoke toward the ceiling, "and you will never discuss it with anyone. The official line is that the information we gather from our MiG evaluation came from a MiG-17 pilot who defected from an Eastern bloc country."

Spencer studied each pilot. "Remember that bit of info."

"Why aren't you using Air America pilots?" Brad asked. "I know there are a number of former fighter pilots flying for the airlines backed by the CIA."

"You're right," Spencer grinned, "but they're all World War Two and Korean vintage, like me. The Pentagon agreed that we should use current military fighter pilots who have recent combat experience . . . and MiG kills to their credit."

Spencer looked at the pilot from Texas. "Lex, do we have any soft drinks in the refrigerator?"

Blackwell twisted around, then opened the door and reached for a Coke. "Yes, sir."

"Folks, help yourselves to whatever you want," Spencer declared, opening his soft drink. "Then we'll get down to the details of the operation."

"This is off the subject," Palmer said, "but I was wondering if the navy is going to send an accident team out here."

"They'll be sending an investigation team," Spencer answered, "after the MiG is gone. They are aware that a bird strike downed the F-8."

Spencer shoved his folding notepad to the center of the table. "For the rest of this week, we will fly the MiG against the Phantom." His gaze narrowed on Blackwell. "Lex, since you're not checked out in the F-4, you'll fly the MiG while Brad and Nick debrief their one-on-ones. Friday, you'll be included in the engagements."

"Yes, sir."

"When the rest of us depart for Laos," Spencer announced, "Lex will be making a whirlwind tour around the carriers and air bases, before he joins us at Wattay. While we're here, we'll meet each evening after dinner to debrief," he looked at Blackwell, "so Lex will have every detail about the MiG etched into his mind."

Nick and Brad exchanged furtive glances.

"That doesn't sound like such a great idea to me," Palmer admitted. "Since Lex will be giving the gouge to the same people we will be trying to evade."

Spencer finally smiled. "Obviously," he pointed the stem of his pipe at Blackwell, "if you breathe a word about the MiG being in Laos, I'll have your ass hung from the yardarm."

Blackwell flushed but remained calm, even though his embarrassment was doubled by Allison's presence. "We got our MiG information from a defector."

Spencer nodded. "This weekend the MiG will be disassembled and flown to Wattay Airport."

"Where is Wattay located?" Brad asked, looking at Allison.

"It's located in Vientiane," she responded. "Wattay is our primary Air America base."

"From there," Spencer disclosed, "an Air America crew will fly the MiG to our isolated landing strip in northeastern Laos, where it will be reassembled." His chair creaked when he reached for a detailed map. He opened the well-worn paper and spread it out on the table. "Right here, next to the border." He tapped his index finger on the map.

"Hot damn," Blackwell exclaimed. "You weren't kiddin' when you said back door."

Spencer adjusted his eye patch. "The runway at Alpha-29, which is still under construction, is one hundred twenty miles from downtown Hanoi."

Brad studied the map, mentally calculating the fuel endurance of the MiG-17. "Cap, we aren't going to be able to loiter very long."

Spencer shifted in his chair and pointed out to the hangar floor. "See those crates behind the MiG?"

The pilots rose to look out the window in the door.

"Those," Spencer informed them, "are drop tanks. You'll have one under each wing, like most other MiG-17s."

"So," Brad replied as he sat down, "depending on our altitude and power setting, we'll have basically another fifteen to thirty minutes of fuel?"

"That's right," Spencer confirmed, and knocked the spent ashes out of his pipe. "We've got another shipment of tanks on the way to Laos, but we prefer that you not punch them off . . . unless you get jumped by someone."

"Someone," Brad asked, "as in Phantom or Crusader?"

"That's right," Spencer cautioned. "Then you had better start steaming for the border."

Spencer looked at the drawings Hank Murray had given him. "Our resident engineering genius has a pet project in the works." He smiled. "One that I am sure you will be interested in hearing about."

Chewing on his pipe, Spencer silently wondered how he would have managed without the brilliant navy captain.

"Nick," Spencer pointed to Palmer, "if a bogey you were engaged with suddenly spewed dense smoke and went into a steep, nose-down spiral, what would you assume, and what would you do next?"

"I would assume that I had a positive kill," Nick hesitated, "and if the sky happened to be saturated with MiGs, I would be looking for other bogies."

"Brad?" Spencer asked.

"Probably the same thing. You can't fixate on one gomer too long, or someone else is going to be on your six . . . pumping cannon shells up your tail."

"Well," Spencer chuckled, "Hank may be a little rough around the edges, but he is sure trying to look out for his flock."

Spencer enjoyed a pull on his pipe. "Hank is fashioning a smoke canister, just like in an airshow airplane, to use as cover in case of emergency."

Watching the three wide grins, Spencer took satisfaction in what Hank Murray and his men had accomplished under the rushed time schedule.

"Is Captain Murray going with us?" Lex asked.

"Yes, fortunately," Spencer answered with a sense of relief. "However, he may have to return if the Agency gets another MiG. In fact, we're going to leave the F-4 here, since two more pilots have been recruited for the project."

"One other item," Allison said. "Leave all of your flight gear here. Southern Air Transport will take it with the MiG."

Brad leaned back in his chair. "I've got a few more questions, if you don't mind."

"That's what we're here for," Spencer assured him. "This is a new adventure for all of us."

Brad noticed that Allison was looking at him.

"From what you said," Brad glanced at Allison, "about the administration not wanting this covert operation to backfire on them, I get the sense that we're going to be abandoned—on our own—if we get into trouble and have to eject."

Spencer drew a breath and adjusted the ever-present utility cap. "I'll try to allay some of your concerns."

The pilots' eyes were riveted to the project officer. Allison quietly slid a sheet of paper to Spencer.

"First," Spencer glanced at the meticulous notes, "I want to assure you that we do not abandon our own, even though you are on loan from the military." He had intended to inject a degree of levity, but no one smiled.

"We can't enlist the military in any search-and-rescue effort," Spencer explained patiently, "because the operation would be exposed."

He saw the look of concern on Palmer's face.

"We are going to use Air America helicopters," Spencer confided, "to get you out . . . if you go down."

Spencer watched their guarded reactions. "I told you we would get back to this subject." He swiveled his chair. "Allison."

"You are going to learn enough Russian," Allison assured them, "to be able to convince the North Vietnamese that you are Soviet advisers, if you land among the troops or civilians."

The pilots glanced at each other with open suspicion.

Brad spoke first. "I would assume, then . . . we're going to be flying around dressed as Russian pilots?"

"That's right," Spencer declared.

"Why are we taking our flight gear?" Brad asked.

Allison fielded the question. "You are going to use your own torso harnesses and g suits, since Hank's crew modified the fittings. Your helmets will be painted to resemble the Soviet headgear." She smiled. "No problem with your boots, and you can use your flight suits to lounge in."

"You'll have Soviet-style flight suits," Spencer informed them, "and Russian documents to help convince the people on the ground that you are Soviet instructor pilots."

"Holy shit . . . ," Lex muttered.

Brad and Nick shook their heads.

"It's a last-gasp measure," Allison added, "to give you time to get to a remote place, so we can get in to rescue you."

Austin caught Spencer's eye. "Cap, I'd like to go back to the subject of selectively stalking their best pilots."

"Sure," Spencer encouraged. "Now is the time to ask questions, before we're neck deep in it."

"Even if we have the descriptions of individual aircraft," Brad looked at Nick and Lex, "it's going to be a complete clusterfu—almost impossible to identify them in the turmoil of battle . . . unless we rendezvous on their wing."

"That's right," Nick added. "It may look easy in theory, but in the real world, at least in my opinion, we'd be better off to take any MiG we can shoot."

"Cap," Austin suggested politely, "if we can't locate and identify specific pilots quickly, I recommend that we go after any target of opportunity."

Spencer pondered the advice. "I have the flexibility to do whatever is necessary to accomplish the mission, but for now, let's stick to the plan as Langley sees it."

Brad shook his head, but remained quiet.

CHAPTER SIXTEEN

Brad followed Allison through the hangar light trap and stopped next to the sentry. The young man wore a .45-caliber handgun around his waist, and carried a small radio transmitter and receiver strapped over his shoulder.

"Any problem," Brad politely asked, "if we take a walk out to the runway?"

"No, sir," the guard assured him, and raised the walkie-talkie to his mouth. "Unit one to all posts. Captain Austin and Miss van Ingen will be walking the runway for . . ." He paused, looking to Brad.

"Twenty minutes."

" . . . approximately twenty minutes. Unit one will confirm when they return to the hangar. Copy?"

When the posts had acknowledged, the sentry nodded his head. "You're all set, sir."

"Thanks."

Allison placed her hands in the pockets of her windbreaker and fell into step with Austin's leisurely pace.

"Brad, I do want to apologize," she offered in a serious vein, "for having to deceive you and your friends. It's standard procedure when we recruit people who are not members of the Agency."

"Apology accepted," Brad said flatly, "but I would like to know one thing."

"What's that?" she said cautiously.

"How did you manage to drink so many martinis and not fall flat on your . . . face?"

Allison gave him a sly smile, then laughed. "I was drinking water. Throw in an olive, and the illusion is complete."

"Very clever," Brad admitted. "Is Allison van Ingen your real name, or does everyone around here have false identities and phony backgrounds?"

"Yes, it's my real name," she conceded, "and I am from Philadelphia. However, my family is not Main Line."

"That's nice to know." Brad looked up at the bright moon and twinkling stars. "I mean, that your name is really Allison."

A pause followed before she stopped and faced Brad. She smiled soothingly. "Is the girl who visited you—Leigh Ann—a steady girlfriend?"

"I guess you could say so," Brad answered with a feeling of pride. "I'm planning to ask her to marry me when I rotate back to the States."

Disappointment showed on Allison's face, but she managed a brave smile. "Congratulations."

"Thank you."

She cast a look at the sky. "I had hoped to have the opportunity to know you better myself."

"Let's not spoil our newfound friendship," Brad suggested, giving Allison a brotherly hug around her shoulders.

She smiled. "I don't give up easily, you know." There was a tone of warning in her voice.

Brad looked down at her smooth, beautiful face. "I don't imagine you do," he replied with a lazy smile. "I'll bet you're a lady who is accustomed to getting her man."

"Well," Allison said, acknowledging the compliment, "I'll have to admit that 'getting my man,' as you call it, has never been a problem for me."

"Look, Allison," Brad said, taking her gently by the shoulders. "Let's keep our relationship on a friendly basis."

"Oops," she teased. "I think I've just been jilted."

Brad shook his head in amusement. "Shall we continue our walk?"

"Yes," she answered eagerly.

They walked quietly, absorbed in their own thoughts, until they reached the end of the runway. After a short pause, they turned to retrace their steps.

"Tell me," Brad questioned, "how did a woman like you get involved with the CIA?"

"It's a long story, but if you really want to know . . ."

"Sure," Brad responded, more curious than ever.

"I come from a very wealthy family—not Main Line, as I told you—but wealthy."

"So the Mercedes, the yacht, and all the trappings of wealth weren't really an act for you."

"No." She laughed softly. "My life, before I joined the Agency, was a series of beauty pageants, debutante balls, and dating only the *right* people from the *right* families."

Brad detected a tone of rebellion in her voice.

"When I finished college," Allison looked at Brad, "all my friends were marrying into the *right* families . . . or buying vans, painting flowers on them, and joining communes."

Allison paused, unsure if Brad really wanted to hear this, or if he was just being courteous.

"Please," Brad said enthusiastically, "don't leave me hanging."

"Well," she continued, "to make a long story short, I inherited a trust fund from my grandfather. With my future financially secure, I practiced my own kind of rebellion and joined the CIA."

"Just like that," Brad questioned, "you gave up the good life . . . for this?"

"That's right," Allison declared, feeling the need to explain further.

"I could be Mrs. Something-or-other the Third right now," she confided in a haughty voice, "but I have never respected men who had it all handed to them, with their parents ensuring their future."

Allison hesitated, expecting some response. When he remained quiet, she continued.

"Brad, people like you are real. You did it on your own, like the vast majority of people I work with in the Agency. Mom and Dad didn't buy your bars or wings for you. Men like you are exciting and alive."

"Well," Brad acknowledged, "I will say that my job is certainly different."

"Then you understand what I mean."

"Yes, I think so."

"I guess I have always had a bit of a rebellious streak," she admitted, "but I worked hard for my degree in international affairs, and the work I have done for the CIA has been very challenging. I had my first falling-out with my family when I got a job—against my parents' wishes—during college."

"What do your parents think about your profession now?" Brad inquired and tossed her a quick glance.

"As you might imagine," Allison conceded, "they never have approved of my choice of careers."

"I'm not surprised," Brad replied as they approached the darkened hangar.

"Thanks for the opportunity to talk," Allison said as they stopped on the ramp, just out of earshot of the sentry.

"My pleasure."

"Brad Austin," Allison kissed him lightly on the cheek, "you're really a nice guy."

"Thank you," Brad replied awkwardly, aware that the guard was probably watching them.

Strapped into the cockpit of the MiG, Brad waved at Nick Palmer in the Phantom next to his left wing. He checked the instrument panel and clicked the microphone. "You there, in the clear-air converter, ready to go?"

"Shoot it the juice, Bruce," Palmer goaded him.

Brad could see the cluster of people on the hangar ramp. They would be closely monitoring the conversations between Nick and himself.

Allison's smile flashed in his mind's eye as he advanced the throttle. Every time he saw her, or talked to her, he had a pang of guilt. Leigh Ann would definitely not have approved of their evening walk.

The MiG lifted from the runway, and Brad went through the exercise to raise the landing gear. A minute later, Palmer rendezvoused on his wing and inspected the MiG.

"All the parts are still in place," Nick observed, sliding under the fighter, "and I don't see any leaks."

Brad examined his engine instruments. "It looks like the fire is still lighted."

"I'm coming out at your three o'clock."

Brad looked past his right wingtip. "Nick, let's set up for a horizontal turning engagement, and see if I can get away."

"What altitude do you want?"

Brad banked right to remain in the restricted airspace. "Fourteen thou," he answered.

Fourteen thousand feet would give Palmer an opportunity to maximize the Phantom's turning capability.

"Roger, fourteen."

They remained quiet until the jets leveled at altitude and accelerated to 370 knots. Both pilots scanned the clear skies, searching for intruders in the restricted airspace.

"Okay," Brad radioed, "angle off, and come back into me. Hard deck is ten thousand."

They would break off at 10,000 feet, terminating the engagement for reasons of safety.

Nick clicked his microphone switch twice and racked the F-4 over ninety degrees.

Brad started a slow turn away, then saw Palmer snap-roll the Phantom back into the MiG.

"Fight's on!" Nick announced.

Watching the airspeed build while he lowered the MiG's nose, Brad waited until he saw 420 knots before pulling into the vertical. Although everyone had agreed not to exceed 400 knots, Brad knew he had a little cushion before the MiG went uncontrollable. He would need every possible advantage if he was going to defeat the Phantom. Nick Palmer was heralded as one of the most talented fighter pilots in the fleet.

Palmer came up with him, canopy to canopy. The fight developed into a rolling scissors as Brad tried to muscle the MiG behind the F-4.

As the two aircraft slowed, Brad used the rudders to nibble away at Palmer's advantage. He slow-rolled the MiG to counter the maneuvers of the powerful F-4.

Nick suddenly snapped the nose of the Phantom down, allowing him to disengage and gain speed and separation.

Floating weightlessly, Brad waited until the last possible moment, then performed a hammerhead turn and shot straight down toward the parched desert below.

"Not bad," Palmer groaned, horsing the Phantom's nose up again, "for a tank driver with two left feet."

"Yeah," Brad countered, "I've got a tally on you. Better check six."

Using the stick extender, Brad pulled steadily until he was in the pure vertical. A second later, Nick popped his speed brakes and went to idle, hoping his adversary would overshoot.

Anticipating the stratagem, Brad rolled the MiG ninety degrees and pulled into the F-4 with all his strength. Without the help of hydraulically boosted controls, Austin was feeling the physical strain. The earth and sky rotated as he performed an aileron roll.

"Jesus!" Palmer gasped, fearing an imminent midair collision. He violently shoved the stick forward as Brad passed over the top of the Phantom. "Yeah," Nick sucked oxygen, "I think that'll work . . . you crazy bastard."

"This is not a contest," Spencer broadcast. "We want to evaluate the MiG . . . not crash it."

Two clicks sounded over the hangar loudspeaker.

The fight continued with each pilot gaining a small advantage, then losing it when the other countered each maneuver. Their instincts and dexterity were finely honed by hundreds of hours of training and experience. In their three-dimensional world, the pilots did not relate to the sky or ground. Each man concentrated solely on his opponent, anticipating the pilot's next move.

On the fourth engagement the aircraft met nose-to-nose. The two fighters flashed past each other with a combined closure rate of 1,100 miles per hour.

Austin placed his feet on the lower instrument panel and pulled with both hands. He heard a loud pop, but the MiG responded to his inputs. A flicker of sunlight glinted from Palmer's Phantom as he forced the F-4 into a punishing turn.

Brad rolled the MiG 120 degrees, then yanked on the stick with all of his strength. Slowly the MiG gained a turning advantage on the heavier American fighter. Austin was within seconds of being in a tracking and firing position when Palmer departed the Phantom.

Watching the F-4 tumble end-over-end, Brad released the pressure on the stick and placed his feet on the rudders. He let the MiG zoom skyward while he rolled inverted to see if Palmer would be able to recover the Phantom.

Brad watched Nick regain control of the fighter as he snatched the nose of the MiG down, diving at the F-4.

"Nice move," Brad panted, feeling the perspiration soak his forehead, "but now you don't know where I am."

"Knock it off! Knock it off!" Palmer radioed when he reached 10,000 feet.

"Roger," Brad acknowledged, glancing at his altimeter. "Let's try twenty thousand."

The radio remained quiet for a brief moment.

"Negative," Palmer replied excitedly. "I've just lost my PC-1. The hydraulic system is going south on me."

"Okay," Brad calmly replied, "let's get it on the ground."

Spencer remained silent, listening to the pilots as Allison and Hank Murray moved closer to the loudspeaker.

Nick closely watched his secondary and utility hydraulic systems while he slowed the malfunctioning Phantom. He waited until he was a mile and a half from the runway to lower the flaps and landing gear.

"Looking good," Brad encouraged, flying next to the F-4. "You've got it made."

"I hope."

When the Phantom slammed into the runway, Brad added power and turned downwind.

He went through the time-consuming process of lowering the landing gear. His thoughts drifted to Allison and the fact that she would be going to Laos with them. If he did not mention it to Leigh Ann, would she find out? Could he innocently neglect to tell her . . . because Allison was not important to him?

Brad completed his landing checklist as he turned on final. Why was he consumed by Allison? Was he refusing to acknowledge that he was attracted to her?

"Concentrate on what you're doing," Brad admonished himself as he flared the MiG, "before you bust your ass."

CHAPTER SEVENTEEN

The temperature in the hangar was becoming unbearable. Engrossed in a detailed map of northeastern Laos, Brad sat across from Nick Palmer. He had memorized the topography of the region, paying special attention to the preferred routes from the clandestine airfield into North Vietnam. Alpha-29, Brad had noticed, was in a remote section of mountainous terrain.

Palmer was examining aerial photographs of the airfields at Kep, Gia Lam, Bai Thuong, Kien An, Hoa Lac, and Phuc Yen. The intelligence brief attached to the photographs stated that the most experienced MiG pilots were stationed at Kep and Phuc Yen. The CIA document, compiled during the previous month, reported that an increasing number of experienced Russian fighter pilots were augmenting the North Vietnamese Air Force.

"Brad," Nick said, looking around to make sure they were alone. "Could I ask you a personal question?"

"Sure," Brad responded, narrowing his eyes. "What's on your mind?"

"I know you and Allison went for a walk on the runway last night . . . and I was wondering—"

Brad laughed, then looked through the open door. "Nick, there's nothing going on, believe me. Allison is a friend—that's all."

Palmer gave Brad a questioning look. "She sure seems to be attracted to you."

"Nick," Brad reassured him, "Allison knows how I feel about Leigh

Ann. I consider Allison a friend—there's nothing else to it, as far as I'm concerned."

"You're sure?"

"Of course I'm sure," Brad responded emphatically. "Why the third degree about Allison?"

"Well," Nick declared, "if she's fair game, I'm going to make a play for her."

"That's your decision," Brad replied. "I sure as hell don't want to screw up my relationship with Leigh Ann."

"I wouldn't either, if I were in your shoes." Nick smiled broadly. "Allison will be a challenge."

"I'm sure it will be an interesting experience."

Brad looked up when he heard Hollis Spencer call Lex Blackwell. A moment later, Spencer and Allison walked into the briefing room, followed by Blackwell.

"Before we get started," Spencer happily announced, "I want to let you know that Grady is doing well. He is in good spirits, and able to converse with the doctors. They are concerned about his lower right leg, but confident they won't have to amputate."

"Would it be okay," Brad replied, "if we stop by Friday afternoon and visit with Grady?"

"I'm afraid not," Spencer grimaced. "We can't risk the chance of even the most innocent questions by his parents or hospital staff. Evasive answers can be as damaging as a real leak. I think you can understand."

"You don't trust us, and I don't blame you," Brad admitted, "but will you tell him that we're thinking about him . . . that we haven't abandoned him?"

"Sure," Spencer assured them, adding, "You could send him a card—he'll understand."

Brad darted a look at his friends. "We'll do that."

Palmer seated Allison, who replied with a pleasant "Thank you, Nick."

"Gentlemen," Spencer said as he took his seat, "I want to give you an update, so we can prepare for our departure."

Brad noticed the message form Allison placed on the table.

"We have been instructed," Spencer informed them, "to expedite Operation Achilles. As I explained before, the MiG will be disassembled this weekend."

Allison gave Austin a hint of a smile, which no one detected except Brad.

"Lex, you will be going out on a military transport on Sunday. Plan to revert to being in the navy at that point."

Blackwell appeared relieved.

"We're going to fly you to Travis early Sunday morning. From there, you'll take the red-eye to Okinawa, where you will catch a hop to Cubi Point, then out to *Coral Sea*."

Spencer consulted the paper lying in front of him. "From that point, the navy is going to fly you from carrier to carrier, then drop you in Da Nang. After that, the air force wants you to make a tour. When you are finished with the briefs, you are to report, in civilian clothes, to the Air America headquarters in Vientiane."

Spencer paused while Blackwell jotted the instructions on a legal pad. "Use your false identification at this point, and simply ask for me. Got it?"

"Yes, sir."

"Nick and Brad," Spencer said as he looked at the two pilots, "will fly commercially to Hong Kong. You will leave on separate flights . . . Nick on Sunday and Brad on Monday. Allison has all the details."

Brad gave her a brief look.

"You'll have a layover in Hong Kong," Spencer continued, "before you catch an Air America flight to our base in Vientiane. Any questions?"

"Yes, sir," Brad replied. "What about the apartment?"

"Turn in the keys and lock the doors," Spencer advised, looking at Allison. "Are the leases being taken care of?"

"Everything has been arranged," she answered, then added, "And you can turn in your rental cars at Los Angeles International— where your flights depart. Your tickets will be at the Pan Am counter."

"I have some additional intel while we're here." Spencer opened his tattered manila folder. "Our observers close to the MiG bases are compiling a thorough log that describes the MiGs you will be hunting."

Palmer clicked his ballpoint pen. "Is there anything in particular— anything that distinguishes their best pilots' aircraft from the rank and file?"

"Yeah," Blackwell advised in an unusually serious tone, "the bright red stars painted on the sides of their fuselages."

Nick shot Lex a look of annoyance. "Lexter, in deference to Allison, I'm going to save my remarks for later."

Allison smiled while Spencer shuffled through his folder. "There is an element of truth in what Lex pointed out." He found the series of attached photographs.

"Here," Spencer spread the pictures on the table, "you can see that the MiGs vary in color, side number, markings, and configuration . . . as far as weapons are concerned."

Brad noticed particularly one MiG-17 with seven red stars forward of the canopy. "Do they know who the pilot is . . . who flies this one?" he said, pointing.

Spencer glanced at the black-and-white photograph. "We believe it is flown by Colonel Tomb, their red-hot ace."

Brad nodded and made a mental note of the MiG's side number. "Cap, I still think that we're making a mistake by trying to identify and selectively kill individual pilots, instead of taking any target of opportunity. The concept is too haphazard."

"We are confident in your ability," Spencer retorted impatiently, "and we are confident that our people can pass the information about individual pilots to you. That's what Langley wants, and that's what we're going to attempt to accomplish."

Austin reacted calmly. "Cap, you've flown fighters. Do you really believe it's going to be so cut-and-dried?"

"What I think," Spencer countered stiffly, "is that we're going to make every effort to accomplish our objective."

Spencer turned to his assistant. "Allison has some additional info for you."

"You may want to take notes," Allison suggested, noting Brad's jaw muscles tighten, "but you will be thoroughly briefed when we get to our destination . . . Alpha-29."

The pilots dutifully prepared to write notes.

"The only armament you will carry," she reminded them, "will be the two Mark-12 cannons that have been adapted to fit the gun pods."

Brad caught the quick glance from Allison.

"Your missions," she confided, "will be coordinated with massive U.S. air strikes. The powers in Washington want as many MiGs in the air, and as much confusion as possible, so you can do as much damage as possible . . . without being detected by the North Vietnamese."

That's great, Brad thought while he watched Spencer. *Dozens of aircraft going in every direction, while we try to locate selected pilots and watch our asses at the same time.*

He shifted his gaze to Allison. She was all business, but Brad found her completely alluring. Allison definitely was not window dressing.

She was obviously an expert in handling covert military missions, even if the planning had been done by others.

"You will take off," she underlined a paragraph on the operations order, "prior to daylight, remain low to avoid radar, infiltrate North Vietnam, and orbit over sparsely populated areas."

"Excuse me," Palmer interrupted. "Isn't it going to look a little strange—to the farmers and so forth—to see an aircraft roaring around a hundred feet above the ground?"

A smile creased the corner of her mouth. "Not if it's a MiG. No one in that country is going to question anything about what a MiG pilot does . . . or how low he flies."

Unconvinced, Nick shrugged and sat back.

"You will monitor preselected U.S. radio frequencies, then zoom into the fray when MiGs are sighted." Allison looked at each pilot, her glance lingering on Brad. "Obviously, you will have to improvise, and make decisions based on what you think you can get away with."

Brad addressed a question to Spencer. "Cap, what if the gomers catch on to our scheme?"

"It would be very difficult for them," Spencer assured him, "to figure out what we are doing, unless you give it away. If you shoot down a flight leader while his wingmen are watching you, that is not good."

"Brad," Allison resumed, "our MiG will be repainted and renumbered after every flight."

That part satisfied him, but he remained skeptical about the entire operation.

"We will constantly change the appearance of the MiG," Allison swept her blond hair back, "from basic camouflage to silver, to dull gray, to a different camouflage. The North Vietnamese use a wide variety of colors and paint schemes. That makes our job easier."

"So," Brad said smoothly, "we are going to be wreaking havoc with the gomers, while F-4s, and a host of other aircraft, are hunting us."

A pause hung in the small room.

"Cold feet?" Allison taunted with a hint of a smile.

Blackwell laughed out loud.

Brad ignored the laugh, focusing his direct gaze on Allison. "No." He arched his eyebrows. "We'll do our jobs, and I trust that you will do yours." Brad hesitated for a moment. "Our lives may depend on it."

"Touché," Allison replied with her throaty laugh.

Lex turned to Nick. "We better get a bucket of cold water for these two."

Spencer started to intervene, then decided to remain silent. He had seen Allison take care of herself in other difficult situations.

"I do understand," she said seriously, "and appreciate your concerns. All of us have a lot at stake, and we are going to do everything in our power to ensure your safety and fulfill the objective of the operation."

Spencer cleared his throat. "We have been cut short on time, so we're going to fly as much as possible before Friday."

Hank Murray stopped by the door. "Cap, we've got the gun sight mounted." He had removed the MiG's sight and installed an optical sight unit from an A-4 Skyhawk.

"Good." Spencer nodded. "How soon will you have the cannons harmonized?"

Murray wiped his hands on a rag. "We're towing the MiG to the firing range now. We'll have it ready in an hour and a half . . . two hours at the outside."

"Okay," Spencer replied, facing the pilots. "We will plan on flying the MiG in two hours."

Spencer waited until Murray had left, then reached for the three packets on the table. "These are detailed backgrounds of three fictitious Soviet fighter pilots. You will memorize every detail about your particular pilot. If you have to eject over North Vietnam, you had better have an A-plus on this homework assignment."

The pilots mechanically reached for their assigned packet. The seriousness of the dangerous operation was hitting home.

"In the meantime, Allison," Spencer suggested with a smile, "how about setting up the Russian language tape."

After a quiet dinner, Brad entered his cramped quarters and listened to the repetitiously dull language tape. He stopped the reel and ran it back a number of times, imitating the monotonous instructor.

Palmer and Blackwell were flying the last hop of the day. Spencer had asked Blackwell to evaluate the MiG's cannons, since Lex had more experience using guns. The F-8 Crusaders he had flown were equipped with four 20-millimeter cannons, while the Navy and Marine Corps Phantoms carried only missiles.

Each of the three pilots was becoming more comfortable with the MiG and its idiosyncrasies. Brad looked forward to testing the drop tanks and smoke canister.

He also wanted an opportunity to fire the newly installed cannons.

Lex and Hank Murray had been having difficulty getting the weapons harmonized. Murray had corrected the optimum firing angle three times during the afternoon. Each time, Blackwell had gone aloft to make strafing runs at the firing range. On the first or second pass of each flight, the vibration and recoil had knocked the cannons out of alignment.

Brad stopped the tape. "*Gde blizhayshaya—*" He paused, hearing a sound in the quiet hallway.

"Hi," Allison greeted, investigating the small room.

"Hello." Brad turned off the tape and looked up. "I mean, *dobriy vecher.*"

She crossed her arms and casually leaned against the door casing. "It is a good evening, especially since it's the last one we have to spend here."

Brad nodded in agreement. "If I left this minute, it wouldn't be soon enough."

Allison glanced at Brad's hazel eyes. There was a rakish, devil-may-care gleam that excited her. "How is your homework coming along?"

Brad cast a glance at the tape recorder and packet of Russian material. "So far, so good. I'm going to concentrate on five or six sentences." He smiled wanly. "If I get shot down, I'll probably forget every single word I've memorized."

"Let's hope that doesn't happen," she said with a touch of concern. "If it does, we're prepared to get a helicopter to you as quickly as possible."

"How is that going to work?" he inquired with a trace of confusion written on his face. "What is the master plan . . . if I have to jettison the airplane over North Vietnam?"

Allison stared into his eyes. "We will have two Air America helicopters to cover each flight." She shifted her position next to the door casing. "One will be airborne at all times. They will orbit close to the border and monitor our preselected frequencies, which will change for each mission."

Brad did not appear convinced. "Will I be able to talk to the pilots if things come unglued?"

"Yes," she declared emphatically. "You'll have two of the standard survival radios that you have been using. If you get in trouble, or have to eject, you will use a call sign and talk directly to the helo pilots."

"Will the call sign change on each flight?"

Allison observed Brad for a moment. "That's right," she said at last.

"We want the confusion factor as high as we can get it . . . so nothing is predictable."

"Good," Brad said firmly. "I like that."

"You'll get to know the Air America pilots," Allison explained, "because they'll be based at our airfield."

"That's even better news." Brad nodded. "I'm anxious to meet them."

"How would you like . . ." Allison winked in a suggestive manner, "a tall scotch and water?"

Brad was dubious.

"In an air-conditioned room," she coaxed, then added with a coy smile, "As friends?"

"Allison," Brad chuckled, "may I ask you a question, at the risk of crossing swords again?"

She showed her usual spirit. "Only if it's personal."

"Do you ever have real relationships with men," he grinned, "or do you just conquer them and then toss them away?"

Allison tilted her head to one side, as if she were pondering a very complex question. "Now that you mention it, I can recall a few times when the hunt was more exciting than the kill."

Brad shook his head. "Well, I guess I've studied long enough. Lead the way."

They walked out of the light trap at the back of the hangar, then crossed the narrow strip of pavement to a small wooden storage shed.

Inside, Brad was surprised to find only a cot, portable shower, miniature refrigerator, and a card table with two chairs. An air conditioner had been mounted in the side of the windowless structure.

"Rather austere," Brad observed after Allison closed the door and switched on the light.

"Yes," she remarked, opening the refrigerator, "but it affords privacy and cool air. Have a seat."

Brad sat at the card table and watched Allison pour two glasses of scotch, adding ice as a final touch.

"Have you heard any more about Grady?" he inquired.

Allison closed the refrigerator and took a seat. "Yes." She handed Brad his drink.

"Thanks."

"You're welcome." She eyed him for a moment. "This afternoon, according to the doctor I spoke with, Grady was doing extremely well."

Brad sipped his drink. "That's good."

Allison lighted a cigarette. "Yes, it is," she inhaled, "and I have another bit of news for you."

"I can hardly wait," Brad teased.

Allison looked at Brad out of the corner of her eye. "Cap has decided that you will be the primary pilot, and Nick will be your alternate."

Brad stared at the ice in his glass before he looked at Allison. "Am I going to fly all the missions?"

"No," she assured him. "Nick will fly some of the time, but Cap wants you to become intimately knowledgeable with the area . . . and how the MiGs operate."

"What about Lex?"

"He will be the backup," she admitted, "if anything happens to you or Nick."

"Thanks for letting me know."

"Cap will talk to you later, but I thought you would like to know."

Brad sat quietly, aware of Allison's gaze.

"I had hoped," she began tentatively, "that you would be the reserve pilot."

Brad slowly turned to Allison. "Why?"

"Because I care about you," she confided with a warm smile, then shrugged her shoulders. "At least I'm honest about my feelings for you."

He met Allison's eyes, but kept his real thoughts about her to himself. "You should have been a fighter pilot, as tenacious as you are."

"Women would be," she replied with a touch of sarcasm, "if you chauvinistic hot dogs weren't afraid of the competition."

"Ouch," Brad said, and winced. "I believe I hit a nerve."

"Think about it, hot shot." Allison forced a smile. "Women could fly fighters . . . if we were given an opportunity to prove ourselves."

"We just hit the hard deck." Brad laughed pleasantly. "Could we call off the fight?"

Allison cocked her head to one side and gave him a beguiling smile. "Whatever you say, Captain."

Brad heard the sound of the jets taxiing toward the hangar. "I guess we better go to the debrief."

Allison extinguished her cigarette. "Yes, I suppose so."

CHAPTER EIGHTEEN

The morning was warm and dry when Brad and Lex Blackwell walked across the hot ramp to the waiting fighter planes. A lone hawk circled high overhead, prompting Austin to look at the blackened wreckage of the F-8 Crusader. He forced himself to concentrate on the present and not dwell on the crash.

"Hey, Lex," Brad said with a serious look, "*Aviatsiya protivovozdushnoi oborony strany.*"

Blackwell laughed aloud. "What the hell was that? 'Let's kick the tires, and light the fires' in Russian?"

"Something about the Soviet Air Force for home defense, I think." Brad observed Nick Palmer speak to Hollis Spencer, then walk toward them. "Anyway, I thought it sounded good when I listened to the tape."

When Nick reached the Phantom, Brad smartly saluted him. "*Zdrastvuytye, comrade. Kak pozhivayete?*"

Palmer gave him a flashy smile and slung his helmet bag over the cockpit boarding steps. "I am fine, comrade . . . and good morning. You must be a fighter pilot in the *Voenno Vozdushniye Sily.*"

"*Nyet.*" Brad squinted into the sun. "*Aviatsiya voenno morskovo flota.*"

"Oh," Nick replied, remembering the words on the language tape. "You're a fleet pilot in the naval air force."

"*Da,* comrade." Brad grinned confidently. "*Aviatsiya osobovo naznacheniya.*" Special-purpose air arm.

"You guys are killing me," Blackwell protested. "I'm sick of hearing your butchered Russian."

"Partner," Nick mimicked Lex, "ya dang sure better learn your Russian, 'cause your Hopalong Cassidy act ain't gonna whack it."

"Let's get on with this," Brad said impatiently, "so we can get the hell out of here."

"I've got an idea," Lex suddenly blurted. "How about an off-to-Laos blowout this evening . . . at the apartment?"

Palmer had started preflighting the Phantom. "Sounds good to me, since we're basically confined to quarters."

"Brad?" Lex asked.

"Sure," Brad declared with a mischievous grin.

"We'll invite Allison," Blackwell suggested, "and throw her ass in the pool."

"I'm not sure she's ready for our animal act," Brad replied with reluctance in his voice.

"I'll invite her." Nick smiled, and looked at Lex. "And we aren't going to throw her in the pool."

Lex started up the side of the F-4, pausing by the rear cockpit. "Brad," he grinned, "are you going to tell your 'lady friend' that Allison is going to Laos with us?"

Brad looked up at Blackwell. "Yes," he laughed, "when the time is right."

Lex belly-laughed. "You mean when you muster up enough courage to tell her."

"You're right," Brad admitted. "It's going to be dicey, to say the least."

Blackwell set his helmet on the canopy rail. "Like spraying a wasps' nest with a garden hose."

Brad nodded his head and walked to the MiG. He placed his helmet on the wing and carefully checked the drop tanks, smoke canister, and cannons. After a thorough preflight of the MiG, Brad mounted the ladder propped against the fuselage and settled into the now familiar cockpit.

The plane captain climbed the ladder, then assisted Brad with his harness straps, g suit, and helmet.

"Have a good flight, Captain," the man said as he backed down the ladder.

"Thanks."

Brad studied the blue sky and puffy clouds leisurely floating overhead. The hawk was still making lazy circles high above the hangar. *I'm going to call Leigh Ann on Saturday and tell her that Allison is a member of this project, and will be going overseas with us.*

The sound of Palmer bringing the Phantom to life brought Austin back to the moment. He ran through the prestart checklist and looked at the plane captain. Holding a fire extinguisher, the man gave Brad a thumbs-up signal.

Austin energized the starter. His adrenaline was as high as it had been prior to his first carrier qualification at night. It was time to become a real test pilot.

Leveling off at 15,000 feet, Brad glanced over his shoulder at Palmer and Blackwell. Their Phantom was stabilized in a standard loose-deuce formation off the MiG's right wing.

Austin meticulously checked his cockpit instruments and switches, paying special attention to the release actuator for the drop tanks. After examining the smoke-canister toggle switch, Brad verified that the armament panel for the cannons was in the off position.

Brad scanned the empty sky, looking for any stray aircraft that might have wandered into the confined airspace. He looked out at the fuel-laden drop tanks. The extra weight of the jet fuel had made his takeoff run much longer than usual. He checked his airspeed at 380 knots.

"Nick," Brad radioed, "drop back in trail, and we'll see if the tanks will stay with me."

"Wilco."

"Here we go," Brad announced, and pulled the nose up fifteen degrees. He executed an aileron roll, followed by a barrel roll, leveled the wings momentarily, then snapped into a knife-edge 360-degree turn. He held 4 g's, increasing the pull to 5 g's during the last quarter of the turn.

"They feel solid," Brad advised Hollis Spencer and the F-4 crew on his tail.

"Copy," Spencer acknowledged. "Put it in a dive and pull out at four hundred knots."

"Roger," Brad replied as he eased the nose up slightly, rolled inverted, then pulled the nose down in a split-S.

"You still with me?" Austin asked Palmer.

"Glued to your ass."

Watching the airspeed indicator spin toward 400 knots, Brad began easing back on the stick. "Coming up," he groaned. Five g's, then 6 g's registered on the g meter.

Austin leveled out and checked the tip tanks. "They'll take at least six g's."

"Okay, Brad," Spencer broadcast, "try the smoke, and then make a couple of firing passes."

"Wilco," Austin answered, and reached for the safety cover over the smoke toggle switch. "Lex, you ready to time this?"

"Go for it," Blackwell shot back.

Brad rolled the MiG and toggled the switch. He let the nose fall through the horizon and continued the spiral. The bleak desert spun around and around in front of his canopy.

"That's it," Blackwell informed everyone when the grayish-black smoke stopped spewing from the tail-mounted canister.

"Eleven seconds flat," Lex reported with a note of disappointment. "The smoke really pours out, but we need to make it darker."

"Copy," Spencer responded, tossing a glance at Hank Murray.

Brad eased back the throttle and turned toward the airfield. "I'm inbound for the firing runs."

"The range is clear," Spencer announced, looking across the runway at the fifteen-foot-high mound of sand.

Murray's men had bulldozed another two feet of sand and dirt on the firing range. The target was over 3,000 feet from the hangar, which afforded a margin of safety for the curious onlookers.

Watching the target sleeve grow larger in his windshield, Brad selected the armed position for the cannons. They would fire simultaneously, causing the shells to appear to converge in the distance.

Brad glanced at the hangar. "I'm in hot."

"Roger," Spencer drawled.

Waiting until the colorful sleeve filled his gun sight, Brad gently squeezed the trigger. The MiG vibrated while a three-second burst of fiery shells erupted from the twin cannons.

"Jesus," Brad said to himself as the tracers ripped across the sand and tore through the middle of the large white and red sleeve.

He yanked the stick back and shoved the throttle to the stop. "They're firing as straight as an arrow, but a little low on the pipper."

"Copy that," Spencer radioed curtly. "Make three passes—all the same airspeed and angle—to see if it changes."

"Wilco."

Brad flew the second pass with the same results. He wished they had an aircraft to tow a sleeve for actual air-to-air gunnery practice, but they were restricted by time. Spencer had vetoed the idea of using the Phantom as a tow aircraft.

"Still low," Brad informed the group on the ground. "I'm going to try something else."

On the third strafing run, he raised the pipper slightly above the target and squeezed the trigger. A stream of fire shot straight at the sleeve, ripping it to shreds as the MiG blasted overhead.

"I think the problem is solved," Brad reported with satisfaction. He disarmed his cannons and made a mental note of where the pipper was when he fired the burst. If he had to, Brad would draw a cross hair with a grease pencil to mark the aiming point.

"That's good to hear," Spencer answered with an audible sigh. "Make a level pass over the firing range, and punch off your drop tanks."

Brad clicked his mike twice and slowed the MiG to 240 knots. He leveled at 1,200 feet above the ground and lined up with the firing range.

"Nick," Brad transmitted, "are you clear?"

"We're at your four o'clock—clear."

Austin craned his neck and looked back over his right shoulder. "Roger that."

Brad glanced at the small group of bystanders on the hangar ramp. "Here they go," he calmly announced as he approached midfield.

A second later, Brad flicked the drop-tank switch. All at once, his worst nightmare flashed through his mind as the control stick violently jerked to the left.

"Son of a bitch," Brad swore as he yanked the stick to the right and snapped the throttle to idle. The left wing continued to drop.

"Your left tank didn't jettison!" Palmer radioed.

Brad fought the controls as the heavy left wing rotated the MiG around its longitudinal axis. The nose fell through the horizon, filling the windshield with a view of the rapidly approaching ground.

Terrified, Brad started to eject, hesitated a split second, then again flipped the drop-tank switch.

The fuel tank popped loose and tumbled away as Brad desperately wrestled the MiG's controls.

"Pull up!" Spencer shouted. "Get the nose up!"

Brad rolled wings level and snatched the stick back. "Oh, God . . . ," he muttered through clenched teeth as the MiG bottomed out at less than a hundred feet.

"Close," Palmer radioed in a hollow voice.

Brad climbed steeply and fumbled through the process of lowering the landing gear. He could feel the adrenaline shock to his heart.

"I think," Blackwell dryly suggested, "we better just weld the sonuvabitches onto the wing."

Brad concentrated on airspeed and lineup as he approached the runway. Against his training as a carrier pilot, Austin flared the MiG prior to touching down. He rolled to the end of the strip and stopped in the turnaround area.

"Do you need any assistance?" Spencer asked, relieved that he did not have to witness another crash.

"Negative," Brad declared, trying to slow his breathing rate. "I'm waiting for Nick to land."

"Roger that."

After the Phantom landed and rolled to the end of the pavement, Brad taxied back up the runway and turned toward the hangar ramp.

A crowd gathered around the MiG immediately after Austin parked. He raised the canopy and shut down the engine.

Brad exchanged a brief glance with Allison as Spencer and Murray climbed the makeshift ladder. Her tanned face was a shade lighter than normal.

"I'm sorry," Hank Murray said glumly. "The tanks worked perfectly during the static tests, but they haven't actually been used before."

Brad tried his voice. "The air resistance," he said as evenly as possible, "probably places too much strain on the attachments."

Darting a look at the taxiing Phantom, Brad turned to Spencer. "Lex is right. The tanks need to be permanently mounted under the wings."

"I concur," Spencer advised Murray. "Hank, we don't have time to screw with the jettison system, so let's bolt the tanks onto the hard points."

Brad's eyes met Allison's. She gazed at him with a smile of relief, aware of her growing attraction to him.

CHAPTER NINETEEN

The party was in full swing when Brad caught a glimpse of Allison's car as she parked in front of the apartment. "She's here, guys."

"Well," Lex responded with an exaggerated sigh, "I guess we'll have to save the story of how Nicholas lettered in croquet at Princeton."

Brad, Nick, and Lex were putting on a great show of cheerfulness, but a strong thread of uneasiness ran under it all. The unknown future was soon to be the present.

Palmer walked to the door and stepped out to greet Allison. "I'm glad you could make it," he laughed aloud, "but I have to warn you that we've been getting," Nick glanced at Lex, "how would you say it, Hopalong?"

"Rowdy," Blackwell replied loudly, and guzzled his beer.

"Don't worry about me," Allison declared with a smile. "I can *rowdy* with the best of them."

No doubt, Austin thought as a smile creased the corner of his mouth.

"Would you care for some wine?" Brad asked Allison after a pregnant pause, "or something a little stronger?"

"Darlin'," Lex exclaimed, "you oughta try a vodka and vinegar, with a ring of Vidalia onion." A grin spread across his face. "It's a south Texas martini."

Allison stared at Blackwell for a long moment. "I believe wine will be fine."

"Pardon me," Brad said to Allison as he motioned Blackwell out the balcony door. "Lex and I are going to have a brief chat."

144

Nick wiped the smile off his face. "Allison, I'm afraid Chablis is the only white wine we have."

"Anything will be fine." She laughed graciously and shook her head with amusement. "How did Lex get in the navy?"

Nick could not quite hear the conversation between Austin and Blackwell. "We don't know, but I think his father must have paid off some congressman."

Palmer poured a glass of wine and handed it to Allison. "Seriously," Nick said with a tone of respect, "Lex is a damn good pilot . . . but his social skills are abominable."

"He's okay." Allison smiled warmly. "Lex is still irritated at me, and I don't blame him for being upset."

The phone rang, and Nick promptly snatched the receiver off the wall. After a short conversation, he cupped the receiver and called to Brad. "Your 'lady friend,' " he announced, using the term that he and Blackwell had adopted.

"I'll take it in the other room," Austin declared as he walked into the living room. "I've got it."

He paused while Palmer replaced the other receiver on its hook. Brad's eye caught Allison's smile as he turned his head.

"Hi, Leigh Ann."

"Brad, I did a little investigating before I left San Diego," she gushed excitedly, "and discovered something very interesting."

"What are you talking about?" he replied, then glanced toward the kitchen.

"The yacht that your friend—Allison—says is her father's yacht is actually leased to the government."

"Leigh Ann," Brad said hastily, "I've got to explain something to you."

She suddenly became quiet. "What?"

"Allison," he carefully selected his words, "is a government security specialist."

"How did you find out?" Leigh Ann asked with a brittleness in her voice. "Did you know that when I was there?"

"No, I wasn't aware of who Allison worked for when you were here," Brad said rather stiffly. "We found out about her job this past Monday."

Leigh Ann didn't respond.

"Allison works for the man I report to," he explained clearly. "She is his assistant, and part of her job is screening people for security violations."

"You're telling me," Leigh Ann replied curtly, "that she works for the CIA?"

"Leigh Ann, I can't discuss this over an open phone line. You'll have to trust me."

"How much longer," she asked in a controlled voice, "are you going to be involved with the project?"

"I honestly don't know," Brad replied, hearing Blackwell and Palmer laugh in the kitchen. He decided to batten the hatches and stand by for action. Brad knew his next statement was not going to be well received, and might even be a breach of security, but he had to risk it. "We'll be going back to Southeast Asia in a couple of days."

"With Allison?" Leigh Ann asked, already knowing the answer.

"Yes," he said evenly, watching Allison out of the corner of his eye. "She is a key member of the team."

The awkwardness between them grew as they remained silent.

"Leigh Ann," Brad broke the long silence, "if you love me, have faith and trust me."

"I do, Brad," she responded with a hollow voice. "But can I trust Allison?"

"Leigh Ann, I can't discuss this right now."

"She's there, isn't she?"

Brad hesitated. "Yes."

"Why don't you call me," Leigh Ann said irritably, "when you *can* discuss it."

The phone connection went dead, and Brad gently placed the receiver down. He hid his concern about the conversation and joined the lively group in the kitchen.

Nick caught his eye. "Things okay on the home front?"

Brad noticed Allison glance at him. "Well, there's always room for improvement."

The evening had been pleasant enough, but Brad remained ill at ease. He wished that he had handled Leigh Ann's phone call better. The situation was rapidly spinning out of control. Leigh Ann already knew more than she should. Brad realized that no matter what he said, she would not be satisfied as long as Allison remained in the picture.

Brad sat across from Allison, exchanging glances with her while Blackwell strummed his guitar and belted out "Your Cheating Heart."

Aside from the affected nasal twang, he sounded better than most lounge singers.

"Lex, you're pretty good," Austin admitted when the song ended. "You obviously have missed your calling."

"Don't flatter him," Palmer protested with a grimace, "or we'll have to listen to this hillwilliam crap all night."

Blackwell slid his bottle onto the table, then addressed Nick. "Here's a little ballad you probably haven't heard at the country club."

"I have no doubt," Palmer countered with a groan.

"It's called 'Whorehouse Boogie,'" Lex proudly announced, prompting a response from Allison.

"Well, things are obviously going downhill from here," she joked good-naturedly, "so I'm going to call it an evening."

Allison rose before Palmer could respond. "Thanks for inviting me, Nick."

"Hey," Palmer protested hastily, "you don't need to go. We'll clean up the songs."

"Lex," Allison said with a smile, "I do like your music, but I have to get some rest." She gave Nick a quick look. "We'll be seeing each other shortly."

She turned to Austin. "Brad, would you be kind enough to walk me to my car? I have a couple of business questions, if you don't mind."

"Ah, sure." His surprised look was evident to the group.

A full, luminous moon cast a bright glow as Brad walked Allison to her Mercedes convertible. He opened the driver's door and waited for her to slip behind the wheel.

"Still driving in style," Brad commented as he closed the door and walked around the sporty roadster.

Allison laughed softly while he got in. "Unfortunately, it goes back to the dealer tomorrow."

Brad twisted in his seat to face Allison. "What did you want to talk about?"

Allison smiled demurely. "Brad, Cap Spencer called me this afternoon. In fact, the phone was ringing when I walked through the door."

Brad gazed thoughtfully into Allison's dark eyes before he spoke. "Is there a problem?"

"That depends," she leaned closer, "on exactly what your friend, Leigh Ann, knows about the operation."

Brad glanced through the windshield, concealing his irritation. He was growing weary of the invasion into his private life.

"Cap is sitting on this," she continued tactfully, "but it's bothering him. He wanted me to ask you in person."

"Why didn't *he* ask me in person?" Austin snapped, then added, "If it's such a big deal."

"Brad," Allison countered with her usual poise, "he is trying to cover for you. Cap likes you, and you're a fellow naval aviator, but you did something that he explicitly told you not to do."

"You people," Brad said firmly, "are too wrapped up in chasing shadows."

Allison found herself wanting to say something sarcastic, but her better judgment prevailed.

"Brad, Cap has a mission to accomplish, and superiors to answer to." She forced her tone to remain steady. "The reason Cap hasn't talked to you is simple. After we left the hangar this afternoon, he received a call from Langley."

"And?" Brad queried impatiently.

"The director for operations, Dennis Tipton," Allison explained, pausing for the information to register, "wanted to know if the operation had been compromised by Grady's crash, or by any breaches of security." She lowered her voice. "Cap told him no, not at this time."

What a bunch of nervous Nellies, Brad thought; so afraid someone will blow their cover.

"Allison, Leigh Ann doesn't know anything about the operation. She only knows that I'm in the military and involved in a special assignment."

"The problem," Allison paused, "is that if anything happens to you, Cap is concerned that your fiancée would start digging for answers . . . that could embarrass the Agency."

"For Christ's sake, Allison, I'm a fighter pilot." He didn't want to reveal that Leigh Ann had made her own deductions and knew that he was involved with a CIA operation. This much Leigh Ann had told him in their last brief telephone conversation. "Leigh Ann, like everyone else, would assume that I had been shot down."

"You're sure of that?"

"Absolutely," Brad countered firmly.

A long pause followed.

"I believe you," Allison finally whispered. Their eyes locked in an unblinking stare. There didn't seem to be anything more to say.

He inhaled deeply and stepped out of the car as Allison shifted her gaze straight ahead and started the engine.

"Drive safely." Brad leaned over and closed the door.

"I always do." She winked, and shifted into gear.

CHAPTER TWENTY

HONG KONG

Nick Palmer, dressed in expensive white loafers, white slacks, polo shirt, and sea-green sports coat, entered the hotel bar and spied Brad. Austin had called his room to wake him.

Brad motioned to the bartender while Palmer slid onto the bar stool next to Austin.

"I gather from the look of your eyes," Brad said lightly, "that you had quite a night?"

Nick slowly moved his head back and forth. "The part I can remember was a helluva time."

Palmer waited until the barkeeper placed the tall Bloody Mary in front of him. "How's Leigh Ann?"

Brad hesitated, trying to squelch the concerns that were bothering him. "I don't have the slimmest clue. I still haven't been able to get in touch with her."

From the look on Austin's face, Palmer decided not to pursue the subject of Leigh Ann. "We had a message from our CIA friends when I checked in."

"What now?"

Palmer stretched his arms to relieve the stiffness in his shoulders. "I'm supposed to catch an Air America flight early this evening."

Expecting a further explanation, Brad sipped his beer and turned to Nick. "What about me?"

"You and Allison are due to leave here tomorrow afternoon." Palmer produced a slip of paper from his jacket pocket. "At twelve-thirty, to be exact."

Brad gave him a puzzled look. "When is Allison's flight due to arrive?"

"Tomorrow morning. Her flight number is the same as yours, so whatever time you arrived."

Palmer finished his drink and signed their bill. "Come on, Brad. We'll have a leisurely lunch, and then tour Hong Kong by rickshaw until I have to catch my flight."

Shortly before noon, Brad stepped out of the small wooden line shack at Kai Tak airport. Carrying his rumpled overnight bag, he proceeded to the C-47 parked at the edge of the ramp. The battered workhorse showed the scars of thousands of landings on rough, short airstrips.

Clad in civilian attire, Brad approached the aging aircraft and was met by a brash young man with a clipboard.

"Name?" the man said curtly.

"Austin," Brad replied firmly, wondering if Allison was already on board. "Are we going to leave on time?"

"Who knows?" came the abrupt reply. "We're waiting for some broad to show up."

Brad flared at the derogatory remark, but let it pass. He walked under the left wing, studying the oil drippings from the big radial engine. He was about to cross to the right wing when he got a glimpse of Allison stepping out of the line shack.

Brad walked briskly toward her, wondering if she would be her usual self or coldly aloof. "Hi, Allison."

"Hello," she responded with a pleasant smile while he grabbed her two bags.

"Are you all set?" she asked the copilot when they reached the airplane.

Brad looked at the copilot, noting the cocky smile on the man's pockmarked face.

"I believe we are, ma'am," he said with obvious effort to be polite. "The captain is ready to crank the engines."

After boarding the aircraft, Allison and Brad selected seats behind the other passengers. The three disheveled men who reeked of alcohol were pilots for Air America. Two had already gone to sleep, while the third man stared vacantly out the window.

After takeoff, the pilot executed a steep turn and began a shallow climb toward the South China Sea. When they had reached the desired cruising altitude, the crew reduced power and trimmed the aircraft for level flight.

Allison leaned close to Brad. "We have another MiG-17, and a twenty-one is on the way," she confided with a gleam in her eye. "That's why I was late."

"Interesting," Brad replied, inclining his head toward her. "Why did you arrange to have me wait for you?"

"You get right to the point." Allison smiled ingenuously. "So I'll do the same."

Brad stared into her deep brown eyes. It was impossible to resist her charm and beauty.

Allison met his stare. "I wanted to talk to you."

Unable to conceal a small chuckle, Brad looked at his watch for a few seconds. "Well, I'm certainly a captive audience for the next few hours."

"I've been thinking about us," she said simply. "I know you were upset with me the night before we left . . . all the questions about your personal life."

He started to protest, but decided to listen to her obviously well-thought-out feelings.

"I just wanted to tell you that I understand how you feel, but I have my responsibilities." She paused and smiled suggestively. "I hope we can still be friends."

Brad nodded attentively, but the warning lights were flashing in his mind.

Allison lowered her eyes without looking directly at him. "We could be friends—close friends—can't we?" Her voice was a soft whisper.

Brad's resistance faded. He reached over and gingerly pulled her head to his shoulder.

"Yes," he answered evenly, knowing full well how difficult a "close friend" relationship would be.

CHAPTER TWENTY-ONE

WATTAY AIRPORT, VIENTIANE, LAOS

Vientiane, the capital of Laos, was a quiet town on the banks of the Menam Khong River where the cultures of France and the Far East blended smoothly. The waterway, better known as the Mekong River, was full of traffic both day and night. Housing in the town was inexpensive and the restaurants were excellent, which prompted many of the Air America pilots to have their wives move to Vientiane.

Hollis Spencer surveyed the muddy airfield while he waited for the two Southern Air Transport C-130s to arrive. He walked to a bench under the trees next to the Air America operations building and studied the variety of aircraft sitting on the parking ramp.

A Curtiss C-46 Commando caught his attention when the propeller on the left engine began slowly to rotate. A few seconds later the eighteen-cylinder radial engine coughed gray smoke, then rumbled to life and settled to a rough idle. Spencer watched a small, single-engine Helio-Courier taxi past while the C-46 captain started his right engine.

Spencer's normally starched and pressed utilities hung from his frame like wet towels. There was no relief from the oppressive humidity. He wiped a rivulet of perspiration from his temple and flicked the moisture away with his finger.

He glanced at the Air America slogan above the entrance to the building: "Anything, Anywhere, Anytime—Professionally."

Spencer felt at home, having helped organize the air support for the

CIA-backed secret army in Laos. Air America had been described by *The New York Times* as a shadowy air subsidiary of the Central Intelligence Agency.

The media had begun investigating the vague and remote operations of Air America after two journalists had stumbled over a covert operation. They had witnessed the CIA airline fly hundreds of Thai soldiers into Laos to bolster the secret army of General Vang Pao. The general's troops were supported by the CIA. Deceiving the United States Congress was standard policy. The Agency did not want the American public to become aware of the clandestine war.

The CIA mercenary army in Laos had been formed at the same time the Pentagon had committed U.S. military forces to fight North Vietnam. The objectives were similar: to oppose Communism and in this region to assist Meo guerrillas in fighting the various Communist factions, including the Pathet Lao. Air America had grown into the largest airline in the world during the prolonged struggle, using fixed-wing aircraft and helicopters to fly supplies and troops while moving masses of refugees to safety.

Millions of dollars in humanitarian foreign aid that Congress thought it was appropriating for the refugees were being used to support this army. The covert operation had expanded on a daily basis and continued to grow as quickly as the money arrived.

Laotian Army General Vang Pao was the driving force. He was not completely trustworthy, but he was a courageous man and a tough warrior, the kind of man the CIA needed to help thwart the Communist insurgency.

Spencer felt a great sense of accomplishment when he thought about the airline. His tireless efforts had resulted in a far-flung, well-organized operation.

Spencer breathed lightly in the suffocating stillness, wishing the monsoon season would end. He glanced at Hank Murray as the navy captain approached the shaded bench.

"How was breakfast?" Spencer asked, lighting his pipe.

Murray sat down next to the project officer. "Pretty good. This place has the best American-style food in Southeast Asia."

Spencer watched an Air America C-123 Provider take off, then heard the distinct, low drone of a Lockheed C-130. "Here they come," he triumphantly announced, pointing to the arriving Hercules.

The men rose and walked to the compound Spencer had set aside for Operation Achilles.

"I only see one," Spencer muttered as he scanned the sky for the second transport.

The C-130 made a long, low approach, touched down, bounced back into the air, then gently settled on the runway.

Spencer and Murray waited patiently while the lumbering Hercules taxied to the restricted area. As soon as the engines were shut down, Spencer walked to the crew entrance door, while Murray went to the cargo ramp.

The project officer mounted the airstair door and climbed the ladder to the cockpit.

"Where's the other airplane?" Spencer asked with a trace of anxiety.

The pilot, a rugged-looking veteran, turned in his seat. "They had to cage an engine. . . . Should be here in a few minutes."

Relieved, Spencer thanked the crew and ducked out of the entrance. He walked to the back of the C-130 and joined Murray and the loadmaster on the lowered cargo ramp.

"How's she look, Hank?"

"Not bad," Murray answered, concealing his irritation. "We've got some minor hangar rash on the right wingtip, but nothing else significant."

Spencer looked at the two wings standing side by side in the cargo bay. The Hercules was packed with the MiG's major components and support equipment.

"Hank, the other flight is due to arrive in a few minutes," Spencer paused to search the sky, "so round up the troops, and let's get ready to move out."

"Will do," Murray replied, glancing at the loadmaster. "I understand the other plane lost an engine."

"That's right," Spencer said at the same time he spotted the second Hercules. "Here it comes."

Both men, along with the loadmaster, watched the C-130 descend toward the runway. The propeller on the outboard engine on the left wing was feathered. The motionless blades were turned sideways, slicing cleanly through the air.

The pilot made a smooth landing, then reversed the two inboard engines as the big turboprop rocked from side to side.

When the Hercules slowed to taxi speed, Spencer turned to Murray. "Hank, if it's going to take long to repair the second plane, we'll go up to Alpha-29, unload, and send the first Herc back for the rest."

Murray looked at the taxiing C-130. "I'll talk to the flight engineer, then we'll know whether to unload it."

* * *

The Southern Air Transport C-130 cruised serenely high above the mountainous Laotian countryside. Hollis Spencer viewed the chains of mountains and plateaus that were intersected by deep, narrow valleys.

Much of the remote land was covered by thick jungle, which was traversed by footpaths. Few roads crossed the landlocked country, forcing the extensive use of airplanes and helicopters to transport people and supplies to remote sites.

Spencer noted that it was an unusually clear day for Laos. The weather patterns of the monsoon season and the windy, dusty summers made flying hazardous and challenging. Depending on the time of the year, pilots had to contend with heavy rain, thick fog, dangerous wind conditions, and the acrid smoke from the farmers' fires.

Standing on the flight deck behind the captain, Spencer looked out toward the runway at the CIA airfield located at Long Tieng. Spencer had helped finalize the initial plans to use Long Tieng as a launching point for clandestine bombing raids into North Vietnam and Laos.

He had a commanding view of the Plain of Jars and the rugged terrain surrounding the luxuriant vegetation. Spencer watched two Royal Lao T-28 fighter-bombers approach, then pass under the left wing. Looking out of the copilot's window, he studied a mountain that reached nearly 9,000 feet.

Spencer let his gaze travel over the nose of the aircraft. He could see a low layer of clouds on the horizon as they flew northeast toward their destination. The crew, who had been instructed not to ask a single question about the MiG, had performed flawlessly.

He glanced at the copilot. The former marine aviator had an operational navigation chart spread across his lap. Spencer had circled the site of Alpha-29 for the pilots.

The highly experienced crew would have to visually acquire the secret base, since the airfield was not equipped with a navigational homing device.

Spencer relaxed for the rest of the fifty-minute flight. He knew that the lengthy repairs to the second C-130 would mean a change in plans, but just what changes he could not tell yet. He thought about Austin and Palmer. Spencer admired and sincerely liked them. He was also concerned for their welfare.

When the captain began his descent, Spencer turned to Murray, who was standing behind the flight engineer.

"Hank," he said in a hushed voice, "I hope we can get under those clouds up ahead."

Murray peered at the horizon. "They do look a bit low, don't they?"

"I'm afraid so."

The flight deck remained quiet while the two pilots conversed over their intercoms.

Spencer closely watched the copilot as the captain banked the Hercules to slip under the overcast. His face reflected a growing concern as the overcast dropped lower the farther north they flew.

Thirty miles from the recently completed airfield, the captain slowed the airplane and descended to 400 feet above the jagged mountaintops. Visibility was becoming a problem as the thick clouds obscured the sun.

Spencer searched ahead and to the right, catching a fleeting glimpse of the outskirts of San Neua. He let his eyes drift across the terrain but could not see any identifiable signs of Alpha-29.

"You better strap in," the captain suggested while he and the copilot went through their checklist litany.

"On our way," Spencer replied, trying not to sound nervous.

He and Murray stepped down into the cargo compartment and settled into the nearest seats.

"Cap," Murray darted a look out the window, "do you think they can find it . . . under these conditions?"

Spencer nodded. "If anyone can, these guys will get it done." But Spencer was not as confident as he sounded. As a pilot, he had faced similar situations many times and knew that finding the airstrip would not be easy.

The Hercules banked steeply while the crew lowered the flaps and extended the landing gear.

Spencer stared through the small window on the opposite side of the cargo compartment. He could see trees and thick foliage flash past, but he could not detect anything that resembled a runway. Water droplets were flowing over the small round window.

The four turboprop engines suddenly became quiet while the flaps were lowered to the landing position. Seconds later, the engines surged and the aircraft climbed at a steep angle, banking sharply over the end of the runway. The flaps transitioned to the approach setting, while the wheels remained down and locked.

Spencer could see what happened. "Hank," he said to the pale-faced engineer, "they saw the runway too late, and tried to salvage the approach."

Murray silently nodded.

"They're flying a tight pattern," Spencer advised, feeling more confident, "so everything should come together this pass." He could see Murray was not convinced.

The Hercules again banked steeply as the crew selected full flaps. Spencer could feel his chest tighten as the engines became quiet.

The captain raised the nose and gently eased the aircraft onto the wet runway.

Spencer let out a quick sigh as the four powerful engines went into full reverse pitch. He looked at the relieved navy officer. "Hank, welcome to our new home."

VIENTIANE

Brad walked into the bar at the Constellation Hotel. The room was crowded with an odd assortment of pilots, CIA personnel, and journalists. Two different dice games were in progress at the far end of the bar. The place reminded Brad of a scene from a smoke-filled saloon in a B-grade movie.

He had no stomach for lighthearted banter. His concern for his relationship with Leigh Ann and anxiety about Operation Achilles—and his survival—weighed too heavily. He stayed just long enough to greet Allison and learn that Spencer had them, along with Nick Palmer, scheduled to fly to Alpha-29 on a C-123 at 7 A.M.

As Brad stood and turned to leave the table, he came face-to-face with two grinning, somewhat inebriated pilots. Allison put a hand on Brad's arm to detain him while she made the introductions. Chase Mitchell and Rudy Jimenez were going to be Operation Achilles' two rescue-helicopter pilots.

Chase Mitchell, a former army Huey pilot, was prematurely bald. He was a small man who wore flight boots with extra-thick soles to compensate for his lack of height. Brad noticed the end of a handgun protruding from a pocket sewn onto the side of Mitchell's trousers.

The other SAR pilot, Rudy Jimenez, was a former air force HH-3E Jolly Green pilot. The highly decorated rescue specialist had become a legendary figure before joining Air America. Quiet and soft-spoken by nature, Jimenez turned into a tiger when he was confronted with a dangerous mission. On the ground, he fueled himself with liberal amounts of tequila, and applied cayenne pepper sauce to everything he ate. He claimed that the combination of liquids eradicated germs from his body.

Even though both pilots were obviously drunk, Brad felt their strength and could see that they and Allison held each other in high regard. He acknowledged the introductions and excused himself.

Austin stopped in the lobby to mail a letter to Leigh Ann. He had not been able to contact her by telephone from Hong Kong, so he had included the address of the Constellation Hotel. The general manager assured him that he would keep Brad's mail in a safe place.

CHAPTER TWENTY-TWO

The C-123 banked gently as the pilot lined up with the runway at Alpha-29. Brad opened his eyes when the landing gear was lowered. He turned sideways and looked out the window next to him, then unstrapped and went to the other side of the weather-scarred aircraft.

"Hey," Brad tapped Nick on the shoulder, "take a look at this place. You won't believe it."

Suffering from an acute hangover, Palmer yawned and flopped his head to one side. "Just let me die in peace."

"This strip," Brad craned his neck, watching the trees and thick foliage flash by, "is in the center of a narrow valley." He went back to his seat and glanced at Allison.

She and two of Hank Murray's men were peacefully asleep.

A moment later, the Provider touched down firmly and the pilot stood on the brakes. The passengers were awake by the time the twin-engine cargo plane turned around.

After the aircraft taxied to a small clearing at the end of the runway, Brad stepped out and helped Allison to the macadam ramp. They lifted their canvas bags and walked clear of the C-123.

Brad gazed around the runway, mentally storing a picture of the high terrain on each side of the valley. He noted a mountain peak to the northwest, guessing its elevation to be close to 6,000 feet. Alpha-29 was strictly a daylight, clear-weather type of strip, he thought. A safe takeoff could be made under the cover of darkness, but a landing attempt at night would be suicidal.

160

"Look." Allison pointed across the runway. "We've got our own stream."

Brad nodded and inspected the steadily flowing channel of water. "This would be an ideal place to film a Tarzan movie."

Allison gave him a thin smile. "It's definitely in the outback, but I've seen worse."

Brad looked at the MiG, which was in the final stages of being reassembled. The fighter sat on a strip of macadam that extended directly to the end of the narrow runway.

Four tall posts surrounded the MiG. The wooden supports were capped by a slanting tin roof. The simple, open-air structure had been painted to match the surrounding foliage.

A camouflaged Quonset hut sat on concrete blocks next to the aircraft shelter. A large round fuel tank had been partially buried on the opposite side of the MiG shelter. Behind the operations center was a congested area consisting of tents, a cookshack, and two generators. Off to the side was a gravity-fed, single-nozzle shower, two portable water containers, and a stack of C-ration cartons. The entire compound was covered by trees and camouflage.

Palmer joined Allison and Brad, then dropped his overnight bag on the pavement. "I noticed that we've got marines surrounding the perimeter."

"Most of them are *former* marines," Allison advised him. "They're our own security specialists."

Brad studied the sandbag-reinforced foxholes with a critical eye. "If we come under attack from both sides, those guys are going to be run over in short order."

Allison's response was interrupted when Hollis Spencer emerged from the Quonset hut. Brad glanced at the Colt .45 hanging from his web belt.

"Welcome aboard," Spencer greeted the trio. "Allison, your quarters are in the Quonset hut . . . back by the radios."

She examined the small building and nodded. "I won't have far to go to work."

"The two of you," Spencer gestured toward the aircraft shelter, "will share the tent next to the MiG. Your flight gear is inside."

The conversation was halted while the C-123 roared down the runway and gracefully lifted off the pavement. The Provider climbed steeply, entered a tight turn to reverse course, then climbed directly over the runway to a safe altitude.

"It looks to me," Brad observed, "like we are going to have to take off in the same direction he did, and land in the opposite direction."

"That's right," Spencer acknowledged with a look of concern on his face. "This is one short strip. We've only got forty-seven hundred feet, plus a little bit of grass overrun at each end. In the MiG," he glanced at each pilot, "if you screw up your approach, you might as well punch out, because you won't clear that ridge line." Spencer pointed at the steep, rugged mountain. He thought about how close the Southern Air Transport C-130 had been to the side of the sharply rising hills.

Palmer noticed some of the security team rush out to place large sections of camouflage on the runway.

Spencer anticipated his question. "From the air," he smiled, "you can't see the runway, or anything else. We can't afford to have someone stumble over this operation . . . from either side."

"Cap," Brad glanced at the nearest foxhole, "I don't mean to tell you how to run your business, but these troops are spread too far apart."

Spencer observed the men. "You're only seeing half of them," he said out of the corner of his mouth.

Brad looked around. "You've got 'em up on each side of the ridges?"

"That's right, and we've got charges and mines buried around the entire perimeter."

The beating rotor blades of an Air America UH-34 helicopter caught their attention. They turned to watch the former Marine Corps work-horse approach the airstrip.

"There's Mitchell and Jimenez," Allison announced, shielding the sun from her eyes. "The other helo will be here as soon as they replace a tail rotor."

Brad watched the bulbous-nosed Sikorsky swing over the ridge line and drop precariously toward the airstrip. At the last second, the helicopter flared before touching down lightly at the intersection of the taxiway and runway.

The battle-scarred helicopter sat on two fat tires connected to struts on each side of the fuselage. The engine was mounted in the nose behind two clamshell doors, while the cockpit was perched above and behind the huge nose.

When Chase Mitchell killed the rumbling engine, Spencer turned to the trio. "After you get squared away, I'll give you an update on the operation."

"Cap," Brad said, darting a look at the helicopter. "I think Nick and I should take an aerial tour and get the lay of the land."

Spencer smiled. "That's already on the agenda."

Brad and Nick sat in the sweltering tent, contemplating their flight suits.

"To hell with it," Brad suddenly blurted, holding the garment at arm's length. "Hand me that survival knife."

Nick gave him a curious look and silently reached for the knife hanging on the end of his cot.

Brad placed his flight suit on the ground and sawed off the legs just above the knees.

"Very stylish." Nick laughed, watching Austin slice through the sleeves above the elbow.

"You can roast if you want," Brad slipped out of his unmodified flight suit, "but I'm not going to croak from heat prostration."

Nick remodeled his gear while Brad donned his creation.

When Palmer was similarly attired, Brad glanced at Nick's boots. "What the hell is that?" Austin laughed, staring at the exposed tops of Palmer's socks.

Nick looked down at his legs. "Haven't you ever seen argyle socks?"

"In the Princeton colors, no less." Brad shook his head. "We better get over to the hut."

They left the entrance flaps open and walked to the operations center. When Brad and Nick entered the screen door, Jimenez and Mitchell burst out laughing.

Spencer and Allison looked up, then gave each other a disbelieving glance.

"Dashing," Allison declared. "Especially your fashion statement, Nick."

"Thank you," Palmer replied without a trace of embarrassment.

Mitchell examined the two pilots while they seated themselves at the planning table. He elbowed his copilot. "They certainly look like fighter jocks to me."

Allison and Cap Spencer joined the foursome.

"Gentlemen," Spencer began with a concerned look, "we originally planned to have you take off under the cover of darkness, but we're going to have to adapt to the timing of the strikes." He paused, displaying a small amount of irritation.

Brad tried to temper his sarcasm. "More politics from the hard-chargers in Washington?"

Spencer looked at the disgusted pilot for a long moment. "It's a combination of politics and secrecy. We're going to have to adhere to normal strike planning, so you'll have to stay low until you can pop up into the action."

"Cap," Austin continued, unable to conceal his worry, "there's a certain amount of lunacy in all this. If the warriors in Washington would let us flatten the MiG bases, we wouldn't have any MiGs to contend with . . . and we wouldn't be sitting out here."

Mitchell and Jimenez glanced in awe at the marine aviator.

Brad's impassioned statement prompted Spencer to sit back and fold his arms across his chest. "Captain Austin, you are free to leave at any time."

No one made a sound.

"No," Brad said firmly. "I want to be the first one up to bat." His jaw muscles were rigid. "But I want to know if I have full authority to operate anywhere I choose, including over the MiG sanctuaries."

Spencer appeared calm and collected. "When you depart from here, you are on your own."

"Good," Austin replied with a flat voice. "No rules of engagement—free to use our own ingenuity?"

"That's right."

Allison gave Brad a look of caution, then glanced at the chart in front of her.

"We've been given the go-ahead," Spencer informed the group, "to begin operations as soon as the MiG is ready, which Hank tells me will be tomorrow morning."

Spencer explained that Allison would coordinate their missions with the operations center in Vientiane. Ops would supply her with the coded times and Route Pack information for the air force and naval strike groups. The details of the missions would be transmitted to Alpha-29 two hours before the scheduled strikes.

Allison would know the exact route the air force F-105 Thunder-chiefs would fly, along with the points of land the navy aircraft would cross. She would trace the routes and times on an enlarged chart of northern Laos and North Vietnam. Brad and Nick would use the charts to position themselves close to the strike aircraft.

Spencer clarified how he would gather the information from the observers close to the MiG fields. When they transmitted their scrambled messages to the EC-121 Warning Star, the airborne radio operator would transmit the information to Alpha-29 in the same form. After the scrambled message was received by Spencer, he would transmit the data, in code, to the MiG.

The MiG call sign would be changed for each flight. Spencer would use a simple code for relaying the type of MiG and side number to Brad or Nick. Only the North Vietnamese MiGs sporting red stars on the nose would be reported to the orbiting Warning Star.

Allison handed the laminated code cards to Palmer and Austin. They studied it, admiring the simplicity. The random alphabetical letters corresponded to numbers from zero to nine,

$$B \quad E \quad T \quad P \quad Q \quad K \quad D \quad V \quad F \quad Z$$
$$2 \quad 6 \quad 8 \quad 1 \quad 7 \quad 3 \quad 5 \quad 9 \quad 0 \quad 4$$

while the MiG airfields had a letter to designate them:

Phuc Yen	H	Bai Thuong	C
Kep	J	Kien An	Y
Gia Lam	M	Hoa Lac	W

Spencer waited a few seconds. "If I have a MiG-17, side number two five two eight, from Phuc Yen, you'll hear it transmitted like this."

He glanced at his code. "I'll first give you the side number, then the type of MiG, followed by the field of origin. Bravo, Delta, Bravo, Tango . . . Papa, Quebec . . . Hotel."

Brad followed the explanation. "Will we reply?"

"Yes, with your call sign," Spencer advised. "The only contact that you'll have, other than that, is a radio check before takeoff, and another shortly after you're airborne. Don't transmit anything else, unless it's an emergency."

Spencer looked at the Air America pilots. "Your call sign, Sleepy Two Five, will remain the same for every mission. I don't want these guys," he gestured toward Austin and Palmer, "to be confused if they have to abandon the aircraft. We'll have you airborne ten minutes after the MiG takes off."

Jimenez remembered a number of risky search-and-rescue missions he had flown. "Where are we supposed to orbit?"

Spencer slid his chart in front of the SAR pilots. "Right here," he pointed at a spot northeast of Muong Lat, "if the mission is around Hanoi or Hai Phong."

The pilots' eyes gave away their feelings.

"Or here," Spencer moved his finger, "over Thiet Tra, if they're going down by Thanh Hoa."

"Cap," Mitchell said with a pained expression, "we'll be over North Vietnam without any air support."

Austin gave Palmer a fleeting glance. Both questioned whether these guys were the red-hot, hard-charging helicopter pilots they appeared to be.

"You'll have air cover if you need it," Spencer assured them. "Allison will give you the call signs and radio frequencies of the SAR people. If you feel you need air cover, use your normal call sign to communicate with the SAR pilots. Operate just like any other Air America flight that needs assistance."

Allison gave them a reassuring look. "I'll have the frequencies and call signs for you before the first mission."

Mitchell considered the information. "Cap, it wouldn't be a problem if we had two choppers. At least we would have a way out if one of them went down."

Spencer gave him a distant look. "Chase, you've been in this business a long time. We never get everything we're promised," he said with resignation. "We're going to operate with one helo until the other one gets here."

"Okay." Mitchell shrugged, accepting the inevitable.

"Right now," Spencer slid his chair back, "I'd like for you and Rudy to take Brad and Nick for a familiarization ride around the local area."

Mitchell and Jimenez exchanged concerned glances.

"Cap," Chase ground a cigarette in an ashtray, "the Pathet Lao have a stronghold about fifteen miles south of here. They're all over San Neua Province . . . and they've got a lot of firepower."

The message was not lost on Brad and Nick. They paid close attention to Spencer's reply.

"Chase," Cap responded with a look of understanding, "I'm not going to pretend there aren't risks, but I want Nick and Brad to know the details of the area. It could save their lives if they have to come in under the weather."

"Okay," Mitchell said with a skeptical look, and turned to Brad and Nick. "I hope you boys brought your flak jackets."

CHAPTER TWENTY-THREE

Brad sat next to the M-60 machine gun in the open cabin door of the helicopter. He glanced up at the winch mounted above the door. Brad studied the hook on the end of the cable and hoped that he would never have to use the rescue device.

Mitchell's usual crew chief, an irascible Air America veteran named Elvin Crowder, had elected to stay behind and inspect the MiG.

Austin adjusted his mind and body to the vibration and steady beat of the rotor blades as the UH-34 struggled to 6,000 feet. He relaxed, checked his seat belt, and looked out to the horizon.

Leaning forward, Brad let the slipstream fan his face. He studied the terrain, memorizing the details of the contour around the landing strip. When they flew over a wide valley leading to the elongated lowland that concealed their base, Brad calculated the distance between the peaks on each side.

Nick Palmer, sitting next to Brad, keyed his intercom switch. "Chase, let's go about ten or twelve miles south, and see if we can slip in from that direction if the weather turns sour."

"He's talking to Cap," Rudy Jimenez replied. "We don't want to go any farther south because of the Pathet Lao."

Brad adjusted his headset.

"Chase mentioned that, but he didn't elaborate," Palmer said, exchanging a look with Austin. "How about filling us in?"

"The Pathet Lao," Jimenez explained in a voice that vibrated in sync with the rotor blades, "has a large contingent of troops at San Neua."

167

The copilot turned the UH-34 to allow Brad and Nick a clear view to the south.

"At the bottom of that tall peak," Jimenez paused to speak to Mitchell, "on the far side, is an ammunition factory and training facility."

Austin and Palmer scrutinized the terrain below them, mentally forming a map in their minds. If they had to eject from the MiG close to Alpha-29, they wanted to be able to orient to the base.

Brad thought about how different the perspective would be if they were on the ground. "Any problem if we drop down and take a closer look at the approach to the runway?"

Chase Mitchell answered, having completed the radio check with Spencer. "We don't want to do that, because there's an estimated four thousand North Vietnamese regulars in this region."

"Yeah," Jimenez chimed in. "If you look straight out at three o'clock low—about a mile and a half—you can see a VC base camp."

Brad scanned the area and was unable to locate the campsite. "I don't see any signs of activity."

Palmer pointed at the encampment at the same time Jimenez spoke to them.

"It's along the east side of the grassy area," the copilot explained, "next to the small village."

The camp was now clearly evident to Austin. "I've got it, but I don't see anyone."

"That's because they can hear us," Jimenez advised. "They are masters at camouflage."

"This is 'Indian country,' " Mitchell informed them as he banked the helicopter to the left, "and we're right in the middle of the reservation."

Brad spied their runway in the distance. "Why haven't the VC or Pathet Lao attacked Alpha-29?"

"Who knows," Jimenez answered over the sound of the rotor blades. "From what I know of them, they're very enterprising and patient people. If they decide to attack our strip, they'll wait until we least expect it."

"Rudy is right," Chase declared as he began a shallow descent. "They're watching the airstrip as we speak. I'm sure—for the time being—that our MiG has them confused."

Austin pulled his headset away from his ear, prompting Palmer to do the same.

"I don't think," Brad yelled over the rhythmic beating of the rotor blades, "that we're getting the whole picture from Cap Spencer."

Nick shrugged and nodded in agreement. "Chase, don't you think the Cong will report the MiG to their HQ?"

"In time, but they may think it's one of their own schemes to hit the Americans close to home."

"You have to remember," Jimenez laughed quietly, "that these guys are out in the boonies . . . and they'll probably be scratching their heads for a while."

"That may be true," Brad admitted with growing concern, "but they aren't stupid."

Nick and Brad continued to examine the mountains and valleys thick with vegetation. Mitchell maneuvered the helicopter to the same point where he had made his original approach to Alpha-29, then started a steep descent. He constantly turned the UH-34 while varying the rate of descent.

Brad was startled by a *ping*ing sound, then saw a ray of light appear above the door opening.

"Oh, shit," Jimenez yelled at the same instant, "we're taking fire!"

Mitchell swore, then dropped the nose of the UH-34. The helicopter plummeted down the side of a mountain as more rounds tore through the fuselage.

PZZING!

Jimenez flinched as a small-arms round ricocheted off the nose directly in front of the windshield. Another shell slammed into the side of the cockpit, ripping open a gaping hole. A half-second later, Mitchell and Jimenez were struck by flying debris when a section of the windshield burst inward.

Off balance, Austin unbuckled his seat belt and slammed into the forward cabin bulkhead. He grasped the machine gun and tried to aim at the muzzle flashes twinkling from the trees.

"You better strap your dumb ass in," Palmer exclaimed, bracing himself against the side of the cabin, "before you fall out of this son of a bitch!"

Realizing that it was impossible to aim and fire under the circumstances, Brad lurched sideways into a seat. He buckled himself in while Mitchell pulled out of the dive 400 feet above the valley.

PZZINNNG!

Another round caromed off the clamshell doors that enclosed the engine. Two more shells pierced the compartment and penetrated the engine.

Brad and Nick could feel the helicopter start to vibrate. Dense black smoke began to fill the cabin as the engine shook violently, then surged and died.

Brad darted a quick glance at Palmer. "Holy shit!"

Nick's eyes reflected the terror that Austin felt. "We're gonna crash!"

Mitchell bottomed the pitch of the rotors, maintaining airspeed while he deftly maneuvered the powerless UH-34 toward Alpha-29. He could see that the autorotation was not going to stretch down the valley to the runway.

"Mayday! Mayday!" Mitchell frantically radioed to Alpha-29. "Sleepy Two Five is going down! We've taken a hit in the engine!"

"We're goin' in!" Jimenez shouted over the intercom as the helicopter settled toward the thick jungle.

Brad could feel his heart pound. Like Palmer, he braced himself for the crash landing and said a silent prayer. *God, let us live through it.*

Hollis Spencer stared at the radio for a moment before he reacted. Hearing the Mayday call, Allison rushed into the compartment at the same time Spencer lunged for the microphone.

"Where are they?" she asked with a look of fear frozen on her face.

"Chase," Spencer suddenly blurted, "say your position! Where are you?"

Rudy Jimenez answered. "We're about four klicks—"

Spencer tried again, then a third time, before he tossed down the mike. "They must be too low. Allison, get ahold of the CO of our security detail and tell him I want his best platoon up here on the double."

"Will do!" she answered, snatching the security walkie-talkie from the corner of Spencer's desk.

Cap leaped to his feet. "I'm going to see if I can spot any smoke," he said in a clipped voice as he rushed for the door.

Attempting to conceal her worry, Allison nodded while she called the security command post.

The belly of the helicopter settled closer and closer to the trees as the airspeed decayed. Mitchell pulled pitch, flaring from the autorotation at the last second. The forward speed had been rapidly reduced before the wheels skimmed the foliage, then began nicking the trees.

Streaming fuel, the helicopter suddenly quit flying and plunged through the trees. The rotors disintegrated as they chopped the tops off the branches, then flew like shrapnel.

The UH-34 yawed sideways, rolled thirty degrees, and slammed into the ground, knocking the wind out of Austin. Stunned, he gasped for breath and grabbed Palmer's arm. "Let's get out of here!"

Palmer clumsily unbuckled his seat belt and crawled on his hands and knees to the cabin door. The fuselage had been crushed by the severe impact, making the exit smaller.

Brad and Nick climbed out of the cabin door and mashed the foliage around them. Engulfed in gray smoke, they struggled over the twisted landing gear to the cockpit.

Smelling aviation gasoline, Brad moved rapidly to free Chase Mitchell. Jimenez had already extricated himself from the wreckage, and was working his way around the nose of the destroyed helicopter.

Austin unlatched Mitchell's harness release and spoke to the groggy pilot. "We've got to get you out of here . . . before this thing goes up in flames."

Chase mumbled and leaned toward the cockpit entrance. Brad noticed a bullet hole in the shattered sliding window, then tugged Mitchell free of his seat. Palmer grabbed the pilot's legs and helped Brad carry him clear of the smoldering wreckage. Rudy Jimenez blazed a trail for them until the foursome was well clear of the helicopter.

Exhausted by the heat and humidity, Brad and Nick gently lowered Chase to the ground and sagged to the grass with Rudy Jimenez. Brad noticed that both helo pilots had various scratches and cuts on their faces and arms.

"Chase," Brad began slowly, catching his breath, "are you okay? Can you talk?"

Mitchell moved his arms and legs, then inhaled deeply and let the air out slowly. "Nice landing, huh?"

A slanted smile crossed Rudy's face. "Yeah, the lucky bastard is okay, as usual."

Brad and Nick gave the copilot a curious look.

"We've gone about . . ." Jimenez paused to count, "five weeks since the last crash."

Palmer laughed nervously and rolled on his back. "That certainly bolsters my confidence."

They rested for a minute while their initial shock subsided. Mitchell propped himself up and leaned against a tree. He had a steady trickle of blood from his nose, but otherwise appeared to be okay.

Nick looked at Brad. "Should we get the machine gun out of the helo?"

"No," Mitchell cautioned, glancing up through the jungle canopy. The telltale smoke from the crashed helicopter was rising straight into the sky. "The bastards who shot us down are on their way here . . . you can count on it."

Brad patted the .38-caliber Smith & Wesson revolver in his shoulder holster. "We need to get the hell out of here, and our little cap pistols are all we've got."

Austin moved closer to the helicopter pilots. "How far are we from the runway?"

Mitchell rubbed his neck muscles. "About two miles—maybe a little farther," he responded, shifting his gaze to Jimenez, "wouldn't you say, Rodeo?"

"At least, from my perspective."

The helicopter suddenly burst into flames, sending black clouds of smoke rising through the dense foliage.

"Let's move out," Brad ordered, glancing at the flattened and burning UH-34, "before we have company."

Austin swiftly rose to his feet. "Chase, you and Rudy take the lead. We don't have any idea what you were seeing when you went down."

Brad handed Jimenez his survival knife and the copilot began the arduous task of chopping his way through the undergrowth. After negotiating two hundred yards of jungle, the pilots were exhausted.

"Shit," Palmer swore under his breath as they again moved forward through the dense growth. "I wish I hadn't cut the legs off my goddamn flight suit."

Brad suddenly stopped. "Rudy, hold it! Stop!"

Ashen-faced, Jimenez stopped in his tracks and turned. "What's wrong?"

"I just remembered what Cap told me," Brad said evenly. "The airfield is surrounded by mines. Take it real easy and slow . . . and maybe we can make voice contact with the security troops."

"I feel a lot better now," Jimenez replied with a touch of sarcasm. "You're the goddamn marine, so why don't you come up here and lead us to the runway?"

"I'll be happy to," Brad answered firmly, "since we've got the general direction established."

After twenty-five minutes, Palmer heard a sound. "Brad," he whispered loudly. "Stop!"

Austin motioned for everyone to hit the ground. He sheathed the survival knife and drew his revolver.

Belly-crawling through the thick tangle, Austin reached a small clearing on slightly higher ground from which he could scan the immediate area. Nothing.

Brad's scratched legs were beginning to bleed, and he could feel the sting of a mosquito bite. A ground beetle crawled across his neck, but he forced himself to ignore it.

Austin stiffened at the sound of voices. The conversation was muffled, but clearly audible and growing closer. He waited, clutching the Smith & Wesson while he strained to hear the words.

With a growing sense of apprehension, Brad caught a slight movement to his right. He cautiously looked and froze in terror. A dark snake, three feet in length, slithered toward him.

Brad involuntarily recoiled and started crawling backward. He instinctively pointed the revolver at the reptile, then stopped himself from pulling the trigger. He felt a knot in his chest as he reached for the survival knife.

The snake momentarily stopped, eyeing Brad before continuing to advance toward him. Austin forced himself to be patient, waiting until the black snake was almost within his reach. Brad lunged forward, driving the sharp blade through the snake and into the soil. Pinned to the ground, the reptile violently thrashed back and forth while Brad crawled away.

The voices he had heard were closer now, and the men were moving rapidly. Austin could hear the sound of a machete as it sliced through the vegetation.

Brad cautiously rose and saw a shadowy form wearing a camouflaged helmet. Brad hesitated, thinking the small man was walking the point for a CIA security squad. Surely they had seen the black smoke and were heading toward the downed helicopter.

Austin started to hail the soldier at the same moment that he recognized the AK-47 assault rifle. The man was a scout for a Pathet Lao or NVA patrol.

Paralyzed for the moment, Brad searched for an escape route, then realized there was no way to avoid the scout.

With his legs spread out awkwardly, Austin gripped his revolver in both hands and aimed for the man's chest. With his heart pounding,

Brad waited for a clear shot. How many soldiers were in the patrol?

He inhaled slowly, held his breath, and gently squeezed the trigger twice. The soldier stumbled backward in wide-eyed astonishment, twisted around, and staggered against a tree.

The two gunshots set off a scene of mass confusion. Amid the screaming and yelling, Brad jumped up and raced back to the other pilots.

"This way!" Austin pointed as a dozen shots rang through the air. "Head straight through there and keep moving!"

Petrified, Nick paused. "What are you going to do?"

"Move it!" Brad ordered as Jimenez and Mitchell thrashed into the deep foliage. "I'll catch up!"

Austin turned to fire another round and heard shooting in the distance. He could distinguish sporadic rifle fire between the bursts from at least two machine guns.

When four soldiers reached their fallen comrade, Brad braced himself and fired two rounds at the group. Not waiting to see the results, Austin chased after the other pilots.

With his lungs heaving, Brad plunged through the tangled jungle. He tried to estimate the distance to the airfield, but his mind kept focusing on the fact that they had to traverse a mine field to reach the runway.

Fighting an insidious feeling of panic, Brad stumbled and fell. He yanked his spare rounds of .38-caliber ammunition out of his chest pocket, reloaded his revolver, and scrambled to his feet.

Brad could hear the thrashing and yelling behind him as he lunged forward. Cut and bleeding, Austin smashed his way through the foliage. His eyes burned from salty perspiration and his lungs were on fire.

A stream of gunfire erupted, ripping through the trees next to him. Fragments of leaves fell on Brad as he tripped over Rudy Jimenez and sprawled on his stomach.

"We're going to stick together!" Nick shouted, firing in unison with Chase Mitchell. Jimenez boldly went to his knees and fired at the enemy.

Unable to speak, Brad crawled around and aimed at their pursuers. Time seemed to slow while Austin carefully made each round count. His instinct for survival won out over the growing panic.

Brad saw three brown faces maneuvering to flank the outnumbered and outgunned pilots. The staccato sound of machine-gun fire startled

Austin. Recognizing the familiar sound of an M-60, Brad squeezed off two rounds at the advancing men. One of the soldiers jerked backward and started screaming.

A fusillade of gunfire erupted as Brad again pulled the trigger. Nothing happened. He frantically reached for the last few rounds in his pocket while Nick and Chase fired at the main cluster of men.

"They're retreating!" Jimenez exclaimed, firing the last of his ammunition. "They're—"

His statement was interrupted by a burst of gunfire that shredded the trees and foliage next to them.

"Those are our guys!" Brad shouted, and cupped his hands around his mouth. "Cease fire! Cease fire!"

Another short burst slammed into the trees, showering debris over them.

"Goddamnit, we're Americans!" Austin yelled at the top of his lungs. "Cease fire!"

The pilots heard the same order in the distance.

Chase twisted around to face Brad and Nick. "That's Spencer . . . thank God."

CHAPTER TWENTY-FOUR

A combined feeling of relief and tension permeated the air in the Quonset hut. The pilots were as grateful for their safety as they were alarmed at the factors that caused the crash.

Palmer and Austin had had a lengthy conversation about the close proximity of the Communist troops. Both felt they had been deceived by Spencer, or at least had not been told the whole truth. No one had mentioned that Alpha-29 was located in the heart of Pathet Lao territory.

Jimenez and Mitchell, familiar with the region, obviously had known about the risks, but no one had explained the situation to the MiG pilots.

"Cap," Austin's glance strayed to Allison, "we need more troops and firepower here. We're sitting in the middle of a potential massacre, and the Pathet Lao don't operate in compliance with the Geneva Accords."

Spencer heard the message loud and clear. "That's why we have the security people spread around the compound. Your job," he said without any visible sign of belligerence, "is to fly the MiG, nothing else."

The only sound in the room came from the fan.

Brad's eyes narrowed. "We just got blown out of the sky less than three miles from here. It certainly got my attention, and I think we should reconsider our security options . . . while we still have them."

"I understand your concern," Spencer replied slowly, "and this *is* a dangerous mission, but you knew that when you volunteered. You're not here in an advisory capacity," he informed Brad, adding, "and you would do well to remember that. Just fly the MiG."

Austin bristled. "May I at least make some suggestions? Just between us?"

"We'll be right back," Spencer announced, sliding his chair back. He followed Austin out the door, and they walked halfway to the camouflaged runway.

Brad was aware that Hank Murray and his men had stopped working, curious about what was happening. When he cast a look in their direction, they pretended to continue with their maintenance chores.

"Captain Austin," Spencer snapped, "you're about a heartbeat away from a one-way ticket out of here."

"I don't really give a shit," Brad flared. "I'm going to tell you what I think, then you can make any goddamn decision you want.

"First," Austin began boldly, "we need at least double the number of troops you've got out here, and a couple of gunships would be nice, if we come under attack.

"Secondly," he continued in a lower tone, "why in the hell do you have a woman out here in the middle of a war zone? Christ, any of us could operate the radios."

Spencer gave him a challenging look. "Allison has a lot of experience with these types of operations, and the two of us are the only ones who have a clearance to receive the strike messages. We're CIA—you're on loan."

Brad paused, then laughed curtly. "Yeah, that makes sense. The rest of us are certainly security risks."

Placing his hands on his hips, Spencer gazed down the runway before facing Brad.

"Austin, I'm going to tell you this just one goddamn time. I'm in charge of this operation, and you are going to get into compliance, or I'm going to ship your ass back to Da Nang."

"I don't think you want to do that," Brad retorted, staring into Spencer's eyes, "because you need me more than I need you, for the time being."

"Don't bet on it," Spencer bridled, then turned for the Quonset hut.

"You must've really hit his hot button," Nick commented while he sat on his cot.

Brad rolled on his back and let his legs dangle from the end of his collapsible bed. "I hope I did. It doesn't take an intellectual giant to figure out that we're sitting ducks if we're attacked . . . and this is the last place he should have brought Allison."

Palmer's eyebrows lifted. "Do I detect that your budding 'friendship' with Allison is growing into something more than a friendship?"

Hearing a clanking noise, Brad swung his legs around and pushed himself to a sitting position.

"May I come in?" Allison asked, holding two loaded M-16 rifles and two magazines.

"Sure," Nick answered enthusiastically, then slid to the end of his cot. "Have a seat."

"Cap wanted you to have these," she declared, handing each pilot a rifle and an extra magazine.

"Thanks," Brad said, propping his weapon in the corner. "I'll feel more secure," he said with genuine appreciation, "having something other than my six-shooter with which to defend myself."

"That's what Cap thought."

Brad gave Palmer a crooked smile. "Nick, do you know which end to point?"

Palmer laughed amiably and checked the safety. "I'll probably figure it out, smart-ass."

Allison reached into the pocket of her khaki blouse and extracted two containers of first-aid cream. "I got these from our corpsman. He said to apply a liberal amount on your cuts and scratches."

"Thanks," Brad replied, "and hadn't we better give one of these to Rudy and Chase?"

"I already gave a tube to each of them." Allison looked around the disheveled tent, taking in the wrinkled *Playboy* magazine on the empty ammunition box. The olive-drab canvas tent was army surplus and well-worn. A pair of jeans and three flight suits hung from a line tied along the roof of the shelter. "Who's your interior decorator?"

"We share the responsibility." Brad smiled, applying the cream. "It's a special talent we have."

"Brad," Allison said with a serious look, "do you have a few minutes? I would like to talk to you."

"Sure."

Palmer quietly coughed and got to his feet. "I know when I'm not wanted."

"You don't have to leave," she assured him.

"Actually," Nick confided, "I'm going to see if I can gag down some of the C-rats."

Allison waited until she and Brad were alone, then gazed at him for a long period of time.

"Brad," she said at last, "I know you had a falling-out with Cap . . . and I've been concerned about it."

Austin silently nodded and placed the top on the ointment container.

"Yes," he responded glumly, "and I suppose I'll have to apologize to him. I've had a lot on my mind, and the crash triggered my pent-up emotions."

Allison sensed that Brad was not going to volunteer much more of his real feelings to her.

"I appreciate your concern for me," she admitted, wanting to touch Brad and confide in him.

"Excuse me?"

"Cap told me about your concern for my safety." Allison waited for a reaction, but Brad remained impassive.

Brad sat back. "And?"

"I told him I want to do my job with the rest of you," she declared, "but I agree with you. We need more security."

He raised an eyebrow. "Did you tell him that?"

"No," she conceded, "but he did confer with the security commander. He's a former marine company commander."

Brad held his response in deference to the experienced ground officer. Although Austin had the fundamental training to be a platoon commander, he had never actually commanded troops in the field.

"Well," he said stiffly, "I'm confident they'll make the right decisions."

Allison studied Brad for a moment. "You mentioned that you've had a lot on your mind. Do you want to talk about it?"

"Not particularly." Brad chuckled. "It's just been one of those days."

"It's Leigh Ann, isn't it?" she inquired coolly.

"Yes," Brad answered truthfully, "and you."

Allison felt an underlying excitement. "What about me?"

Brad grew cautious. "Allison, I appreciate your efforts to smooth things over." He rose from his cot. "I'm going to see Cap and apologize."

"Okay," she replied, concealing her disappointment. "Perhaps we can talk later."

He felt a compelling desire to speak freely to her, but he resisted. "Sure."

The fan was humming at full blast when Brad entered the warm Quonset hut. Hollis Spencer was seated at one of the four radios, having a brisk conversation. He motioned for Austin to have a seat.

Brad sat down next to the long table that dominated the middle of the room. He felt conspicuous as he waited for Spencer to conclude his conversation. Brad idly inspected the relief maps on the wall until Spencer signed off and removed his headset.

Austin rose from his chair. "Cap, I want to apologize." He extended his hand. "I have no excuse for my behavior this afternoon."

Spencer shook Brad's hand. "Let's put it behind us. Have a seat, and I'll fill you in on the latest."

After Spencer sat at his desk, he opened a lower drawer and propped his boots on it. "We've got another thirty troops arriving tomorrow afternoon."

"Great." Brad could not suppress his grin. "I really think we'll need them . . . if anything happens."

"However, the UH-34s—they're scrambling to get another one— will be the only air cover we'll have."

"Cap, I appreciate your efforts," Brad responded, adding wryly, "and we'll do the best we can with what we've got."

Spencer observed Austin, then picked up a pencil and absently tapped the eraser on his desk.

"Brad, I know you've had one hell of a day—all of you—but I'd like to discuss a personal matter," he paused, "if you don't mind."

Austin tensed in anticipation. "What is it?"

"Allison hasn't said anything to me." Spencer said, and smiled politely. "Hell, she doesn't have to. I've known her for a long time, and it is obvious to me, and probably everyone else, that she has fallen for you."

Maintaining his composure, Brad searched for a response. "I recognize that, Cap, but she knows that I have a relationship with someone else."

"Don't get me wrong," Spencer declared, sitting upright. "Whatever the relationship is . . . is none of my business, unless it affects our mission."

Spencer pulled out his pipe.

Brad started to tell Cap about his walk on the runway with Allison and their discussion about Leigh Ann, but he decided not to. He waited impatiently while Spencer lighted his pipe.

"Brad, I can't monitor your feelings or your actions," he paused to exhale the smoke, "but, believe me, the more you can keep your total concentration on our work, the better your chance of survival."

"Sir," Brad said, wishing there was an easier way to extract himself from the conversation, "I get the message."

"I'm relieved, Brad." Spencer smiled warmly. "Get some rest."

In the damp stillness of the early morning, Brad listened to Nick's uneven breathing. Believing his tentmate was having a nightmare, Brad reached across the aisle and prodded Palmer. Nick rolled onto his side and his breathing smoothed.

Brad listened to the buzzing sounds of the insects and reviewed the events of the last four days. The CIA reinforcements had arrived and the replacement helicopter had been flown to the field. The ferry pilots had remained overnight and flown back on the C-123.

Unable to sleep, Brad gazed at the top of the darkened tent. Spencer had finally been given permission to launch the MiG. Before midday, or shortly thereafter, Brad would be airborne in a MiG-17 over North Vietnam. This was going to be the first testing of the feasibility of Operation Achilles.

He let his mind drift to Leigh Ann, but could not afford to let himself dwell on her. Brad hoped that she would receive his letter and address at the Constellation Hotel in the next few days.

From Leigh Ann, his thoughts shifted to Allison. After his conversation with Spencer, Brad had purposely avoided Allison. He had spent most of his time around the MiG, except for a brief visit to the security command post. He had left feeling a renewed confidence in the combat-experienced ground officer and the men under his command. Over sixty percent of the security detail were former marine infantrymen.

"Ah, shit," Brad swore as he swatted a mosquito on his forearm. He checked the mosquito netting and pulled the drawstring tighter.

Clad only in his shorts, Brad felt sweaty and irritable. He heard Nick stir. "Are you awake?"

"Barely," Palmer uttered, then sneezed. "I hope I'm not coming down with malaria or some shit like that."

"You don't sound like a happy camper."

"This is ridiculous," Nick snorted.

"What?"

Palmer sat up and slapped a mosquito. "I joined the navy to fly from carriers, and I'm sitting in a goddamn mosquito-infested tent in the middle of shitville." He swatted his ankle. "Surrounded by thousands of gooks who would like nothing better than to kill me."

Brad reached up and cupped his hands behind his head. "Look at the bright side."

"Don't piss me off," Nick said curtly.

"You're not damaging your liver at the O club bar," Austin stated emphatically. "You'll probably live an extra ten years . . . if someone doesn't shoot you."

Brad heard Nick thrashing through his belongings. "What are you doing?"

"I'm trying to find my gun," he sneezed again, "so I can blow your worthless brains out."

Brad extended his arm. "Let me bum one of your cigarettes."

"Since when did you start smoking?"

"Just give me the cigarette," Brad insisted. "Maybe, if we can create enough smoke, it'll drive these goddamn bloodsuckers out of here."

Nick lighted two cigarettes, handing one to Brad. "Are you nervous about today?"

"Naw," Austin replied, puffing steadily. "I normally stay awake all night."

CHAPTER TWENTY-FIVE

Alpha-29 sweltered in the soaring heat of midmorning when Brad stepped out of his tent. His flight suit, tailored to resemble a Russian flying garment, clung damply to his torso. He checked the security of his revolver and patted the pocket containing extra .38 rounds.

Brad paused to watch Hank Murray direct his men as they pulled the MiG out of the makeshift shelter. The aircraft had been painted in camouflage similar to that of MiG-17s stationed at Gia Lam, the highly active air base on the northeastern edge of downtown Hanoi.

Walking toward the Quonset hut, Brad glanced at his watch. The longer he waited to take off, the higher the air temperature would be. Each degree of heat would increase his takeoff distance. Another four degrees would place the MiG at the maximum limit for the altitude and length of the runway at Alpha-29. Weight was the critical factor, and Brad did not want to dump fuel before his takeoff roll. He would need every ounce of jet fuel Murray could squeeze into the tanks.

When he entered the Quonset hut, Hollis Spencer was hunched over a radio at the far end of the room. Nick Palmer was sitting at the briefing table with the helicopter pilots. Allison glanced up at him and smiled as she retrieved a piece of paper from her desk and sat down with the group of pilots.

"We've just received permission," she informed them in a steady voice, "to launch the MiG in coordination with a carrier-based strike at Phu Ly. The target is a major shipping and storage facility."

She handed Brad a chart with a line from the strike group coast-in point to the target.

Austin studied the map, noting that the attack pilots would cross the shoreline at Quan Phuong Ha on their way northwest to Phu Ly. He looked at a circle over the foothills west of Nam Dinh, then saw one to the east of Phu Ly.

"What do these circles represent?" Brad asked Allison.

Nick leaned closer, examining the circles and target area.

"That's where the fighter cover will orbit," Allison explained, pointing to the foothills. "Another group of fighters will be circling east of Phu Ly, over the Red River at Phu Vat."

Brad rose and looked at the relief map on the wall. "Nick, take a look at this."

Nick joined Austin and looked at the valley above Brad's finger. The valley and the river were ten miles west of the fighter escort near Nam Dinh.

"I'm going to stay below the ridge line," Brad explained as he examined the terrain near Nam Dinh, "because I can turn at each end . . . and stay on the deck until the right moment."

Nick measured the distance from Alpha-29 to the valley. He calculated the time to cover the ninety-five nautical miles at a fuel-saving speed. "If you don't have to deviate, you'll be there in twenty-five minutes."

The helicopter pilots stepped to the detailed map. Jimenez looked at the area around their holding point at Thiet Tra. "If you can stay in this area, we'll only be thirty-five to forty miles from you."

Brad gave him a thin smile. "That's easier said than done. If I get jumped by a couple of Fox-4s, or Crusaders, I'll be all over the place."

"If you'll have a seat," Allison suggested, "we can finish this before Cap joins us."

Everyone returned to the table while Brad spread his chart in front of him.

"The strike is planned for twelve forty-five," Allison looked at Brad, "so you'll have to take off at fifteen after the hour."

Brad computed the probable temperature and corresponding distance needed for the MiG to get safely airborne. "I'm going to be on the ragged edge, as far as the heat goes."

"You're the pilot," Allison asserted, "so it's your call."

Austin cracked a smile and looked her in the eye. "That's correct . . . fortunately."

Spencer placed his headset down and stepped through the entrance to the radio shack. "It's a twelve-fifteen go, Brad," he said excitedly. "Jot down these call signs," he instructed, glancing at his hastily written notes.

"Your call sign is Tabasco," he read while he seated himself next to Allison.

"The strike leader is Rock Crusher." Spencer adjusted the patch over his eye. "The west F-4s are Montana, and the F-8s east of Phu Ly are Sugarloaf."

Austin circled Tabasco and hurriedly wrote the other call signs on his dented kneeboard.

Spencer looked at Mitchell and Jimenez. "The SAR flight is Sandy Five Seven. If you have to contact them, call the flight leader on Guard." Guard was the military emergency frequency, 243.0, which was monitored by a separate radio receiver in each aircraft, including helicopters.

"Brad," Spencer handed him the radio frequency for the strike group, "write that down."

Austin would use his number-one radio to monitor the strike aircraft, while the second radio would be tuned to the discrete frequency selected by Spencer. The frequency and MiG call sign would be changed for each mission.

"We'll do a radio check before takeoff," Spencer advised Brad, "and another as soon as you're airborne."

Brad gave him a dubious look, but remained quiet. *If I get airborne.*

"Any questions?" Spencer asked, anxious to commence the covert operation. His nerves were beginning to fray.

"Yes," Brad answered with a calmness that belied the churning in his stomach. "What's the weather like?"

Chagrined, Spencer covered the oversight with a quiet laugh. "Sorry. The guessers said that you can anticipate cumulus buildups around the target area."

Brad exchanged a brief glance with Allison. Her soft brown eyes reflected her concern.

"Well," Brad shoved himself back from the table, "it's almost showtime."

The surface of the MiG's skin was blistering hot when Brad peered into the bifurcated engine-air intake. He continued the preflight as he walked around the fighter and climbed into the cockpit. The metal on the canopy rail burned his hands, causing him to flinch. *Next time*, he thought, *I'm going to have Murray keep the plane under the shelter until I'm ready to start the engine.*

Palmer climbed the boarding ladder to help strap Brad into the ejection seat. "I was going to ride in the helo, but Cap gave me an emphatic no."

Brad looked up, wide-eyed. "Holy Christ, you're crazier than I am."

Perspiring profusely, he donned his reconfigured helmet and checked his watch. Four minutes to go. Brad strapped on his kneeboard and ran through the prestart checklist. He glanced at the hand-lettered asterisk at the bottom of the list, then felt the Russian identification papers in his breast pocket. The documents identified him as Kapitan Sergey K. Yefimov.

Nick patted him on the helmet. "Don't do anything stupid."

Brad gave him an incredulous look. "Do you think what I'm about to do is *intelligent?*"

"Put some Marine Corps on 'em," Nick said with gusto as he dismounted the ladder.

Brad rolled his eyes and energized the starter. He carefully watched the engine gauges while Nick carried the ladder to the MiG shelter. After a systems and flight-controls check, Hank Murray gave him a thumbs-up.

Brad taxied to the runway and turned toward the grass overrun. He wanted to have as much speed as possible before he reached the macadam.

He turned the MiG around and saw Jimenez and Mitchell climbing up the fuselage of the helicopter. Elvin Crowder, their scruffy-looking crew chief/gunner, was shutting the clamshell doors around the engine.

A crowd of curious onlookers had gathered in front of the Quonset hut. Brad watched the security troops crawl out of their foxholes. Most of them were eating their C-ration lunches. The big event was about to take place. The unexpected audience served only to heighten Brad's anxiety.

Switching the number-two radio to Alpha-29's discrete frequency, Brad keyed his microphone. "Alpha Base, Tabasco One, radio check."

"Tabasco," Spencer replied in a clear voice, "Alpha Bravo reads you loud and clear."

"Roger," Austin responded, rechecking his trim and flap settings. He looked through the armored-glass windscreen at the runway, noting the shimmering heat waves rising from the macadam. This was going to be a maximum-effort takeoff.

Brad smoothly advanced the throttle to the stop, waited until the engine spooled up to maximum power, checked the gauges, then released the brakes. "I'm on the roll."

Burdened with a heavy fuel load, the MiG accelerated slowly. The fighter bounced over the edge of the macadam and continued to gain speed at a sluggish rate.

After rolling 3,000 feet, Brad knew he was committed to attempt the takeoff. If he tried to abort at this point, the MiG would overrun the grassy area and slam into the trees near the winding stream. The resultant conflagration would consume the aircraft and pilot.

Brad watched the airspeed indicator as he neared the end of the runway. 80 . . . 85 . . . 90 . . . He stopped glancing at the airspeed as he prepared to time his rotation.

A half second from the end of the macadam, Brad snapped the control stick back. The fighter staggered into the air and wobbled twice. Brad gently eased the stick forward as the MiG mushed through the air. He slowly let out his breath. *Holy Mother of Jesus . . .*

Brad went through the procedure to raise the landing gear, then retracted the flaps. He kept the MiG in a shallow climb to allow it to accelerate to normal climb speed. Brad keyed the radio that was tuned to the discrete frequency.

"Tabasco One up."

"Five by five," Spencer replied briskly.

Brad would be able to monitor both the discrete and strike-group radio frequencies.

Keeping his climb profile shallow, Brad raced low over the tops of the trees. As his speed increased, Brad reduced the power setting to conserve fuel. Flying low used more fuel than climbing to a higher altitude, but he could not risk being discovered by radar.

Reaching the border of Laos, Brad topped a 5,850-foot mountain at an altitude of 6,000 feet. He smoothly lowered the nose and eased the throttle back. Brad intently scanned the skies as he entered the airspace over North Vietnam.

HANOI

Edmund Graham-Rawlings, a career CIA officer, adjusted the tripod under his Strobel binoculars. His identification card stated that he was a correspondent for the British Broadcasting Corporation. The CIA had, in fact, arranged to have an occasional story published in Britain to substantiate his role as a journalist.

The North Vietnamese officials had thoroughly checked the Englishman's background, finding that his published articles were unbiased and well-written. The Hanoi censors closely examined Graham-Rawlings's work, but found that he did not report anything objectionable. The officials were quite pleased that he portrayed the North Vietnamese government in a favorable light.

At three inches over six feet, with tousled snow-white hair, Graham-Rawlings looked the part of a distinguished journalist. Wire-framed glasses and an unfashionable sports coat, which he wore every day, capped the disguise.

He leaned down and looked at the aircraft ramp at the Gia Lam air base. His second-story apartment near the MiG field had taken a year and a half to acquire. After convincing the press corps officials that he needed to be close to the action, they offered him the apartment.

Although his view was partially blocked by another building, Graham-Rawlings could see over half of the flight line. Most important, he could watch for red stars on the fuselages of the MiGs as they taxied for takeoff.

The dimly lighted living room was sparsely furnished. A cluttered table with a manual typewriter was the centerpiece of the room.

Graham-Rawlings turned the binoculars' range-finding reticle to focus on the MiGs as they scrambled for the runway. He wrote down the side number of the MiG-17 with three red stars on the nose, then continued his inspection of the fighters.

He scribbled another four-digit number when an aircraft sporting two stars turned onto the runway. After scrutinizing the last MiG in the procession, Graham-Rawlings placed the binoculars in the bedroom closet.

He walked into the kitchen, emptied the contents of the refrigerator onto the cabinet, then tilted the appliance forty-five degrees against the wall. Enclosed in the false bottom was a radio with the capability to scramble his message to the EC-121 high over northern Laos.

ABOARD THE WARNING STAR

Lieutenant (junior grade) Gary Lawson heard the scrambler activate. He yanked a government-issue pen from his flight-suit pocket and patiently waited.

After the garbled message was translated back to English, the junior officer transmitted it to the new listening post in northeast Laos. MiGs were scrambling from the base at Gia Lam. He was curious why the side numbers of two MiGs were being sent to a listening post in Laos.

A moment later, Lawson received a message confirming that MiGs had taken off from Phuc Yen. Again, the side number of a particular aircraft was sent. *This is a new twist,* Lawson thought as he relayed the information.

Alpha-29

Hollis Spencer wrote as fast and legibly as he could, then turned down the volume on the radio and hurriedly finished his notes. He checked the code twice to make sure that he had not made any mistakes.

Allison, nervously smoking a cigarette and chatting with Nick Palmer, continually checked her watch. Her gaze became fixed on the helicopter as the rotor blades developed a crescendo of noise.

The UH-34, delayed with a starter problem, clattered into the air and passed over the Quonset hut.

Spencer moved to another radio and adjusted the headset for that transmitter.

"Tabasco One. Tabasco One, stand by." He looked at the code and spoke slowly. "Kilo . . . Foxtrot . . . Papa . . . Zulu . . . Papa . . . Quebec . . . Mike . . ."

Allison walked to the door and stared across the stream while Spencer sent the rest of the message.

Nick walked to her side. "Don't worry, he'll be all right."

She turned and exchanged a smile with him. "I wish I could believe that."

CHAPTER TWENTY-SIX

Too low to take his eyes off the terrain and look down at his knee-board, Brad printed the first letter of each word in the phonetic alphabet. When Spencer finished, Austin keyed his mike. "Tabasco copy."

He raised the nose slightly, climbing to 300 feet above the rugged mountains. Brad quickly read the coded information. Two MiG-17s from Gia Lam with side numbers 3014 and 3022. One MiG-17 from Phuc Yen bearing the number 2531. They had one thing in common: red stars on their fuselages.

Monitoring both the discrete frequency and the strike frequency, Brad carefully scanned the horizon to the southeast. If the strike leader was on time, the A-4 Skyhawks would be crossing the shoreline. The radios remained eerily quiet.

When Brad neared Chi Ne, he heard the strike leader call the fighter cover.

"Montana, Rock Crusher Three Oh Three is feet-dry."

"Copy," the F-4 flight leader drawled. "We're orbiting at fifteen thousand."

"Sugarloaf," the Crusader leader called, "is over the Red River at sixteen."

"Roger," the Skyhawk pilot acknowledged, then talked to his flight. "Crushers, arm 'em up."

"Two."

"Three's hot."

"Four."

Craning his neck, Brad searched the cloudy sky for the Phantoms at 15,000 feet. The Target Combat Air Patrol (TARCAP) fighters would be circling in loose combat spread.

Austin armed his cannons and entered the valley west of Nam Dinh. Concentrating on flying low over the river in the valley, Brad listened to the radio calls.

"Rock Crusher, Montana Two Zero Seven has a visual on you."

"Copy."

Austin blasted over a group of boats and rocketed out over the foothills. He noticed a smokestack in the distance as he racked the MiG around in a punishing turn.

"Montana and Sugarloaf, Red Crown on Guard. You have MiG activity, Hanoi one seven zero for thirteen miles."

Red Crown was the U.S. early-warning radar stationed aboard a navy cruiser in the Gulf of Tonkin. The MiGs from Phuc Yen and Gia Lam had remained low to avoid radar detection. The North Vietnamese pilots had popped onto the radar screen when they commenced a zooming climb.

"Sugarloaf, switches hot."

"Two."

Brad felt his pulse quicken as he hurtled back up the narrow valley. He was anxious to intercept the MiGs now that Operation Achilles was underway.

"Montana, switch 'em."

"Two's hot."

Flashing over the boats, Brad saw a number of people wave. *They think they're getting a private air show.*

"Skeeter Four Fifty-three is in," a calm, low voice announced. Skeeter 453 and his wingman were the Crusader pilots assigned to flak suppression. Their job was to pound the air defenses around the target before the bombers commenced their attack.

"Rock Crusher's in hot," the A-4 leader called, rolling into his strike on the supply center.

Raising the nose, Brad flew above the ridge line and looked toward Phu Ly. He saw concentrated streams of red tracers slashing through the sky. A barrage of white, puffy-looking antiaircraft fire saturated the air over the target.

A few moments later, Austin saw a flash, followed by a billowing black cloud. *The strike leader sure as hell hit something big.*

Brad checked his fuel gauge and lowered the nose, skirting close to the ridge line. His thoughts turned to timing his attack to coincide with the confusion of the initial aerial engagements.

"Two's in."

Brad listened to the attack pilots while he maneuvered through the valley.

"Bandits!" someone called. "We've got MiGs at one o'clock, eight miles, climbing!"

"Patience," Austin said to himself. "You've got to be patient . . . for this to work."

"Montana has a tally! Stroke the burners!"

Inching his throttles forward, Brad rechecked his cannon switches. All he had to do was squeeze the trigger when he got a MiG in his gunsight.

"Paul, take the one on the left!"

Brad recognized the drawl of the Phantom leader.

"I've got him!" a strained voice replied, then added, "I'm overshooting—goin' high!"

Banking toward the aerial engagement, Brad listened to the garbled radio calls. The strike aircraft had completed their attack and were exiting the target area. Large columns of dense smoke were rising into the air over Phu Ly.

"Sugarloaf has a tally! Four at two o'clock!"

"High or low?" the wingman queried.

"Slightly low—breaking into us!"

"Got 'em!"

Brad tweaked the nose up, searching for the other fighters. He swiveled his head from side to side, unsure if he was heading in the right direction.

"I've got a tone," the F-4 wingman shouted.

Feeling a moment of indecisiveness, Brad checked for aircraft behind his MiG. Relieved to see empty sky, he turned his head at the instant an orange-and-black fireball erupted four miles in front of him.

"I got him!" the Phantom pilot exclaimed. "I got him!"

Brad saw the burning remains of the MiG spin crazily toward the foothills. He slapped the stick to the left and started a tight 360-degree turn. Austin did not want to become entangled in the middle of a multiple-aircraft fight. His mission was to seek out and destroy pre-selected MiGs.

"Sugar Two is hit! I'm disengaging!"

Brad listened to the frantic call and quelled his instinct to help the F-8 pilot.

"Jim, go for the beach!" the Crusader flight leader barked. "Your six is clear!"

"Copy! Where is he?"

"Diving for the deck. How's your fuel?"

"Okay for now," the wingman paused, "but I'm losing my hydraulics."

"Hang in."

Completing his turn, Brad was startled to see a MiG-17 flash past his right wing. *Where the hell did he come from?* A second later, Austin caught the blurred image of a Phantom as it sliced over his cockpit. He would recognize the distinctive planform anywhere.

"Oh, shit . . ." Brad swore softly, then mumbled to himself, "How did this happen?" He selected afterburner and searched the sky.

"Dash Two," the F-4 leader blurted, "you've got a seventeen on your nose."

Brad looked through the windscreen and spotted the oncoming Phantom. Pulling into the vertical, Brad saw the F-4's nose rise to match the MiG.

"I've got him," the wingman assured his section leader.

Both aircraft shot straight up, gaining thousands of feet while the airspeeds rapidly decayed.

With his head tilted back, Brad looked at the Phantom crew. He watched the pilot, hoping that he would drop the F-4's nose before both aircraft stalled.

The MiG was almost out of kinetic energy when the Phantom pilot, afraid that he might lose control of the fighter, snapped the nose down. Brad rudder-rolled the MiG and pulled into a firing position on the F-4.

"Montana," the Phantom pilot gasped, "I've got a MiG on my six . . . right on my ass!"

Brad watched the F-4 accelerate away in full burner.

"Go for separation," the Phantom leader shouted. "I'm coming around."

Watching the wingman go supersonic, Brad reefed the MiG into a hard nose-low turn. Austin caught sight of the other F-4 at the same time the wingman called.

"Lead," he said in a calmer voice, "I'm reengaging the son of a bitch."

"Negative," drawled the flight leader, "I've got him."

Caught in the deadly vise, Brad dived for the deck. He pressed the airspeed to 430 knots, then shallowed his descent. His only hope was that neither of the Phantom pilots could get their missiles to lock on in the ground clutter.

"Watch the bastard," the wingman cautioned as the lead F-4 closed rapidly on the slower MiG. "He's good."

Heading straight for Hanoi, Brad could feel the perspiration soaking his cheeks. He leveled at 30 feet and screamed over a highway. Brad raised the nose and glanced behind him. The Phantom was overtaking him at an alarming rate.

"I can't get a steady tone," Montana Lead complained, "but when I get close enough, I'm gonna kick off a couple of 'Winders."

Brad frantically craned his neck. The F-4 pilot, flying faster than the speed of sound, was almost on him. Instinctively, Brad simultaneously snapped the throttle to idle, deployed the speed brakes, and cross-controlled the aircraft. The MiG shuddered and rapidly decelerated as Brad continued straight on course.

"What the shit!" the flight leader shouted, finally recognizing the overshoot. He did not want to fly out in front of the MiG.

"I told you he was good," the wingman radioed, pulling up into a high yo-yo.

The flight leader yanked his power back and deployed the speed brakes. "Check my six, while I get this asshole."

Watching the F-4 rapidly close, Brad pulled up in a displacement roll.

"Shit," the wingman shouted. "What the fuck is he doing?"

The Phantom leader sucked the speed brakes in and went into afterburner. "I'm going to nail his ass . . . if I have to run over him."

Brad retracted the speed brakes and selected burner while the Phantoms maneuvered for another shot.

Continuing straight ahead, Brad watched the two F-4s join in loose combat spread. They turned in from his eight o'clock position, flying on the deck.

"I'm going to shoot a 'Winder," Montana 207 drawled, "regardless if I get a tone."

Brad counted the seconds, then keyed his mike. "Montana flight, break right! Break right!"

Both Phantoms snapped over into knife-edge flight and turned hard right.

"MiGs! MiGs!" Austin radioed. "Ten south, cutting you off from your five o'clock!"

"Say again, Red Crown," the F-4 leader demanded. There was audible confusion in the request.

"Red Crown," the radar controller declared in an even voice, "did not broadcast a MiG call."

Brad continued toward Hanoi while the confusion persisted.

"This is Montana Lead," the harsh voice fumed. "Who called MiGs?"

The radios remained silent.

"Skeeter, you up?" Montana 207 asked.

"That's affirm," the Crusader pilot said curtly, "but we didn't call MiGs."

"Goddamnit, Red Crown," the Phantom pilot said angrily, "what the hell is going on?"

Gaining separation, Brad began to breathe easier. He climbed a hundred feet and forced himself to be calm.

"Montana, Red Crown did not—repeat—did not broadcast a MiG call." The normally pleasant voice sounded annoyed.

A moment later, the EC-121 Constellation radar-surveillance aircraft over northern Laos called the bewildered F-4 pilot.

"Montana Two Zero Seven, Disco. We've got the transmission on tape."

"Roger that."

Brad was watching the skyline of Hanoi approach when Red Crown again broadcast.

"Montana and Skeeter flights," he began hastily, pausing for another radar sweep, "you've got activity bearing zero two zero, your position . . . coming out of the Hanoi area."

"How many?" the Phantom pilot snapped.

Starting a shallow climb, Brad searched the sky for MiGs. He spotted three MiG-19s four miles east of his location.

The controller waited until he had confirmed the initial radar image. "I show four targets south of Gia Lam, and I'm picking up three returns six miles in-trail."

"Copy," Montana 207 replied, then added, "Red Crown, get the closest BARCAP up our freq."

"Stand by."

Remaining low to avoid detection, Brad turned to parallel the three MiGs Red Crown had detected. A few seconds passed before he heard the barrier combat air-patrol flight leader.

"Montana, Ragtime Two Oh Four with you."

"Ah, Ragtime." He paused. "Tally! I've got a tally at twelve, level!"

His wingman spotted the four MiG-17s. "I've got 'em!"

"Ragtime," the Phantom leader said excitedly, "we need you in here."

Brad scanned ahead of the MiG-19s and caught sight of the four MiGs Montana had located.

"Ragtime," Red Crown radioed, "steer three zero zero."

"We're buster three double oh," the F-4 BARCAP leader replied, selecting afterburner. Buster meant expedite.

Easing back on the power, Brad watched the Phantoms engage the four MiG-17s. One section of MiGs broke left, while the other two aircraft began a weave.

"We're going after the ones to our left," the Phantom leader grunted under the heavy g force.

"Montana, Red Crown," the controller said urgently, "you've got bandits closing from your four o'clock, five miles."

"Roger," came the terse reply.

Brad could see that the MiG-19s were going to be in a perfect position to attack the outnumbered Phantoms. He applied full power, accelerated to 390 knots, then raised the nose. *This is going to be a cluster fuck.*

"Paul," the F-4 leader groaned, "disengage—disengage to the southeast."

"Montana, Red Crown. I show another bandit closing from the northwest! He just popped up!"

Brad knew the controller was referring to his MiG. He was equally sure that the North Vietnamese pilots were being informed of his presence.

Two of the MiG-19s turned toward Brad, recognized the lone MiG-17, then reversed to pursue the hapless Phantoms.

"Montana, Ragtime has a tally!"

Brad heard the desperate pilot click his mike twice.

"Montana, break hard starboard," the BARCAP section leader instructed, "and we'll have 'em bottled up."

"Roger!"

Brad saw the two F-4s snap over at the same time the Ragtime flight leader fired a Sparrow radar-controlled missile. The MiGs scattered in various directions. Their ground controllers had obviously informed them about the Phantoms approaching at supersonic speed.

Snatching the stick into his lap, Brad hauled the MiG around in a gut-wrenching circle. He spotted a lone MiG-17 diving for the ground.

"Ragtime, Montana is down to four point six on fuel. We've gotta hit the tanker."

"Copy. The gomers are running out, so we'll rendezvous on your port side."

"Bring 'em aboard," Montana 207 acknowledged. "Red Crown, give us a steer for the Whale."

The Whale was a carrier-based KA-3B twin-engine refueling aircraft.

"The tanker is one one zero," the controller paused, "for a hundred and fourteen."

"SAMs!" Montana warned. "We've got two SAMs at three o'clock. Take 'em down!"

Austin risked a quick look. He saw the billowing trail of the two surface-to-air missiles, but could not locate the F-4s. One streak of fire continued to accelerate through the hundreds of tracer rounds, while the other flashed brightly into a mushrooming black-and-orange explosion.

Brad cringed. *Sweet Jesus.*

"Ragtime Two is down!" the flight leader shouted in anguish. "They took a direct hit!"

"Any chutes?" Montana called. "Paul, you guys see any chutes?"

"Negative," came the sad reply. "They didn't get out."

With the throttle to the stop, Brad checked his fuel gauge as he gained on the lone MiG-17. He saw another MiG in the distance, but the aircraft was slowly angling away.

Coasting into position on the MiG's starboard wing, Brad was startled to see three red stars painted on the fuselage. The numbers 3014 on the nose of the fighter corresponded with the first set of numbers he had copied. He was astounded by his close proximity to the enemy pilot.

Alerted by a ground radar site, the MiG pilot turned to look at Brad. The North Vietnamese airman raised his goggles and tapped his right earphone.

Austin pointed to his helmet next to his left ear and shook his head no.

With a toothy smile, the Communist pilot cocked his head and nodded his understanding. His new wingman's radio was not functioning properly.

Skirting the edge of a band of cumulus clouds, the North Vietnamese pilot descended rapidly.

Drifting backward, Brad steeled himself and moved swiftly to center the gun sight on the MiG's fuselage and right wing root. *How am I going to feel after deliberately shooting this guy in the back?* With the gun-sight pipper centered at the trailing edge of the wing, Brad held his breath and squeezed the trigger.

The cannons emitted a stream of molten lead as the shells ripped into the fuselage and tore through the cockpit and canopy. Debris flew off the stricken fighter and flashed past Austin's aircraft.

Brad released the trigger and watched the MiG trail black smoke, nose over and roll inverted, then fly straight into the ground. The explosion and blinding fireball mesmerized him while he yanked the stick over.

Banking steeply, Brad dove and hugged the ground as he raced for the Laotian border.

He switched to the discrete frequency for Alpha-29, resisting the temptation to talk to someone. The more he thought about the cold-blooded killing, the more it twisted his insides. Brad tried to rationalize the act by persuading himself that the MiG pilot would have killed him under the same circumstances. Besides, many former fighter aces gained many of their kills by approaching from behind and below their adversaries. The victims never knew what hit them.

Thundering along the jagged mountaintops, Brad attempted to concentrate on flying the airplane. He finally faced the reality of his act. He had been trained to kill the enemy in any manner possible, and he had vanquished another MiG. Brad would not receive credit for the kill, but he felt the satisfaction of knowing the North Vietnamese pilot would not be adding a fourth red star to his airplane.

Threading his way through the cumulonimbus buildups, Brad ran through his landing checklist. After establishing his position on the chart, he commenced a shallow descent, then lowered his flaps and landing gear.

The visibility between the towering clouds was becoming a concern as he neared the base. Brad wondered if the UH-34 was still orbiting

Muong Lat. Unsure of the location of the helicopter, Brad decided to break radio silence. The last thing he needed was a midair collision with the UH-34.

"Sleepy Two Five, say posit."

A long pause followed, tempting Brad to call again.

"About twenty due east of the field," Rudy Jimenez finally responded.

"Copy," Brad replied with relief. "No factor." He needed to talk with Spencer about coordinating his return with that of the helicopter. A simple one-word call, with an acknowledgment from the UH-34 pilots, would suffice.

Two miles from the runway, Austin reduced power and stabilized his approach speed. He remembered what Spencer had said about trying to go around after he committed himself to land. If he overshot the runway, Brad would have to eject before the MiG plowed into the steep mountainside at the far end of the field.

Brad deployed the speed brakes and settled into a low, flat approach to the runway, aiming for the grass overrun. He knew the MiG would float in ground-effect when he flared to land. The cushion of air would carry him to the runway.

Passing through thirty feet, Brad reduced the throttle to idle and gently walked the rudder pedals in an attempt to slow the fighter.

The MiG touched the macadam sixty feet from the end and Brad quickly lowered the nose. He stepped firmly on the brakes.

What the shit is wrong?

The left brake was soft. Hurtling down the short runway, Brad pressed hard against the right brake until the MiG slewed toward the right side of the narrow strip.

"Easy," Austin said to himself, letting off the pressure to correct the heading.

Brad rapidly thumbed the air valve on the stick while he pressed and released the right brake. The tire began to skid intermittently as the MiG rapidly neared the end of the landing strip.

Correcting far to the left, Brad stood on the right brake and skidded into the grass overrun.

The MiG bounced, swung to the right, and ground to a halt.

"Beautiful," Brad said disgustedly as he added power to complete the turn. Standing on the right brake, he noticed the audience that had gathered to watch the landing. *That must have impressed them.*

When he reached the macadam, Brad was surprised to hear Hank Murray's voice over the radio.

"Austin, the right brake is smoking," Murray said excitedly. "Taxi slowly to the end and turn around and taxi back. I don't want that brake to seize."

What an ignominious arrival. "I'll taxi to the end, but you can tow it back. The left brake isn't working."

CHAPTER TWENTY-SEVEN

Brad left his helmet in the steamy cockpit and clambered onto the wing. He slid off and inspected the smoking brake, then walked to the other wheel.

Finding nothing obvious, Brad turned toward the Quonset hut. He saw Allison and Nick hurrying down the runway.

Austin unzipped his Soviet-style flight suit, slipped his arms out, and tied the sleeves around his waist.

"How'd it go?" Palmer asked, glancing at the helicopter as it passed over the MiG. "Did you have any luck?"

"I got one, but it isn't as easy as everyone thought it was going to be," Brad replied in a tired voice. "We're going to have to discuss strategy."

"We were relieved," Allison said with a tightness in her throat, "to hear your voice."

Brad looked at her for a second, then smiled. "We had better huddle with Cap and sort through a few miscalculations on our part."

The steady hum of the fan masked the conversation between Spencer and Murray when Austin held the screen door open for Allison and Nick. Brad tossed a casual wave to the helicopter crewmen.

The debrief was already in progress when the trio sat down.

"Did you have any success?" Spencer nervously asked. He was unusually hesitant.

"Yes," Brad answered mechanically. "The People's Army of Vietnam Air Force is shy one pilot with three kills to his credit."

"No shit?" Chase Mitchell blurted with undisguised excitement. "You got a gomer?"

"Yes," Brad said stiffly, "but not without a close call," he paused to catch Spencer's eye, "that may have jeopardized our operation."

A long silence followed.

Spencer's face was devoid of expression. "What happened?"

Brad explained what had happened, including the last resort tactic that he had been forced to use to get the Phantoms off his tail.

Murray gave Austin a grave look and challenged him. "Why didn't you use the smoke canister? We spent a helluva lot of time engineering it to give you a way out if . . ." He trailed off, seeing Brad's features harden.

"Captain," Austin began patiently, as if explaining something to a child, "it isn't very convincing—turning on smoke—when no one has shot anything at you."

Murray's chubby face flushed as an uneasy quiet settled over the room.

Spencer broke the silence, erasing the tiny smile etched in the corner of his mouth. "Brad, we didn't hear you say anything over the strike frequency."

Having vented his ire, Austin's expression softened. "I was too low . . . right on the deck. If I had been at ten or fifteen thousand, you would have been able to hear me."

Brad shifted, suddenly uncomfortable in the flight suit. "I know Red Crown and Disco have it on tape, because Disco told the F-4 leader."

Spencer rested his elbows on the table and pressed his fingertips against each other. "Well, it may or may not be a problem. We'll have to see what develops."

"Cap, I'm not kidding," Brad declared in an attempt to convince him of the seriousness of the incident. "The F-4 pilot was a second away from hosing me when I yelled for his flight to break. He was madder than a Tasmanian devil."

Spencer showed no emotion.

"Also," Brad continued uneasily, "the North Vietnamese radar controllers know that an aircraft they could not communicate with," he hesitated as Nick nodded in understanding, "flew next to one that crashed. I dropped off their radar at the same time the other MiG hit the ground."

"Well," Hank Murray ventured, clearly irritated by the pilot, "they may believe that both of you were shot down."

Brad calmed himself in an effort to be respectful. "Perhaps I didn't point out one important factor."

Murray glared at him.

"The North Vietnamese controllers," Brad said evenly, "could see that the American planes were going in the opposite direction."

Brad felt the stares from around the table. "The people in those radar shacks were communicating with the pilot after I joined on his wing to see the side number." He stopped and turned to Murray. "What do you suppose he told them . . . Captain?"

Murray was flustered. "That was pretty stupid on your part, along with talking on the radio."

Spencer started to speak, but Brad waved him off. Everyone sat in stunned silence, waiting for the explosion.

"Captain Murray," Brad said evenly, "I yelled for the Phantoms on my ass to break because of a primal instinct. I wanted to live."

Brad's voice dropped as he fixed Murray in his gaze. "After that experience, maybe I wasn't thinking clearly . . . and I offer no excuse. But, with your wealth of combat flying experience, you would naturally have done something else . . . right?"

Murray turned beet-red. "You're flirting with insubordination."

Spencer rose from his chair. "We're going to take a break, so I'll see all of you after dinner."

The tension in the room slowly dissipated as chairs were pushed back. Allison and the three pilots gave Austin and Spencer quiet glances while Murray flashed Brad a warning look.

"Brad," Spencer said firmly, "I need to go over an operational question with you."

"Yes, sir," he answered, concealing his anger. *Why is that son of a bitch sitting in on the operational briefings? His job is simply to oversee the airworthiness of the fighter.*

Allison knew Hollis Spencer well enough to follow the group out of the building.

"Pull a chair over," Spencer said as he slipped behind his desk and placed his pipe on top.

Brad complied, feeling drained from the emotional strain of aerial combat.

Spencer reached into a bottom drawer and extracted a half-empty bottle of bourbon. He placed it on the top of the desk and put an empty coffee mug in front of Brad.

"Help yourself." Spencer forced a smile, then reached for his pipe. Brad looked skeptical. "Cap, I don't need any booze."

"Relax," Spencer encouraged, "and have a drink." He lighted his pipe and reached for a paper cup on the counter behind him. "In fact, I'll have one with you."

Reaching for the bottle, Brad hesitated before pouring a few ounces of the bourbon in the mug.

"Tell me something," Spencer leaned forward for the bottle, "what do you really think about this operation . . . after what you experienced today?"

Brad looked at the mug for a moment before shifting his gaze to Spencer. "It has merit, but I believe we are going about it in the wrong way."

"How so?"

"The idea of trying to be selective in our pursuit, in my judgment, isn't feasible."

The project officer took that criticism in stride. "Do you think the operation has been compromised?"

"No question," Brad replied, forgetting the bourbon. "I made a mistake, and I'm sure there are going to be a number of questions raised when our folks listen to the tapes."

Spencer glanced through the screen door at the MiG as it was towed past the Quonset hut. "What would you suggest we do?"

Brad thought about the situation. If the administration wanted to keep the operation secret, Spencer was going to have to be cautious and more conservative.

"Cap, I would stand down for a couple of days, and see what filters down the pipeline."

"I agree." Spencer tasted the warm bourbon. "If this operation is exposed, heads are going to roll in Langley . . . and I might as well kiss my ass good-bye."

"In my estimation," Brad advised in a respectful manner, "the best we can do is disrupt and confuse the MiG pilots, and take them out if the opportunity presents itself . . . without compromising the operation."

Spencer nodded in agreement. "Trying to selectively kill their aces is too ambitious, huh?"

"I know you spooks work in mysterious ways," Brad ventured a smile, "but this is stretching it fairly thin."

Spencer leaned back and studied the ceiling for a period of time.

"What would you suggest we change?" he asked without taking his eye off the overhead light.

"I would keep the MiG low, to keep from being detected by radar, and pick off any stragglers," Austin paused, "or targets of opportunity that I could find . . . regardless of their side number."

"Keep it simple?" Spencer turned the statement into a question.

"Well," Brad responded cautiously, "I wouldn't call sneaking around North Vietnam in a MiG a simple project."

"That's true." Spencer swirled the amber liquid in his cup and tossed back the entire contents.

"Brad, let me pose a question to you," Spencer mused while the bourbon warmed his throat.

"Yes, sir."

Austin watched Spencer's expression. He looked tired and worried. The project officer had somehow changed since his arrival in Laos. There was a tenseness and reserve that Brad had not seen before.

"Hypothetically," Spencer began with a hint of apprehension, "what would you do with the MiG," he turned to Brad, "if you had the final decision?"

The question aroused Brad's suspicion. "You've already told me that when I leave here, I'm on my own." He noticed the strain in Spencer's taut neck muscles.

"What would you most like to do," Spencer asked, pouring another liberal shot of bourbon, "since you're in a MiG without any identification to link you to the United States?"

Brad listened to the whirring blades of the fan while he separated the whole into sections and analyzed each. Hollis Spencer, he thought, wanted him to commit to something without directly asking him.

"From what information I know," Brad declared, "body counts and kill ratios are very important to the administration."

"You're not answering my question."

Brad's mouth felt dry. "I want to get everything into the proper perspective, since I'm not privy to the intel you receive on a regular basis."

"Fair enough."

"If it were left to me," Brad glanced at a relief map of North Vietnam, "I'd use the MiG as a psychological weapon, and increase the kill ratio at the same time."

Spencer nodded.

"What we're trying to do now sounded implausible in California,"

Brad said stiffly, "but I went along because I figured the CIA knew what they were doing."

The project officer shrugged. "A lot of things that are developed in the classroom don't work on the battlefield."

"That's true," Brad agreed, then countered, "but I suspect that you—the Agency—had a broader scheme in mind anyway."

Spencer accepted the statement as a compliment. "Tell me what you have in mind, since we have almost one hundred percent impunity."

Brad did not feel comfortable with Spencer's statement. If he had to eject over enemy territory and the helicopter could not rescue him, it would not take the North Vietnamese long to figure out that he was an impostor.

"Cap, we can have a tremendous effect on their emotions and behavior by shocking the hell out of them."

"I'm listening."

There was an awkward moment of silence while Brad decided to say exactly what he thought.

"I've got an idea that will give us the advantage," Brad confided, "but the Hanoi regime will howl in protest."

Spencer's eyes narrowed as he responded with a taunting inquiry. "What's the culpability factor?"

"Low, if we do it right."

"It better be," Spencer asserted, "because that is the bottom line in the White House. This has to be a covert operation, with no ties to the administration."

A low rumble of thunder distracted Brad for a brief moment. "Cap, if I go in prior to a strike, keeping low to avoid radar, I could strafe at least two airfields while the pilots are manning their aircraft."

Spencer's face brightened. "Or while they're taxiing for takeoff. There would be total surprise."

"That's right," Brad agreed. "You can bet that they will get a major dose of total confusion and distrust . . . and it won't be the last one, if we're careful."

Spencer grabbed the bottle of bourbon. "After I hear from the Warning Star which airfields are active, we can use the helicopter to relay my message to you."

"We'll have to use the helo relay, since I'll be too low to pick up a direct transmission from you."

Feeling a degree of concern, Brad observed Spencer fill the cup to the brim.

"The one thing we have to have," Austin continued, "is instant communications in regard to when the MiG pilots scramble. I damn sure don't want to strafe a field if they already have fighters in the air."

"No, that wouldn't be good."

"It will work, Cap." Brad paused when a flash of lightning and an accompanying thunderclap announced the arrival of a torrential rain-storm.

"They can complain to the world," Brad suggested with a taut smile, "but it's still a MiG-17 that is causing chaos and confusion. The MiG will have to be in a different paint scheme for each flight. We'll strike from different directions, and we'll vary the times between raids . . . from days between attacks to twice in one day."

Spencer beamed with pleasure. "If you happen to shoot someone down who has time to report that he's being attacked by a MiG, it would create even more confusion."

Brad nodded. "They'll experience the entire gamut of emotions—from hostility to confusion, to betrayal, to knowing they're being had—and can't do much about it, unless they maintain a combat air patrol from daylight to dusk."

"I like the idea." Spencer took a swig of bourbon and sighed. "A MiG shooting up MiG bases, and no one can prove who is doing it."

"Unless I get shot down," Brad added, glancing at the deluge of water cascading off the small roof over the door. "Cap, when pilots are confused and forced to constantly look over their shoulder, they aren't as sharp and focused as they would like to be."

"Which means," Spencer suggested, "that our pilots can take advantage of the confusion to increase the kill ratios."

Without blinking his eyes, Brad stared at Spencer while the rain pounded the Quonset hut. "Precisely."

CHAPTER TWENTY-EIGHT

Due to a lack of sleep, exhaustion was beginning to sap Brad's energy. He found it hard to maintain interest even in his own recommendations for strafing enemy air bases. The excessive humidity and sweltering heat had made sleeping almost impossible. He had also lost his appetite.

Brad watched a small spider crawl across the top of the tent. He wondered what Leigh Ann was thinking about their relationship. Brad hoped to have some mail from her waiting for him at the Constellation Hotel in Vientiane when he returned.

Outside the sagging tent, Hank Murray supervised the replacement of the right main-gear tire on the MiG. It had been flat-spotted when the brake locked several times during Austin's landing incident.

The MiG's camouflage paint scheme had been repainted and the last two of the four numbers on the nose had been changed. The fighter now appeared to be silver-gray.

During the wait for a replacement tire to be flown to the airfield, Nick and Brad had played gin rummy for hours, discussing the strafing tactics they were going to employ. Palmer had agreed with Brad's theory and was looking forward to flying a mission.

Allison and Hollis Spencer had spent a number of hours arranging the change in strategy, then forwarding the request to Langley. Everyone was waiting impatiently for a response to the request to strike the enemy airfields with the MiG.

Brad turned on his side and propped his head in the palm of his hand. Nick was lying on his stomach with his arms and head hanging over the end of the cot. He was carefully examining a photograph of the Playmate of the Month.

"Nick."

Palmer turned the page. "Don't bother me when I'm trying to solve Einstein's unified field theory."

"If you could be anywhere right now," Brad covered his mouth to conceal a yawn, "where would you pick?"

Nick pondered the question. "At Mustin Beach, Friday-afternoon happy hour, holding a chilled martini, and surrounded by a half-dozen women." The Mustin Beach Officers' Club in Pensacola, Florida, is a naval aviation landmark.

Austin heard Spencer's voice and sat upright while Palmer flipped his magazine aside.

"We haven't got the word to strafe the fields yet," Spencer informed them when he entered the cluttered tent, "but we've got a mission laid on for tomorrow."

Brad and Nick remained quiet, silently guessing the details of the next flight.

"Nick, I want you to fly this one."

Palmer nodded his acknowledgment.

Spencer gave each pilot a brief look. "As soon as you get dressed, come on over and we'll go over the latest information we have. From what we know right now, tomorrow is going to be an eventful day."

When the project officer left, Brad and Nick slipped into their self-tailored flight suits.

"Brad," Palmer pulled the edge of the tent flap open and looked at the Quonset hut, "have you noticed a recent change in Spencer?"

"Yes," Austin answered, zipping the front of his flight suit closed. "It's the pressure, and I suspect there is more to this operation than he has told us."

Palmer looked puzzled. "What do you mean?" he asked with a hasty look. "Do you know something that I don't?"

"No, not really," Brad confided while he thought about Spencer's subtle but steady personality change. "I can only guess at the various strategies that have been discussed for using the MiG, but I suspect this operation is a make-or-break point in Cap's career."

Nick placed his revolver in his shoulder holster. "What do you really think they—the CIA people—are going to do with the MiGs they acquire?"

"Probably the same thing I suggested," Brad chuckled softly, "but on a larger scale."

"How so?"

Brad bent to tie his boots. "If they can get their hands on a number of MiGs, why not use them to raise hell with the enemy's air force?" Austin continued before Palmer could answer. "Especially if the pilots don't carry identification . . . and the chances of their long-term survival are nil."

"Yeah," Palmer agreed with a wry grin. "The gomers—out of desperation at some point—would end up shooting down each other."

"Let me tell you something," Brad lowered his voice, "that Allison told me on the flight from Hong Kong."

Palmer's eyes narrowed. "This should be juicy."

"She said that U.S. Air Force pilots are flying T-28s for the CIA on missions over Laos."

Nick looked at him with a degree of skepticism. "You're shitting me?"

"No, I'm not kidding," Brad countered. "Apparently, the CIA can't find enough qualified pilots to support their secret war against the Communists, so they're dipping into the military . . . just like our situation."

"Unbelievable," Palmer uttered.

"Allison explained," Austin said clearly, "that the pilots' air force records are placed in some type of limbo file while they are on loan to the CIA . . . and they're paid in cash—same as us. If they get shot down, they will be carried as missing in action over Vietnam."

Nick was speechless for a moment. "How in the hell is the CIA keeping their war from the public? And why would she tell you about it?"

"According to Allison," Brad answered with a shrug, "*The New York Times* has stumbled onto the operation, and the *Washington Post* is hot on the trail."

Austin reached for his M-16. "I suppose she told me . . . because that's her way of showing me that she trusts me."

"Well, it's going to get interesting," Nick replied with a straight face, then glanced at his watch. "We better get over to the briefing."

They went to the water cistern and had a long drink before entering the Quonset hut.

Allison greeted them with a faint smile and lighted a cigarette. Brad noticed that her fingers trembled with an unusual clumsiness.

"Gentlemen," Spencer began hastily, "we're going to do the same thing on this trip." He looked at Palmer. "Stay low and see if you can pick off a MiG or two."

Spencer turned his attention to Austin. "Your plan is still being reviewed at Langley, so all we can do is wait and see what they decide."

A radio call prompted Allison to go into the small communications room.

"The air force," Spencer advised, pointing to the chart Allison had prepared, "is going to hit a target right here, halfway between Thai Nguyen and Hanoi."

Brad studied the map. "It looks like they're going after the railroad that parallels the road north of Phuc Yen."

"That may be true," Spencer agreed, "but we don't know the exact target. We know the time of the strike, along with the route the F-105s will follow to the target area." The F-105 Thunderchief, affectionately known as the Thud, was a supersonic fighter-bomber.

"Right down Thud Ridge," Palmer observed as he traced the line of flight north of Yen Bai, then down to the target area. "They're probably coming out of Takhli."

Spencer gave the chart a fleeting look. "I don't know if they're from Takhli or the Avis Wing at Korat, and it doesn't make any difference."

Both pilots sensed the growing impatience in Spencer. His behavior was definitely changing.

"Nick," Spencer explained, tapping the map with a pen, "you're going to orbit along the west side of the Black River near Song Huan."

Palmer examined the terrain.

"Cap," Brad said with a look of concern, "we better have the helicopter stationed farther north if Nick is going over by Thud Ridge."

"I agree." He hesitated, straining to hear Allison as her voice rose. "After talking with Chase and Rudy, I've decided to have them orbit near Chieng Pan."

Allison appeared from behind the partition. "Langley sent the word that we'll have an answer about strafing within twenty-four hours."

GULF OF TONKIN

The carrier was steaming in an elongated pattern around Yankee Station when Lex Blackwell arrived in the COD. He had been informed by the copilot that the air-wing commander had the pilots standing by on the hangar deck.

Blackwell went belowdeck and walked forward in the hangar bay. He was greeted enthusiastically and delivered his MiG brief, then answered questions for fifteen minutes.

After the brief was completed, a thin, long-limbed fighter pilot approached Blackwell and introduced himself.

"Lex, I'm Ev Wetherbee," drawled the lieutenant commander.

Blackwell instinctively looked at the rectangular insignia on the left side of the pilot's flight suit. Below the gold wings, Lex read:

Evert "Ev" Wetherbee
Montana
LCDR   USN

"Have you got a minute?" the Phantom pilot inquired with a friendly smile.

"Yes, sir," Blackwell replied politely.

"I'd like to ask you a few questions," Wetherbee declared, "if you don't mind going to my stateroom."

"Sure thing," Lex said with a look of confusion.

The rangy pilot caught Blackwell's expression. "I'll explain when we get to my stateroom."

"Okay," Lex responded, and followed Wetherbee down a ladder and through a maze of passageways to his room.

"Have a seat," the Phantom pilot offered, gesturing toward the bottom bunk.

Blackwell sat down while Wetherbee sat at his desk.

"For the past few weeks," Wetherbee began with a sense of wariness, "we've heard rumors that the CIA—actually, Air America—has an operational MiG."

Lex was caught off guard, but kept from showing any sign of surprise. It was virtually impossible to keep anything secret in naval aviation. The small community had always been tight-knit and open with each other.

"Is that true?" Wetherbee asked bluntly.

Blackwell guarded his answer. "Well," he drawled, "I don't know anything about that. All I know is that the operational and technical information came from a MiG-17 pilot who defected from an Eastern bloc country."

Wetherbee stared at Lex for a moment. "I had an interesting experience a few days ago," he reached for a tape recorder, "that I'd like to share with you. By the way, my call sign is Montana."

Lex nodded reluctantly. *What the hell does this guy know, if anything?*

"I was about to stuff a Sidewinder up a MiG-17," he punched on the play button, "when my wingman and I heard this."

"Montana flight, break right! Break right! MiGs! MiGs! Ten south, cutting you off!"

Lex attempted to conceal his initial shock at hearing Brad Austin's voice.

"Say again, Red Crown."

"Red Crown did not broadcast a MiG call."

"This is Montana Lead. Who called MiGs?"

The tape remained silent for a moment before the rest of the recording confirmed that no one had admitted to making the frantic call.

Wetherbee snapped the recorder off and gave Blackwell a cold look. "You seem surprised."

"Well," Lex said innocently, "I am surprised, but I'd have to speculate that the gomers have at least one English-speakin' pilot . . . probably educated in the States."

Wetherbee gave him a dubious look. "Or the CIA is screwing around with a MiG flown by an American pilot."

"I guess that's always a possibility," Lex countered, thinking about a way to contact Hollis Spencer and tell him the truth. *They're onto you, and I'm being forced to lie about it.* "But I don't work for the CIA, so I wouldn't know the answer to that. My job is to pass along the gouge about the capabilities of the MiG-17."

Ev Wetherbee was unconvinced, and it showed in his suspicious smile and unblinking stare.

CHAPTER TWENTY-NINE

When Nick Palmer selected afterburner, Brad and Allison plugged their ears while they watched the beginning of the takeoff roll. A blazing stream of white-hot exhaust gases shot from the tail pipe of the MiG as the wheels bounced roughly over the uneven ground.

The fighter's new silver-gray paint blended perfectly with the leaden-gray overcast. The weather forecast had predicted a seventy percent chance of rain by midmorning.

With the cooler temperature of early morning, Brad was confident that Nick would not have any problem getting safely airborne from the 4,700-foot airstrip.

Allison and Brad watched the MiG slowly gain momentum before it rotated and accelerated low to the ground. Seconds later, with the landing gear transitioning to the up and locked position, Palmer executed a steep, climbing turn.

Brad glanced over his shoulder when Chase Mitchell started the noisy Sikorsky. Rudy Jimenez tossed Allison and Brad a friendly salute and slid his side window closed.

Smiling, Austin returned the gesture and followed Allison into the small operations building. He was very much aware of her physical presence. Brad acknowledged to himself that he was becoming more and more attracted to her.

Sitting in the communications room, Hollis Spencer waited for Palmer to check in on the strike frequency being used by the air force. The Warning Star reconnaissance aircraft would continue to supply the information about the MiG activity at the airfields, but Spencer had decided to ignore the side numbers of the aircraft. At the appropriate time, he hoped, the word would be passed to the CIA observers to stop including the numbers and concentrate on catching the first signs of a fighter scramble.

"Buckboard is up," Palmer reported in a flat, expressionless voice, "and everything looks good."

Spencer adjusted the volume on the auxiliary speaker. "Read you loud and clear, Buckboard."

Nick clicked his mike twice.

"I hope this goes well," Allison commented to no one in particular before she lighted a cigarette.

Brad waited until the clattering UH-34 lifted off and accelerated down the runway.

"Nick's one of the best," Brad assured her, and then quietly sat down. In Austin's mind, he was in the cockpit of the MiG, flying the mission.

"Sleepy Two Five," Jimenez radioed.

"Alpha Two Niner copies you loud and clear," Spencer tersely acknowledged.

Sliding a chart next to him, Brad drew a mental course line from Alpha-29 to Song Huan. Computing the speed of the MiG and the time that had elapsed since takeoff, Brad followed the MiG across the face of the map. *Don't get bagged, Nick.*

Palmer leveled the fighter low over the lush green rain forest and adjusted the elevator trim tab. The low overcast was solid, but the visibility beneath the rain-swollen clouds was reasonable. He compared a prominent mountain peak with the chart on his kneeboard. Exactly on course for his holding point near Song Huan.

Checking the cockpit gauges and indicators, Palmer wondered if the weather would cause the strike to be canceled.

Passing northeast of Chieng Pan, Nick heard Rudy Jimenez in the helicopter.

"Buckboard, activity," the copilot relayed for Hollis Spencer. The *whomp-whomp-whomp* sound of the whirling rotor blades made his voice quiver.

"Buckboard copy," Palmer calmly replied even as he experienced a rush of adrenaline.

Regardless of the weather, the air force was forging ahead. The MiG pilots had been alerted when the sixteen F-105s, flying at 22,000 feet, had passed close to Yen Bai and turned toward Thud Ridge. The fighter-bombers from Korat Air Base, Thailand, would parallel the 5,000-foot-high mountains that led to the Red River Valley.

When Nick approached his orbiting point, the murky overcast forced him to alter course to the north. A few minutes later he passed over the karst west of Song Huan. The eroded limestone sinkholes and caverns provided a sharp contrast to the luxuriant tropical forests.

Palmer finally found a break in the clouds along the ridge line. He whipped the MiG around in a left 270-degree turn and slipped between the overcast and the ridge.

He looked across the expanse of surrounding countryside and decided to move closer to the target area. When the action started, he could not afford to be too far away. Palmer knew that it was in his best interest to hit and run.

"Lance broke out at twelve hundred feet," the flight leader of the first four Thunderchiefs reported to the following flight. "We've got a ragged ceiling around eleven hundred to twelve hundred feet."

"Buick has a copy," the metallic voice responded.

Nick pushed the throttle forward and headed directly toward the airfield at Phuc Yen. He wanted to take advantage of the disorder the first strike would cause.

Passing over the Red River between Viet Tri and Dong Sang, Nick heard the radio chatter erupt in confusion.

"Lance is rolling in."

"SAMs!"

Dense puffs of antiaircraft fire filled the sky.

"Multiple launches!"

"Watch it—one o'clock!"

"Take it dow—" was interrupted when another F-105 pilot attempted to talk at the same time. Surface-to-air missiles were being launched from several locations.

"SAMs at two and nine!"

"Watch out!"

A series of garbled radio transmissions heightened the confusion.

Palmer stared at the target area through the MiG's armored-glass windscreen. The sky below the overcast was ablaze with tracer rounds. He knew that many of the gunners were chained to their guns, which motivated them to achieve a high degree of marksmanship. Nick had never seen such concentrated firepower. The horizon seemed to be illuminated by flashes of lightning.

"MiGs! Three o'clock, coming up!"

"SAM, SAM. Two o'clock!"

The nonstop radio chatter was almost impossible to decipher. Many calls were blocked when a number of pilots attempted to talk at the same time.

"We've got four MiGs at our eight," a high-pitched voice warned. "They're comin' around to our six!"

"Two's hit!"

"Say again!"

Transfixed, Palmer selected afterburner as the MiG blasted over a series of villages and small rice paddies. He could see the workers stop and stare as the fighter swept low over them.

"Who's hit?"

"Carl!" the flight leader barked.

The last pilot, tail-end Charlie, in the first wave of Thuds called clear of the target.

"Lance Zero Four is off the target," the pilot reported briskly.

"Buick is one minute out," the leader of the second four-plane flight replied excitedly.

"Carl, you're on fire!" someone radioed. "Get out of it. Eject before it blows!"

"Negative!" came the agitated reply. "I'm gonna stay with it as long as I can."

"SAM launch, seven o'clock!" another voice chimed in. "Get down—coming hard right!"

"Look out, Duane!"

Nick's eyes darted in every direction, constantly searching for a threat. The sky was solidly peppered with flak.

"See 'em?" a distraught voice shouted.

"No!" someone growled. "Call it again!"

"Duane went in!"

"He get out?"

"Negative—exploded and went straight in!"

Palmer saw a billowing black cloud of smoke rising. He knew it marked the impact point of the Thunderchief.

Detecting a dark blur and a bright light to his right, Palmer scanned the sky. He spotted an F-105 thundering over the Red River. The Thud was trailing a yellow-white sheet of flame from midfuselage to thirty feet behind the tail pipe. *Must be Carl.*

Nick tuned out the chaotic radio calls while he searched for MiGs. A moment later, he saw two Thunderchiefs approaching head-on.

"We've got a MiG at twelve," one of the pilots shouted over the radio.

"Shit," Palmer exclaimed when he saw the left side of one of the Thunderchiefs twinkle. He cringed when the tracer shells from the Vulcan cannon flashed past, followed by the supersonic fighter-bombers.

"Buick is rolling in."

Palmer noticed a trace of fear in the pilot's voice.

A second later, another barrage of surface-to-air missiles and dense cannon fire filled the sky over the target.

"SAM on the nose!" warned the Buick flight leader. "Watch it—right up the pike."

"MiGs! We've got four crossing right to left!"

The radio calls again became unintelligible.

Palmer spotted two MiG-17s in a hard turn. They were closing on an F-105 that had just pulled off the target. Nick turned to track the MiGs, then froze when three MiG-17s descended out of the clouds in front of him.

Nick snatched the stick into his lap in an effort to pass behind the MiGs and reverse into them.

Without warning, the starboard wingman pushed over and dove toward his sanctuary at Phuc Yen.

Palmer snapped the fighter over and closed to firing range on the remaining MiGs. He was about to squeeze the trigger when the two MiGs broke hard right.

Out of the corner of his eye, Nick caught sight of the Thunderchief that had attacked the MiGs. The F-105 pilot fired a burst of shells at the tight-turning aircraft, then reversed toward Palmer.

Nick turned into the Thud and dove under the fighter-bomber. He settled into a trailing position on the fleeing MiGs and frantically searched for the F-105. The aircraft had vanished for the moment.

Palmer steadied the pipper on the wingman and squeezed the trigger. The MiG's cannons vibrated as a streak of fire shot forward to the trailing aircraft. The shells ripped through the wing and fuselage. The MiG immediately began streaming fuel and smoke as the stunned pilot pushed the nose down.

Nick pressed his stick forward and squeezed the trigger again. Shards of metal flew off the damaged MiG as the flight leader came to the realization that a MiG was pumping cannon shells into his wingman.

Palmer hesitated, then again squeezed the trigger. *The game is over. We might as well start strafing airfields and supply ships.*

Flames erupted from under the belly of the fighter at the moment the flight leader began an evasive maneuver to distance himself from the rogue MiG. Palmer pursued the flaming aircraft until the pilot ejected.

Nick savagely snatched the stick back to miss the pilot and searched for the other MiG. *He has to be under me.*

The multiple radio calls from the departing Thunderchiefs were distracting Palmer. He rolled the MiG inverted when he reached the bottom of the overcast.

Nick swore to himself when he saw the MiG flight leader raise the nose to track him. The jet intake appeared to sparkle when the MiG's cannons started spewing 23- and 37-millimeter shells. Nick felt a series of jolts as a number of the rounds impacted the aircraft.

Shoving forward on the stick, Palmer groaned from the force of the negative g's. A continuous stream of red-orange fireballs slashed by the cockpit. Entering the clouds inverted, Nick rolled the aircraft and instinctively scanned the instrument panel.

The attitude indicator, which provided the pilot with an artificial horizon, had failed. The instrument had tumbled, giving Palmer an instant case of vertigo. He pushed the stick forward and looked at the altimeter.

Nick felt a twinge of panic before the MiG emerged from the dark clouds. He raised the nose and racked the aircraft into a steep turn. *Where is that son of a bitch?*

Three-quarters of the way through the turn, Palmer saw the MiG turning into him. Nick pulled with all his strength, then squeezed the trigger and felt a short vibration before the cannons jammed.

"Damnit!" Palmer exclaimed as an F-105 streaked under the two airplanes. He aimed straight at the nose of the approaching MiG and jinked up and down and left and right.

Passing sixty feet apart, Nick rammed the throttle into afterburner and dove for the deck. Palmer kept swiveling his head while he raced across the countryside. Without the use of the cannons, he was helpless to defend himself. He heard another flight of four Thunderchiefs roll into their attack.

After a minute that seemed more like an eternity, Nick started to relax and pulled back the power. He flinched when a battle-damaged Thunderchief passed him off the left wing and then shot straight up through the ragged clouds.

CHAPTER THIRTY

Brad Austin inspected the low overcast and fought the temptation to check his watch. He looked the length of the runway and prayed for Palmer. The MiG would be running low on fuel by this time, and the weather at Alpha-29 was growing worse by the minute.

After a short conversation with two of the security men, Brad walked toward the Quonset hut. Although he tried to force himself to think positively, a gnawing concern about Palmer would not go away.

Allison rushed out of the building when Austin approached the entrance.

"We heard from Nick," she announced exuberantly.

"Good," Brad said casually. The nonchalant reply was an effort to conceal his overwhelming relief.

After a long look at the dark clouds, Austin joined Allison and Hollis Spencer in the cramped communications post.

"How far out is he?" Brad asked while he and Allison sat down beside Spencer.

"I'm not sure," Spencer answered with a look of concern. "He's trapped on top and unsure of his position."

Austin realized that if Palmer was flying above a solid deck of clouds and could not find an opening to descend through, he would not have a way to locate the airfield. Without a homing device to guide him to Alpha-29, Nick would have to rely on visually sighting the runway.

"Cap," Brad said, formulating a plan, "how much fuel does he have left?"

Spencer keyed his mike. "Buckboard, say fuel state."

The speaker remained quiet for a long moment.

"Fifteen to twenty minutes," Palmer responded at last, "if the gauges are accurate."

Brad grabbed a chart. "Where's the helo?"

"Sleepy Two Five," Spencer radioed, "how far out are you?"

"Ah . . . Two Five is approximately fifteen miles out," Rudy Jimenez stated. "We're barely maintaining VFR."

The weather was making it difficult for the helicopter crew to fly by visual-flight rules.

"Cap, let me talk to them," Austin said hastily.

Spencer gave Brad a questioning look, then handed him the headset. "What have you got in mind?"

"Let me set it in motion," Austin declared while he adjusted the bulky headset, "and then I'll explain."

Spencer nodded and looked at Allison.

She shrugged and turned her attention to Brad.

"Buckboard and Sleepy, this is Alpha Two Nine, copy?"

"Roger," Palmer answered.

"Copy," Jimenez replied, recognizing Brad's voice.

Austin hid his uneasiness. "Two Five, when you reach the field, can you climb on top?"

"Buckboard, what are the tops?" Jimenez asked coolly.

"It's varied," Palmer informed them while he surveyed the layers of thick clouds, "but I'd say around fifty-five hundred to six thousand . . . in the general direction of the field."

Rudy and Chase Mitchell conferred for a moment.

"Sleepy Two Five," Jimenez explained, "can get on top, but we can't guarantee that we'll be directly over the field."

Brad thought for a second. "That's okay. If Buckboard can get a visual on you, I can work him from the sound of his engine . . . the same for you."

There was a pause at the same time Spencer gave Brad a doubtful look.

"You must dream in technicolor," Jimenez said with a trace of sarcasm.

Austin ignored the remark. "Two Five, have you got flares?"

"That's affirm."

"When you break out on top," Brad continued, "pop a flare every thirty seconds."

"Wilco."

Slowing to think, Brad keyed the mike. "Buckboard, when you're directly overhead—I'll call it by sound—I want you to go outbound on runway heading for one minute, do a procedure turn to the left, then let down when you turn inbound."

"A homemade approach," Palmer grumbled.

Austin could tell Nick's confidence was slipping away at a rate equal to his fuel consumption. "Descend until you break out."

"Or crash," Palmer replied in a flat voice.

"That's the best I can do," Brad said evenly, then added, "on the spur of the moment."

"What's the ceiling?" Palmer queried. "There's a lot of rocks in these clouds."

"Stand by," Austin said mechanically and yanked off the headset. He rushed outside and examined the overcast, noting that it was beginning to rain.

Returning to the radio compartment, Austin was surprised when Spencer confronted him.

"Brad, this is crazy," he said emphatically. "You're going to kill him if he can't find a hole to get under this stuff. And getting the helo down is not going to be an easy task."

Austin spoke slowly. "We shouldn't have launched him in the first place, since the forecast looked like shit."

"That's past history," Spencer retaliated in self-defense. "And not your responsibility, if you recall."

Allison tensed and reached for her cigarettes.

"Let's let Nick make the decision," Brad offered bluntly, "since it's his life."

"Fair enough." Spencer gestured to the headset.

Austin sat down and replaced the earphones. He would give Palmer the current ceiling and visibility, then let Nick make the decision.

"Buckboard, we've got approximately four hundred over, with light rain," he paused, "and the vis is at least three-quarters of a mile."

Brad caught Allison's pained look.

"We can try the approach," Brad said with as much confidence as he could muster, "or I'll attempt to vector you over the field . . . and you can jump out."

Austin heard the helicopter race across the runway and begin a steep climb.

After a long silence, the speaker came alive.

"I sure as hell hope your ears have a good sense of direction," Palmer's voice cut through the soggy air, "because I'm not inclined to jettison the airplane."

"Buckboard," Jimenez interrupted, "Sleepy is over the field, climbing with everything pegged."

"Thanks," Palmer replied in a voice laced with trepidation.

Brad rose and handed the headset to Spencer. "Cap, if you will man the radio, I'll go outside."

Austin turned to Allison before Spencer could reply. "I'd appreciate it if you could stand outside the door to relay the word to Cap."

She nodded and extinguished her cigarette.

"We've got to be right on the money," Brad declared as he rose from his chair and started toward the door.

"Buckboard," Spencer advised Palmer, "your cohort will be feeding me instructions for you."

"Roger that."

Craning his neck, Palmer looked out over the white-and-gray expanse of clouds. There was an occasional buildup where a vertically developed cumulonimbus was producing a thunderstorm with heavy rains.

Nick purposely avoided looking at the fuel indicator. He concentrated on scanning the sky ahead of the MiG, keeping his eyes constantly moving. It was easier to spot an object by sweeping the horizon than by staring at a specific area in the sky.

The minutes seemed to drag while Palmer waited to hear from the helicopter. He reduced power to idle and began a shallow descent. *God, if you're watching over me, I'm going to need a little help this morning.*

"Buckboard, Sleepy is on top at fifty-four hundred."

Palmer breathed a sigh of relief. "I'm looking."

"We're popping a flare," Jimenez advised while Elvin Crowder shot a single flare out the entrance door. "It's away."

Nick studied the tops of the clouds in his desperate search. Seconds ticked by while the flare arched over and entered the thick overcast.

"No joy," Palmer said in a hollow voice.

"We'll try again in twenty seconds," Jimenez assured him, wondering how he and Mitchell would fare during their descent in instrument conditions.

Beginning to wonder if he had overflown the airfield, Nick considered reversing course. He took a quick look at the fuel supply and decided to follow his flight plan. The fuel gauge indicated that he would flame out in a matter of minutes. He had to follow his instincts, and Austin's bold idea, if he was going to get the MiG down in one piece.

"Buckboard," Jimenez said soothingly, "we're going with another flare in five seconds."

"Copy," Palmer replied with a dry mouth. He let his eyes drift from forty-five degrees to the right of his heading, to forty-five degrees to the left, then reversed and scanned across the tops of the clouds.

"I've gotcha!" Nick rejoiced, turning toward the reddish-orange glow. "I'm at your eleven o'clock, high."

"Tally," Chase Mitchell exclaimed before Jimenez saw the descending MiG. "We're pointed in alignment with the runway, so make a pass by us for your initial heading."

"Wilco."

"Buckboard, we hear you," Spencer informed Palmer after Allison relayed Brad's words.

Nick tightened his turn, popped his speed brakes, and flew past the helicopter. In order to avoid a possible collision, the UH-34 would have to remain above the cloud deck until Palmer was safely down or had ejected. No one wanted to admit that Nick might hit the side of a mountain while he was descending in instrument conditions.

Palmer lowered the landing gear and flaps, the retracted the speed brakes as the fighter settled into the menacing clouds. He wanted to concentrate solely on flying the approach. Distractions could kill him because of the less-than-reliable instruments.

Austin heard the MiG approach and relayed the message to Spencer.

"Nick, you're passing directly overhead," Spencer radioed in a studiously calm tone, "slightly to the right of the runway . . . but definitely in the ballpark."

"Copy," Palmer replied with a tight voice.

Descending and correcting to the left, Nick counted the seconds to himself. The instrument panel did not contain a clock.

Three seconds short of a minute, Nick was startled by Spencer's voice.

"Start your procedure turn."

"Roger," Palmer said, turning left forty-five degrees to a heading of 075 degrees. He leveled off and counted to himself. The clouds grew darker, and Nick knew that he was approaching a thunderstorm cell.

With his heart in his throat, Palmer began a smooth 180-degree turn to the right at the forty-five-second mark. Rain cascaded across the canopy before Nick rolled out on a heading of 255 degrees.

Brad heard the MiG returning to the field. He glanced at Allison and hesitated while he listened. "Tell him to turn inbound—now!"

Palmer attempted to slow his breathing rate as he turned to the inbound heading after counting forty-five seconds.

"Buckboard," Spencer said hastily, "turn inbound!"

"I have," Nick responded while he concentrated on holding a heading of 300 degrees.

"Tell him to turn on his landing light," Brad yelled as he walked toward the runway.

Palmer swore to himself when Spencer relayed the terse message. He flipped the light on and gradually reduced power to slow the fighter.

Brad said another silent prayer while he strained to see the landing light. Soaked to the skin by the deluge of rain, Brad rejoiced when he saw the dull glow of the bright light.

"Turn slightly to the right!" he said excitedly to Allison, then froze when the light disappeared. "Pull up! Pull up!"

She yelled at Spencer.

Nick saw the hill a second before Spencer's frantic call. He snapped the stick back and shoved the throttle forward as the MiG skimmed the top of the small ridge.

Brad saw the light reappear when the MiG passed over the crest of the hill. He shouted to Allison.

"Get off the power!" Spencer relayed for Brad. "Slip it!"

Palmer felt as if he had been hit in the chest by a giant sledgehammer. He yanked the throttle to idle and extended the speed brakes. He saw the end of the runway rushing up from his right.

Nick cross-controlled the aircraft, dropping the right wing and raising the nose to sideslip the jet. The fighter sliced toward the runway at an alarming rate of descent.

"Flare, goddamnit," Brad said under his breath as Allison ran toward him.

Palmer waited till the last second to level the wings, then smashed onto the narrow runway. The MiG hydroplaned on the wet macadam and went off the right side of the airstrip.

Spencer rushed outside as Nick fought to regain control of the careening MiG.

"Oh, shit," Brad swore, grabbing Allison's arm and pulling her toward the other side of the runway.

After a half-dozen steps, Austin abruptly stopped when he saw the MiG slew around and head toward the runway.

"Run!" Brad shouted as he tugged Allison toward the Quonset hut. Reaching the entrance, the trio watched Nick hurtle past and slide the distance of the grass overrun. The MiG stopped with the nosewheel in the stream.

After Palmer shut down the engine, a sudden quiet settled over the airstrip.

"Well," Brad sighed with a nervous laugh, "it wasn't pretty, but at least he's on the ground in one piece."

While Austin and Spencer talked the helicopter pilots down, Allison and Hank Murray and his men raced through the rain to the side of the MiG.

Palmer had slid the canopy open and was crawling out of the cockpit when Allison ran around the end of the wing.

"Nick, are you—" She stopped in midsentence when he slipped off the fuselage and tumbled into the stream.

Palmer sat up in the shallow water and looked at Allison. "A perfect ending," he tilted his face into the rain, "to a perfect flight."

Allison, accompanied by Murray and his technicians, belly-laughed in relief.

After showering and changing into his custom-tailored flight suit, Nick Palmer joined Brad under the small roof over the entrance to the Quonset hut. A steady drizzle persisted after the rainstorm that had followed Palmer's haphazard landing.

Nick turned to Brad. "Thanks for saving my bacon."

"We were lucky this time," Austin admitted while he glanced at the low overcast. "We—the two of us—are going to make the final decision about weather from now on."

"I agree," Nick said, "or one of us is going to bust his ass trying to salvage a homemade approach."

They watched Hank Murray direct his men, along with twenty security personnel, in an effort to extract the MiG from the muddy stream. The ends of a thick rope had been tied to the struts of each main landing gear. Murray centered the rope at the tow tractor, flipped a knot in the line, and attached the cord to the tug.

The driver backed away from the fighter's tail pipe until he had a solid strain on the line. When Murray gave the signal, the tug driver floored the throttle while two dozen men pushed on the leading edge of the wings.

The rain-soaked men heaved and grunted while the tow vehicle spun its tires in the grass and mud. Slowly but steadily, the MiG's nosewheel emerged from the stream. After the aircraft was twenty yards from the edge of the water, Murray halted the tug driver. After removing the rope from the two struts, Murray directed the driver to attach his tow bar to the nosewheel.

The exhausted working detail trudged back to their posts while the MiG was towed to the shelter.

Brad and Nick entered the Quonset hut and joined Cap Spencer, Allison, and the helicopter pilots at the cluttered briefing table.

"Nice GCA," Chase Mitchell said, referring to a radar-guided ground-controlled approach. By sound alone, Austin had directed the pilots through an instrument descent to an uneventful landing.

"Thanks," Brad replied while he sat down.

Palmer recounted the mission in detail up to the point where he attacked the two MiGs. His face did not reveal the mixed emotions he felt. He was pleased that he had downed another fighter, but disappointed that the MiG ruse had been discovered by the enemy.

"Cap," Palmer lightly drummed his fingers on the table, "they're onto us—the MiG drivers."

All eyes looked at Palmer, then shifted to Spencer. The project officer's irritation was evident.

"How did that happen?"

Nick replayed the event in his mind. "I had two MiGs—in formation—directly in front of me, and I thought I could get both of them."

Spencer tugged on his eye patch. "Go on."

"I got the wingman," Palmer declared in a low, even voice, "but the flight leader saw what happened."

A long silence hung in the air.

"He engaged me while I was trying to finish off his wingman." Nick stopped drumming and shrugged. "When I went one-on-one with the leader, my cannons jammed. I was damn lucky to get away, and there's no doubt the gomer is blowing the whistle as we speak."

Spencer studied Palmer for a brief moment. "If we receive permission to implement Austin's suggestion—strafing the airfields—we'll be okay, as far as the Agency is concerned. If we don't get the go-ahead, you've done the best you could . . . and you got another MiG."

Before Palmer could answer, Hank Murray stepped through the door. His wet utilities were plastered to his overweight body.

Cap Spencer glanced at him. "How's the MiG?"

"I'm afraid it's going to be down for a few days." He slid a chair out and sank into it. "We've found the problem with the cannons, but we're going to have to repair or replace the attach points for the nose-gear strut."

Murray turned his attention to Palmer. "Lieutenant, you're lucky to be here."

Appearing to be unfazed by the remark, Nick remained quiet. He was not about to ask why.

"We've got five holes to patch," Murray continued, "and one of them is less than two inches above a fuel line."

Palmer shifted uncomfortably in his chair, but kept his poise and remained silent.

Spencer evaluated the situation, knowing that if Langley approved the plan to strike the airfields, he wanted to move swiftly. "Do you have the necessary equipment to repair the nose gear?"

"No," Murray answered glumly. "We can jury-rig it, but a hard landing would collapse the strut and damage the cannons . . . beyond what we could repair here. I need to send the strut to Vientiane so a brace can be fabricated. In the meantime, we can patch the MiG and do some preventive maintenance."

Spencer rose and walked to the front entrance. He looked at the rain and low overcast for a moment before turning to Murray. "I'll contact Vientiane and have an aircraft standing by," he fumed impatiently. "As soon as this goddamn weather clears, we'll get a one-twenty-three in here." Spencer had already decided to request that a C-123 Provider be stationed at Alpha-29.

Rudy Jimenez could not resist the opportunity. "Cap, since the MiG is going to be down, how about if we—"

Spencer interrupted him with an understanding smile and a wave of his hand. "All of you, including Allison, could use some time off. Just be damn sure that you're ready to leave Vientiane the minute the strut is fixed.

No one tried to conceal their excitement.

CHAPTER THIRTY-ONE

CIA Headquarters, Langley, Virginia

Dennis Tipton hurried toward the office of the deputy director of the Central Intelligence Agency. Tipton, recently promoted to the position of director for operations, sometimes called the "Department of Dirty Tricks," was a highly respected intelligence analyst who had a reputation for gleaning critical information from the most unlikely sources.

He had the responsibility for overseeing the Agency's various clandestine operations, such as counterintelligence, recruitment of defectors, political intervention, espionage missions, and covert actions like Operation Achilles. He was the primary link to the Agency's wide array of field officers.

Conservative by nature, Dennis Tipton was dressed in a dark-gray suit and plain black shoes. Of average stature, he wore bow ties and wire-rimmed bifocals. The thick lenses made his sensitive blue eyes look out of proportion to his gaunt face. An avid tennis player, Tipton maintained a trim physique for a man in his late forties. His graying hair and receding hairline were the only obvious clues to his age.

The son of a wealthy attorney from Topeka, Kansas, Tipton had attended Culver Military Academy, and later graduated from Harvard. After serving a stint as an intelligence officer in the army, Tipton was hooked by the intrigue of research and analysis in the intelligence community.

Upon leaving the army, he applied to the CIA and was accepted as an apprentice analyst. Tipton quickly distinguished himself by displaying an uncanny ability to dissect a plethora of seemingly unrelated data and draw accurate conclusions. His rise through the ranks in the CIA had been a textbook case of how to balance an eccentric personality with patient diplomacy. Dennis Tipton was one of the few people who had worked in both the analysis and operations sides of the Agency.

When Tipton reached the office suite of Drexel McCormick, he had time for only a glance at the Potomac River before McCormick's secretary announced his arrival and ushered Tipton into the spacious office.

The deputy director of the CIA motioned for Tipton to have a seat while he concluded his telephone conversation.

Drexel McCormick was a tough-talking, back-room politician who had bulldozed his way to his present position. Short and pugnacious, the bald-headed McCormick was fiercely competitive and hated losing. Raised by his no-nonsense Irish grandmother, McCormick had been a barroom brawler who had come up the hard way.

"Morning," Drex McCormick said gruffly as he dropped the telephone receiver into its cradle.

"Good morning," Tipton replied, carefully charting his course. The deputy director was not in a pleasant mood this morning, Tipton thought, but then again, he never was in the best of spirits at this early hour.

McCormick stabbed at his intercom button. "Betty, hold all my calls, unless The Man calls." McCormick always referred to the director of the CIA as The Man.

"Yes, sir," the faint voice immediately responded.

McCormick leaned back from his oversize walnut desk. "Dennis, we've got a hell of a storm brewing on the horizon."

Tipton had not had time for his morning brief by the watch officer. "The Achilles Operation?"

"That's right," McCormick answered, shoving a pile of paperwork and messages aside. "The North Vietnamese, through their Information Ministry, have lodged a complaint to the international press, charging the U.S. with breaching the rules of engagement to gain an unfair advantage in the air war."

He saw the pained expression on Tipton's face. "They haven't actually accused us of using a MiG yet," he squinted, testing the resilience of the politically adept director, "but you can wager your last goddamn nickel that they're going to try to knock our MiG down . . . and make us look like fools."

McCormick spun his chair around and grabbed his coffee urn. "The word from the White House is that we better not have another U-2 incident," he said brusquely while he filled his mug, "and cause a political embarrassment."

The American reconnaissance plane that was shot down deep inside the Soviet Union in May 1960 had been the catalyst for Nikita Khrushchev to cancel a joint summit conference with the United States, Great Britain, and France. The CIA received a major blow when the downed pilot admitted that he was flying for the Agency.

"I understand," Tipton replied with no show of emotion. He felt a sense of foreboding settle over him as his mind raced to sort through the consequences if the MiG fell into enemy hands.

"You," McCormick let the word hang in the air, "are charged with the responsibility to ensure that Cap Spencer keeps the lid on this operation . . . at all costs."

Tipton quietly nodded. He and Hollis Spencer had worked together for over a year in the Agency's Directorate for Plans.

"The White House," McCormick said at last, "has issued a press statement to the effect that we categorically deny the unfounded allegations. The United States has not breached any rules. Period."

Tipton was already thinking about contingency planning. "What has been decided in regard to Spencer's request?"

"The Man believes it's a good idea, if we can pull it off without getting caught." McCormick stared over his steaming mug at Tipton. "What do you think? Can Spencer keep the Agency from getting shit splattered on it?"

Tipton grew cautious, knowing what McCormick was suggesting without actually saying the words. "It's a pretty ambitious plan, but I'm confident that he can keep the situation under control." Tipton was not that confident, but he was not going to reveal that to McCormick.

"That's good," McCormick forced a smile, "because the White House sent word that they thought the strafing idea had merit, if we make damn sure that we can get away clean."

"Well," Tipton replied matter-of-factly, "it certainly will have a profound effect on the enemy's morale and fighting effectiveness."

"That it will, Dennis." McCormick looked at the huge brass clock mounted on the far wall. "Get in touch with Spencer and pass the word to get on with his idea."

Tipton started to remind McCormick that Spencer had made it clear that one of the pilots had originated the strafing idea. Instead, he decided to remain silent.

"You make sure," McCormick's voice cut through the quiet office, "that Spencer understands the gravity of this situation."

"I will."

"If Hanoi gets ahold of one of our MiG pilots," McCormick scowled and leaned forward, "the White House is going to disavow any knowledge of the operation . . . and then blow our asses right out the door."

"I understand," Tipton answered in a hollow voice, aware of the burning in the pit of his stomach. Between the Agency's clandestine war being waged in Laos, the continuing buildup of Air America, and the secret MiG operation, Dennis Tipton had developed a peptic ulcer.

"Another thing," McCormick said dryly. "The people over on Capitol Hill are starting to shake the administration's trees . . . with the hope that something will fall out."

"Or someone," Tipton ventured, "like SECDEF." He was referring to the ongoing turf battle between the secretary of defense and congressional leaders. The festering issue was the conduct of the air war.

Military leaders and key political leadership wanted to greatly expand the air war, while the secretary of defense wanted to use a piecemeal approach.

"If they convene a Senate Committee to question the air war," McCormick said with a touch of contempt, "and SECDEF has to testify under oath, the Agency could be in for a thorough housecleaning."

Tipton's stomach was beginning to feel more uncomfortable. The secretary of defense was aware of the CIA's activities, and he was also aware that Congress was being hoodwinked.

"That's why," McCormick continued, "we can't afford any mistakes—none." He let the message sink in. "You've got to plug every hole—airtight."

"I fully understand," Tipton muttered, feeling a sudden revulsion. He was going to have to do something that he had never done before.

WATTAY AIRPORT, VIENTIANE

When the C-123 taxied to a stop at the Air America maintenance facility, three of Hank Murray's technicians unloaded the MiG's nose strut. They carried the bulky strut into the hangar while Allison and the four pilots accepted a ride to the Constellation Hotel in an Air America van.

Allison made reservations for the maintenance men while Brad inquired about his mail.

The shy Laotian woman apologetically informed Austin that she was unaware of any mail for him.

Disappointment showed on Brad's face as he and Nick carried their bags to the room they would share.

Palmer cast a look at his friend when Brad closed the door. "Nothing from Leigh Ann?"

"No," he replied listlessly. "Maybe she didn't get my letter." *Or, Brad thought as he crossed to the window, she is still upset with me.*

After Austin and Palmer each had a leisurely hot bath and changed into fresh clothes, they made arrangements to have their laundry sent out, then went to the noisy bar.

Chase Mitchell and Rudy Jimenez were engrossed in a lively conversation with three other Air America pilots. The reunion promised to be both drunken and boisterous.

"Let's sit at the bar," Palmer suggested, noting Austin's glum expression, "and play some liars' dice."

"Okay," Brad replied without his usual enthusiasm.

Nick ordered drinks and asked for one of the dice cups behind the counter.

The bartender returned with their drinks as Allison entered the smoky room.

Palmer saw her first. "Here's Allison," he announced.

Brad turned to see her wave at the inebriated helicopter pilots. They returned the greeting while she approached Palmer and Austin.

Dressed in a simple khaki skirt and powder-blue blouse, Allison looked radiant. Her blond hair, which had been pulled back in a French braid since her arrival at Alpha-29, flowed loosely across her shoulders.

"Mind if I join you?" she asked with a perky smile.

Brad slid off his bar stool so Allison could sit between them. He stood next to her.

"Please do," Nick replied, letting a smile crease his face. He shoved the dice cup away. "What would you like?"

"I think I'll be adventuresome," she said innocently, "and have a martini."

"A real one?" Brad chuckled.

Allison laughed softly. "Yes, a real one."

The din of noise steadily increased as the late-afternoon crowd gathered at the popular watering hole. Brad was about to excuse himself when Lex Blackwell sauntered into the smoke-filled room.

"Lex," Austin shouted over the bedlam, "over here."

Blackwell spied Brad, then worked his way toward the packed bar. His civilian clothes were wrinkled and his left arm was in a sling.

"It's good to see you," Palmer said, slapping Lex on the back while Brad shook Blackwell's right hand.

"What happened to your arm?" Austin asked while he motioned for the bartender. "Did one of your feisty girlfriends break it?"

"No." Lex saw Allison's subtle smile. "I broke my wrist at the O club," Blackwell answered sheepishly, "carrier-qualin' some air-force jocks."

Naval aviators traditionally carrier-qualify at officers' clubs by heaving each other down long tables placed end to end. The object is to slide down the beer-soaked "deck" and catch the wire (tablecloth or rope) before you fly off the end of the table. The fun is multiplied when the carrier aviators have the opportunity to "qual" air-force pilots.

"Must have been impressive." Brad laughed while Lex ordered a beer.

After a toast and catching up on lighthearted events, Lex surveyed the bar and stepped closer to Brad and Allison. Nick leaned around her to hear Blackwell.

"I probably shouldn't say anything in here," Lex said just loudly enough to be heard over the unrestrained conversations, "but the horse is outta the barn."

"What are you talking about?" Allison asked, aware that no one was paying any attention to them.

"I had a guy—at one of the briefin's I gave—play a tape of an engagement he had with a MiG."

Blackwell looked at Brad for a moment.

"And my voice was on it," Austin said evenly, then added, "and his call sign is Montana."

Blackwell's eyes widened. "That's right, so what the hell's goin' on? I heard that Washington flat denied that the U.S. has broken any rules . . . but the scuttlebutt on the carriers is that we have MiGs."

"Lex," Palmer responded in a hushed voice, "Hanoi knows that we've got at least one MiG-17 roving around in their backyard, and they've obviously lodged a complaint."

Allison nodded. "I'm sure Hanoi—at some point—will accuse us of using MiGs against them."

Blackwell looked down the bar, then to Brad and Allison. "What's that mean to us—the operation?"

"We don't know yet," she answered patiently, careful to keep her voice low. "We're waiting for permission to use the airplane to strafe their airfields while the MiGs are scrambling for takeoff."

Lex paused while a drunken patron next to Austin turned to order a drink. "How'd we go from the plan of takin' out their ace pilots to strafing airfields?"

"Well, partner," Nick drawled in his best Lex Blackwell impersonation, "buy me a drink, and I'll set you in step with the times."

"That sounds like a great idea," Allison said hastily, "because Brad is going to take me to dinner, aren't you, Captain?"

Austin slowly turned to her and arched an eyebrow. "I was just about to ask."

FALLS CHURCH, VIRGINIA

"Ouch!" Dennis Tipton glanced at the portable television, then examined the nick above his upper lip. Tired from a sleepless night, Tipton listened to the newscaster and finished shaving. He had sent a coded message to Hollis Spencer and expected a reply before the end of the day.

Reaching for a bottle of mouthwash, Tipton paused when he heard the word "MiG."

"Administration officials have denied that the U.S. military or CIA has access to any MiG fighters." The anchorman waited for his cue. "Our White House correspondent, Susan Forrester, has an update."

The well-dressed, serious-looking woman pursed her lips. "A White House spokesman has admitted that military sources have obtained operational data about the Communist fighters, but disclaim that they have possession of a MiG.

"In related news, the North Vietnamese Information Ministry has made new claims of repeated attacks on Hanoi by American-flown MiG fighters." The distracted woman paused to listen to a voice off camera.

"I'm being told that key congressional leaders are asking for an investigation into the MiG allegations. This latest development comes on the heels of continued questions concerning the effectiveness of the air war."

Tipton turned the television off and sat on the edge of the bathtub. He had a premonition of impending disaster. Yielding to his burning stomach, Tipton went to the kitchen for a glass of milk. Hollis Spencer would have to take the necessary steps to protect the Agency and preserve their jobs and reputations.

CHAPTER THIRTY-TWO

Allison and Brad left the small restaurant and walked along the bustling waterfront. The shops along the river were crammed with evening shoppers, many of whom were American wives.

"Well," Allison finally broke the silence, "what did you think about dinner?"

"The sour-pork salad was good," he answered with his usual candor, "but the steamed duck was . . . certainly exotic."

Allison gave him a breathy laugh and slid her hand under his upper arm. "Are you aware that a good number of these shoppers are Communist soldiers?"

Brad found himself responding to her gentle squeeze. "You're kidding me."

Tilting her head slightly, she smiled evenly. "No, I'm not kidding. It's crazy, but true."

More curious than cautious, Brad nonchalantly looked at the shops and open-air markets.

"I can't believe this," he said lightly as two soldiers in tattered field clothes purchased vegetables. "We're walking through the middle of hundreds of Communist troops while they're doing their shopping."

Allison hugged his arm and smothered a laugh. "That's right, and they know who you are—actually, they think you're another Air America pilot."

"Holy Christ," Brad replied under his breath. "How did this come about?"

She steered him toward a popular night spot that overlooked the Menam Khong River. "I'll tell you all about it over our after-dinner drinks."

"I can't wait," he replied as they turned to enter the darkly lighted establishment. After they had been seated at the outdoor bar, Allison moved her chair closer to Brad. He could smell the fresh scent of her perfume.

"The CIA originally rigged an election," she said in a voice just above a whisper, "to place a right-wing puppet government in Laos. When the arrangement didn't work to the satisfaction of the State Department, the CIA removed the Laotian leaders in a quiet coup."

Austin paused for a moment. "I had no idea."

"Few people know the real story," she continued, "including the members on Capitol Hill."

Brad shook his head. "Incredible."

"Part of the reason that I'm here," Allison said quietly, "is because of the contacts I made when Cap and I were here before. I have a number of sources who supply us with information about what is going on in the enemy camp." She glanced around, then smiled. "The Agency pays the informers very well."

"Interesting."

"At any rate," she went on in a hushed voice, "after the coup, the State Department and the CIA really butted heads, which resulted in each backing different political leaders."

Brad had a question written on his face. "Are you saying that the State Department backed a Communist faction?"

"They didn't intend to," Allison gazed into his eyes for a moment, "but the end result was that two Laotian princes—they were actually half brothers—sided against each other, and one backed the Communist opposition forces."

"I see," Brad replied slowly.

Allison glanced at the river traffic. "That resulted in both sides deciding to make Vientiane a neutral zone."

"What a mess." Brad said in wonderment. "Two sides at war . . . and they shop together."

"It's total confusion most of the time," she declared with a shake of her head. "The leaders on both fronts are in constant flux, which only fuels the confusion. It has become a way of life here."

Brad finished his cognac and studied Allison's face. "And Air America continues to grow?"

"That's true," she answered, and slipped her fingers over Brad's hand, "but I would rather talk about you."

"You would, huh?" he replied, beginning to feel the warm inner glow of the cognac.

Allison's consuming passion for Brad caused her to cast aside her caution. She had tried to be patient, but that effort had its limits.

"Brad, I'm going to be candid. My feelings for you are not going to go away, and they are real."

He tried to suppress the physical desire he felt for Allison. "Let's both be candid."

She gently squeezed his hand. "We're alike—the two of us—and I think you do care about me." There was a tone of defiance in her voice. "Tell me I'm wrong."

Brad was, at that moment, confused and unsure of his feelings. Indeed, he was attracted to Allison. What man, in his right mind, would not be drawn to her? The disappointment and hurt he felt over not receiving any mail from Leigh Ann caused him to doubt her commitment.

"No, you're not wrong," Brad said boldly, and slid his chair back. "Let's talk about this in private," he smiled broadly, "if you don't mind."

Allison was at first stunned, then beamed and kissed him lightly near his ear. "I know just the place," she murmured.

Hollis Spencer accompanied the company commander of the security forces to the posts surrounding Alpha-29. Both men sensed the need to begin rotating the weary soldiers to Vientiane for rest and relaxation.

Preoccupied by the disturbing message from Dennis Tipton, Spencer suggested that the former marine officer select a few men to board the C-123 on the next flight to the Air America base. Now that the Provider he had requested was at his disposal, Spencer could operate a steady R & R shuttle to the Laotian capital.

Unable to concentrate on the conversation, Cap Spencer politely excused himself and returned to the Quonset hut. After opening a fresh bottle of bourbon, he again read the urgent, top-secret message.

The usual dry language had been replaced with words such as "imperative" and "plausible deniability." Spencer had known Dennis Tipton long enough to know that he was operating under a tremendous amount of stress. The normally amiable director for operations, from the text of the message, had suddenly become demanding and openly hostile.

Spencer lighted his pipe and reread Tipton's decoded communication.

TOP SECRET CIA

FM: DIR OPS CIA
TO: ACHILLES PROJECT OFFICER
INFO: DEP DIR CIA

ACHILLES OPS

1. YOU ARE HEREBY AUTHORIZED TO CONDUCT STRAFING SORTIES IN ACCORDANCE WITH YOUR REQUEST.
2. IMPERATIVE THAT PILOT IS UNIDENTIFIED AT ALL COSTS. NO PLAUSIBLE DENIABILITY FOR WHITE HOUSE IF PILOT IS TAKEN PRISONER AND CONFESSES.
3. YOU ARE DIRECTED TO ENSURE THAT OPERATION ACHILLES IS NOT EXPOSED.
4. RESPOND IMMEDIATELY. DIR OPS SENDS.

"Goddamnit," Spencer said to himself as he filled his coffee mug with bourbon. He stared blankly at the top of his desk. It was obvious, he thought, that the existing powers in the CIA were getting the *we don't know anything about it, but go ahead* message loud and clear from the White House. The chiefs at Langley, in turn, wanted to continue the covert MiG operation but did not want to jeopardize their careers.

He sipped the warm bourbon and tried to make sense out of the current state of affairs. The situation, at least in his mind, was getting out of control. He had seen similar situations many times in government service—everyone scrambling to cover their asses, while the ultimate responsibility for an operation flowed down to the lowest person in the chain of command.

Spencer let his mind explore the hidden message under the surface of Tipton's communication. There was a sense of desperation in the text. Hollis Spencer knew without a doubt that his career was on the line, and now it was obvious that Dennis Tipton's future was also at stake if Operation Achilles was discovered.

There was a strong message disguised in the wording of Tipton's priority dispatch. The subliminal directive was obvious to Spencer. If a pilot went down and could not be rescued, he should commit suicide.

There would be a loud cry from the North Vietnamese Information Ministry, but there would be no way to positively identify the body. The State Department would call the charges fabricated and unsubstantiated. If Hanoi transferred the body to an international organization for identification, the CIA would have possession of the corpse within minutes.

Yes, Spencer thought while he poured more bourbon, it was an ugly business. He stared at his watch for a moment, then rose unsteadily and went in search of Hank Murray. Hollis Spencer needed to talk with someone he trusted before responding to Dennis Tipton's message.

Brad prepared fresh drinks and surveyed the small, softly lighted room, noting a small bottle of perfume and other personal articles sitting on the dresser. He opened the window and stared at the star-studded sky while he listened to the muffled sounds from the hotel bar downstairs. Turning, he looked at the bed before carrying their glasses to the single nightstand.

Slipping off his shoes, Brad settled comfortably on the bedspread and propped himself against the wooden headboard. The gentle breeze from the ceiling fan cooled his face while he tasted his drink. Strangely detached, Brad let the chilled scotch trickle down his throat while he tried to dispel thoughts of Leigh Ann.

The bathroom door opened and Allison appeared in a beige dressing gown made of pure silk.

"I see that you've made yourself at home," she said with a provocative smile. "Mind if I join you?"

Brad caught his breath and extended his arm. She sat on the edge of the bed and folded herself into his arms.

She nuzzled his chest and teased him with a smile. "What are you thinking?"

He pulled her next to him and tilted her chin up. "Allison, I have to be honest with you."

She kissed him lightly on the lips and looked searchingly into his eyes. "I expect you to be honest, and I know you're experiencing some guilt."

"That's true," he conceded, "and I'm not sure this is such a good idea."

"Brad," she purred while she began to unbutton his shirt, "we're risk takers . . . you and I. For us, each tomorrow is a precious gift."

He groaned when she ran her tongue slowly down to his navel. He untied the thin belt to Allison's dressing gown and slipped the garment off her shoulders.

"Don't deny your feelings," she whispered soothingly as he slowly undressed her. "Let's enjoy the moment, because we can't predict the future."

Prolonging their mutual hunger, Brad caressed and tasted Allison's skin as he uncovered each new area of her body.

The temporary maintenance hangar had wide sheets of waterproof canvas draped over the sides to conceal the lights. Spencer listened to the electric generators while he lighted his pipe, then pulled a section of the tarpaulin aside and entered the MiG shelter.

Hank Murray concluded his conversation with two of his men and walked over to talk with Spencer. He could tell by the downbeat look on the project officer's face that something was wrong. Very wrong.

"Cap, are you okay?"

"Yeah . . . physically. Have you got a few minutes?"

"Sure. What's on your mind?"

"Let's go over to ops."

Spencer and Murray walked to the blacked-out Quonset hut in silence. After Cap poured himself another bourbon, he turned to Murray.

"Hank, can you afford to take the rest of the night off?"

"No problem," he answered hastily. "We're ready when the strut gets here."

Spencer nodded and fixed Murray a drink.

"Hank, I know this isn't your area of expertise, but I need a sounding board."

Murray accepted the cup and studied his friend. He had never seen Hollis Spencer so glum. "I'll give you the best shot I can."

"Take a look at this," Spencer said tautly as he handed Murray the priority message, "and tell me what you make of it. I have to respond soon, and I would like someone else's opinion. How do you view it?"

The dimly lighted room forced Murray to put on his glasses. He read the contents of Dennis Tipton's harsh communication, then let out a low whistle.

"Well, you finally have permission to conduct the strafing missions." He looked at the message again and slowly removed his glasses. "I'd say, from what I'm reading," Murray grew cautious, "they're telling you to terminate the pilot . . . if he's shot down and the helo crew can't get him aboard the helicopter."

Spencer looked over the rim of his mug at the maintenance director. "That, or ask him to kill himself."

Cap watched Murray's eyes widen.

"But there are two major problems, as I see it," Spencer continued after a pause.

Murray remained quiet, unsure if he should be discussing the contents of a CIA directive with the project officer. Hank Murray had attained his present rank by avoiding complicated decisions. He was a clever officer who always left himself a way out of any controversial situations.

"First," Spencer said scornfully, "I've never asked anyone to commit suicide, and these men would think I was insane. They aren't the type of people who would take their own lives. These guys would fight to the bitter end."

Murray looked at his cup and continued to keep his thoughts to himself. He knew, from what Spencer had said in previous conversations, that the CIA had no qualms about killing expendable field personnel in the interest of secrecy. The Agency referred to the slayings as "terminations with extreme prejudice."

"And secondly," Spencer swallowed deeply, "I seriously doubt if Mitchell or Jimenez would carry out an order to have their gunner shoot Austin or Palmer if they couldn't get them into the helicopter."

"Cap," Murray paused to measure his words, "I don't know anything about the politics involved in the CIA, but isn't there a way out . . . for you?"

Spencer rubbed his shoulder. "Hank, if I can manage, somehow, to get through this operation unscathed, I have no doubt about my future. I'm in line," he continued, letting his pent-up emotions surface, "for a cushy desk job at Langley, while someone else moves up to take over my shit details."

Murray was taken aback by the open contempt Spencer displayed toward the CIA. He had never expressed any negative feelings about the Agency before.

"If we get through this," Spencer confided while he tried to regain his composure, "I'd like to see you retire from the navy and join me at Langley."

"I'd be honored," Murray beamed, excited at the prospect of

supplementing his retirement pay. "You say the word, and I'll submit my papers."

Spencer gave Murray an appreciative smile. "I'm happy to know that, Hank. For now, we've—or more to the point—*I've* got to take every precaution to make sure this operation doesn't blow up in our faces."

Murray nodded his understanding. "Cap, let's look at all the options and see if there isn't some way to pull this off without endangering your future."

"Hank, this operation could go on for a long time." Spencer lifted his mug, then placed it back on his desk when he noticed his hand shake. "Even if we lost the MiG and got the pilot out safely, they'll probably send over another MiG."

After a short hesitation, Murray spoke in a slow, deliberate manner. "As I see it, the only worry we have is the pilot—the weak link."

Spencer gave him a curious look. "What are you suggesting?"

"Cap, if you instructed Elvin Crowder to . . . eliminate the pilot if they couldn't get him into the helo, you wouldn't have to discuss it with Jimenez and Mitchell. Crowder is the kind of sea slug who would carry out the order. There wouldn't be anything the rotorheads could do about it, after the fact."

The idea had already occurred to Spencer, but he had discarded the thought. If the helicopter was close enough to allow the gunner to shoot a downed pilot, eight out of ten times the crew would be able to safely extract the man. Besides, Spencer had known Crowder a number of years and had learned to not trust him.

"The problem with Crowder," Spencer sighed and ran a finger under his eye patch, "is that he and the pilots have no secrets. He'd go straight to them, and I'd probably have an open rebellion on my hands."

"What about one of your security troops?" Murray countered. "You could have the CO appoint his best marksman to serve as a door gunner, then instruct him to dispatch the pilot if they can't get him on board."

Self-consciously, Spencer tilted his head back and stared at the ceiling. "What am I talking about?" he suddenly blurted, and cast his glance on Murray. "My only choice is to rely on Austin and Palmer. They're good—damn good—but if one of them goes down, I've got to count on the helo crew to get him out." Spencer turned to Murray. "If Hanoi gets one of them alive, the roof will blow sky-high in Washington, and my ass will be as good as dead."

The maintenance chief was far from convinced that Spencer should leave the fate of the operation to divine intervention. Hank Murray had another idea in mind, one that he was positive would ensure the secrecy of Operation Achilles and protect the project officer.

Spencer tilted his cup to his mouth and finished the bourbon. "This operation, as I'm sure you're aware, is being denied by the White House."

Tension filled the room. Both men knew the consequences if one of the pilots was downed and identified as an American.

Spencer reached for the half-empty bourbon bottle. "Hank, I'm really out on a limb this time."

"Don't worry about it, Cap." Murray felt obligated to use his resources to make sure that a pilot shot down would not give the project away. "Just keep doing what you've been doing, and it'll work out fine."

CHAPTER THIRTY-THREE

The first hint of daylight was filtering through the open window when Brad awakened with a start. Allison moaned softly and nestled her back against his chest.

Brad listened to the overhead fan for a few minutes while he gathered his thoughts. Luxuriating in the warmth of Allison's firm body, Brad cupped a bare breast and brushed her neck with his lips.

She stirred and reached behind the small of his back, pressing him next to her.

Brad still had mixed feelings about their sexual encounter. He loathed the weakness that allowed him to break the bond he had with Leigh Ann. He had questioned her commitment; now he questioned his own. Maybe Allison really was the woman he desired most . . . or was she just convenient?

"Good morning," she said in a sleepy voice.

Brad nibbled her earlobe. "It's a great morning."

She turned in his arms and ran her hand between his thighs.

"Tell me something," he said, pulling her close to him. "Which was better . . . the hunt or the kill?"

Allison smiled and squeezed his thigh. "This one is a close call," she teased with a small chuckle. "The hunt was a real challenge, but the kill was incredible."

They laughed and then remained quiet, each absorbed in their own thoughts before Allison broke the silence.

"Brad, be honest with me," she paused a moment, "about us—your feelings for me."

Brad's answer was interrupted by the metallic clinking of the telephone.

Allison sprawled across Brad and fumbled with the phone receiver. "Hello."

Brad smoothed her hair while he listened to the short conversation. The pressure of her breasts on his chest aroused him, and he pulled the bed sheet over Allison's back.

"I take it," he said sadly when she replaced the receiver, "that our visit in paradise is coming to an end?"

"Unfortunately." Allison sighed, and pressed a leg between his thighs.

"That was Lo Van Phuong, the hotel manager. He just received word that we're scheduled to depart at seven-thirty." She rose slightly, barely touching his chest with her breasts.

Brad gazed at Allison's heavy-lidded eyes, then gently bit her lower lip and met the pressure of her mouth. "You're insatiable," he murmured.

Exhausted and suffering from a splitting headache, Hollis Spencer examined the rough draft of the message he had sent to the director for operations. The dirty feeling again washed over him as he read the carefully worded response.

ACKNOWLEDGE STRAFING AUTHORIZATION. EVERY PRE-CAUTION BEING TAKEN. CONFIDENT THAT INTEGRITY OF OPERATION WILL NOT BE COMPROMISED. ANTICIPATE RE-SUMPTION OF MISSION WITHIN 48 HOURS. ACHILLES OPS SENDS.

His emotions, after drinking until shortly before dawn, had changed to fear at what would happen to him if the operation collapsed in an international embarrassment.

Should he resign and protect his many years of exemplary service to the Agency, or roll the dice and hope to retire from a senior position at Langley?

If he left now, with his reputation intact, Spencer was sure that he could land a secure job of equivalent pay and prestige in the private sector. His alternative was to stay the course and pray that he emerged unscathed from the highly explosive MiG operation.

After anguishing over what course he should pursue, Cap Spencer had finally decided to stick with the Agency and take his chances. If Austin and Palmer, who both believed and trusted in him, were willing to risk their lives, he certainly could put his career on the line.

He wadded the handwritten draft into a ball and threw it into the trash. "Screw the bastards. . . ."

The door was ajar when Brad reached his room. Nick Palmer was closing his overnight bag when Austin entered the cramped quarters.

"Well," Nick grinned mischievously, "the wandering Lothario has returned to his lair."

Brad ignored the remark and quickly tossed his belongings into his bag. He glanced at his watch, then stepped into the tiny bathroom and splashed water on his face.

"You can go ahead," Palmer said with a beguiling smile, "and make out an allotment to me—half your paycheck will suffice."

"What are you talking about?" Brad muttered while he dried his face.

"Half your money," Nick teased, "or there's going to be hell to pay when I tell Leigh Ann about this."

Brad gave him a warning look. "Are we checked out?"

"As soon as you're ready."

Lex Blackwell knocked on the door and stepped inside. He glanced at Brad and laughed. "You look like you've been rode hard and put up wet."

Austin heaved his bag off the bed. "Let's go."

When the trio reached the front desk, the general manager approached Brad.

"Mister Austin, I must apologize," Lo Van Phuong said with a trace of embarrassment. "I saw your name on the guest register this morning, and . . ."

The courtly man handed Brad a letter. "Miss Chieu was not aware that I was keeping your mail in my office." He bowed politely. "My apologies, sir."

Brad flushed when he saw Leigh Ann's handwriting on the envelope. He darted a quick glance at Palmer, who gave him an *I told you so* look.

"That's okay. No need to apologize." He stuffed the letter into his shirt pocket. "Thanks for keeping it safe."

The manager turned to greet Allison as she entered the crowded lobby.

"Good morning, Lo Van," she replied cheerfully. "It's good to see you again."

Austin quietly slipped out of the hotel and walked to the waiting Air America van.

"Brad, my boy, you're in deep shit," he said under his breath while the driver tossed his bag into the back of the rickety van.

The steady roar of the big Pratt & Whitney radial engines lulled Brad into closing his eyes. He was anxious to read Leigh Ann's letter, but did not want to open it in front of Allison. She sat across the aisle from him, talking to the technicians about the nose strut.

Brad thought about going to the cockpit to read the letter, but dismissed the idea. He would wait until he could open it in the privacy of his tent. Brad opened his eyes and glanced at Allison, then closed them again. He was not proud of himself.

Palmer and Blackwell had had the good sense, at least in Allison's presence, to act as if nothing had happened. Their apparent innocence made the situation easier, but a nagging guilt weighed heavily on Brad's mind.

His thoughts drifted as the Provider neared Alpha-29. *You're a real son of a bitch.*

After the C-123 had landed and parked, Brad smiled at Allison and quietly went to his tent.

Palmer followed Austin into their quarters and dropped his bag. "I'm going to take Lex over to see Cap, then give him a tour of the ville."

Brad appreciated Nick's consideration. "Thanks. I need a few minutes of privacy."

Palmer grinned good-naturedly and walked out.

Listening to the sounds and voices coming from the hangar, Brad stretched out on his cot and opened Leigh Ann's letter.

Dear Brad,

I was thrilled to receive your letter today. There are so many things I want to tell you, but I don't know where to begin. The thoughts and feelings are there, but it is so difficult to translate them into words on a page.

Let me begin by telling you that I'm sorry I missed your calls. After our last telephone conversation, I received a call from my parents. My uncle in Atlanta passed away. We left on Saturday morning to attend his funeral. I tried to call you from Atlanta, but the operator said your phone had been disconnected.

Speaking of our last telephone conversation—I behaved like a spoiled, jealous brat. You have never done anything to make me doubt your loyalty. That was very unfair to you, and I hope you will accept my apology.

Brad placed the letter on his chest and closed his eyes. *Yeah, I've been a real prince.* A sense of shame consumed him as he thought about the previous night. He imagined Allison's face smiling at him. He opened his eyes and continued reading.

Brad, I miss you so much, and I've been thinking about our relationship. I could fill pages pouring out my deep feelings of love for you, but I suppose the best way to describe my thoughts is to say that I'm miserable without you.

I want to go to Vientiane. I don't know how far it is from where you are, but if your mail goes to the hotel, you must pick it up occasionally. When you do, I want to be there and feel your arms around me.

I have applied for a visa and expect it to be granted by the end of the week. As far as I'm concerned, graduate school can wait. What is most important to me, at this stage of my life, is being with you and experiencing your world.

Since I haven't made travel arrangements yet, perhaps you could give me some pointers about the best way to get there.

Brad, I am so anxious to see you. Please write soon.

With all my love,

Leigh Ann

Brad carefully folded the letter and slipped it into his shirt pocket. He was relieved to know that Leigh Ann considered their relationship to be on solid footing, but he was concerned about her desire to join him.

He thought about the feasibility of having Leigh Ann reside at the Constellation Hotel. Vientiane was safe enough, and there were a number of American wives living in the city. He was sure that she would adapt to the environment and make friends. That is, he thought at length, if Allison did not interfere.

For a half hour, Brad weighed the positives and negatives of having Leigh Ann come to Vientiane. The more he thought about the idea, the more appealing it sounded. He was growing more frustrated by having to conduct their relationship via correspondence, and who knew how long he would be in Laos?

"I'm going to invite her to Vientiane," he said to himself and reached under his cot for the legal pad that he and Nick used to take notes. He would ask the C-123 pilots to mail the letter for him when they returned to Vientiane. Leigh Ann could contact the hotel's general manager to make reservations.

In the heat of the afternoon, Hank Murray's technicians replaced the nosewheel strut while Hollis Spencer and the five pilots discussed the upcoming strafing missions. The project officer had informed them that the Agency thoroughly endorsed the strafing campaign, but he had kept the actual contents of the message to himself.

Allison manned the radios and compiled the detailed information about the air strikes planned for the following day. The final Route Pack information concerning the strike groups would be transmitted to her two hours prior to the scheduled attacks.

Spencer had told Lex Blackwell that he could return to Vientiane until his wrist healed. Characteristically, the gritty fighter pilot turned down the offer and volunteered to help in any way he could. Spencer, grateful to have additional administrative assistance, assigned Blackwell to oversee all supplies for Alpha-29.

"Brad," Cap Spencer said while he drew a circle on the map spread on the table, "from the information we have received today, the navy is going to clobber the Ham Rong bridge at Thanh Hoa late tomorrow afternoon."

The fabled bridge was eighteen nautical miles southeast of a major MiG airfield at Bai Thuong.

"When the Warning Star or Red Crown," Spencer went on, "confirms that the MiGs at Bai Thuong have gone to strip alert—when they've fired up and they're ready to taxi for takeoff—we'll pass the word to you."

The reason for waiting until the MiGs were manned was twofold.

The CIA wanted to destroy the Communist fighter planes on the ground *and* kill the pilots at the same time.

Austin studied the detailed map while Spencer briefed the group. "Cap, I'm going to have to be fairly close to the field if I'm going to catch them on the ground."

"That's true," Spencer replied, tracing a short line across the map. "The navy is going to have a four-plane F-4 TARCAP about ten to fifteen miles north of Bai Thuong, along with some F-8s northwest of Thanh Hoa, so I suggest that you stay right on the deck and orbit about seven miles south of the field."

The three fighter pilots scrutinized the terrain features south of Bai Thuong and selected a spot where they all agreed Brad should loiter.

"You'll be monitoring the strike frequency," Spencer explained quietly, "so if you hear the bomber group call feet dry before you hear from us, press the attack and get the hell out of there before the navy pilots see you strafe the field."

"Okay."

Brad noted that the runway was oriented southeast to northwest. He could increase his speed while he made a sweeping left turn, strafe the MiGs, then continue straight out toward Alpha-29.

"Duck soup," Lex Blackwell stated.

Brad and Nick let their glances slide to the Texan.

"You haven't been on one of these fire drills," Palmer said dryly. "It's not exactly a walk in the park."

A sudden burst of automatic-weapons fire stunned the group. Seconds later, two loud explosions forced Brad to react.

"Get down!" Austin shouted while he scrambled across the floor to his M-16. "Nick, follow me!"

Palmer lunged for his rifle as a steady volume of fire erupted. He snatched the M-16 from the edge of a chair and stumbled out the door on the heels of Austin.

They crouched and ran a few yards, then spread-eagled on the ground in a firing position.

Total confusion reigned, with people screaming and yelling over the blazing gunfire. Brad and Nick were unsure where to direct their fire until Austin spotted a number of Communist soldiers high on the hill across the runway.

"Up there!" Brad pointed, and began squeezing off rounds.

The soldiers threw grenades while Nick fumbled with the safety on his M-16. The Chicoms penetrated the trees and exploded near one of the perimeter foxholes.

Chase Mitchell and Rudy Jimenez raced toward the helicopter, yelling at Elvin Crowder to man the M-60 machine gun.

In the middle of the maelstrom, Cap Spencer tumbled out of the doorway with his M-16 and sprawled on the ground. "Where are they?"

"Halfway up the hill," Brad shouted above the hail of gunfire. "Just above the trees—past the perimeter line!"

Someone was yelling for a medic as Mitchell cranked the blades of the UH-34.

Brandishing his .38 revolver, Lex Blackwell followed Spencer out of the Quonset hut, dropped to his knees, then rolled onto his good arm. Although the handgun was basically ineffective at the distant targets, Blackwell selectively aimed and fired until he was out of bullets.

Palmer and Austin poured fire into the area where the soldiers had disappeared moments before. Brad swore when he ran out of ammunition. He frantically belly-crawled toward his tent, cursing himself for not carrying the extra magazine clip with him.

Reaching the bullet-shrouded tent, Brad slapped a new clip in place as Chase Mitchell yanked the helicopter off the ground. Elvin Crowder was firing his machine gun as Mitchell climbed for altitude and maneuvered the UH-34 to give the crew chief the best firing position.

Brad rolled out of the tent and began firing where he thought the enemy might be dug in. He heard the whine of high-powered rounds, then a solid *crack* as a bullet slammed into one of the supporting posts for the hangar.

Brad stole a look around the perimeter of the field. Everyone was pinned down by the heavy fire. He had a lump in his throat as he crawled back into the tent and grabbed Palmer's extra magazine. The thought that the security forces might be overrun was foremost in his mind.

After jamming the second clip into the breast pocket of his flight suit, Brad thought about Allison. Was she okay?

He rapidly crawled back to where Palmer and Spencer were sprawled. Brad was sighting in on a fleeing soldier when Allison spilled out of the Quonset hut with her own M-16. Austin paused in amazement while she methodically selected targets and calmly fired at the attackers.

A round hit directly in front of Brad, snapping him back to the present as dirt and grass showered his face.

Elvin Crowder poured a barrage of machine-gun fire into the

Communist soldiers, causing them to begin retreating. Two powerful explosions marked the spots where the withdrawing attackers stepped on mines.

Horrible screams punctuated the gunfire as the Communist forces stumbled over mines in their hasty retreat. They had carefully marked the Claymore antipersonnel mines during their stealthy advance, but overlooked them in the panic of withdrawing from the firefight.

An incredibly long burst of gunfire accompanied the uphill charge of two perimeter security squads. They routed the attackers, decimating them with a hail of small-arms fire and hand grenades.

Brad heard another call for a corpsman as the fighting slowly dissipated. He watched the helicopter circle low overhead while Crowder kept up a relentless stream of fire.

As quickly as the direct assault had begun, the fighting decreased to sporadic exchanges of gunfire. The attack had been sudden and brutal, leaving everyone feeling numb and vulnerable.

Expecting the worst, Spencer followed Brad and Nick toward the security command post. The commanding officer, who had taken a round through his right forearm, was sitting on the ground in a state of shock. A corpsman was treating the CO's wound while the acting executive officer, former gunnery sergeant Salvador Rodriguez, was on the company net talking to the outlying posts.

Rodriguez barked an order into his handset and spun around to face Cap Spencer.

"Get the one-twenty-three fired up," he ordered, stepping over the CO. "We've got three casualties and five wounded to medevac."

Wordlessly, Spencer turned and ran toward the Quonset hut.

Brad reached into his pocket, then snapped Palmer's spare magazine into his rifle. "Gunny, where's the M-16 ammo?"

Rodriguez glared at the pilot. "I don't have time to fuck with you right now."

"Goddamnit!" Austin flared as he snatched Rodriguez by his utility collar, "where's the ammo?"

"You," the gunnery sergeant pointed to one of the men. "Get the captain some ammo—on the double."

Preparing for another possible onslaught, Rodriguez ignored the pilots and continued shouting orders to the men in the field.

Nick and Brad grabbed the extra magazines and trotted toward the compound. When they reached the Quonset hut, the C-123 crew had the engines running. Chase Mitchell brought the helicopter to a quick hover, then dumped it onto the grass next to the Provider.

Palmer and Austin hurried to the transport and helped load the wounded on board, then assisted the CO into the airplane. There was a moment of confusion when the pilots started to taxi, then abruptly stopped when three bodies wrapped in poncho liners were carried out of the treeline.

After the casualties were placed aboard, the pilots taxied rapidly to the end of the field, swung the Provider around, and roared down the runway. The propwash blew the camouflage off the macadam, spinning the matted foliage in a violently destructive whirlwind. The aircraft banked toward Vientiane before the landing gear was completely retracted.

The sudden stillness seemed foreboding to Brad. Was the eerie quiet a calm before another storm? Would the Communist forces regroup and assault the field again? Now was the opportune time for them to attack, Austin told himself, with part of the men on R & R, and eight others either dead or wounded.

Nick and Brad walked to the Quonset hut in a daze. Rudy Jimenez was overseeing the refueling of the helicopter, while Mitchell and Crowder loaded the UH-34 with fresh rounds of 7.62-millimeter ammo for the machine gun.

"I'm going to find an E-tool," Brad declared as they entered their ops building, "and we're going to dig us two deep foxholes." E-tool was the nickname for a short shovel called an entrenching tool.

"I may not stop digging," Palmer said flatly, "until I surface in Kansas."

CHAPTER THIRTY-FOUR

The atmosphere in the Quonset hut was strained when Hollis Spencer stepped out of the communications compartment and approached the briefing table.

Outside, evening was settling over the airfield as Hank Murray and his disgruntled men prepared the MiG for the upcoming mission. The aircraft technicians, who had been shaken by the frightening Communist assault, were losing confidence in the CIA security forces.

The stubby fighter, which was in the process of being repainted in camouflage colors, had weathered the attack with minimal damage. The blast-protection plate between the cannons and the engine-air intake had been dented, and the leading edge of the right wing had a scratch from a ricocheting shell.

Cap Spencer shared the anxiety expressed on the faces at the table. Allison and the three fighter pilots looked numb and shaken from the stress. The prospect of being killed or maimed was now a reality.

Chase Mitchell and Rudy Jimenez, along with their crew chief, were manning their idling helicopter. They had hurriedly stockpiled more ammunition, patched four bullet holes in the fuselage of the UH-34, and were prepared to launch at the first sign of another assault.

Brad could not erase the gut-wrenching feeling of watching the dead and wounded being evacuated. One minute the men were alive; the next minute they were either dead or scarred and disfigured for life.

Austin looked at Spencer while he relived some of the same visceral scenes of the dead and wounded being flown out of Da Nang Air Base. "Cap, where do we stand?"

Spencer sat down with a forlorn look on his face. "The Pathet Lao forces range far and wide in this part of the country. We've obviously got their attention, and this landing strip would be prime real estate for them—especially since the site is so close to their stronghold at San Neua."

"Cap, I know there's an explanation," Brad began slowly in an attempt to conceal his growing concern, "but would you mind explaining why Alpha-29 was developed in the middle of an area crawling with thousands of Pathet Lao soldiers?" *Christ, they know we're Americans and we've got a MiG-17. It won't take long for Hanoi to figure out where the phantom MiG is based.*

Spencer nodded and rubbed his good eye. "The decisions were made at Langley, and they were based on the distance from Hanoi to the nearest suitable landing site in northeastern Laos. They—actually the director of the Agency—thought the risk to us was outweighed by the risk of trying to stretch the range of the MiG and exposing it to possible observation for extended periods of time."

Brad exchanged a look of uneasiness with Palmer. "Well, that certainly answers my question, but what do we do to solve our immediate problem?"

"We're going to have replacements flown in in the morning . . . ," Spencer answered flatly, "as soon as an airplane can get in here."

"Is there any chance," Austin asked in a respectful tone, "that you could get some marines or army troops to augment our security forces?"

Spencer shook his head. "No. We have to use our own people, because of the secret nature of this operation."

"Brad," Allison explained in a hushed voice, "our people have top-secret clearances, and they are well paid. They keep their mouths shut to protect their jobs. We can't control what anyone else might say when they leave here."

Austin grudgingly accepted the explanation. Was the covert operation worth risking the lives of so many people? "My guess is that they're going to be back," he said without showing any emotion, "and in greater force next time."

"Gunny Rodriguez," Spencer replied lamely, "is leaving their bodies out there as a reminder for anyone who might want to try it again. He's also stringing more trip-wire, and I've requested a large supply of flares."

Brad refrained from responding and turned his mind to what had to be accomplished in the next few hours. The first thing he planned to do was borrow an E-tool and dig a fighting hole.

"We had better get some rest," Palmer suggested, and reached for his M-16.

"You're right," Spencer agreed, trying to maintain a show of optimism. The facade did not convince anyone.

A ray of moonlight occasionally penetrated the luminous clouds while Austin labored in their foxhole. The parapets around the deepening hole steadily grew larger as Brad continuously shoveled dirt over the lip of the shelter.

Nick Palmer, who had been helping Brad dig, rested on his back next to their bullet-perforated tent. He rolled onto his side and rested his head in his hand. "What do you think is going to happen?"

Brad paused and dropped the shovel, then flopped against the side of the hole. "As I said before, my guess is that the Pathet Lao—or whoever they are—will be back. They're patient little assholes, and they've got us right where they want us."

"When?"

"Who knows?" Brad shrugged and took a deep breath. "A week . . . two weeks—three at the outside." He looked up at the few stars shining through the clouds. "As soon as they get their shit together."

Palmer lighted a cigarette and kept it cupped in his hand. "And you think they'll come back en masse?"

"Nick, I don't know any more than you know, but I think we'd better dig in and be prepared for the worst."

Palmer looked around the compound. "How did we get ourselves into this mess?"

"We," Brad forced a thin smile, "volunteered to be test pilots . . . remember?"

Nick quietly cursed himself and stared at the drifting clouds. "Oh, yes. The roar of the crowd and smell of the greasepaint."

Austin handed Palmer the shovel. "Would you care to take over as excavation engineer?"

"Sure. As soon as I finish this cigarette."

The conversation ceased when Allison approached from out of the darkness. She carried her M-16 in one hand and clutched a C-ration container in her other hand. "Do you mind having a guest for dinner?"

"Have a seat," Brad encouraged, patting the soft dirt around the foxhole. "It's time for a break."

"Where's Lex?" Nick asked, pushing himself up to a sitting position.

"He's still working with Cap." Allison carefully placed her rifle on the ground, then crossed her feet and plopped onto the embankment surrounding the hole.

Palmer slowly ground his cigarette into the soft dirt and wearily struggled to his feet. "Guess I'll go see what they're up to."

Austin watched his friend walk toward the Quonset hut before turning to Allison. "I don't want to sound pushy, but I firmly believe that you should be on the next flight out of here . . . wouldn't you agree?"

She avoided his gaze and opened the C-ration container. "No, I don't agree."

"Allison, be reasonable, for Christ's sake."

"Brad, we've been through this before. I have a job to do, just like you."

"I'm telling you," he insisted with a look of exasperation, "this is no place for a woman. Do you have any idea what they would do to you if we were overrun?"

Allison shoved the C-ration carton aside. "I can hold my own . . . and I can fire a rifle about as well as most of the men around here."

Brad exhaled sharply. "I suppose, with proper training, you could fly the MiG, too?"

"That's right," she asserted, "and you could probably type as well as I can, with *proper* training."

In frustration, Brad grabbed her by the shoulders and pulled her into the foxhole. "Allison, if you really do care about me, then you'll—"

"I'll leave," she smiled and cupped his face in her hands, "if you'll go with me."

Brad slowly pulled away from her. "I can't leave . . . and you know that." He remained silent for a moment, preparing himself for what he had to tell her about Leigh Ann. "The whole operation revolves around the MiG."

Allison studied his eyes in the pale moonlight. "It's your decision, but I'm not going to leave without you."

He looked away for a moment, then stared into her eyes. "Allison, I had a letter from Leigh Ann."

Sensing a threat, she tilted her head and gave him a quizzical look. "When?"

"The hotel manager gave it to me when we checked out." Brad maintained eye contact with her and steeled himself. "He had been saving it for me, and I didn't know it was there when I checked in."

Allison concealed the sudden pain and anger that welled inside of her. She had convinced herself that she and Brad had a future together. "What are you telling me—where does that leave us?"

"I'm going to ask Leigh Ann to marry me," Brad answered more calmly than he felt, "and I want to be honest with you . . . so there are no surprises."

They locked glances while an awkward silence settled over them. The message was clear to both of them.

"You bastard!" Allison hissed, and slapped him across the mouth, splitting the inside of his lower lip.

She scrambled out of the foxhole while Brad recoiled from the blow. He tasted the warm, salty blood on his tongue and wiped a trickle off his chin.

"Allison," he said steadily, "will you sit down and talk with me for a minute?"

She kicked the C-ration carton at Brad, showering him with dirt and food. "There's nothing to talk about, you son of a bitch!" Allison leaned over and yanked her M-16 off the ground, then angrily walked away.

After spitting a mouthful of blood in the dirt, Brad slumped against the edge of the foxhole and closed his eyes. "You're doing just great. . . ."

Lex Blackwell, who had commandeered his own tent, was busy setting up his shelter when Brad awakened with a groan. Nick Palmer was supplying the raw muscle, while Lex steadied the sagging tent.

Brad touched his tender lip and stiffly sat up on his cot. Allison's rage rushed back to linger in his mind. It was his own fault for letting himself get into the embarrassing position in the first place.

Feeling groggy from his restless sleep, Austin grabbed a clean flight suit and his dopp kit, mumbled "Good morning" to Lex and Nick, then walked to the shower stall.

Fifteen minutes later, Brad returned freshly shaved and showered. Using the water from his canteen, he gently brushed his teeth and rinsed his mouth.

All activity on the field came to an abrupt halt when the sound of the C-123 reverberated across the valley. Brad shielded his eyes and searched the sky above the morning haze layer. He spotted the Provider as the pilot commenced a steep approach to Alpha-29.

Nick and Lex joined Brad, and they watched the transport plane briefly flare, then smoothly touch down with a chirp from the tires.

"Not bad for a 'trash hauler,'" Blackwell said lightly, then caught a glimpse of Austin's swollen lip.

"What happened to you?"

Uneasy with his sense of guilt, Brad hid his feelings with a careless smile. "I forgot to duck."

When the C-123 taxied to a stop, twenty-three CIA employees in fresh jungle utilities leaped out and reported to Gunnery Sergeant Rodriguez. The second-to-last man out of the aircraft sported a new uniform that was at least three sizes too large.

"Well," Blackwell ventured dryly, "they must've shanghaied the mess cook."

Brad gave Lex a sidelong glance. "At least we've got more firepower," he observed, then walked over to inspect the MiG.

CHAPTER THIRTY-FIVE

Brad felt the perspiration on his forehead as he preflighted the venerable fighter that he had come to respect. The mission briefing, with Allison sitting across from him, had been difficult for both of them. He was certain that everyone in attendance was aware of the strained relationship between the two of them.

The aircraft technicians had repainted the airplane in a standard terrain camouflage of black, white, and gray with North Vietnamese national markings on the fuselage and outboard on the wings. They had also repaired a small fuel leak in the left drop tank and tightened the bolts that held the right tank to the wing.

Reaching the tail pipe, Brad inspected the smoke canister and paused. Thoughts of Allison entered his mind. The last thing he had wanted to do was hurt anyone, but he had had to be straightforward with her. Brad hoped that after the flight she would give him a chance to talk with her. At the moment, though, he had to concentrate on the immediate future.

The navy strike force would launch from the carriers at 1600. Accompanied by F-4 Phantom and F-8 Crusader fighter aircraft, the A-6 Intruders and A-4 Skyhawks would strike the Thanh Hoa Bridge and the supporting antiaircraft sites at approximately 1635.

Although Operation Achilles was ancillary to the air-force and navy strike forces, Austin felt confident that he could contribute to the air-war effort in a meaningful way.

Climbing into the cockpit, Brad started the engine and ran through his pretakeoff checklist, then taxied to the runway. He avoided looking at Allison and the other spectators near the Quonset hut, but noticed that Nick and Lex had positioned themselves near the middle of the airstrip.

After a quick radio check with Cap Spencer, Brad made a maximum-performance takeoff and headed for his holding point south of Bai Thuong.

The weather was partly cloudy with good visibility underneath the clouds. The extended forecast had indicated no change in the next twelve hours. When the airborne radio check had been completed, Brad tuned one radio to the strike-group frequency and the other to Sleepy Two Five.

Austin glanced at his watch when he passed his first checkpoint. It was time for Mitchell and Jimenez to lift off the ramp. The rescue helicopter would be over the border between Laos and North Vietnam five minutes before Brad was expected to strafe the MiG base.

Bright sunshine filled the MiG's cockpit, causing the temperature to climb in the cramped space. Brad looked out along the forty-five-degree swept wings and checked both slipper-type drop tanks. They appeared to be secure and showed no signs of fuel leakage.

Austin carefully followed his progress on his operational navigation chart. He had cut the map down to a fraction of its normal size, eliminating everything more than twenty-five nautical miles on either side of his route.

Passing Ban Na Mang, Brad hugged the tops of the rugged mountains and slipped into North Vietnamese airspace. He had another sixty miles to travel before he would be on station south of Bai Thuong.

Brad continued to monitor his speed, time, and fuel as the sun gradually disappeared above the clouds, leaving only faint holes in the overcast. The MiG's pale camouflage would blend perfectly into the grayish clouds.

Waiting for the fighter activity call from the UH-34, Brad tightened his chest harness and seat strap. He decided to arm his cannons early so he would not forget the important step in the heat of battle.

Squinting through the thick, armored-glass windshield, Austin began to distinguish the runway at Bai Thuong from the surrounding terrain.

Brad altered course to the right and again glanced at his watch. When was he going to hear the strip-alert call? The strike group should be nearing the coast-in point. After passing the last mountain summit, Brad eased the throttle forward and kept his rate of descent shallow as he let down toward Bai Thuong. Better to be early than late.

"Tidewater One, Rock Crusher. Weather check."

Tidewater was the call sign for the navy F-4 target combat air-patrol fighters. They had previously crossed the shoreline and were in a position to view the target area.

"Crusher," the Phantom flight leader replied, "no problem with weather. We'll be on station in about two minutes."

"Roger," the strike group leader answered, then added, "Crushers will be feet dry in three minutes."

"Copy."

A moment later, the other TARCAP flight came up strike frequency. "Ragtime copies," the F-8 Crusader leader chimed in. "We're on station and anchored at eleven thou."

Brad looked high in the sky north of Bai Thuong. "Come on, Spencer . . . time's running out." A minute and a half later, he heard the flak suppressor flight leader check in on strike frequency.

"Ah, Skeeter Four Fifty-one is crossing the beach—starting our run-in."

"Roger," the strike leader said in a controlled voice. "I've got you in sight."

Searching for the F-4 Phantoms, Austin was startled when Rudy Jimenez suddenly called on the other radio.

"Top Cat, Sleepy Two Five. Activity."

Brad thumbed his radio switch. "Top Cat—copy."

"Go get 'em."

Banking toward the MiG base, Austin lowered the nose and let the airspeed increase to 410 knots. He could feel the airplane tremble as it approached 425 knots.

"SAMs," someone called. "We've got SAMs up!"

"Watch it, Tony!"

"I've got 'em," an emotionless voice answered.

Brad managed a look toward Thanh Hoa before he turned his attention to the MiG runway.

"Well, shit," Austin swore when he saw a MiG-17 lifting off the runway. "I'm going to be late."

The urgent radio calls from the strike group became impossible to understand, forcing Brad to mentally tune out the incessant chatter.

Another North Vietnamese fighter was commencing his takeoff when Austin lined up with the runway. He saw a string of MiGs bunched together for takeoff as he flattened his dive.

"Keep it together," Brad coached himself as he placed the gun sight on the first of the MiGs. Squeezing the trigger gently, Austin felt his fighter vibrate as a stream of white-hot shells ripped through the line of MiGs.

He let the incandescent tracers walk the length of the field, then made a snap decision. Releasing the trigger, Brad whipped the thundering jet into knife-edge flight and executed a punishing 6-g, 360-degree turn to again align himself with the runway.

"MiGs! We've got MiGs airborne!" a voice shouted. "On the deck—comin' from the north."

"Tidewater has a tally. We're engaging."

Focusing his attention on the airfield, Brad was surprised to see two columns of black smoke rising into the gray sky. Three more fighters had reached the runway, with two of the aircraft rolling for takeoff. The rest of the MiGs waiting for takeoff were scattered like bowling pins. People were running in every conceivable direction.

"Ragtime has the MiGs. We'll cover you, Tidewater."

"Jump in whenever you want!" the F-4 pilot shot back. "There's plenty for everyone!"

"Brownie," another voice broke through the confusion. "Bandits—check your four o'clock!"

"SAMs! Two more at eleven!"

Brad boresighted the two fighters on the runway in his gun sight and held the trigger down. A bright streak of molten fire tore through one of the fighters, then Brad raised the nose, tracking the MiG that had become airborne.

Everyone on the base who had a weapon fired at Brad's MiG while the others watched his cannon fire rip the lead aircraft to shreds. The MiG slow-rolled to the left, caught a wingtip on the ground, and cartwheeled into a blazing inferno.

"Watch out, Ski!" a high-pitched voice warned. "You've got a MiG coming around to your six."

The other MiG Brad had hit staggered into the air and began a steep, climbing turn, then reversed and dove for the deck. Brad was about to chase the damaged fighter when two dark forms flashed overhead.

Snapping his head up, Brad saw two MiG-17s blast across the end of the airfield. They had to have come from another base, Austin thought while he lowered the nose and raced toward the Laotian border. He heard the flight leader of the Rock Crushers order his charges to head for the beach. It was time for everyone to exit.

Brad winced when tracers flashed over his right wing. Expecting to see an F-8 on his tail, Brad craned his neck in time to see the muzzle flashes from one of two MiG-17s.

Someone at Bai Thuong had radioed his position and description to the fighter pilots who had been patiently waiting for the fraudulent MiG. The enemy pilots, who Brad guessed had fair hair and blue eyes, were obviously from the first string, and certainly spoke fluent Russian.

Brad yanked the stick into his lap and slammed it hard to the left. The nose snapped up and the horizon rotated three quarters of the way through a roll before Brad centered the stick and then pulled with every ounce of strength in his arms.

The MiG flight leader, who was the designated shooter, overshot Brad's aircraft. Austin dove for airspeed and separation, but he could not shake the wingman. The two fighters worked in perfect harmony, with one attacking while the other pilot called the fight and flew high cover. When Brad reversed, the enemy pilots simply switched roles.

Knowing that it was only a matter of seconds before they would shoot him down, Brad frantically searched for the TARCAP F-4s or F-8s. In desperation, he keyed the radio tuned to the navy strike frequency.

"Tidewater, say posit!"

"Five north of Bai Thuong," the Phantom flight leader gasped as he executed a high-g turn. "We've got bogies—engaging bandits coming from the north." The F-4s were busy with MiGs from the airfields at Phuc Yen and Gia Lam.

Brad slipped and skidded the MiG, then snap-rolled the aircraft and popped the nose up and down in a reflexive effort to elude the intense cannon fire. There was no escape from the two expertly flown fighters.

"MiGs airborne over Bai Thuong!" he called, then wrapped his aircraft into an uncoordinated displacement roll. "We need cover— MiGs north of Bai Thuong!"

A different voice, which sounded calm and soothing, cut through the garbled radio transmissions. "Ragtime is on the way. Say your call sign and position."

Brad caught a glance of the runway as he shoved the nose down and then violently yanked the stick back. He again rolled the airplane and keyed his mike. "Two north of Bai Thuong," he inhaled sharply, "coming back across the field." He purposely avoided using a call sign.

"Roger that."

Breathing rapidly, Brad pulled the MiG into the vertical before cross-controlling and extending the speed brakes. He yanked the throttle to idle and shoved the stick forward, causing the aircraft to depart from controlled flight.

"Oh, shit . . . ," Austin blurted as one of the MiGs flashed directly over his canopy. His first priority was to recover control of the fighter before it hit the ground. Brad was violently slammed around the cockpit as the MiG tumbled end-over-end, wallowed in a yaw, then rolled inverted.

Fighting the crushing g forces, Brad slammed the throttle forward and let the nose fall below the horizon. The airspeed rapidly increased and he rolled the MiG upright, searching for his attackers.

He felt a solid jolt followed by a blinding white flash, then experienced a searing pain in his right arm as more tracers slashed past the canopy. Austin also saw what he hoped would be his salvation. Two F-8 Crusaders were turning tightly to engage Brad and his two adversaries. The American fighter pilots obviously had no idea that two MiGs were attacking another Communist fighter.

"Ragtime has a tally! Engaging three seventeens north of Bai Thuong."

Turning to face the F-8s head-on, Brad waited a second before beginning a shallow, nose-low turn. He twisted around in time to see the other two MiGs break off to avoid fighting the supersonic Crusaders.

"Come on, Ragtime," Brad said to himself through clenched teeth, then pulled the nose up. "Jump the bastards . . . so I can get the hell out of here."

"Jimbo," the Ragtime flight leader yelled to his wingman, "I'm taking the one coming up on the right! Stick with me and clear our six."

"I'm with you, Skipper!"

Austin swore under his breath when he realized that Ragtime One, the commanding officer of a Crusader fighter squadron, had elected to pounce on his lone MiG.

Deciding to try his last means of escape, Brad turned north and raced toward Hanoi and the sanctity of the MiG bases that were adjacent to the capital city.

The F-8 pilots selected afterburner and knifed through a climbing reversal. Rolling out of the tight turn, the Crusaders accelerated past the speed of sound and quickly caught Austin's slower MiG.

Hugging the terrain, Brad hoped the pilots would not be able to get their heat-seeking Sidewinder missiles to lock on to his fighter. Seconds later, the lead F-8 fired two bursts from his 20-millimeter cannons.

When the stream of tracers flashed past, Brad toggled the MiG's smoke canister. *You're cutting it too damn close.* He raised the nose slightly above the horizon, then started a lazy roll while the oily smoke poured from his tail pipe. Austin watched the ground rise to meet him and counted the seconds. Seven . . . eight . . . nine . . .

"Jimbo," the F-8 leader shouted, "I've got a smoker goin' down. See him?"

"I see him," the wingman exclaimed, "but we've got two bandits high at four o'clock!"

"Ragtime is coming around," the exuberant pilot announced. "Are they the same ones who broke off?"

"Ahh . . . can't tell."

Austin ignored the radio calls and snap-rolled the diving MiG upright. He bottomed out on the deck and turned toward the Laotian border. *Thank you, God.*

Climbing to clear the approaching mountains, Brad slowed his breathing and felt his heart pounding in his chest. The smoke subterfuge had worked, but the North Vietnamese were obviously gunning for the impostor. Brad swiveled his head in search of possible attackers and unconsciously shoved on the throttle.

Aware of the numbing pain near his right elbow, Austin cautiously looked down. Blood soaked his forearm, staining his Nomex and calf-skin glove. Brad gingerly felt his bicep while he wrestled the MiG on course. His eyes swept the instrument panel, noting the damaged section near the left side of the windshield. Whatever had penetrated the cockpit next to his right arm had impacted under the canopy rail.

To hell with radio silence. He tweaked the volume up on the UH-34's frequency.

"Sleepy Two Five, Top Cat."

After a short pause, Brad was relieved to hear Chase Mitchell's voice.

"Sleepy up."

"Top Cat's been hit," Austin said briskly as he passed low over a village. He tried to calm himself. "Request your position for rendezvous en route."

"We're on course line," Mitchell responded dryly, "turning toward home plate." Course line was the direct route from Alpha-29 to Bai Thuong.

Brad looked at the blood-splattered chart on his kneeboard and glanced at the mountain peak to his left. He was approximately seven miles north of course. "Say altitude."

"Six thousand," Rudy Jimenez answered for Mitchell. "You'll catch us in a few minutes. What's the extent of your damage?"

"I think the airplane is okay . . . for the time being. But I've been hit in the arm."

The disclosure was met with a moment of silence from the helicopter crew. Finally, Jimenez keyed his radio. "Hang in there. We're not far from home."

Austin clicked his mike twice. *Settle down,* he told himself while he methodically scanned the engine gauges and checked the fuel quantity. Everything appeared normal and fuel was not a factor. For the first time, he noticed specks of blood on the starboard electrical control panel and lower instrument panel.

The minutes dragged on while Brad probed the sky in search of the helicopter. He was about to call the UH-34 when he spotted a slow-moving speck on the horizon.

He steadied the MiG at 5,800 feet and flexed his right hand. The pain was becoming more acute, forcing Brad to concentrate on the task of flying the airplane.

"Sleepy, Top Cat has a tally."

"Roger. Do you want us to look you over, or do you want to go straight in?"

Brad looked out at the wings, noticing a hole in the right inboard wing fence. He could not see any other apparent damage. "I'll go straight in."

"Copy."

Passing to the right of the helicopter, Brad rocked the wings in a salute and lowered the nose. He felt something wet on his right thigh. A quick glance confirmed that blood was dripping from his wrist.

"Top Cat," Hollis Spencer's voice boomed in Austin's helmet. "We're taking sniper fire from the top of the ridge on the south side of the field. Do you have enough ammo for a strafing run?"

A kaleidoscope of thoughts ran through Brad's mind. *This is crazy—goddamn insane.* He slowly inhaled, then let his breath out in a rush. "Affirmative."

Brad looked at his armament panel, then swore to himself. In his eagerness to escape from the F-8 Crusaders, he had left the cannons armed.

A mile from the threshold of the runway, Brad eased the stick to the left and lined up with the jagged ridge. He leveled at 200 feet above the crest and deftly lowered the nose. A series of muzzle flashes winked at him from the trees as he squeezed the trigger.

Two streams of tracers converged ahead of the MiG, walking straight through the bright flashes. Brad pulled off to the right and bent the MiG around for a firing run in the opposite direction.

Halfway through the strafing pass, Brad felt the vibration from the cannons stop. The ammunition bin was empty. He reduced the power to idle, then clumsily lowered the flaps and landing gear.

Brad widened his turn to the airfield and rechecked to be sure that his wheels were down and locked. Feeling light-headed, Austin focused on the narrow runway and concentrated on his lineup.

"Stay with it," he muttered as he nudged the throttle to arrest a high sink rate. The MiG impacted in the grass overrun and bounced onto the macadam in a bone-jarring landing.

Austin braked evenly, stopping near the entrance to the taxiway. He opened the canopy and turned onto the short strip, then shut down the engine and slumped in his seat. Oblivious to the approaching men, he tilted his head back and breathed the fresh air.

CHAPTER THIRTY-SIX

From the top of the briefing table, Brad opened his eyes and stared at the dim light bulb dangling from the ceiling. His lower back ached and his right arm was sore. He raised his head a few inches, then let it fall back on the sweat-soaked pillow. What time was it?

Austin brought his left wrist to his chest and waited for his eyes to adjust. Eleven-fifteen. The Quonset hut was dark and quiet, so it must be nighttime.

He cautiously glanced at his upper right arm, which was resting on a second pillow. The sleeve of his Soviet-style flight suit had been cut off at the shoulder. He studied the thick gauze bandage that was neatly wrapped around his arm. The loosely woven fabric extended from above his elbow to under his armpit.

Brad closed his eyes and sighed. He felt drowsy from the effects of the morphine, and he let his mind drift back to the mission. The events suddenly rushed back as he replayed the terror in slow motion.

"How are you feeling?" a soft voice said from somewhere off to the side.

His eyes blinked open and he turned his head in the direction of the sound.

"Allison?" Brad uttered, searching through half-closed eyelids. His mouth seemed as dry as a barren desert and his tongue felt swollen.

"Yes," she replied quietly as Hollis Spencer stirred from his nap. "Would you like some water?"

Brad attempted a smile. "Yes . . . thank you."

"I'll be right back."

Cap Spencer stretched and walked to Brad's side when Allison went outside to the water cistern. He looked haggard when he sat down in the chair next to Austin.

Spencer placed his hand on Brad's left shoulder. "Things are looking up. Our ace corpsman says you're going to be as good as new in a week or two."

Austin gave him a feeble grin. "This is the worst hangover I've ever had." He rubbed his eyes in an attempt to clear his vision. "How bad is it?"

"You've got a couple of deep cuts," Spencer explained warmly, "and a small hole where the doc removed a piece of metal. He cleaned and sutured your wounds, but we need to medevac you to Vientiane in the morning to have a real doctor check you over."

Before Brad could respond, Allison returned, followed by Lex and Nick. She poured a cupful of water while Palmer and Blackwell stepped next to the table.

"Ah, yes," Nick said with a haughty smirk, "now we have two goldbricks in the outfit."

Brad thanked Allison and thirstily sipped the cool water. He handed the cup back to her and gazed at Spencer.

"Cap, I don't want to go to Vientiane and lie around on my ass." The challenge was underscored by the determined look in Brad's eyes. "I'll be okay in a few days."

Blackwell, who had not wanted to return to Vientiane and be viewed as a shirker, jumped to Austin's defense. "He's right, Cap. Hell, I've seen the clodhopper hurt himself worse fallin' off a bar stool."

Brad smothered a laugh. Lex Blackwell, the garrulous fighter pilot from Texas, would never change.

"Have it your way." Spencer chuckled, then rose from the chair. He clearly understood the guiding principles of a naval aviator. "But you've got to rest and have the dressing changed every morning. That," he said emphatically, "is an order, Brad."

"Yes, sir," Austin replied, and again accepted the cup of water from Allison.

"Yeah," Palmer smiled at Brad, "all of us can rest, since you thoroughly trashed the airplane."

"Okay, everyone out except Allison," Spencer insisted. "We'll get together in the morning."

Nick turned serious and clutched Brad's left arm. "Glad you're okay."

"Thanks."

When the pilots left and Spencer returned to his cubicle, Allison sat down next to Brad. There was a pronounced awkwardness until she initiated the conversation.

"Nurse van Ingen," she said offhandedly, "at your service."

Tension hung in the air while Brad tried to assess her mood. Still dulled from the anesthetic, Brad was having a difficult time formulating a reasonable response.

"Allison, I really appreciate your consideration," he said somewhat indistinctly, "but I'll be okay as soon as my head clears."

She nodded somberly and crossed her arms. "Nick brought your cot in, if you feel like moving to it."

"That's okay," he replied, and raised his left hand to plump the pillow under his head. "I'll just stay here for a while . . . until the grogginess wears off."

"Suit yourself," she countered, and rose from the chair. After a few steps, Allison paused and turned, then walked back to his side.

"Brad," she began in a hushed voice, and gently gripped his left hand, "I apologize for what I said to you."

He rolled his head to look at her gloomy face. She blinked back the tears that filled her eyes.

"You don't need to apologize. I deserved it."

"Brad," her voice shook from pain and frustration, "I will always love you."

He had never felt such deep moral anguish in his life. He squeezed her hand. "Allison, I—"

"Please," she said emotionally, and pulled her hand away, "don't make it more difficult than it is."

Allison silently accepted for the first time that all the promise of their future would never be.

CIA HEADQUARTERS

Dennis Tipton stared blankly through the smudged windshield of his car as he turned into the basement parking garage. His stomach felt as if he were on a pitching and rolling fishing schooner in a North Atlantic storm. The deputy director of the CIA had been unusually agitated when he called to rouse Tipton out of bed.

He parked in his designated spot and quickly walked to the

entrance. The early-morning dampness made him shiver as he greeted the security guard.

When Tipton reached the top floor of the building, he hurried to Drexel McCormick's office. He slowed when he saw the open door. McCormick, who was loudly berating someone on the telephone, abruptly hung up when he spotted the director for operations.

"Dennis, have a seat."

Tipton nodded silently while he unbuttoned his topcoat and slipped into one of the chairs facing McCormick's desk. He could feel his neck muscles stiffen while he mentally prepared himself for one of McCormick's verbal onslaughts.

"The President called The Man on the carpet a few hours ago," he growled, and furrowed his brow. "Our MiG was almost shot down and the pilot was wounded."

Dennis Tipton looked confused. "This is the first that I've heard about it."

"That's because Cap Spencer didn't tell us about it, goddamnit!" McCormick was beet-red.

Tipton cast his eyes down and remained silent. He knew from experience that it was not in his best interest to say anything until his boss had vented his initial anger.

"Damnit, the White House had the information before we knew anything about it," McCormick snorted. "Do you know what that makes us look like?"

"Yes, sir." Tipton inwardly cringed, wishing that he had never placed his stamp of approval on the operation.

"It makes us look like a bunch of half-witted, knuckle-dragging amateurs," the deputy director bellowed. "The Man didn't like that," he snarled in a harsh whisper, "and he knocked fire from my ass!"

"What's the current situation?" Tipton ventured, concealing his growing contempt for McCormick.

"The situation is this," he said while he lighted a cigar. "The White House wants us to get a handle on this Chinese fire drill, or get the hell out and make everything vanish."

The red-faced deputy director, for the first time Dennis Tipton could remember, looked genuinely scared. The White House was rolling the dice, trying to get an edge in the air war while they maintained an appearance of unwavering integrity.

Tipton was aware of the devastating Communist attack on Alpha-29, but the news of the narrow escape of the wounded pilot was a major blow. He decided to change the subject slightly. "Have we got the damage assessment—what the pilot destroyed, if anything?"

McCormick squinted and chewed on his cigar. "Reconnaissance photographs have confirmed that five enemy fighter planes have either been destroyed or damaged at Bai Thuong, but we came close to losing the MiG . . . and that goddamned Spencer didn't even inform us!"

Tipton was afraid that the North Vietnamese were setting up an ambush for the lone MiG, and was deeply concerned that the pilot might be captured alive and tortured to the point of making a confession.

The operation, he decided after thinking about the miraculous escape by the pilot, was becoming more of a liability than an asset for the Agency—one that was exposing their own Achilles' heel. "In my estimation," he said cautiously but with resolve, "it's time to cancel the operation."

McCormick tapped his cigar on the edge of an ashtray and fixed Tipton in his stare. "That's what The Man thinks, too. But he wants some straight answers before he makes the decision to pull the plug, because the White House wants to get everything they can out of the MiG operation."

"What kind of answers?"

"The entire complexion of Achilles has changed," McCormick said curtly, "and The Man wants *you* to assess the viability of continuing the operation . . . or shutting it down before the lid blows off."

"Me?" Tipton's color faded.

McCormick glared at him and absently flicked ashes from his cigar. "You're the goddamn director for ops," McCormick snapped, then continued very slowly. "It's that simple, Dennis . . . or would you rather tender your resignation?"

The question stunned Tipton, and it was obvious. He felt his stomach twist into a knot while he contemplated his answer. Were they— the director and McCormick—using this crisis to force him out of the Agency before he reached his normal retirement date? After all the years of politically savvy moves and fostering the right connections, was he being shoved out of the CIA?

Throwing caution to the wind, Tipton gritted his teeth and gathered his strength. "What is it—precisely—that I am expected to do?"

"Get your ass over there," McCormick insisted impatiently, "and eyeball the operation—make a goddamned decision to continue the ops or slam the lid."

Tipton's mouth sagged open. "You want me to go to Alpha-29?"

"That's right," the deputy director glowered. "There's a jet, which the President authorized, standing by at Andrews. They'll take you to Honolulu, then you'll catch a commercial flight to Hong Kong. From there, our people will fly you to the site."

They remained silent for a long moment.

"I'll need to pack some things," Tipton protested in vain. "I can't just race off to—"

"Everything you'll need, including work khakis, is being loaded on the plane." McCormick shoved himself up from his wide chair and handed Tipton a sealed manila envelope. "There's a car waiting for you at the main entrance."

Tipton silently reached for the thick packet. In all the years he had been with the Agency, no one at his level had ever been dispatched to a field operation. A premonition of bad fortune crossed his mind.

"Dennis, I expect to hear from you," McCormick declared in an openly belligerent manner, "as soon as you step foot on Alpha-29."

Tipton turned and walked out of the office. Everything was going too fast, and he was caught in what he considered to be a no-win situation. Operation Achilles was spinning out of control, and no one seemed to have the guts to end the operation before it exploded in their faces. If he recommended that Achilles be canceled, what type of repercussions could he expect? He had to find a way to distance himself from the approaching debacle.

When Tipton reached the main entrance, he paused to look at the spectacular yellow-orange and pink glow on the horizon. The pale light filtered evenly into the dark-blue and purple sky. The striking sunrise marked the beginning of a day that Dennis Tipton would never forget.

CHAPTER THIRTY-SEVEN

ALPHA-29

The time had passed slowly while Hank Murray's team repaired the severely damaged MiG. When the holes in the fuselage had been patched, the men painstakingly inspected the turbojet engine and stripped off the camouflage paint. After restoring the airplane to a dull-silver finish, Murray completed an engine run-up, checked all the systems and controls, then pronounced the MiG airworthy.

Nick Palmer had flown the refurbished airplane on a mission to coincide with a strike by Task Force 77 aircraft from Yankee Station. The targets had been a series of truck convoys traveling between Phu Ly and Ninh Binh. The "truck busting" operation had been canceled at the last minute because of low ceilings and limited visibility in the target area.

The flight leader, who temporarily ignored the targeting restrictions, had led the sixteen aircraft along the coastline in search of targets of opportunity. After expending their ordnance, the navy pilots and their fighter escorts had returned unscathed to the aircraft carrier.

Nick had followed the action over the radio while he tried to find a hole in the clouds near the airfield at Bai Thuong. He never found an opening in the swollen clouds, or saw any MiGs above the overcast, so he returned to Alpha-29 and made an uneventful landing.

It was a quiet group that sat around the foxhole in front of the tent that Austin and Palmer shared. Brad mechanically curled his rifle to strengthen his right arm while Nick swapped stories with Lex Blackwell and Rudy Jimenez. Chase Mitchell was in the helicopter, ready to start the engine at the first sign of another Pathet Lao assault. Gunnery Sergeant Rodriguez had viewed the dead bodies from the previous attack and identified them as Pathet Lao.

Jimenez, Mitchell, and Elvin Crowder were sharing the responsibility of having at least one crew member in the UH-34 twenty-four hours a day. The cumulative effects of the fatigue and strain were beginning to weaken their camaraderie.

The sun was slipping below the mountaintops when a loud boom echoed across the valley.

"Sonuvabitch!" Blackwell exclaimed while he and Jimenez scrambled into their foxhole.

Nick and Brad collided when they rolled into their shelter. They raised their eyes above the dirt embankment a second before a mortar round exploded next to the Quonset hut. They ducked as the concussion blasted over their heads.

The entire compound security force opened fire in the general direction of the initial booming sound. People were yelling back and forth while everyone tried to pinpoint the location of the Communist mortar team.

Brad leaped out of his fighting hole at the same time Jimenez raced for the helicopter.

"What are you doing?" Palmer shouted as Austin ran toward the Quonset hut.

The helicopter engine was revving to full power when Brad reached the entrance to the building. He abruptly stopped when Allison stumbled through the open door in a daze. Spencer was close behind her. Wide-eyed and deafened by the explosion, they followed Brad back to the foxholes. Spencer dove into Blackwell's shelter while Brad pulled Allison into his.

The steady rain of rifle and machine-gun fire slowly subsided when Gunny Rodriguez passed the word to cease fire.

Moments later, as the UH-34 became airborne, another loud bang announced a second incoming mortar round.

"Get down!" Austin shouted as he huddled in the corner with Allison and Nick.

The ground shook from the explosion next to the MiG hangar. A tremendous volume of machine-gun fire erupted as dirt and debris shot over the tents and foxholes.

"Come on, Crowder," Brad encouraged as he cautiously peeked over the dirt mound. He saw a steady stream of muzzle flashes coming from the open hatch of the helicopter. "Pour it on 'em!"

The crew chief raked the trees on the hillside with a devastating volume of fire. After three passes, Mitchell maneuvered the UH-34 to a position over the end of the runway and waited for the mortar to fire again.

Alpha-29 had come under intermittent sniper fire for days, but this was the first time a mortar attack had been launched at the compound.

The temporary lull in the action was shattered by a sudden burst of automatic-weapons fire halfway up the hill. Two explosions reverberated across the narrow valley as the security forces fired M-79 grenade launchers at the mortar position. The seasoned men, led by a former platoon sergeant, had worked their way to a forward position in hopes of catching the Pathet Lao off guard.

After four minutes passed without any further shelling, Chase Mitchell gently sat the helicopter down and everyone breathed a collective sigh of relief.

"Allison," Spencer said as he crawled out of his shelter, "you stay there until it's completely dark."

"No argument from me," she responded boldly.

Spencer went to the Quonset hut while Lex Blackwell made his way to the other foxhole.

"I love it," Nick grumbled while he brushed the loose dirt from his hair.

Lex squatted on the parapet. "I don't know about the rest of you, but I'd say it's past time to close shop and get back to civilization."

"I agree with you," Brad replied evenly, "because I've got a feeling they're preparing for a full-blown frontal assault."

Palmer cast Brad a worried glance. "Great."

Brad turned to see Hank Murray rush by with one of his men. The technician was holding the side of his head and muttering unintelligibly.

"Oh, Jesus," Blackwell exclaimed, "he's bleedin' like a stuck hog."

They watched the two men approach the damaged building while Murray yelled for a corpsman.

Nick hesitated for a moment, then turned with a false calm to face Austin. "Well, your last prediction was right. When do you think they'll hit us again?"

Brad gave his dressing a cursory inspection. "If I were their honcho," he glanced at the crest of the opposing mountain, "I'd wait until the helo and the MiG were gone."

Blackwell swung his legs over the side of the hole and adjusted his arm sling. "Yeah, 'cause they've been watchin' us, and they know that when they're both gone . . . we're a bunch of sittin' ducks."

Hollis Spencer hurried out of the Quonset hut as the corpsman rushed around the corner of the building.

"I think it's time to talk with Spencer," Palmer suggested, and looked at Allison. "What do you think?"

She shrugged and cast a look at her boss. "You know that I'm very loyal to him, but I have to agree with you."

The security forces were still jogging from post to post around the field when Spencer knelt by the foxhole. He had a piece of paper rolled in his hand and he looked pensive.

"The director for ops is on his way here," he declared with a pained expression. "The word just came in."

"Dennis Tipton," Allison tilted her head, "is coming to Alpha-29?"

"That's what the message says."

Brad studied Spencer with a curious interest. "Would you mind filling us in?"

He looked at Austin and spoke in a subdued voice. "You know as much as I do, but it's highly unusual for a director to go to the field."

Searching for the right words, Brad decided to form his thoughts into a question. "Cap, do you think we're pushing our luck beyond a reasonable limit?"

Spencer sighed heavily and examined the MiG for a long moment. "Probably."

"You're the boss," Austin said warily, "but I think it would be in everyone's best interest to consider the gain from this operation . . . for the risk involved."

Spencer suddenly felt the built-up pressure and unending tension. Had his personal ambition to make Operation Achilles a success clouded his decision making? Was Dennis Tipton on his way to Alpha-29 to relieve him of command?

"For the moment," Spencer replied in an effort to convince himself as well as the others, "we'll go ahead with tomorrow's mission, then we'll stand down until the director for ops gets here."

Brad and Allison exchanged a cautious glance, but kept their thoughts to themselves.

*   *   *

The C-123 Provider had been used to transport the seriously wounded aircraft technician to Vientiane. The airplane was due back at sunrise with supplies and ammunition.

After darkness had enveloped the airfield, Allison returned to the Quonset hut while Nick, Brad, and Lex slipped into the hangar to inspect the MiG. The fighter had sustained only superficial damage from the mortar-shell explosion. After leaving the blacked-out hangar, the three pilots selected a variety of C-rations and then congregated in front of their foxholes.

When the trio had finished their unappetizing meals, Spencer approached and asked them to join him inside, then walked to the helicopter to get Mitchell and Jimenez.

"I know you're tired," Spencer said patiently as the pilots entered the building and slumped into their chairs, "so I won't keep you long.

"Allison just received our preliminary ops instructions for the strikes tomorrow." He tugged on his eye patch and scanned the wrinkled document. "The air force has been tasked to hit a number of targets in Route Pack Six . . . around the Thai Nguyen area near Thud Ridge."

Spencer paused to point to the target area on the wall-mounted chart.

"And the carrier groups are launching an Alpha Strike aimed at targets around Haiphong." A weary smile creased the corner of his mouth. "Their primary target is the airfield at Kien An, so we can expect a lot of MiG activity."

Brad rested his chin on the top of his knuckles and examined the map with a critical eye. The enemy air base was located five miles southwest of the bustling port city of Haiphong. "Who's scheduled for tomorrow?"

"You are," Spencer answered without hesitation, "if your arm isn't bothering you."

Brad looked at the small dressing he still wore. The wounds were not completely healed, but they would not prevent him from flying. "I'm fine, as long as I keep the dressing in place."

"Good, because we need to make this mission a big success."

Austin slowly rose and walked to the chart. "Cap, I have a suggestion—actually, it's an idea that I've been hashing around since my last flight."

"It's your mission, Brad," Spencer conceded with a slight nod, "so you'll be calling the shots."

"The air force is obviously going to have a number of Wild Weasels trolling around Thud Ridge," Austin explained while he surveyed the area north of Phuc Yen, "so there's going to be a lot of confusion between Phuc Yen and the target area."

Wild Weasels were F-4 Phantoms that had been highly modified to act as surface-to-air missile-suppression and electronic-counter-measure aircraft. They had the unenvied responsibility for jamming enemy search or fire control radar sites.

"In my estimation," Brad continued almost soothingly, "we might as well go for a grand slam . . . when we get up to bat."

No one said a word while they waited for his explanation. Blackwell and Palmer never blinked an eye.

Spencer reasoned that Austin sensed the mission would be their last one. "Brad, let's do the best we can, without unnecessarily endangering the operation."

Austin fell silent for a moment. Spencer noticed that Brad was absently flexing his fingers.

"Cap, let me throw my idea on the table," Brad countered in a low, even voice, "and if you don't agree with it, I'll be happy to listen to whatever you have in mind."

"You have the floor," Spencer replied with marked apprehension.

Austin caught Palmer's pained expression, but decided to say what he thought in spite of the subtle warning. If he was going to risk flying the mission, he might as well do as much damage as possible.

"What I have in mind is going in low and fast—as usual." He traced his proposed route on the chart. "Hit Hoa Lac, continue straight over downtown Hanoi, strafe Gia Lam, turn hard northwest to strike Phuc Yen, then pack it out of there down in the trees."

With the North Vietnamese ground units and air force alerted to watch for suspicious MiGs, Austin would be extremely lucky if he managed to attack all three airfields and survive.

Lex Blackwell let out a low whistle. "You're gonna give Uncle Ho's boys a bad case of the runs," he drawled with a straight face, "but they're liable to jump on you like buzzards on a gut wagon."

"Cap," Brad said in an impassioned plea, "if I can hit Hoa Lac seven minutes before the first air strikes, I'll be off the last target when they roll in. The gomers will be in shock, which should help keep our losses to a minimum."

Spencer thought about the proposal while the other pilots quietly talked among themselves. The odds were against Austin's being able to successfully strafe three airfields and get away clean.

"I'm not comfortable with your idea," Spencer said at last, "but I'll go along with it, if you feel confident that you can pull it off."

"Cap, I don't have any doubt. I know I can make it work." He hesitated, listening to Allison's faint voice as she talked on the radio. "I want to create an atmosphere of pure pandemonium . . . and let them think about it every time they crawl into their cockpits."

Spencer gazed thoughtfully at Brad, his eye questioning what the pilot was really thinking. There was an intense determination in Austin's stare.

"Okay, Brad," Spencer said at last, "we'll go over the details in the morning." He glanced at the other men. "Get some rest."

When the pilots had left, Spencer poured a coffee mug full of bourbon and sat in silence. He quietly prayed that the director for operations would arrive in the morning and call off the operation, before it was exposed, or someone died.

The air force Special Air Missions jet cruised serenely at 39,000 feet over the tranquil Pacific Ocean. Dennis Tipton sat quietly, gazing vacantly out the window at the tops of the moonlit clouds. He had made an agonizing decision over the past few hours.

To hell with McCormick, Tipton thought bitterly, and to hell with the internal politics of the Agency, and his precious retirement. He had a documented medical problem; a peptic ulcer that could easily lead to perforation and peritonitis of his abdominal cavity.

"May I get you anything, sir?" the male air-force flight steward asked.

Startled, Tipton looked up at the smiling staff sergeant. "Sure. I'll have a Bloody Mary, and make it extra hot."

"A rocket Bloody Mary it is," the soft-spoken man replied, then added, "We'll be on the ground at Hickam in an hour and twenty minutes."

"Thank you," Tipton replied with a calming sense of relief.

Having made his decision, Dennis Tipton looked forward to his first drink in weeks. The spicy concoction would certainly inflame his ulcer and exacerbate his already delicate medical condition. No one could possibly deny the seriousness of his stomach problem.

When the steward returned with his drink, Tipton took a small sip and finalized his plan. He would ask the pilot to contact Hickam Air

Force Base and demand that a physician be standing by when the VIP transport landed.

Tipton would explain his condition to the doctor and request immediate hospitalization. Someone else could deal with Operation Achilles while he was undergoing treatment for his ulcer.

Tipton raised his glass and drank half the contents in three quick swallows. He would cover his ass, and no one could question his actions. Especially after the doctors documented his condition.

CHAPTER THIRTY-EIGHT

Brad examined the wall chart and jotted notes while Allison prepared the detailed mission brief for him. The final instructions for the massive air strike had arrived only minutes before.

Working at a feverish pace, Allison neatly printed call signs and radio frequencies on Brad's kneeboard cards. The weather, both en route and over the targets, looked good and was steadily improving.

Hollis Spencer and Lex Blackwell had walked to the hangar to inspect the MiG and talk with Hank Murray. The project officer wanted to make sure that the MiG was in perfect flying condition before Austin stepped into the cockpit.

Allison had maintained an air of casual friendliness with Brad, but there was an easily recognized aloofness about her. She was cautious in his presence and measured her words when they conversed.

"Can you spare a minute?" Austin finally asked when she paused to light a cigarette.

"Sure."

"What do you think Cap is going to recommend when the director for ops arrives?"

The expression on Allison's face abruptly hardened. "He's under a lot of pressure. I think he'll recommend that we cancel the operation."

Austin started to respond, but held his thoughts when Palmer entered the building.

"Nick," Brad said with a quick smile, "you're just the guy I wanted to see."

Palmer gave him one of his slanted grins. "Don't tell me—you need a loan?"

"Thanks, Allison," Brad said briskly and caught Nick by the arm. "I'll be back as soon as I get into my zoom-bag."

She nodded and returned to her work.

"Nick," Austin said as they stepped out of the Quonset hut and turned toward their tent, "I've got a favor to ask."

Palmer became suspicious when he noted Brad's sober tone. "Should I brace myself, or open my wallet?"

Brad slowed to a stop and lowered his voice. "I asked Leigh Ann to come over here."

Palmer cocked his head. "To Vientiane?"

"Yes," he replied, casting a glance at the MiG hangar. "I haven't told anyone, and I was—"

"Brad, are you sure you want to do that? We don't know what we're going to be doing from one day to the next."

A tense smile creased Austin's face. "That's my point, and she's on her way here as we speak." Brad thought about the number of days that had passed since he had sent the letter to Leigh Ann. "In fact, she may have already arrived at the Constellation. At any rate, who knows what is going to happen day by day, or if they're going to halt the operation and ship us back to fighter squadrons."

Palmer rolled his eyes, but remained quiet for the moment.

"Leigh Ann wanted to come to Vientiane," Austin continued evenly, "and she has every right to be here. It's safe in the city, and she'll have plenty of American wives to visit with."

Brad paused when Blackwell and Spencer emerged from the hangar. "Let's go to the tent."

Palmer and Austin exchanged greetings with the two men and entered their open shelter.

"If she's here, or on her way," Brad reached for his Soviet-style flight suit, "and I get knocked down—or can't get back right away—will you make sure that she's okay?"

Nick observed the rigid look on his friend's face and swallowed a sarcastic remark. "You're going to be fine . . . but if something goes wrong, I'll take care of things, so don't worry about it."

"Thanks, Nick," he said while he slipped into his flight suit, then saw Blackwell saunter out of the Quonset hut. Lex gave them a thumbs-down indication.

Brad glanced at Nick, then let his eyes follow Lex. "What's that supposed to mean?"

"Beats me." Palmer laughed quietly and then turned serious. "Maybe the mission has been scrubbed."

"Naw, couldn't be." Brad responded uncomfortably. "That would make things too easy."

Blackwell approached them with a grim look on his face.

Palmer nudged Austin. "Your request to fly for the Blue Angels," he said out of the corner of his mouth, "must have been turned down."

Brad reached for his holster. "Right."

"Cap is fit to be tied," Lex announced dryly. "From what I could gather—he's still goin' over the message—the Agency's chief bureaucrat what's-in-charge has mysteriously gone medically down in Hawaii."

"Tipton?" Brad inquired while he checked the rounds in his service revolver.

"Yeah, the op's heavy," Blackwell replied with a shrug. "Convenient place to drop anchor . . . 'specially if this shit hole is your ultimate destination."

Palmer shook his head in resignation. "I guess we continue to march," he said curtly, "until someone makes a decision about our future."

"Or until we bust up the MiG," Lex solemnly observed.

WATTAY AIRPORT, VIENTIANE

Leigh Ann, tired and frayed by the series of grueling flights, hailed a taxi to the Constellation Hotel. After her luggage had been loaded into the rusting cab, she slid across the backseat and thought about what Brad had suggested in his letter. She would ask the general manager of the hotel to give her some assistance in getting settled in Vientiane.

The happy-go-lucky taxi driver kept up a running commentary in broken English as he made his way through the sparse traffic. His nonsensical rambling was occasionally punctuated by a turn of his head and a smile at Leigh Ann.

She would force a smile in return, then attempt to concentrate on the scenery in the quiet, almost sleepy city. She was astounded by the endless open-air markets and relaxed atmosphere. There seemed to be no sense of urgency. The capital of Laos was certainly not what she had envisioned when she left Memphis for the Orient.

When the taxi stopped in front of the hotel, Leigh Ann felt a rush of excitement. Maybe Brad would be waiting for her. She quickly paid the driver, then grabbed her two suitcases and hurried into the lobby.

Her initial excitement waned after she met Lo Van Phuong and the friendly general manager explained that Mister Austin was not registered in the hotel at the present time.

She thanked him for his kindness and was surprised when he insisted on carrying her luggage to her room. Lo Van Phuong had given her one of the best rooms in the hotel.

Leigh Ann unpacked slowly, then filled the tub with bubble bath she had bought in Hong Kong. She watched as the hot water stirred the scented bubbles into a frothy mound, then undressed and reclined in the warm bath.

Leigh Ann rested her head on the rounded edge of the tub and let her tired body go limp. She closed her eyes and thought about Brad, remembering the first time she had met him. Leigh Ann smiled when she thought about that special morning at the Royal Hawaiian Hotel.

Now, she thought while she brushed the bubbles away from her chin, *how am I going to tell him that I'm pregnant?*

Brad Austin watched the dense vegetation flash under his left wing, then shifted his eyes to scan the partially repaired instrument panel. He paid close attention to the engine gauges and listened to the steady whine of the turbojet. The fighter was performing flawlessly.

His thoughts momentarily turned to Leigh Ann as he passed his first checkpoint. He hoped that she would not encounter any major problems during her long trip. Maybe Spencer would allow him to catch a ride on the C-123 the next time it returned to Vientiane.

Brad continued to closely monitor his course while he waited to check in with the helicopter. Passing a rugged ridge of limestone karst, Austin noted the time and keyed his radio.

"Sleepy Two Five, Safari."

"Sleepy copies," Jimenez replied hastily.

Brad clicked his microphone twice and wet his dry lips. At his present speed of 340 knots, he would be three miles from the end of the runway at Hoa Lac in ten minutes and forty-five seconds. He would select afterburner at that point and accelerate to 420 knots, timing his attack to commence exactly seven minutes before the navy and air-force strikes were scheduled to begin.

Checking to ensure that his shoulder straps were properly snugged, Austin ran a critical eye around the cockpit, then armed the cannons. He watched for the next route checkpoint and glanced at his watch when the fighter raced over the tiny village. Eight seconds fast. He gently nudged the throttle back a fraction of an inch.

The minutes ticked by while Austin felt a mounting tension. He reviewed his meticulously drafted plan, running it through his mind again and again. Off Hoa Lac, a slight right turn to pass over the southern edge of Hanoi, a hard left turn to align himself with the runway at Gia Lam, a sweeping left turn to set his pipper on Phuc Yen, then a hard left turn toward the Laotian border.

Turning the volume up on the radios, Brad selected the air-force strike frequency on one and the navy frequency on the other. If he needed to communicate with Mitchell and Jimenez, he would switch the number-one radio to their discrete channel.

When the Black River was visible through the fighter's thick windshield, Brad made a last-second course adjustment and waited for the runway at Hoa Lac to come into view.

"Okay, everything looks good," Austin said to himself as he concentrated on skimming the tops of the trees. He spotted the airfield and went to afterburner as he approached the lake adjacent to Hoa Lac.

Brad watched the runway fill his gun sight. "Hang on . . . and take your time."

Three MiGs were beginning to taxi while seven other fighters waited to follow them to the runway.

Austin allowed the airplane to climb slightly, then placed the pipper below the first of the stationary line of aircraft. He waited until he could see the pilots.

"Now!"

Brad squeezed the firing button and watched two streams of high-explosive shells rip through the parked fighters. One of the airplanes blew apart and was immediately engulfed in billowing black smoke.

A line of tracers tore past Austin's canopy as he released the trigger and banked to the right. He lined up with the southern fringes of Hanoi and shot a glance at the instrument panel. No apparent problems at the moment. He heard the navy strike leader check in with Red Crown.

Antiaircraft fire began filling the sky with shimmering lines of tracers. Brad figured that air-raid alarms must be going off over the entire Hanoi area. He concentrated on his next turn-in point and watched two tall towers flash past his left wing.

Hurtling over a large truck depot, Austin felt a round smash into the fuselage. He was almost at eye level with the crews of the camouflaged gun emplacements. Brad saw a Fansong missile-guidance radar unit at the same instant a half-dozen weapons opened fire from the perimeter of the SAM site. He instinctively ducked when a sparkling row of tracers arced over his head.

"Oh, mother of Jesus," he said, forcing the words out of his throat as he zoomed over the revetted gun positions.

The antiaircraft fire quickly faded as other gunners hesitated to fire at the lone airplane. Even though the gun crews had been warned about a MiG-17 that was purportedly being flown by a Yankee air pirate, most were hesitant to shoot at a MiG that was not presenting a direct threat. The North Vietnamese gunners knew that if they shot down one of their own aces, they would not live to see another sunrise.

Austin was approaching the parallel highway and railroad leading south from Hanoi when he heard the leader of the air force F-105s call his fighter cover.

"Chicago Zero One, Spooky Lead." The hollow voice sounded calm and professional.

"Spooky, Chicago is making a sweep down the ridge."

"Roger."

From his briefing cards, Brad knew that Chicago 01 was the flight leader of the "Triple Nickels" from the 555th Tactical Fighter Squadron. The F-4C Phantoms were trolling for MiGs along Thud Ridge.

Austin snapped the agile fighter on its left wingtip and boresighted the runway at Gia Lam. Leveling the wings, Austin thundered over the rooftops and trees. The low-flying aircraft, at least to the gun crews, appeared to be a definite threat. The element of surprise was gone.

A barrage of tracers suddenly danced around Brad's fighter. The North Vietnamese had done a thorough job of alerting every single gunner about the MiG's description.

Whump!

Brad swore when a flak burst rocked the airplane. He saw a single MiG diving toward the airfield from the opposite end of the runway. Had the enemy pilot spotted him?

Rocketing across the Red River, Austin held his breath and waited to fire. A brilliant flash caused him to wince and glance through the top of the windshield.

He stared in amazement as the oncoming MiG, trailing flames and spinning out of control, plunged into the ground and exploded near the runway. The frightened gunners were firing at everything.

Brad heard the Chicago MIGCAP flight leader call bandits in sight over Phuc Yen.

Austin pressed the firing button as the radio frequency crackled to life. The cannons spewed a seemingly solid line of shells into the MiGs that were staggered for takeoff. He could only imagine the confusion and fear spewing from the radios in the North Vietnamese cockpits. He watched pieces of debris fly off the fighters as he swept low over the field.

A rapid series of bright flashes caught Brad's eye when he passed over the river bridge north of Gia Lam. More bright stars winked at him from the gun emplacements spread along the highway leading to Kep airfield.

Brad cringed when a solid wall of white-orange puffs erupted directly in front of him. There was no way he could avoid the menacing flak trap.

"Get down!" he exclaimed as he popped the nose down and snapped the stick over. His heart skipped a beat when he saw a number of wide-eyed faces looking straight at him from their windows. Brad snatched the stick back to avoid colliding with the apartment building. He missed the edge of the roof by less than the length of his wingspan.

The erratic NVA gunners, in their desperate attempt to shoot down the elusive MiG, blasted a dozen people on the top floor of the building into oblivion.

Momentarily disoriented, Austin frantically scanned the terrain to the northwest. In the continuing chaos of SAM launches and fierce antiaircraft fire, he had lost sight of Phuc Yen. The sky was ablaze with flak and missile plumes in all quadrants.

"God . . . don't leave me now."

He maintained a shallow bank to the left and witnessed a bright orange-and-black explosion mushroom high overhead. The trail of smoke leading to the ball of flames meant a surface-to-air missile had found its target.

Brad searched for his last target while he listened to a frantic voice yell for someone to eject. He gave in to curiosity and looked up. He saw a number of MiGs in the vicinity, then froze when he recognized two sections of Phantoms diving toward the enemy fighters.

The runway at Phuc Yen suddenly appeared off to his left. Brad racked the airplane into a tighter turn and focused his concentration on the aircraft that were waiting to get airborne.

Steady. Hold what you've got.

Ahead, on the perimeter of the airfield, a gun battery opened up with a continuous burst of fire. The deadly tracers approached in a flat arc and swept over the canopy. The shells slowly corrected and slammed into the tail of the MiG, blasting a gaping hole in the vertical stabilizer.

Brad felt the stick tremble before he squeezed the trigger. He fired a long burst into the closest fighter and gradually walked the rounds through the remaining aircraft.

The cannon shells ripped through the planes like a buzz saw, tearing off chunks of metal and rupturing fuel cells. In awe, Brad saw a taxiing MiG career into a drainage ditch and erupt in towering flames.

He released the trigger and made a sharp feint to the right, then yanked the airplane over into a punishing left turn.

Austin could feel a constant vibration in the control stick as the damaged fighter screamed low over a highway. *Just stay together a few more minutes.*

Two MiGs suddenly appeared from the left, ascending in a shallow, high-speed climb. Brad instinctively tweaked his nose up and fired the last of his ammunition in a sweeping arc. He cursed himself when the tracers went under the two planes.

Both pilots broke hard into Austin, prompting him to reef the fighter around to pass under them nose-to-nose. Seconds later, the two MiGs pulled up in a steep, climbing turn and Brad craned his neck to watch them. What he saw pumped a new surge of adrenaline through his veins. A pair of Phantoms had spotted the MiGs, and two other F-4s had obviously seen Brad's airplane. The second section of fighters were about to engage him in combat.

"Chicago One has a tally—two at eleven o'clock and climbing!"

"Three has one on the nose! We're going down to get him!"

"Roger—" The acknowledgment was garbled and followed by, "'areful."

Brad decided to use his transmitter while he still had the capability to communicate with the UH-34. He needed to give Mitchell and Jimenez his current location and direction. Turning the radio to the rescue helicopter's frequency, Austin lowered the nose and dove for the deck. Hugging the ground in a last-ditch effort to escape, Brad ventured a quick look over his shoulders.

Like prehistoric predators stalking their prey, the Phantoms were rapidly closing on the crippled MiG.

Austin twisted his head around to face a wall of fire and flak bursts. He was so low that the gun crews on opposite hills were raking themselves in a cross fire.

"Sleepy Two Five, Safari!"

No answer.

A missile from one of his pursuers streaked over the right wing and detonated in front of the MiG. Brad glanced rearward as the airplane buffeted from the missile concussion.

"Oh, shit!"

He started to toggle the smoke canister when a tremendous explosion rocked the MiG. The right wing dropped and Brad desperately tried to raise it.

"Come on, don't lose it now!"

Austin simultaneously muscled the stick to the left and pulled it back. The flight controls were sluggish, and the wounded fighter trembled under his inputs. Slowly, the wings leveled while he kept the stick pressed to the left and shoved on the rudder to correct the yaw.

Terror gripped Brad as he turned to look behind him. One Phantom had disintegrated in a huge fireball and the other F-4 was executing a vertical reverse. Two men, who had no idea that they were chasing another American, had died instantly in the explosion.

Gulping air, Austin raised the nose a few degrees and then felt the engine surge. The MiG was dying a slow, agonizing death. He had to climb as high as possible as quickly as possible.

"Stay together . . . just a little longer," he said as he unconsciously clinched the stick grip.

Brad faced the nightmare he had often thought about. He would have to abandon the aircraft in the heart of enemy territory. Could he maintain the guise of being a Soviet instructor pilot until Mitchell and Jimenez located him?

Climbing for altitude, Austin relied on his instincts and ignored everything but his plan for ejecting. He would stay with the airplane as long as the engine was running.

Locating his position on his chart, Brad checked to make certain that his primary radio was tuned to the frequency of the rescue helicopter. Praying that the transmitter would work, he gingerly keyed the mike.

"Sleepy Two Five, Safari," Austin said excitedly.

"Safari, Sleepy copies." It was Mitchell's voice.

The turbojet surged, and Brad felt a severe vibration in the airframe. He knew that he was about to lose the struggle.

"Sleepy, I've got an emergency."

Brad's headset was silent for a long moment.

"Say again."

"I'm going to have to eject," Austin shot back as his mind raced to verify his position. "I'm west of Dong Sang—approximately six miles east of the Black River."

"Roger. We're on our way." Mitchell's voice had a definite trace of caution. He and his crew had never penetrated so far into North Vietnam without a backup rescue helicopter. "Give me your position before you jump out."

Brad strained to see as far ahead as possible. "Wilco." He tipped the right wing down and saw a narrow river that flowed into a small lake. Then he spied the point where the Black River joined the Red River. "I'll be over the Black River—seven to eight miles south of where it meets the Red—in about a minute and—"

A muffled explosion jolted the airplane. Austin took a deep breath and banked the MiG into a shallow turn, then cast a wary glance behind him. His suspicions were confirmed when he saw the telltale sign of an engine fire. Fed by raw fuel, the conflagration in the turbojet pumped volumes of black smoke into the sky.

"I've got to get out! I'm on fire!"

"Understand," Mitchell said above the beating rotor blades, "that you're on fire and ejecting at this time?"

"Affirmative!"

Brad glanced blankly at the instrument panel and braced himself for the ejection. He closed his eyes and pulled the ejection handle. Nothing happened.

With strength born from a sudden, overpowering fear, he again yanked on the handle, then yanked once more.

Panic momentarily swept over him as he realized that he was trapped in the burning airplane. The seat was not going to fire. He could not simply jettison the canopy and bail out manually. His parachute was not capable of opening without going through the ejection sequence.

"Chase," Brad said as his mind struggled to find a means of escape, "my seat won't work—I can't get out!"

"You can't eject?" Mitchell blurted in amazement.

"That's affirm!" Austin's voice was harsh as he fought to remain calm. "I'm trapped in the cockpit . . . and I'm on fire."

CHAPTER THIRTY-NINE

Alpha-29

Everyone in the room sat in stunned silence when they heard Chase Mitchell's radio call to the MiG. Lex Blackwell rose from his chair and followed Allison to the edge of the door to the communications room. Nick Palmer and Hank Murray remained seated at the briefing table.

Cap Spencer turned the volume up on the radio and exchanged an uneasy glance with Allison. Her face reflected a deep alarm, but she kept her thoughts to herself and silently prayed for Brad's safe return.

Spencer swallowed and keyed his mike. "Sleepy, Blue Devil," he said without waiting for a response. "Confirm that he cannot eject."

"That's affirmative, and he's on fire. Stand by one."

Hollis Spencer stared at the radio for a moment and then turned to Murray.

"Hank, is there a way he can . . ." Spencer's words trailed off when he saw the strain on Murray's face. The blood had drained from his skin, turning his complexion pale and pasty. His mouth opened, but no sound came out.

A synapse flashed in Spencer's mind. He felt as if he had been hit in the forehead with a baseball bat. "Hank—"

"Cap, I did it to protect the operation," Murray uttered defensively. "We had to have insurance . . . and I didn't think it would ever be detected."

With a combination of disbelief and mounting rage, Palmer turned and faced the heavyset officer. "You disarmed the ejection seat?"

Murray's eyes gave him away. He had deactivated the seat's firing mechanism to help ensure that the North Vietnamese would not get their hands on a live pilot. Murray had bet that no one would have known if the MiG had been shot down. He had been confident that a pilot could not transmit his plight if the airplane was blown apart or was spinning out of control.

Facing the shocking reality that Murray had allowed Brad to take off with an inert escape system, Palmer leaped to his feet and exploded across the table.

Murray was only halfway out of his chair when Nick swung wildly, smashing Murray straight in the face. The two men tumbled backward over the chair and slammed into the wall.

"Did I fly with a bogus seat?" Palmer said venomously, and slugged him with a staggering blow.

Murray's eyes bulged in pain when his broken and bleeding nose was again flattened.

"You low-life son of a bitch!" Palmer yelled as he repeatedly pounded Murray's pulpy face. "I'm going to kill you, you worthless bastard!"

Reeling from shock, Blackwell and Spencer lurched across the room to separate the men. Allison stared in horror and tried to restrain her anger. Brad was trapped in a burning airplane that had been sabotaged by the chief of maintenance. She could see that Palmer was literally trying to kill Murray.

"Goddamnit, Nick," Lex shouted as he attempted to grab Palmer around the neck. "Get aholt of yourself!"

"Back off!" Nick warned as he pummeled Murray's bleeding face. "I'm gonna kill this chickenshit!"

Spencer straddled Palmer's back while Blackwell tried to pin his friend's arms. Nick tossed Spencer off and fell sideways when Lex leaped on top of him.

"He's almost unconscious!" Blackwell gasped as he held Palmer in a headlock. Nick continued to shake from anger, but looked at Lex.

"Okay." He breathed heavily, trying to calm himself. His hand felt like it was broken. "Let me go . . ."

After Brad had lowered the flaps and secured the blazing engine, he turned off the fuel valve and dove for the ground. The tail pipe of the MiG continued to burn while he fought off his rising fear and searched for a place to crash-land the stricken fighter.

He scanned the area toward the river and spotted a long section of rice paddies. Immediately, Austin calculated the distance to the landing site and set up for a steep descent to align himself with the first row of paddies.

He thumbed his mike and heard a side-tone. The battery was still powering the radios.

"Chase," he exclaimed firmly, "I've got to stuff it in a rice paddy on the east side of the river."

"Copy," Mitchell responded while Brad twisted the last bit of horsepower from the screaming engine.

Rudy Jimenez transmitted a call a few seconds later. "Understand you are going to land seven to eight miles south of where the rivers intersect?"

Brad jabbed the mike button. "That's affirm—east side of the river in the rice paddies."

"Keep the faith," Jimenez encouraged, then added, "We're moving as fast as we can."

Austin clicked his mike twice.

Feeling an increase in the intense heat, Brad quelled his panic and concentrated on his approach. He would leave the landing gear retracted and belly the airplane into one of the flooded fields. He gradually raised the nose to arrest his swift descent.

He could feel the airspeed bleeding off rapidly as the powerless MiG became a silent glider. Realizing that he did not have enough altitude to execute a standard flameout approach, Brad entered a modified base leg.

Darting a look at the small village next to the irrigated fields, he decided to stretch his glide as far as possible. In the distance, toward the bridge where the two rivers joined, he could see a convoy of military trucks.

Austin kept the control column jammed to the left and maintained a steady pressure on the rudder. The MiG continued to descend in a relatively stabilized manner, but it was settling much faster than he had anticipated.

The searing heat from the blazing fire in the fuselage was steadily consuming the aircraft. Brad was beginning to feel the first effects of being cooked alive when he aligned the flaming aircraft with the rice paddy.

Dense smoke began to seep into the cockpit, filling the small space with an acrid smell. With his vision becoming blurred, he reached down to his left and grabbed the canopy jettison knob.

I'm going to roast in here! Brad's mind screamed as he jerked the semi-hot release knob.

The canopy slid backward a few inches before the wind blast ripped it from the railings. The heavy canopy slammed into the vertical fin and horizontal stabilizer, then plummeted toward the road that led to the river.

"This isn't looking good," Brad uttered as the MiG shook from the impact of the canopy. The intense heat was unbearable and the controls were becoming mushy.

"Just a few more seconds," he groaned as he fought the controls. The fighter was slowing and beginning to nibble on the edge of a stall. "I've got to hang on. . . ."

The UH-34

Chase Mitchell concentrated on flying low and fast while Rudy Jimenez plotted their course to Austin's reported landing site. The engine was straining at full power while Elvin Crowder inspected his weapons and checked the rescue hoist. He was not comfortable with the idea of going into North Vietnam without their usual backup helicopter.

"Chase," Jimenez said over the intercom as he handed the pilot a folded chart, "what do you figure was the problem with the ejection seat?"

Mitchell glanced at the course line his copilot had drawn on the map and altered course five degrees to the right. "Beats me. It's old technology, but someone should have examined the firing system."

"Well," Rudy shook his head in disgust, "I guess it's all academic now."

"Yeah, but it doesn't change our job."

Jimenez looked at the fuel gauge. They would have only five to ten minutes to locate and rescue Austin when they reached his last known position. If they stayed any longer, the helicopter would most likely run out of fuel before they could reach Alpha-29. "I just hope he got down okay . . . and didn't bust his ass."

Mitchell eased the nose up to clear a ridge as he skimmed the tops of the trees. "I'll be relieved if he comes up on his survival radio."

Absorbed in his fuel-endurance calculations, Jimenez noted the time and turned to Mitchell. "I hope he's out in the boonies—away from civilization."

With a look of concern, Chase glanced at his friend. "Rudy, he's landing near the river, and that means lots of people in the area."

Jimenez studied the rugged landscape and nervously fingered his round-wheeled flight calculator. "I wish we had some North Vietnamese insignias to slap on the side of this bucket."

Brad pulled back the control stick and sailed over a walkway at the edge of the rice paddy. Focusing on his likely point of impact, he saw a number of farmers running in a frenzied attempt to escape the burning MiG.

"Easy . . . nice and easy . . . ," Brad coaxed as the MiG's belly caressed the water, skipped twice, then settled into the irrigated field with a huge splash.

Warm water shot through the engine-air intake and slammed into the blazing turbojet. The resultant explosion blew the tail off and partially extinguished the raging fire.

Austin was violently thrown into the instrument panel as the tailless MiG slid the length of the paddy, caromed over a narrow dike, then slewed sideways and struck another levee.

A tidal wave of water and mud showered Brad as the airplane careened to a stop against the embankment.

An eerie quiet suddenly settled over the paddy. Brad could hear voices, but they seemed to come from a distance. He opened his eyes and saw only blurred images in front of him. He wiped his face with a mud-splattered flight glove and shoved himself upright. There was a trace of blood on his glove and the forearm of his flight suit.

Jesus, Joseph and Mary, I'm still alive.

With a sense of urgency, he moved his eyes to view the cockpit. The sturdy MiG had survived the forced landing remarkably well. He cleared his head and ripped off the soaked gloves, then removed his helmet and tossed it onto the wing.

Reaching for the windshield bow, Brad attempted to hoist himself up. His legs would not cooperate with his mind.

Why can't I get up? Am I paralyzed from the waist down?

"You dumb shit!" he blurted as he snapped his seat restraints loose and scrambled over the side of the cockpit. He landed in the squishy mud next to the dike and took a quick look around the area.

The startled villagers were hurrying toward the burning MiG. Austin unsnapped his kneeboard and tossed it and the attached charts into the residual fire. Mechanically, he struggled clumsily out of the mire and forced himself to think like a Soviet instructor pilot. Be calm and take charge of the situation. He tried to recall the Russian phrases he had studied, but drew a complete blank.

ALPHA-29

Hollis Spencer had sent for the corpsman and then walked Hank Murray to his quarters in the hangar. Spencer knew that he had to keep the battered maintenance chief separated from the pilots until he could decide how to handle the crisis.

After explaining to Murray that he would be confined to his quarters for his own protection, Spencer rushed back to the Quonset hut.

When he entered the building, he could feel the growing animosity. Allison was desperately trying to contact the helicopter while Lex Blackwell wrapped Palmer's swollen and bleeding hand in gauze.

"Allison," Spencer said in a terse voice, "they're probably too low to pick up our signal. I'm sure they'll call us as soon as they can."

She nodded glumly and stared at the radio.

Nick tried to restrain himself, but gave in to frustration and anger. "Cap, we've got to stop playing games and get the search-and-rescue people involved . . . if we're going to get Austin out of there."

Spencer gritted his teeth and gave Palmer a stone-faced look. "Lieutenant, if you give me just half a reason, I'll place you under armed guard, so help me God."

Palmer bridled, and Blackwell stepped between the two men.

"Nick," Lex said soothingly, "let's go outside and have a cigarette."

Palmer glared at Spencer for a long moment, then rose and quietly walked to the door. It required all of his self-control to keep his contempt from overriding his better judgment.

After Blackwell followed Nick outside, Allison eyed her boss with a glimmer of displeasure. "Cap, what are you going to do about Murray?"

"Allison," he replied in an exhausted manner, "I'll deal with that after we know about Austin." He slumped in his chair and reached for his pipe. "First things first."

She tried unsuccessfully to conceal her irritation. "Are you going to chalk it up to fierce loyalty, or are you going to call it what it is . . . attempted murder?"

Spencer knew what was appropriate, but he needed time to sort through all the possible ramifications. He felt in his heart that he was through, and hoped that all of them could escape unharmed from the operation.

"I'll take care of it," he responded sadly, knowing that he could not keep Murray's incident under wraps for long.

CHAPTER FORTY

When the first of the villagers reached the twisted and torn MiG, they stopped on the levee and gawked at the burning fighter plane. It had left a long trail of destruction through the paddies during its wild slide.

They turned to look at the pilot, expecting to see a fellow Vietnamese. The looks on their faces changed to surprise when they saw Austin, but no one showed the slightest hint of fear or aggression.

Brad calmed himself and glanced around. He needed to get away from the black smoke rising into the sky, but he had to act his part and move cautiously.

When the Vietnamese began chattering and walking toward him, Austin held up his hand.

"*Stoy.*" Stop. His mind raced, hoping the heavy accent would convince the men and three teenage boys that he was indeed a Soviet pilot.

"*Mi pravil'no yedem v krasnaya ploshchad?*" Are we on the right road for Red Square? It was the best he could do under the circumstances, and he prayed that it was good enough. Hopefully, the strangers could tell the difference between English and Russian.

The blank looks on the villagers' faces reinforced Brad's decision to move out while he had the chance. He gently dabbed the cut over his right eyebrow and wiped the blood on his mud-splattered sleeve.

When the chattering continued, Austin waved his hand back and forth and pointed to himself. "*Kapitan Maksimov . . .*" he grunted stiffly, "*Aviatsii—Hanoi.*"

A few of the Vietnamese nodded while the others surveyed the pilot and the wreckage. The crash landing had stunned them, and now the magnitude of the damage to their crops was beginning to dawn on the farmers.

Sensing no immediate threat, Austin boldly walked through the middle of the Vietnamese and continued the length of the dike. With his adrenaline pumping, he leaped across a slit in the levee and started up an incline toward the road next to the small village.

When he reached the dirt strip, Brad shot a look up and down the road and nonchalantly strolled toward the cluster of trees on the opposite side.

He quickened his pace when he noticed a truck approaching from the direction of the convoy he had seen earlier. When he reached the trees, Austin squatted under the middle of the clump and quickly yanked out his survival radio.

With trembling hands, Brad switched on the radio and cupped it to his mouth. "Sleepy Two Five, Safari."

The noisy army truck slowed and rumbled to a stop on the side of the road.

"Sleepy Two Five, Safari. Copy?" *Come on, guys.*

"Safari," the speaker crackled, "you're weak, but readable. Say your posit and condition."

Brad watched two men get out of the truck to look at the burning wreckage of the MiG. *God, please don't let them go down to investigate the crash site.*

"I'm in the same location that I gave you before I went down." He leaned against a tree trunk and flicked a drop of blood off the bridge of his nose. He tried to slow his breathing before he spoke. "Approximately seven miles south of where the rivers meet. I'm on the east side of the river, near a large marshy area."

Austin cast a wary glance at the truck. A half-dozen NVA soldiers had struggled over the tailgate to join the two men from the cab.

"I'm okay . . . physically," Brad continued in a hushed voice, "but an army truck just stopped near the airplane. Also, there's a large convoy of trucks headed this way—traveling north to south."

"Copy that you're okay," Rudy Jimenez replied with a tone of confidence. Downed and frightened airmen needed to hear a strong, positive voice. "We estimate being over your position in—ah . . . twelve minutes."

Brad felt his heart sink to the pit of his stomach. Twelve minutes sounded like an eternity, especially when he was facing death or torture and imprisonment. "Roger. When I have you in sight, I'll direct you to my position before I come out from under these trees."

"Okay, Safari." It was Mitchell's reassuring voice. "Take it easy . . . and give us a holler when you hear the helo."

Austin froze when the group of soldiers began walking toward the blazing fighter. "Will do, Sleepy. Thanks."

"Just stay put."

Brad clicked the mike twice and eased back into the foliage and branches. He watched the eight men disappear down the incline leading to the rice paddies. His intuition told him that the situation was ripe for disaster. The villagers would obviously tell the NVA regulars which way the pilot went, and, most important, that the airman was not Vietnamese.

He quickly glanced down the wide river and guessed that it was at least a quarter of a mile around the marshy recess to a wooded area next to the shoreline. *I don't think it's a good idea to stay here.*

"Sleepy, I've got company nearby—need to get away from the immediate vicinity. I'm going to head south, along the shore. The MiG is sending a plume of black smoke into the air, so you'll probably see it before I hear you."

"Roger that," Jimenez responded evenly. "We'll hit the river a couple of miles south of your position, then work north toward you."

"I'm on my way," Brad said as he stuffed the radio inside his flight suit, then hunched down and began running around the perimeter of the marshy cove.

Looking across a vast expanse of forested ridge lines, Chase Mitchell decided to drop into a valley leading to the flatlands west of the Black River. His eyes ranged over the sky and horizon, searching for enemy aircraft or signs of tracers.

The air-force and navy strike groups were exiting the area, but the threat of MiG activity was always present. The UH-34 would be no match for a fighter, especially one flown by a competent pilot.

"Rudy," Mitchell said after a long silence, "there's a major roadway that runs along the west side of the river."

Jimenez looked at the chart and tried to forget the rapidly dwindling fuel supply. "We better steer clear of it. It's a basic supply route that'll be crawling with guns."

"That's what I plan to do." Mitchell pointed when he caught a glimpse of the river in the distance. "We'll stay about a mile and a half west, as low and fast as we can go, then pop over the river when Austin hears us." He gave Rudy a questioning glance. "What do you think?"

Jimenez was skeptical, and it showed in his eyes. His legendary reputation as an air-force SAR pilot had been earned from a wealth of experience gained from many dramatic rescues.

Although Mitchell was senior to Jimenez, he respected his copilot's knowledge and judgment. "Rodeo, if you've got a better idea, now's the time to sing out."

Rudy studied the chart. "Chase, I think we'd be better off to cross the road and the river here." Jimenez pointed to a 4,200-foot peak on the east side of the river. "We can skirt along the edge, then shoot straight up the east side of the river. There aren't any roads, until we get close to Austin's position."

Rudy handed the chart to the pilot. "The area is sparsely populated, so I wouldn't expect much in the way of small-arms fire . . . if some gomers recognize us. The closer we get to the water, the more people we're going to overfly."

Mitchell looked down at the chart and thought about the plan, then nodded in agreement. "Makes sense to me."

"Elvin," Mitchell cautioned, "keep an eye out. We're going to cross the river and go for a quick snatch. If he's in an open area, I'll go into a hover and you yank his ass aboard. If we have to use the winch, let me know as soon as he's in the sling. We'll drag him to a safe area before we hoist him up. Got it?"

Crowder rested a gnarled hand on the M-60 machine gun and scanned the sky. "I've been doin' this shit," he growled over the intercom, "since your mother was a virgin."

Jimenez rolled his eyes to Mitchell. "Why do we put up with that shitbird?"

"Because," Chase gave him a tense grin, "he's saved our asses a couple of times."

Brad kept up a steady pace as he doggedly splashed through the shallows of the marshland. He leaped over a rotting log and tripped, then caught himself before he sprawled face-first in the muck. He paused, thinking that he had heard the beat of helicopter rotor blades. He listened intently, but the only distinguishable sound was a jet engine high overhead. He started running again.

Without warning, a shrill whistle stopped him in his tracks. Austin glanced over his shoulder and felt a chill run down his spine. A lone soldier was standing on the lip of the road. He was holding a whistle to his mouth and motioning for Brad to come to him.

Overwhelmed with raw panic, Austin started to reach for his revolver, then stopped to weigh his chances of reaching the trees near the river. The longer he hesitated, the more suspicious the soldier would become.

An insidious feeling of doubt began to creep into Brad's mind. His confidence in masquerading as a Soviet pilot was quickly evaporating. What if there was a Russian adviser in the group?

When the other seven men gathered on the road, Brad made a split-second decision to run and take his chances. He bolted forward and raced toward the nearest trees.

Austin heard muffled shouts as he scrambled up a small rise and tumbled down a steep, water-filled ravine. He sloshed across the ditch and crawled out as shots rang through the air. The North Vietnamese had finally cornered the culprit who had inflicted so much damage during the time he had flown the mysterious MiG.

Stumbling blindly toward the treeline, Brad was suddenly spun around and knocked to the ground. The round from the AK-47 had torn through the side of his right upper thigh. The hunters had their quarry at bay.

"There it is," Rudy Jimenez gestured wildly. "I see the smoke!" The dark cloud had risen at an angle and was spreading horizontally with the wind.

Mitchell made a slight course correction. "Yeah, I've got it." He hit his mike switch. "Safari, we have the smoke. Give us a sit rep." He wanted a situation report before they attempted the rescue.

After a long moment, Mitchell tried again. "Brad, if you hear me, click your transmitter. We're almost there."

Silence.

"This doesn't look good," Jimenez muttered as he caught sight of the line of army vehicles in the distance. "I've got the convoy. They're almost to the downed MiG."

Mitchell banked the helicopter toward the water. "Rudy, do you see any power lines over the river?"

Both pilots strained to see any indication of towers along the shore-lines. An unseen power line could send the UH-34 crashing into the river.

"No, just some small boats up ahead."

Chase Mitchell gripped the collective tighter and keyed the radio. "Brad, we need to know your location."

The radio remained quiet.

Austin heard the radio calls while he fumbled for his revolver. The searing pain in his thigh had changed to a dull numbness as the enemy troops approached. If he died here, it would only be after he had used every means to resist. If he lived, Leigh Ann would be waiting for him.

He moved his bleeding leg and felt that it would support him. The bullet had ripped through the fleshy part of his thigh, but it had not hit the bone.

Fueled by adrenaline and cold fear, Brad shoved himself to a sitting position, aimed at the center of the group of soldiers, then fired two rounds.

He was amazed when one of the men staggered sideways and collapsed. When the soldier hit the ground, his assault rifle dis-charged a wild burst of fire. A dumb-luck shot from the revolver, accompanied by the spray of rifle shells, had sent the infantrymen diving for cover.

Seizing the moment, Brad scrambled to his feet and awkwardly limped toward the foliage near the trees. A volley of shots rang out, and he waited for a bullet to find him.

"Try him again—keep trying!" Chase Mitchell ordered while he con-centrated on flying ten feet above the water. "We've gotta make a decision, Rudy . . . before we get sucked into an ambush."

"Brad," Jimenez pleaded with an emotional intensity in his voice, "we're almost there. Say your position. Repeat, say your position!"

Recalling the time he had been lured into a North Vietnamese trap during a SAR mission, Jimenez was cautious but determined to go above and beyond their duty.

"Chase, they may have captured him," Rudy said sadly, "but we owe it to him to go in—to find out."

Mitchell knew Jimenez was right. They would never be able to live with the guilt if they aborted this close to the downed pilot. "We're going in."

CHAPTER FORTY-ONE

Stumbling and weaving, Brad Austin blindly plunged into the dense undergrowth and fought his way through the branches and thickets. Ignoring the shells that ripped through the vegetation, he turned and fired another two rounds at his pursuers.

When they dropped to the ground, he crawled through the underbrush leading to the river. With his lungs heaving, Brad stopped to peer through the leaves. His hopes sank when he saw some of the soldiers moving to his left and right. They would soon have him surrounded.

In the distance, he heard the familiar beating sound of rotor blades. The helicopter was only seconds away. *Oh, God, give me the strength to hang on.*

He fired his last rounds at the infantrymen nearing the edge of the water, then dropped the revolver and groped clumsily for his survival radio.

"Chase, open up with the machine gun! I need cover fire along the riverbank!"

His plea was answered by three short, distinct bursts of fire across the water next to the shoreline. The trail of splashes turned to mud splatters as the rounds walked up the bank and through the men.

When the advancing soldiers stopped and began shouting at each other, Brad plunged toward the riverbank. He plowed through the thick foliage, dragging his leg and clutching the survival radio.

"I'm close to the water!" he gasped as a bullet ricocheted off a tree trunk in front of him. "Next to the shore—north edge of the trees!"

Brad heard the metallic voice from the radio, but he ignored it in his desperate attempt to reach safety. Another high-powered round whined past his head and exploded a leaf a foot away. *My luck is going to run out.*

Expending the last of his energy, Brad charged through the maze while he heard the staccato sounds of the M-60 raking the shoreline. He also heard someone scream in agony.

He dropped the radio and lowered his head, forging his way through the last of the obstacles. Suddenly free from the entanglement, Brad fell facedown on the muddy bank. He clawed his way toward the river and flinched when a row of geysers blasted across the water next to him.

Brad looked to his right and saw his tormentor disappear in a hail of machine-gun fire.

Above, the helicopter was slowing to a hover and the rescue sling was skimming the water. Brad crawled into the water and rose to his knees. He frantically waved his arms at the helo, but the crew had already spotted him.

Elvin Crowder continued to decimate the soldiers while Mitchell maneuvered the sling toward Austin. It dangled tantalizingly close, just out of reach.

Brad tried to get to his feet, then lunged at the horse collar. He missed and fell headlong into the water. He struggled to his knees and gagged when he swallowed a mouthful of water.

Rudy Jimenez was acting as a backup on the flight controls when the helicopter unexpectedly tilted steeply and slid sideways. The tips of the rotor blades nipped the water for a split second.

"Chase!" Jimenez gasped as he clutched the controls and righted the helo. "You 'kay?"

Mitchell groaned, then slumped in his harness as his arms went limp. A single hole in the windshield marked the entry point of the round that had struck the pilot in the neck.

"What's goin' on?" Crowder demanded while he continued to blaze away at the soldiers.

Rudy ignored the gunner and skillfully moved the rescue sling over Austin. "Grab it, Brad," he said to himself as another round hit the top of the windshield. "They're going to blow us out of the sky when we run out of ammo."

Movement to the left caught his eye. "Sonuvabitch," he swore out loud when he saw the convoy grinding to a halt.

When the machine guns mounted on the trucks commenced firing, Jimenez squeezed down in his seat and concentrated on flying smoothly.

The sling was skipping toward him, but Brad was blinded by the spray churned up by the rotor blades. When the harness bumped him, Austin frantically grabbed it and stuck his arm through the opening.

"Go!" he yelled into the gale-force wind, then grappled with the unwieldy horse collar. He felt himself being pulled through the water before he could get his head and other arm through the sling.

Sweet Jesus, I'm not going to make it! Brad clutched the sling in the crook of his right elbow and used his other hand to seize his wrist in a death grip. He closed his eyes and prayed for renewed strength.

Supporting the weight of his soaked flight suit, Brad strained when his body was yanked from the river. His feet bounced off the water a couple of times as the helicopter swiveled and gained speed.

He twirled precariously on the end of the winch line as the helo climbed and accelerated. *I can't hang on forever.*

"Is he secured?" Jimenez barked over the intercom. He could not afford to climb too high or go too fast if Austin was not securely in the sling.

Elvin Crowder braced himself against the cabin door and leaned into the wind. "Shit no. He's only got one arm through the collar."

Jimenez swore under his breath and searched for a relatively safe place to make a quick landing. He glanced at Mitchell and thought he detected a tentative movement.

"Chase, can you hear me?"

The only response from the wounded pilot was a slight flicker of his eyelids.

"Is Mitch hit?" Crowder snapped.

"Yes," Jimenez answered bitterly. "I'm going to land just ahead—about a mile—and get Austin aboard."

"You better make it now," Crowder said with a touch of sarcasm, "'cause our boy is about to take a big dive."

Brad alternated between thanking God for watching over him, and calculating his chances for survival if he lost his grip. The throbbing pain in his thigh had diminished to an unpleasant tingling sensation.

He found if he closed his eyes and concentrated, he could hear and see Leigh Ann laughing on the beach at Waikiki. It seemed like a hundred years ago.

A moment later, Brad felt the helicopter begin to slow. He opened his eyes and saw that he was descending toward a partly submerged bank of mud extending out from the shoreline.

When the helo finally hovered above the shallow water, Brad let go of the collar from a height of three feet and fell backward in the deep mud.

He staggered to his feet and plodded unsteadily toward the helicopter. The UH-34 moved sideways and hovered, with the main tires barely touching the mudflat.

Austin lowered his head into the windblast and trudged forward a few more feet before he felt Elvin Crowder grab his arm. The crew chief helped Brad to the open hatch and boosted him inside.

With a visceral sense of relief, Brad collapsed in a heap while Jimenez pulled pitch and sucked the wheels out of the quagmire.

After a couple of minutes, Crowder leaned over the mudsoaked pilot. "How ya' feelin'?"

Brad had to shout over the noise from the thrashing rotor blades. "Great," he grimaced from a sudden stab of pain. "Never felt better."

"Good," Crowder grinned for the first time Austin could remember, "because you look and smell like you crawled out of a benjo ditch."

Brad mustered a weak smile. "You guys are first on my Christmas list . . . thanks."

Crowder nodded and ran an experienced eye over the trickle of blood next to Austin's leg. The crew chief spoke briefly to Jimenez and then opened a first-aid kit. "Looks like you got a little scratch."

"Yeah," Brad replied in a tired, hoarse voice. "It's been one helluva day."

"I ain't much of a doc," Crowder grumbled as he extracted a dressing, "but I'll patch you up best I can."

The look in Brad's eyes showed his appreciation.

* * *

Rudy Jimenez forced the battle-scarred helicopter to ascend at its maximum rate of climb. He kept the helo close to the rising mountains while he waited to gain enough altitude to head directly for Alpha-29.

He scanned the engine instruments and maintained a careful vigilance for any signs of trouble. If the MiG bases had been notified of the rescue effort, the fighter pilots would be searching for the American helicopter.

Jimenez glanced at Mitchell and saw that his color was gone. The cockpit floor was awash in dark blood and the pilot's half-closed eyes were fixed in a vacant stare. Chase Mitchell was dead, but Jimenez refused to accept the fact. *Maybe the medics can help him when we get to Alpha-29.*

He could taste the bile in his throat as he turned to a westerly heading. Since there was not a passageway between the cabin and cockpit, Mitchell would have to remain strapped into his seat. "Elvin, keep an eye out for MiGs."

"Will do, but it's gonna be easy to spot us."

"Say again."

"We're trailin' a thin stream of smoke. From the color, I reckon it's comin' from the engine."

Rudy shot a look at the engine-temperature and oil-pressure gauges. The cylinder-head temperature was slightly higher than normal, but the oil pressure remained unchanged. "We're looking good . . . at least for the moment."

Crowder leaned out of the hatch and watched the faint streak of oily smoke. "How's Mitch doin'?"

Jimenez looked at the fuel gauge and spoke softly. "Not so great. What's Austin's condition?"

"He'll make it, but he's got a nasty thigh wound. We'll have to get 'em medevacked as soon as we hit the ground."

If we have enough fuel to reach base, Jimenez thought with a calm fatalism. *All of us may die before the day is over.*

CHAPTER FORTY-TWO

ALPHA-29

A palpable tension hung in the air as Hollis Spencer slowly drummed his fingers on his desk. He looked around the room, then stared at the second hand on his wristwatch while it completed one full sweep. Letting the silence build, he stopped and methodically packed fresh tobacco into his pipe. At last, he snapped his lighter open, puffed repeatedly, and swiveled to face Allison.

"Let's give them a call."

Nick Palmer shared a glance with Lex Blackwell. They knew the odds were against a successful rescue deep in the heartland of Northern Vietnam. Their worst fear was that Brad Austin had been killed in the crash landing.

Allison slid her chair close to the radio and adjusted the volume control for the overhead speaker. "Sleepy Two Five, Blue Devil. Do you copy?"

The speaker suddenly crackled with a garbled static, but the message was sporadic and unintelligible. The random noise served as a ray of hope.

"Let's wait a few minutes," Spencer said with a rush of enthusiasm, "and try again."

Surprised by the distorted radio transmission, Rudy Jimenez

answered the call while he nursed the helicopter higher. He would keep climbing and call Alpha-29 every thirty seconds until he could hear clearly.

He thought about calling in the blind, hoping someone at a higher altitude would relay his message. After careful consideration, he elected not to risk exposing the operation. Making contact with the base would bolster his morale, but it would not get them home any sooner.

Jimenez watched the altimeter as the laboring helicopter struggled for every foot of altitude. He felt the tension that knotted his neck muscles.

"Blue Devil, Sleepy Two Five."

He listened to the sound of the engine and cast a hesitant glance at the oil-pressure gauge. His eyes were playing tricks on him, or were they? The indicator seemed immobilized, but he was sure it had been slightly higher the last time he looked at the pressure.

"Blue Devil, Sleepy radio check. How do you read?"

Finally, Allison's excited voice filled Rudy's earphones.

"Sleepy, we copy. Is Brad on board, and where are you?"

Jimenez gave Chase Mitchell a quick glance and felt his stomach tighten. Rudy could not admit to himself that he and the best friend he had ever had would never again go barhopping together.

"Blue Devil, we're a couple of miles southeast of Chieng Pan." Jimenez stared at the oil-pressure indicator. He was certain it had dropped a fraction of an inch. "Austin is on board, and we have two wounded. We need the doc standing by, and the dollar-twenty-three ready to medevac. Copy?"

"Read you loud and clear. Stand by."

"Wilco."

The oil gauge had definitely moved. Jimenez could see the pressure dropping. He eased back on the throttle to try to conserve the precious fluid. He searched his chart for a reasonable place to make a forced landing. Rudy computed the time to Alpha-29 and concluded that it was his only choice. At the rate the pressure was dropping, it would be a close race between landing at the remote base and running out of oil short of the field.

"Sleepy, say nature of the injuries and your ETA."

"Austin has a gunshot wound to his thigh," Jimenez said, knowing how Allison felt about Brad, "and Chase has a severe neck wound." Rudy glanced at Mitchell once more. "Chase needs an immediate medevac."

"We're making preparations as we speak. Say your ETA." Her voice was thin and cracked, but the emotional relief was clearly evident.

"I'd say eighteen to twenty minutes," Rudy estimated while he studied the engine instruments, "if this thing holds together that long."

"What's the problem?"

Jimenez raised his arm and wiped his cheek on the sleeve of his flight suit. "We've got an oil leak, and the engine temp is going out of sight. I'll keep you informed."

"Roger that," she replied in a hollow voice.

Watching each minute slowly drag by, Rudy decided that in the event of total engine failure, he would broadcast a Mayday call over an emergency frequency used by the Air America pilots. If he did not get a quick response, he would switch the frequency to 243.0 and send out a distress call. To hell with the goddamn MiG operation.

Nick Palmer rose from his chair a moment after he heard a loud swooshing sound. He and Lex Blackwell froze in place, then dove to the deck when machine-gun fire flayed the Quonset hut and surrounding area.

"Get down!" Hollis Spencer exclaimed as he grasped Allison's arm and pulled her to the floor.

"Stay down!" Palmer ordered while he yanked the briefing table over on its side. "Over here—get behind the table and stay low!"

Blackwell quickly discarded his cumbersome arm sling and grabbed the nearest M-16, then belly-crawled to the entrance. He cautiously peered above the kick panel and ducked when a mortar shell made a hit on the hangar.

"Holy shit!" Lex gasped as he scrambled behind the tabletop. "They scored a direct hit on the hangar. We've gotta make it to the foxholes!"

"Not yet," Palmer shouted over the ear-splitting machine-gun fire. "Hang on a minute!"

Spencer waited for a lull in the fighting before he decided to venture from behind the desk. He crawled to the field security radio while Allison hurriedly snatched her rifle and rejoined the pilots.

"Nick, we better make a run for it," Blackwell declared as another hail of gunfire erupted.

"We can't go outside right now," Palmer shouted above the crackling fusillade of automatic-weapons fire. "They'll rip us apart before we get twenty feet!"

Their mouths turned dry while Spencer yelled into the Command Post radio. Gunnery Sergeant Salvador Rodriguez barked orders in return.

A series of thundering concussions pounded the operations building as mortar rounds rained on the hangar and adjacent sleeping quarters.

Spencer cursed and tossed the handset down when a barrage of shells lashed the Quonset hut. He sprawled on the floor a second before a spray of shells riddled the wall.

"The CO—Gunny Rodriguez says we have to withdraw!" Spencer flinched when two rounds smashed into his desk. "We're being over-run!"

Smelling the stench of his damp flight suit, Brad Austin closed his eyes and captured a mental image of Leigh Ann. How was he going to be able to contact her? Maybe the C-123 pilots would do him a favor and tell her where he had been taken for medical treatment.

An unexpected shudder ran the length of the fuselage. Brad suddenly opened his eyes and let his questioning glance slide to Elvin Crowder. He could tell by the tormented look on the crew chief's face that something was wrong.

Before Austin could speak, another solid vibration ran through the airframe. His adrenaline, which had slowly begun to ebb, shot through his system with renewed vigor. *What the hell is happening?*

Brad gestured to Crowder when another tremble convulsed through the helicopter.

"What's wrong?"

The grizzled gunner reached for the overhead and leaned down. "We're losin' oil at a perty fair clip."

Crowder moved to the open hatch and peeked out to see if the UH-34 was still emitting white smoke. The telltale vapor had completely disappeared. He stepped back to Brad.

"The engine is probably dry, 'cause we ain't trailin' no more smoke."

Austin silently nodded. The forced landing and harrowing rescue had left him badly shaken. Now, after surviving that ordeal, he had to face the possibility of another forced landing. Without a second helicopter, Brad knew their chances of being rescued before they were captured were nonexistent.

He cringed inwardly, remembering a downed air-force pilot who had had his rescue helicopter shot out from under him. He and the SAR crew had been plucked from certain imprisonment by a gutsy Air America pilot.

A succession of tremors wracked the helicopter, marking the final minutes of flight.

Brad struggled to sit up, pushing himself upright by sheer will. "How much longer . . . to the field?"

Crowder shrugged and opened a pouch of chewing tobacco. "Don't much matter, if the motor ain't runnin'."

Reaching for a loose M-16, Nick Palmer flipped off the safety and inched toward the screened door. A deafening explosion knocked him backward into Blackwell, Allison, and Spencer.

With their ears ringing, the foursome stared through the dust at a cavernous hole in the wall. They could see the twinkle of muzzle flashes as the Pathet Lao boxed the compound with a curtain of red-hot steel.

"We've got to make our way," Lex shouted above the explosions and chaos, "to the one-twenty-three."

Palmer and Spencer looked through the smoldering hole in the wall. The cargo pilots had already started one engine and were taxiing toward the runway. Nick watched while the individual fire teams from the perimeter safety unit made an orderly retreat toward the C-123.

The twin-engine transport, which was configured to carry sixty-one passengers, would be overloaded if the majority of the evacuating personnel boarded the aircraft.

"Let's make our move," Spencer said boldly, and raised to one knee, "while we still have some cover fire from our troops."

Allison turned and looked at him with wide-eyed contempt. "We can't leave until the helo lands. You can't leave them here to die."

Palmer interrupted Spencer's reply. "Allison, we'll work our way toward the airplane—using the foxholes—and hope the helo gets here before the cargo plane takes off."

She was outraged as fire flashed in her eyes. "Nick, of all the people I would have thought—"

"Goddamnit, Allison," Palmer blurted in frustration, "we can't sacrifice an entire plane packed with human beings for four people. They'll have to find another place to set down."

"Allison," Spencer said hastily, "we can't afford the risk of having everyone annihilated. We've got to get on the plane while we can."

She gave him a defiant look and crawled toward the communications room.

With a knot tied in his stomach, Rudy Jimenez watched the cylinder-head temperature peg at the top of the scale. The oil pressure registered zero, and he could smell the hot engine as the helicopter began to shake.

Come on, sweetheart . . . don't give up yet.

He left the power set, fearing any abrupt change might cause an immediate engine failure. He watched the altimeter begin to unwind as the screaming engine ground itself to pieces.

Something flashed in the distance and caught his attention. Smoke was rising from the general area of Alpha-29. Jimenez was about to call the airfield when Allison's voice exploded in his headphones.

"Rudy, we're under attack! How far away are you?"

"Five minutes, if the engine holds together." He could feel the vibrations becoming more violent. "We won't be able to provide any cover fire."

"We're being overrun—everyone is evacuating the base," Allison yelled over the crackle of gunfire. "Land next to the cargo plane!"

Jimenez was horrified. If the UH-34 held together long enough to reach the airfield, would he be forced to land in the middle of the enemy troops?

He started a shallow descent to gain some speed. "I've got the field in sight."

"Hurry, Rudy! We can't hold on much longer!"

The odor of the overheated engine was beginning to sting his nostrils. "We're almost there!"

"I'm signing off, Rudy," Allison exclaimed, and crawled back to the overturned table. She stared Spencer in the eye. "Cap, we aren't leaving them."

Nick Palmer swung around at the same time another mortar round exploded next to the building. "It may not be our choice to make."

She gave him a quizzical look. "What do you mean?"

Nick saw Lex Blackwell glance at him. "Allison, when the last person the pilots can see is on that airplane, they're going to be shoving the throttles through the instrument panel . . . trust me."

"He's right," Lex added, and flattened himself on the floor when a round ricocheted through the room. "They aren't gonna be takin' roll call."

CHAPTER FORTY-THREE

Brad studied the Spartan interior of the lumbering helicopter, noting that everything was buzzing from the continuous vibration. The shaking fuselage was even rattling the machine gun and ammunition belt. *If the engine blows, I hope this thing can autorotate.*

He watched Elvin Crowder speak into his lip mike. The crew chief swore over the loud banging and turned to Austin.

"They're retreatin' from the strip."

Brad experienced a pang of fear. It seemed that somehow they were not destined to make it to safety. "Our security troops are pulling out?"

Crowder checked his sidearm. "Everyone is jumpin' in the plane and haulin' ass." His face reflected a degree of disdain. "If they cut and run 'fore we get there, I'm gonna do some serious ass-kickin'."

A new rhythm to the vibrations developed into uncontrollable shaking. A moment later, the screaming engine thrashed itself apart in a series of violent explosions.

Jimenez immediately reacted to the loud explosions and pushed the collective down to neutralize the rotor-blade pitch angle. With the pitch flat, the main rotor blades would aerodynamically continue to spin during the emergency descent. The autorotating blades would provide the pilot with some degree of control during the descent and flare to land.

If the collective was held in the normal flying position after an engine failure, the rotor blades would rapidly slow and fold upward. At that point, the helicopter would have the same flying characteristics as a bowling ball.

Brad felt the deck cant downward at the same time he heard the sound of the wind whipping around the cabin door. He let his head sag for a moment, then gripped the sides of the bulkhead in preparation for an emergency landing. The irony of two crash landings in one day consumed him while the helicopter autorotated toward Alpha-29.

"Is everyone ready?" Nick Palmer asked when the withdrawing security men momentarily halted the advancing Pathet Lao forces. The C-123 was on the runway and a number of the CIA troops were making a stand thirty yards from the transport.

Spencer glanced at Allison, who was crouched beside him next to the shattered door. "Wait until I reach the first foxhole before you run for it. We'll give you as much cover fire as we can . . . so don't hesitate."

She nodded and inched toward the door. "There's no time like the present."

A thunderclap of noise shook the building and knocked a clipboard off Spencer's desk.

"Here goes," Lex Blackwell muttered, and charged through the hole in the wall. Spencer waited a few seconds and dashed through the opening.

"Go!" Nick told Allison when the small-arms fire began to decrease.

She rose and darted through the door while Palmer poured a long burst of fire into a line of enemy soldiers crossing the stream.

When Allison disappeared into the ground near the tents, Nick sprinted toward the foxholes in the midst of another mortar attack. Twelve feet from the first hole, Palmer was blown off his feet by an explosion that nearly leveled the Quonset hut.

Rudy Jimenez tightly gripped the collective and breathed deeply. He talked to the helicopter, coaxing as much distance as he could from the silent machine.

"Elvin, when we land, I'll get Chase out," Jimenez looked at Mitchell's lifeless body, "and you take care of Austin."

"Are we gonna make the strip?"

"It'll be close," Rudy answered calmly. "Man the gun and give us everything you've got."

"I'm locked on it now."

From his current altitude, Jimenez was unsure if he could reach the airfield. He ignored the streaks of tracers in his path and concentrated on stretching the autorotation as far as possible. *Come on, baby. You can do it. . . .*

A blazing streak of fire ripped chunks of dirt into the air as Palmer tumbled into the foxhole. He landed on top of Blackwell, knocking both of them on their backs.

Lex scrambled to his knees and looked at Nick. "Are you okay, partner?"

Palmer groaned, then blinked his eyes and swallowed hard. "I can't hear you."

After checking Nick for wounds, Blackwell grabbed him by the shoulders and helped him to a sitting position.

The gunfire was continuous as the security teams slowly backed toward the C-123.

Lex sneaked a glance over the rim of their shelter. "You've still got all your parts, but your rifle is about twenty feet out in the boonies."

Unsteady and dazed, Palmer propped himself on one knee and carefully rose to peer above the pit. "There they are," he shouted, pointing to the descending helicopter.

"Cap," Blackwell yelled to the adjacent foxhole. "Are you and Allison ready to go?"

"Yes," Spencer shouted over the gunfire and booming concussions that buffeted the compound. "We've got the helo in sight!"

"Let's wait—" Lex ducked when a round blew dirt across the top of his head. "Let's wait until the helo hits the ground—then go for it!"

"Okay," Spencer hollered above the din of noise.

Nick shook his head in an attempt to clear the ringing sound. He gingerly cast a glance over the embankment, then snatched Blackwell's M-16 out of his hand.

"What the—"

Palmer opened fire, killing two men clad in black near the remains of the hangar. When they dropped their AK-47s, Nick noticed something else. "Oh, God . . ."

Lex looked and spotted the twisted bodies of Hank Murray and one of his technicians. They had been blown outside the hangar and were lying next to the fuel dump.

Palmer absently handed the rifle back to Blackwell while they watched the approaching helicopter. Under the circumstances, there would be no way to retrieve all the bodies.

With infinite patience, Jimenez skillfully guided the powerless helicopter straight at the cargo plane. He caught a glimpse of billowing white smoke as the pilot cranked the second engine. Relief swept over him when he saw the propellers settle into a steady idle.

"Brace yourselves!" Rudy cautioned over the intercom while he pulled pitch to slow their descent. He could hear Crowder's M-60 spewing a steady stream of fire.

Without warning, a continuous burst of tracers slammed into the stricken helo. Jimenez swore and stomped on the tail-rotor control pedals when the helicopter started to swivel. *I'm going to have to dump it!*

Palmer grimaced when he saw the UH-34's tail rotor blades chewed off by the intense machine-gun fire. Without directional control, the fuselage was beginning to rotate around the axis of the main rotor blades. Nick and Lex watched in horror as Jimenez tried to salvage the landing.

Blackwell sucked in his breath. "I hope they make it."

"He's too fast," Nick declared, using body English to align the fuselage with the direction of flight.

The helicopter slammed into the ground near the cargo plane and bounced across the taxiway. The struts and wheels flew in different directions as the helo slid to a halt with a wrenching tear of metal. The jarring impact had collapsed the main rotor blades and severed the tail-rotor pylon.

With sheer determination, Brad crawled from the crumpled wreckage and reached back to help Crowder through the crushed entrance.

"I'm okay," the crew chief grunted as he struggled free. "Let's get Rudy and Chase!"

Austin rose and went to the sliding window at the side of the cockpit. He and Crowder lowered Chase Mitchell to the ground while Jimenez leaped out the other side entrance.

"They're out," Palmer yelled to Spencer when he saw the four men were clear of the demolished helicopter. "Cap, you and Allison take off!"

"We're going!" Spencer replied as he and Allison crawled out of their refuge. They sprinted toward the transport while Blackwell fired the last rounds in his rifle.

"Let's go," Lex said when the M-16 stopped firing.

Palmer jumped up and over the embankment, then dashed after Blackwell as rounds kicked dirt up a yard in front of him. Nick could see that the cargo plane was being riddled by small-arms fire. The CIA men were holding their own, but if the Pathet Lao regrouped and charged, they would overwhelm the outnumbered Americans.

Brad hobbled behind Jimenez and Crowder while the two of them carried Mitchell's inert body toward the idling C-123. He saw Allison and Spencer racing for the airplane, followed by Nick and Lex.

Then it happened. A hail of gunfire cut Allison's legs out from under her and she awkwardly tumbled to the ground.

Time and space seemed to slow as Brad ran toward her, limping as fast as he could. Spencer turned back and Brad waved him toward the cargo plane, then dropped next to Allison. She was moaning softly and trying to shove herself to her feet.

"Allison," Brad's voice cracked, "don't try to move!"

"Brad," she coughed, "I can't get—"

Ignoring the heavy gunfire, he scooped her up and felt the blood run down his arm. "Hold on to my neck."

She raised one arm and clasped his neck. "Brad . . ."

"Just a few more yards," he gasped while he limped toward the C-123. He saw Spencer turn and run toward him.

A staggering blow knocked Brad off balance, and his wounded leg buckled under him. He stumbled twice before they collapsed in a heap.

Brad pushed himself to his hands and knees, then stared in shock and disbelief at Allison. She had taken the brunt of the rounds that had ripped into the two of them. "Allison . . . oh, God, Allison."

He tried to lift her, but fell back when his limbs failed to respond to the sensory inputs. Brad saw a blurred image of Nick and Lex, then the dark settled over him.

Palmer and Blackwell, with assistance from Spencer, carried Allison and Brad into the airplane. They heard the distinct sound of bullets impacting both sides of the fuselage.

"Easy," Nick said as the three men, with the help of Crowder and

Jimenez, gently placed Brad and Allison on the flight deck next to Chase Mitchell.

When the last soldier leaped through the door, the cargo pilots fire-walled the big radial engines and released the brakes. The airplane leaped forward and slowly gathered speed in a hail of gunfire.

Three-quarters of the way down the runway, the Provider shuddered from the concussion of a mortar shell that exploded near the right wing.

Just as the aircraft rotated, a small-arms round penetrated the fuselage and struck a soldier next to Blackwell.

The pilots kept the plane low, accelerating as they raised the landing gear and flaps. With a sudden lurch, the C-123 pitched up in a steep, climbing turn to clear the rising hills.

After five minutes, the pilots leveled the battered airplane and reduced power. The right engine was smoking and running rough, but they kept it going in order to expedite getting the wounded to Vientiane.

Gunny Rodriguez lay mortally wounded near the rear entrance to the cargo bay. He had been the last person to board the battle-damaged airplane.

Brad opened his eyes when Lex and Nick moved him to a long bench seat. Vaguely he became aware of where he was when he heard Palmer speak to Blackwell. He also heard the cries and groans from the severely wounded soldiers.

"Brad." Nick leaned closer and carefully examined his friend's eyes. "How are you feeling? Do you want something for the pain?"

Austin had never seen Nick Palmer's face look so pale and full of sorrow.

"Is Allison okay?" Brad asked in a flat, guttural voice.

Nick gave her a furtive glance. Cap Spencer had cupped Allison's small hand between his while Rudy Jimenez tearfully covered her face with a utility jacket. She hadn't made it. Operation Achilles was over, and Hollis Spencer would carry the guilt with him for the rest of his life.

Palmer hesitated and glanced at Blackwell, then snapped out of the paralysis of anguish. "She's in good hands, Brad. Try to relax."

Brad noticed the pained expression in Nick's eyes. He choked and struggled to speak. "Please tell Leigh Ann . . ." he swallowed twice and coughed, "where they are taking me . . . which hospital."

"I will." Palmer strained to keep his composure as Lex gloomily shook his head. "You rest . . . and save your strength. We'll be on the ground soon."

Brad nodded weakly and closed his eyes. "Thanks."

CHAPTER FORTY-FOUR

The lights of the city were beginning to twinkle brightly as the sunlight dissipated over the Menam Khong River. The narrow streets were becoming clogged from the early-evening hustle and bustle in the open-air markets. The lewd jokes and loud noises from the partying crowd drifted from the raunchy bars and settled over the river traffic.

Nick Palmer paid the taxi driver, then hefted his bag of new toiletries and clothes and entered the Constellation Hotel. He walked straight to the front desk and set his belongings on the floor.

"Is Miss Leigh Ann Ladasau registered?" he asked when Lo Van Phuong turned and gave him a toothy smile.

"Mister Palmer, good to see you again." The general manager concealed his astonishment at seeing Nick dressed in a ripped and soiled flight suit. He glanced at the pilot's bandaged hand, pretending not to notice it.

Nick acknowledged the pleasantry and gazed toward the commotion coming from the crowded, smoke-filled barroom. He was not in the mood for small talk.

Sensing Palmer's restraint, the amiable man erased the smile from his face. "Yes, Miss Ladasau staying with us. She check in today." He glanced at his wristwatch. "She go to dinner maybe ten, fifteen minute ago. She say she be back soon."

"Thanks," Palmer said while he reached for his wallet. "Do you have any rooms available?"

"Yes." He smiled and reached for a key.

"When she returns," Palmer said wearily, "please don't mention that I inquired about her."

Lo Van Phuong smiled innocently. "As you wish."

After Nick had signed the guest register, he went to his room for a quick shower and a fresh change of clothes. He would wait to talk to Leigh Ann until she had finished her dinner and returned to the hotel.

Donning a clean shirt and khaki slacks, Palmer went to the front desk. Leigh Ann had not returned from dinner.

Deciding to go into the bar, Nick ordered a double scotch on the rocks and took a seat where he could observe the entrance to the lobby.

He thought about Brad Austin and all the experiences they had shared since they had first met on board the aircraft carrier. The memories cascaded through his mind, and he took another sip of his drink.

Still reliving their close calls in the air and their humorous times on liberty, Nick suddenly became aware of someone entering the lobby. He looked up to see Leigh Ann walk to the front desk.

Forgetting his drink, Palmer rose from his chair and quietly left the bar.

Leigh Ann stopped in midsentence and turned to see who was approaching her.

"Nick," she exclaimed excitedly while reaching out to hug him. "What a pleasant surprise!"

Palmer awkwardly embraced her and stepped back with a trace of a smile on his face. "You're as beautiful as ever."

"Thank you, Nick." She laughed, then added, "Always the gentleman." She noticed his bandaged hand. "You look great, too, but what happened to your hand?"

"Just some minor damage," Nick answered uncomfortably, then fell silent.

"Is Brad with you?" she beamed before noticing the pained expression on his face. "Nick, what's wrong? Has something happened to Brad?"

Hesitantly, he took her by the arm. "Leigh Ann, let's go to your room . . . if you don't mind."

"Nick," she said somberly as they walked down the hallway, "has there been an accident?"

"Yes."

The color drained from Leigh Ann's face as she shakily placed her key in the lock and opened the door.

"Tell me the truth, Nick," she said with a strained intensity.

He absently closed the door and gently took her by the shoulders. "Leigh Ann, Brad just came out of surgery . . . and he's in serious condition."

She stared at Nick with a mixture of confusion and disbelief written on her taut face. "Is he going to be okay . . . ? What happened?"

He paused while he framed an answer. The doctors had been cautiously optimistic about Brad's chances when he was taken to the recovery room. "It's a long story, Leigh Ann." Nick thought about the events of the last few hours and shook his head. "We're not going to know much until tomorrow, but the initial report sounded good."

Relieved that Brad was alive, Leigh Ann inhaled deeply. The room seemed to be spinning as Nick reached to steady her. When he took her in his arms, she buried her face against his chest and sobbed. He held her tightly and felt the shudders that tortured her body.

Nick could hear the faint sounds from the bar as the dull noise mixed with the street traffic. He shared her concern and silently prayed that his friend would be okay.

"Go ahead, let it out." He pressed her head into the hollow of his shoulder and gently stroked her hair.

Glancing at the IV bottle hanging next to his bed, Brad Austin focused his eyes and took inventory. He had both feet and both hands, so he obviously had his arms and legs. His bruised stomach hurt, and his chest felt as if someone had dropped an anvil on it.

He slowly raised his head off the damp pillow and surveyed the spotless room. A sudden chill ran through him as he remembered seeing Allison fall to the ground and struggle to get to her feet. His head plopped back on the pillow, and he heard a distinct voice.

"Captain Austin," the unsmiling nurse said while she checked his dressings and the IV, "you have visitors, if you feel up to having company."

His first attempt at talking came out as a croak. He tried a second time. "Sure."

The terse woman walked out, and a moment later Leigh Ann appeared in the doorway, followed by Nick Palmer.

Brad's eyes reflected his happiness. "Leigh Ann . . . Nick." He lifted his hand a few inches above the bed.

As shocked as she was to see Brad in his condition, Leigh Ann maintained her poise while she walked to the bed and clasped his outstretched hand. "You had us worried."

Nick remained by the door. "The drill sergeant . . ." He coughed and cleared his throat. "The nurse gave us five minutes, so I'm going to step outside. I'll see you later."

Austin turned his head to look at Palmer. "How is Allison?" He felt Leigh Ann squeeze his hand at the same instant Nick lowered his head and quietly replied.

"Brad, Allison didn't make it."

Brad stared blankly at the ceiling, then glanced at Leigh Ann while Nick stepped from the room.

She fought the tears that suddenly filled her eyes. "Brad," Leigh Ann patted his hand, "Nick told me you did everything you could for Allison."

He forced the pain and anguish deep inside him and kept his thoughts to himself. No one could know the guilt he felt about Allison.

Leigh Ann leaned over and gently kissed Brad on the forehead. "The doctors told us that you're going to be fine . . . and I'm going to take you home as soon as you're able to travel."

Brad smiled, and his eyes glistened. "I'm ready now, if you can smuggle me out of here."

Leigh Ann laughed softly and wiped a tear from her cheek.